No

Regrets

Not Now or Ever

Cyberworld Publishing

www.cyberworldpublishing.com

Cyberworld Publishing
Toronto
Australia

NO REGRETS

NOT NOW OR EVER

A memoir of Orlando, Count of Madelaine, Consort of the
Emperor and Cokeeper of the Keys to the Gates of Time.

Stephen Bush

CONTENTS

PREAMBLE

It hasn't been hard for me to decide where to begin this story of myself, but you will probably be disappointed with my decision. To you it will seem as if I begin with events in which you have no interest, happenings which have no connection with those things that have made me known to you. But all things have a beginning, and I know precisely the events that have led me, inexorably, to where I am now. That have made me what you think I am.

To myself I am just a man, and I have struggled to be a man, to be such a simple, yet astoundingly difficult, thing and nothing more. To you I am Orlando, Count of Madeleine, companion to the Emperor of the Confederation, Cokeeper of the keys to the Gates of Time, which sounds like something a great deal more difficult than just being a man.

But I assure you it isn't.

CHAPTER 1

In which I suffer the death of youth and prepare to write Report 509

In life there are moments never to be forgotten, moments that are burned so deeply into us that they can never be erased. If I die, and they preserve my brain and at some time resurrect its contents, I know with certainty of half a dozen moments that will be recoverable whatever its condition. I have lived for a very long time, yet three of those unforgettable moments occurred in the year after the woman was murdered.

She was killed near the end of a hot summer, and I remember summer passed slowly that year, fading into a gentle autumn, before sliding into a short mild winter, with only brief and occasional falls of snow. And emblazoned on my mind is the vivid memory of one day, one day early in the following spring, when I am standing before one of the windows in my study at the Chateau gazing out through the ancient imperfect glass at the park beyond.

It is late afternoon, or very early evening, depending on how you want to look at such things, and the greens and browns of the grass and trees are rich and strong in the fading light.

Several hundred yards away I see an apparently carefree man and woman moving across the lawns, strolling lazily arm in arm through the fading heat of the day. She wears a long, brilliant, golden-yellow dress and carries a straw hat in her free hand; he appears lean and tall but nondescript in brown breeches and waistcoat.

A slight movement draws my eyes to the left. A flock of a dozen or so sheep are emerging from a small stand of trees, followed by the shepherd and his dog. The man is walking at a leisurely pace, swinging his long staff, while the dog trots back and forth, driving the sheep before him. The sheep pause occasionally to graze as I watch them travel slowly across the park, and I know that they will spend the night sheltered from wolves and other animals in a stone walled pen at the Chateau farm.

Suddenly two small, longhaired, black and white dogs with big ears flapping come bounding out of nowhere. They run at the small flock and begin barking and charging at the sheep. The sheepdog leaps into action, barking back at them and chasing them through and around the sheep. Some sheep stand rigid with fear, others leap over an imaginary obstacle before heading off across the park at an amazing speed. And a couple, ones that must be deaf and blind with age, continue grazing, totally ignoring the tumult about them. The shepherd is running about frantically, waving his long staff and yelling.

Faint echoes of the commotion below carry up to me on the breeze. Then as suddenly as they have appeared, the two small terrorists are charging off to cause trouble elsewhere, with the sheepdog in halfhearted pursuit. The shepherd throws his staff to the ground in disgust and continues to yell abuse after them. Then he collapses onto the grass and lies down for a rest while his dog does the work of rounding up the strayed sheep and the remainder of the flock continue to graze. I look over and see the man and woman laughing, holding each other as they do, then turning to kiss.

And in that moment I know that I have lost myself.

As I watched them I realized that I was no longer the man I had been only weeks before. I could no longer feel or laugh as I once did, I had become a wiser and sadder man. And I no longer felt part of that world.

That is one moment, the last of those three moments, which occurred in the year after the woman was murdered. That day was the 17th of April, and I know it was the point at which my life turned from one direction to another. I continued to stand there watching the world until the sound of birds beginning to flock in the trees outside, before settling for the night, came through the open space at the top of the window.

The other two moments?

One was when I saw the woman lying dead and had to touch her, the first time I ever touched someone whose life was ended by another's hand. There is a difference.

The other moment was no one instant, no single image or event; it was instead a long period when I was drowned in a feeling, and the feeling was about completing something secret to which my commitment was total and private. I was apparently normal to everyone about me, yet I was hardly aware of them for so long that the moment burnt into my mind is one of a lonely apartness. I know it was a time when I was entirely true to myself; yet I thought more about someone else.

It happened slowly, it ended on the 17th of April. One long moment ends, and while it still fades, another is imposed over it, brightly, unforgettably, and I understand what has happened.

There is a report in the Administration archives; I have just reread it, fifty years after I wrote it. Report 509, Region Madeleine: Report into the death of Louise Lanoir. Prepared by Count Orlando and Clerk Lambert, signed and dated on the 17th of April. A lovely spring day, I know, warm with a gentle breeze, a day like the day before had been. A day when things ended and others began, a day when I discovered I was unable to laugh at a comic scene played out before me in a timeless place I loved.

I was Count Orlando of Madeleine then. Officially, I still am, though I was gone from Madeleine and my job was temporarily taken by another within six months of that day. I have returned to Earth once since then, to come alone to the Administration's archives. Why did I come? Because I wanted to know if what I remembered was real.

What sort of man was I before the woman died? Vain, proud, obsessive, thoughtful, diligent. I think I filled my position well, managing my region of Madeleine for the Administration. I enjoyed my life immensely; I tried to ensure the other residents of Madeleine could enjoy theirs. I know I tried to do what I thought was right, as I still do.

What am I like now? I do what I believe is my duty; I do it as well as I can. I know that I am not now so vain, nor so proud or obsessive as I once was, but I think I am still diligent. Above all else I now have a much wider vision of humanity and the universe—and humanity's place in it. And I secretly long for the past I lost.

Were those last months of apartness a sort of preparation for what has happened since? I have had to set aside aspects of my own life so I can think always of others. There is always a choice, but at the beginning the alternative for me was almost no choice. I would have liked things to be different since that time; I would like them to be different now. I would have liked them to have been easier. I am not a god, and sometimes I have doubts about what I have done and still need to do.

But I move too quickly ahead, thinking about that year is still painful, thinking about the day before the 17th opens a door into a room where I can bear to do no more than stand on the threshold looking in. It is a room in the house of my life about which I can have no feelings. I have no regrets for what I did, not then, not now, not ever.

My life is like a house of many rooms and corridors.
Near the entry it has rooms full of life and light,
rooms of warm firelight and loving company.

But also in the house of my life,
I have passed alone through rooms without windows
through rooms of darkness, which no light can ever penetrate

And I have walked winding corridors
whose length is unseen
that have no doors offering me either egress or entry.

Here in these pages, so old-fashioned now to write on paper, I have set out to tell a story of myself, to increase my own understanding of what I am and how I have become that. And I shall begin it at the beginning, where this part of my journey through life began for me.

Though I may be a familiar name to you from some history class, I shall perhaps mention little of what you know me for. What you know of are only odd moments along the way, moments that were merely the public and unexpected result of other far more important private things.

I begin properly

I begin my tale long ago in the days when I was really the Count of Madeleine, when I lived the fantasy of that place as if it were real life, as of course it was. In those days I know I was seldom at home in the afternoons. Occasionally I would be able to ride or walk in the grounds of my Chateau for pleasure. Sometimes I could join my great friend, Leonardo, my gamekeeper, and his huntsmen as they hunted wild pigs and deer in the forests nearby. Not healthy deer, only the old and unsound, and in late autumn those young late born ones who were unlikely to make it through the coming winter.

Sad, but no one should ever forget that nature is universally an unfeeling mistress. Only foolish men expect her to be otherwise.

I fenced, practicing often, in the early morning with Leonardo, but also occasionally in the afternoons with some other members of my household.

Mostly, though, my afternoons were not taken up with my own pleasures. Usually they were spent doing what a Count of Madeleine is there for, doing the paperwork required by the Administration, inspecting things or attending meetings.

There were many things to inspect.

At my small, beautiful Chateau I was responsible for inspecting the gardens, the restoration work on the murals and ceilings, and the quality of the gilding being done to restore the ornate plaster and wood decoration. I would discuss progress and plans with the engineers where they were working on their drawings, talk to artists and sculptors, to plasterers and plumbers. As I felt it to be appropriate, I would cajole or compliment them, admonish them or admire their work.

It was my purpose, my life, to be responsible for ensuring that the whole fabric of the Chateau, its bricks and mortar, plaster and paint, furnishings and ornaments were kept in good condition. This was, of course, so that the whole creation would still be there in another five hundred years. So that people then will still be able to admire it, see it much as it was meant to be when the original builders and artists created it.

The Historical Societies of Earth

I know there are people who seem to have no knowledge of the historical societies, which have existed on Earth for the last two centuries. Many people are not aware that they have their origins in the cultural and environmental preservation movements of the twenty-first century. And were made possible by the declining population of Earth caused by various laws and the exodus to the colonies.

All humans have the right to apply to live in them, and basic information is given in schools. But many people have told me they thought that what they were told was only meant to be for the information of serious students of history. This is not true. The societies are for anyone who is willing to contribute his or her labor to them and abide by their rules.

A large part of the duties of a position such as mine involves maintaining the historical and social integrity of a region's society. In the historical societies this is of paramount importance and must be dealt with sensibly. In all of these societies, not just Madeleine, but all of them, including ancient Greek, pre-Christian Roman, American Indian, the religious monastic societies, Zarathustran, Japanese Imperial, Zulu, and all the others, people may only change societies by leaving them. It is fundamental that they don't change the society itself, because the society remains constant while there are sufficient people wanting to live in it.

People were forever trying to invent eighteenth-century ways of making plentiful electricity and other things, wanting to "'improve'" Madeleine. Making them stop and understand that's not appropriate could sometimes be very difficult.

Of course all of the historical societies are nothing but elaborate delusions; they remain part of the whole planet and are responsible to the Administration. They must follow today's laws when it comes to serious crimes, and only exist with the Administration's approval. How some of the bizarre societies one heard about ever got approved and allocated space will always be a mystery to me.

Madeleine and St Louis themselves are certain to be around for a long time; eighteenth-century rural France seems to have an enduring romance associated with it. Without the horrors that many had to endure in the original, the latest in medical care, plumbing, and the active encouragement of casual relationships they offer a wonderfully simple, yet culturally and sensually rich lifestyle.

I was also responsible for looking after the villages, towns, and countryside of my region, my Madeleine. Inspecting them, again, which was always a great pleasure, but unfortunately also doing what was not always a great pleasure—meeting with the Society for the Preservation of Native Forests, an admirable bunch of enthusiastic fanatics obsessed by ancient descriptions of trees. Or being browbeaten by the members of the Committee for the Removal of Inappropriate Exteriors, passionate devotees of prenineteenth-century architecture, who hated any structure not completely original.

So impractical to be that pedantic when we were required to have and house a certain population, and when old poorly made buildings of little architectural value were always having to be replaced. Or worst of all, the Society for the Removal of Exotic Flora and Fauna, who were equally obsessed about thistles and bears. (Who knew what weeds had been there in the region in 1790 anyway?) Sometimes I thought there should be a Society for the Preservation of the Sanity of Counts.

I attended many meetings. Too many meetings.

Then there were those times when I would be away, traveling about my region with Lambert, the region's Clerk, and a couple of his assistants, in my large coach with a wagon and half a dozen riders to accompany us. Staying away for two or three weeks at a time, carrying out inspections again, of the countryside and the villages. But also acting as magistrate and arbitrator.

Rarely taking ladies with me for company, as I did not want too much distraction.

In my first months in my position at Madeleine, I had taken two lovely women with me on such an inspection trip. It seemed natural to take them with me in a place where I was able to, and I was very much encouraged by the ladies concerned to do so. Unfortunately, we had enjoyed ourselves so thoroughly and so often that when we returned after the allotted fortnight, I had done virtually nothing I had planned. Embarrassed at my delinquency, I had to leave again as soon as possible; alone this time, trying not to seem too foolish at reappearing again in places I had so recently visited.

After that I satisfied myself with the wonderfully pleasurable company of women I found where I was, when the time allowed, when I wanted it, which sometimes led to interesting interludes and sometimes not.

Memories float up in my mind of a cool misty morning when I discovered three milkmaids relaxing in a stone barn, low roofed and filled with the warm, sweet smell of cows. They joined me, (the milkmaids that is) in a wonderful abandonment of couplings, full of laughter and fun.

But that summer afternoon of the 26th of August, when I first heard the news that the woman had died, was an exception, as I was occupied by none of the aforementioned activities. Lambert, Alain, the senior clerk from region St Louis, and myself were in my study peacefully reviewing the Madeleine and St Louis region's production for the coming harvest. Both our regions were virtually self sufficient, but St Louis made much better wines than Madeleine and grew more temperate climate fruits in their hillside orchards. On the plains of Madeleine we easily grew a variety of grains and fine vegetables. So we would meet together several times a year and arrange to trade this for that so we could all enjoy the best of everything.

Alain's arrival the previous afternoon had been an excuse for a more enjoyable evening than usual. Not a ball, but a reason to put more thought into the evening's entertainment than was normal, especially as Alain himself was a competent musician and a singer of some ability.

I had no reason then to know that there was anything special about that night, anything to cause me to note it particularly. So I know that my memories of it now are probably an amalgam of a hundred such gatherings that had occurred at my Chateau over the years.

But I shall describe it here in as much detail as I seem to recall it—my last night of careless pleasure. Which I am sure could have been no more pleasurable if I had known it would indeed be my last.

There were more candles lit than normal so the salons of my were ablaze with light. Through their crystal facets the chandeliers refracted the thousand small flames into a flickering rainbow of dazzling light reflected back from the many mirrors. Cecile organized for a very fine dinner to be brought from the kitchens, which she oversaw as mistress of the house.

That was her position there, and it had nothing to do with her relationship with myself. My position in Madelaine and the Chateau was that of count, responsible for the management of the region, while Valentin was master of the Chateau, making him responsible for supervising the gardeners and grooms and outdoor staff, while Cecile supervised the cooks and maids and indoor staff.

That night we dined on freshwater fish and fowl of a dozen sorts, accompanied by salads, cheeses, pastries, breads, and a small amount of venison. Not the normal food, I admit, for the period in which we pretended to live. But it was what we ate (and I believe they still do eat there), because it was clean and healthy and allowed us to best maintain the countryside about us, which was our duty.

It was all served with fine wines from the cellar, which had been laid up for such special occasions. We ate throughout the evening, drank more than was usual, and were wonderfully entertained with music and song. The latter were provided by Alain alone, a fine voice; by Alain with my small orchestra; by Alain and the singers from Madeleine; and by everyone together. The singers sang unaccompanied, old medieval songs and modern ones. Then my musicians played and we all danced.

The ladies of the household were a fine sight in their full, long, gathered, and beribboned, or lace-trimmed skirts. Their equally adorned tight bodices gave them fine small waists and pushed the soft mounds of their breasts above the tight fabric. They were a pleasure to watch skipping and swaying in time to the music as they danced their way through the figures of the time.

The men were a handsome sight too, in their breeches and embroidered, brightly trimmed vests and coats, with fine linen and lace at their necks and wrists, swinging the ladies about energetically when the dance called for it, turning the dance floor into a wild sea of flying skirts and petticoats with an occasional glimpse of milky white legs.

Rebecca, our brilliant embroideress, sang beautifully that evening, as she always did, and after she had sung the old French song "Margot in the Vineyard," I'm sure I pulled her to me and whispered in her ear, enquiring if she was free to join me for the night. She laughed musically as she always did, then made a solemn sad face and whispered back that she had already promised herself elsewhere and was looking forward to it too much to forgo that assignation for one with an old man like me. I sadly told her I was devastated and would be inconsolable without her. Then she sang a very lewd song, and there was much laughter and more dancing, which I joined in energetically.

At that time I physically appeared to be a fit and healthy man of between forty and fifty—dark haired, stocky.

Now? I still look much the same as I did then, though noticeably grayer perhaps, and paler from the lack of sun. In truth I suppose I look more fifty now.

I took advantage of "refreshing" from when I was only twenty-three. It had just then become available and I determined to take advantage of the process, which effectively allows us to recover four of every five years we live. Now everyone has access to it, of course, but in the beginning it was hugely expensive, and the young all know they will live forever or want to die young and beautiful and don't care, so few young people availed themselves of it then. Now as each year passes and fewer of my generation remain, I find myself more alone in my memories of that distant past.

I am one of the first, of the first generation.

But to return to my last night of careless pleasure—perhaps a rather exaggerated description, but I don't care.

At some time I sat down again, and Cecile was there beside me and twined her arms about my neck and caressed the skin behind my ear with her warm breath and her tongue, and I rose and wished the company a good night. She had emptied my mind of all thoughts except of her and my bed, and I escorted the mistress of my Chateau up to my apartment for the night.

Was that place my idea of heaven? Yes, yes, and yes again. Even then I knew it was as close as a man such as me could come to heaven. I am not a fool who needs always to lose something before he knows its true value.

I was woken briefly at the first light of dawn, and as I was awake, I rolled over and made sure Cecile was too. Afterward I slept a while, and it was a pleasant and relaxing morning to have after a lively and enjoyable evening.

Washed and dressed, I was in my study at the time that was scheduled for the meeting to begin between Alain, Lambert, and myself. Lambert was already there, as he usually was, and Alain arrived in a rush a few minutes late. I had a suspicion that he might have been Rebecca's irresistible engagement of the previous night. He was certainly handsome, which was quite common for the members of Count David's household. But most of them preferred the intimate company of members of their own sex.

Count David's Chateau in the St Louis region was, as you can imagine, exquisitely magnificent, making my lovely Chateau at Madeleine look dowdy in comparison. There everything was the best and maintained to perfection. And the residents—already generally more attractive—were dressed more richly and more elaborately than those of my humble household ever managed to be.

A visit there was always interesting, especially as being a way off, it required one to stay overnight. It was an adventure to approach a beautiful woman with thoughts of pleasure. So many of those who appeared to be beautiful women were actually men that one had to use all sorts of odd tactics if one wanted to avoid the women of that type. For those who didn't care, the adventure was to see what they had when the truth was finally revealed. If it ever was, as some had once been one thing but were now another and what they had been was of no relevance anymore.

I admit now that I only ever stayed there once. I disliked the place; it depressed me. Now I know why, but it is of no relevance.

We had spent several hours talking over trade matters and had eaten a light lunch, but of course when the news of the most dramatic crime I ever had to deal with came, I was at the bathroom. As I reentered my study, I saw Lambert looking pale, and he rose and greeted me with the announcement of the women's death.

He told me in such an unemotional way that initially I wasn't sure if he was serious.

And I shall tell you that it has been my experience in life that on such occasions, real people often display little emotion. I think this may be because they are in a state of mild shock; most people's emotions seem to require some time to ferment before they overflow in passion.

I confess this was something that always surprised me. I was brought up in a society that was what is called the "real world." This was before the historical societies existed, and it was a world where such announcements were usually portrayed in the media and on the stage as full of deep and meaningful expressions, gasps, and strained voices.

The background music telling you this is a "dramatic moment" and the camera or lighting focusing on the faces of the actors showing the look of deep shock on the face of the recipient of the announcement, the stunned voices, the screams or gasps.

Having grown up with that image frequently before me, it was naturally how I ever afterward expected real life to be. But as I said, I have since found it isn't so. When people announce a death or a terrifying experience, they are frequently almost expressionless and quite calm, and

24

the words are ordinary everyday ones. We make the exceptional and cataclysmic from the same stuff as we make a complaint about the weather.

There have been two times in my life when I have heard those true spontaneous wails of grief such as Greek and aboriginal women of another time made. But they were rare even in my real world. Few people even then had the passionate blood that carries them.

Anyway, "Pardon?" I said. How inane. Lambert repeated himself, and the second time around I did comprehend him and sat down dully.

What Lambert told me was that there was a young woman dead at the nearby village of St Clair. The death of any young person is usually a shock and always sad, but this was worse. Dr. Malwi believed that another person was involved in causing this particular young woman's death, and that it was not likely to be accidental.

I put my face in my hands and prayed that it had been an awful accident, though I didn't really believe in a God even then.

With Alain's and Lambert's help and the assistance of the servants, Lambert and I managed to depart for St Clair a short while later. It was one of the very rare occasions when I longed for a faster means of travel than the horse. But I also realized that the woman was already dead and the speed of our arrival could never change that. Only turning back time would.

From the idiotic things I have read about myself, written by people I have never met, there are some who would be surprised that this is an ability I've never had.

The hour and a half ride to St Clare on a good horse and over a well-maintained stretch of road should have left my mind sufficiently free to determine a course of action. But there seemed to be too many unknowns for me to do this.

Was her death an accident or not? And if her death wasn't accidental, I imagined we would arrive at the village to find everything explained, with her killer filled with remorse and horror for what had occurred.

It would be difficult to deal with that person, or persons, I thought. Even if it was an accident, it was a serious matter, and I did not look forward to having to deal with anyone directly involved in it. The first objective would be to reduce the stress on them and the rest of the villagers that the woman's death had caused. But, and here I hesitated to think too far, such a situation would be far easier for me and everyone else to cope with than if her death were not an accident.

Following the main road from the Chateau we entered St Clair at its northern end just before the inn and then wound on around the small lake in the center of the village to the large manor house at the southern end of the village, known as the Jones farm.

It had been known as that for only about twenty years then, even though Beryl Jones came to run it forty-odd years before. It's always like that for us humans, isn't it, that delay between habit and change. But I have found it is not so with some other species.

We were met outside the house by a small group of people consisting of James and Simone, who had discovered the body, Beryl Jones, and Dr. Malwi. Everyone else who lived there had been sent back to work in the fields as far from the house as possible. The villagers had been encouraged to keep away and had generally obliged, though we had observed several small groups of people lurking around St Clare as we rode through it.

"Thank you for coming so quickly, Orlando," Beryl said, clutching at my hand briefly, looking pale and uncertain, something I had never known her to be before.

James and Simone fidgeted nervously in the background, and Dr. Malwi looked grim. I greeted them all and made appropriate noises of concern. Then Beryl led us inside the house, through the spacious hallway, and into a small parlor, where there was water in a large jug, some glasses, a basin, and small towels. It had been a hard ride, and Lambert and I washed the dust of late summer out of our throats and off our hands and wiped its yellow buildup from our faces.

I was told that no confession had been made yet, no one coming forward to explain what might have happened. We assured each other quietly that it was early yet and anyone involved might still be in shock.

"A few more hours, a sleepless night," I murmured reassuringly, and we all wanted to believe; believe that whoever was responsible would come forward freely.

Then it was time for me to ask questions.

"Who is she?"

"Her name is Louise, was, Louise Lanoir," Beryl stammered.

James and Simone were there because they had found the woman's body, and as they were likely to have little information as to the way she died, I spoke to them briefly.

Then I asked, "Will you show us where she is?" and Beryl led the way, followed by me, Dr. Malwi, Lambert, and the two young people, all trudging reluctantly up the main staircase to the scene of Louise's death.

When we came to the doorway of the room where she was, we remained on the threshold looking in. Her body no longer looked human. It was oddly twisted where it had partly slipped from the bed onto the floor and resembled some stained and discarded doll. I felt ill seeing the dark livid blotches about her face and neck.

Kneeling down, Lambert opened the small case he had brought with him and, taking out the visual recording device it contained, passed it to Dr. Malwi, who fiddled for a minute before starting it.

"Please describe the scene as it was when you found her here?" I asked James and Simone, so their response could be recorded on the device.

Nearly fifty years later as I watched the visual record we made that day I saw them nervously answering me. So strange to see those images for the first time, to see a brief glimpse of myself caught at the edge of the picture. I stopped the recording and went back to that frozen image of myself, mesmerized by myself as another person, in another life, with no idea of what is already happening to him.

I am privileged that I was able to return to Earth briefly and given complete access to all the records of that time that are held in the Administration's archives. But I wonder if, in fact, it was another punishment, seeing myself so unaware, at the height of my power and pleasure. Knowing as I do now that I had already started to fall, had begun the arduous journey to where I am, as I watched the record we made, and saw myself as I was then.

What is up and what is down? Most people would think I am mad, that I have not fallen, that I have risen instead above anything I could ever have imagined then. There is a truth in that, but I have risen in a way that is not personal, I am seeing myself in another way.

I was happy then, and independent, doing just what I wanted to be doing, living as I wanted to. Now I am not independent and can never be like that again. How I live now and what I do are not what I would have chosen. There is nothing dreadful about my life, but it is not the one I would want, yet I could not have chosen otherwise about other more important things.

Choices are built on other choices; they pile upon each other like the bricks in a wall. And some cannot be removed if the wall is to remain strong.

Others can't know the price I have been obliged to pay for everything that has changed for humanity. That is what this story is about, perhaps. I am telling myself about the price, which is insignificant to humanity and the Empire, but means something to me.

Apparently, Louise's position when James and Simone found her had been much as it still was, as we recorded it when we arrived, only the discoloration was far worse.

"I knew she was dead immediately I saw her." James said, but he went in to look at her anyway and had felt for a pulse at her neck and found her cool and still to his touch.

There was no need for them to remain any longer, and I asked Beryl to find them something to do until Lambert and I were ready to interview them properly.

We stayed outside the room and watched Dr. Malwi visually recording the body, all of us instinctively whispering instructions, not speaking out loud. Once everything had been recorded as it was in there, we had to go in and help him to move Louise's body around so he could record her image from all sides. Right side, left side, and back. He recorded the bed under her, the floor under her foot, where it hung down.

The strange, little, brushing-slapping sounds our hands made on her dead flesh and clothes as we grasped and turned her and the spongy cool feel of her body made me gag.

As I have said already, this is one of the moments burned into my mind.

I pressed my tongue to the roof of my mouth and thought of nothing. All that existed while I worked was total concentration on handling her with care, with reverence, turning her so Dr. Malwi could record the appearance of her body, back and front, head to toe. Then he recorded the outside of the room, the passage, the access ways, and the adjoining rooms.

Lambert took over the recording and continued down the main staircase and then returned and went down the small servants' staircase at the back of the house, and finally he recorded the exterior of the house. Lambert also took measurements of the room and building in preparation for making a detailed plan of the house. Once the two men had finished, it would be possible, if it were necessary, for someone who knew nothing of who or where we were, to examine the body and the scene of the crime in detail.

Watching it again in the Administration's archives I thought the record they made achieved that. For me it was like being there again, and as I have said I had to stop it after only a few minutes and wait, overcome by my emotions, before I could continue.

The wagon carrying Louise's coffin arrived from the carpenter before we were finished, and I ordered it taken upstairs and laid outside the room where her empty shell lay covered with a sheet, and then I sent the two drivers off to the inn to wait for us to finish. When the visual recorder had finally been put away, Dr. Malwi and Beryl wrapped her body in a clean linen sheet, and Lambert and I helped them place it carefully in the coffin. That task complete, Lambert went in search of James, and the boy ran and fetched the drivers back from the inn.

We all helped to carry her coffin downstairs and load it onto the wagon. We were a sad, sorry group as we watched it drive off, a small cloud of pale yellow dust rising into the late-afternoon air and twisting in the breeze behind it, partially obscuring it. Louise's journey took her underground to meet the train, to return in a couple of days for her funeral. Wherever she went in between, they

30

would do whatever they could to determine the story of how she had died.

By then all I wanted to do was to return home. But first I had to interview Jones and the two young people who had found the dead woman, and after that I would have to talk to Dr. Malwi.

Lambert recorded the interviews I conducted in the journal he had brought for that purpose. Like the report, I was able to reread it recently, and I could almost hear the constant sound of his pen scratching furiously across the paper as he endeavored to take down everything that was said.

From experience I knew his writing pace and tried to proceed with the interviews at a speed such that it was only occasionally that he demanded a break, or for a question or response to be repeated. He was obsessive about recording everything, which pleased me.

I saw James first. Except for the people working on domestic duties in the farmhouse, everyone was working away that day.

"I was in the apple orchard clearing grass from about the trees with Luc Denisovic. We returned to the farmhouse for lunch at about a quarter past twelve," he told me.

Then he had a brief wash outside the stables with a couple of other men before joining Simone for lunch. In the summer a couple of long trestle tables were set up in the cobbled yard behind the house, and the farm's thirty-odd residents ate a cold lunch outside. At harvest time the food was taken out to the golden fields where they worked among the ripe grain. Or into the shady orchards. In winter and on rainy days, they ate a hot lunch inside in the main hall.

When he and Simone had finished lunch, they went upstairs with the intention of spending some time together in James's bed before going back to work. Instead, they had found Louise's body.

James had not noticed that Louise was not at lunch, nor had he any idea of where she would have been that morning. He hadn't seen anyone leaving the house while he ate or washed. His only interest was in Simone. He was able to tell me exactly what she had for lunch and what she had said before and after they found the body and gave me a vivid description of how she reacted to the discovery.

Simone was next and had little to add. She had been checking the fences around the large wheat fields with Phillipe Pao Lin. They had been fortunate to get a ride back to the farm on a wagon. This got them in at a little after noon, and she had saved a seat beside her for James.

Simone knew exactly what James ate for lunch but had no idea of who may have come out of the farmhouse or whether Louise had been at lunch or what she would have been doing for the day. She could also recite every word James said and was unstinting in her admiration of his bravery in confirming Louise was dead and then waiting alone with her body while Simone went to get help.

I wondered how soon this pair of lovebirds would decide to move from Madeleine with its casual relationships, on to a society oriented toward monogamous couples and families. I gave them six more months at the most, and I confess it gave me amused pleasure to see their obvious mutual adoration and happiness.

Poor Beryl Jones was obviously deeply upset by what had happened, but she had to provide details about everyone's duties for the day and where they should have been. She had thirty people living in the big house and working on her farm, and fortunately she had a rough program written out for each day. She and Lambert sat down with it at a small table in the parlor under the main window, and together they went through it and prepared a rough map of the farm with everyone's supposed location on it.

Three people were away from the farm that day. Henrietta, the housekeeper, under whom Louise worked performing household duties, had left that morning, gone to the market in the village of Du Lac and taking two young men, Raoul and Jacques, to help her and drive the wagon. They had taken the light wagon suitable for the chores of collecting some piglets and cooking pots and were not expected to return until the middle of the next day.

Beryl did remember noticing that Louise had not been at lunch that day, but it was not odd. Having worked in the house all morning, she could have eaten in the kitchen earlier in the day if she had wanted to. On a personal note she advised that she had spent the night with her on occasion and had been close to her without being involved. She also considered herself to be one of the girl's few close friends—which added to her distress.

"Louise was young and could be foolish," Beryl unhappily admitted, "But everyone was used to the odd ways she occasionally had, no one would have hurt her because of them."

When Dr. Malwi rejoined us, he gave his opinion that Louise had not been sexually assaulted nor was she pregnant as far as he could tell. From his records, she had been refreshed about six months before, her physical age reduced by therapy as everyone's is every five years or so. She appeared healthy, and he knew of no significant illnesses since she had come to the village several years before.

"While you were busy interviewing the others, I went for a slow walk around the village. I've lived in St

33

Clair for some time, and I think I'm generally well liked and trusted by the villagers. I hoped that whoever caused Louise's death would take the opportunity of being able to talk to me discreetly to do so," he informed me. But unfortunately that hadn't happened.

A number of the residents had approached him, but it was to express their shock and fear and enquire about the cause of her death and whether it could happen again.

"I still hope it was an accident, but as she was dressed at the time, I find it hard to imagine what they could have been up to. Is your imagination better than mine, Count?" Dr. Malwi asked.

"Perhaps they were having a dry run at something dangerous," I replied sarcastically

"Do you really think that likely?" Lambert enquired, with a look of disapproval on his face.

"No, I don't think so," I replied, and I was serious when I continued, "But I also don't yet want to accept that I may have allowed a person capable of killing her, deliberately killing her, to come and live here. I have been responsible for accepting and admitting most of the people who live here now, in St Clare, in the whole region of Madeleine. In the years that I have been count I have radically refined the selection process they must undergo, I have set and reset the tests they take, and I have decided the degree of psychological stability I consider acceptable in new arrivals.

"I am responsible in every way for what has happened if a resident of this village or of this region has deliberately killed this young woman. Whether they killed her because of love or hate, greed or jealousy, I am still ultimately responsible." I sounded pompous even to myself, but I took myself very seriously then. I took my position very seriously. It was my life, my passion, my world. "I feel the responsibility Lambert, and it is a very heavy one to bear. If I sound flippant, it is because this is a terrible business and I am not yet ready to accept my part in it without rebelling, if only with sarcasm."

"If you will arrange the horses for our return to the Chateau, I will have a few private words with the doctor before we leave," I added.

Lambert now had his lips tightly pressed together in a thin line of anger. He gave me a small, sharp bow before leaving the room, and I knew he thought I was being ridiculous. I ignored him and looked at the doctor.

"If no one has yet confessed their involvement, then I think it unlikely that it was an accident. Nearly everyone has finished working by now and should have returned home, but no one has come forward to say they know anything," I said to him, then tried to reassure myself by adding, " It's still possible we may hear something in the morning."

"So if it was deliberate, where do you go from here?" the doctor responded.

Dr. Malwi liked to play the part of a revolutionary. Though we suffered none of the wrongs that the French people of the actual eighteenth century had, he saw the political ferment of the time before the French Revolution as an intrinsic part of the period in which we pretended to live, even if no one else did. He expressed this by regularly denigrating my position, and me. But he apparently had no qualms now in dumping full responsibility for investigating this matter squarely on me, as count.

Of course in the petulant mood I was in, I had to goad him about this.

"Are you sure the aristocracy can be trusted to investigate this matter fairly, Doctor? As the most educated and respected person in St Clair, shouldn't you remain involved to ensure that your fellow villagers are treated justly?" Valuing earned respect and education above any formal position was a favorite stand of his.

"Normally I would, Count, but over the years that you have been here, I have come to regard you as a just man." He looked at me in that superior way he had at times. "If all the aristocracy were as enlightened as you, I believe that equality, et cetera, et cetera, for all Frenchmen would probably have been gained through peaceful means. Without the need for a bloody revolution." He leaned back and gazed benevolently at me across interlinked fingers, his hands held before his chest while he rested his elbows on the arms of the heavily carved chair he occupied.

We were talking in the small parlor of Beryl's farmhouse, a cozy room with dark timber paneling three-quarters of the way up the walls and plain whitewashed plaster above. The ceiling had some simple decoration, and it was a pleasant private room.

"But isn't the denial of equality intrinsic in the very concept of an hereditary aristocracy or ruling class?"

"A minor point, Count." He obviously did not wish to proceed with his usual political diatribe.

"Of course, I am not actually an hereditary ruler, am I?" This afternoon I wanted the last word.

"You represent an hereditary ruling class." He was going to have the last word after all. "Will you stay in the village tonight?"

I gave up. It was a stupid discussion to have at any time. "No. We shall return to the Chateau. I need to come to terms with what has happened and organize the paperwork for the investigation. Lambert must obtain the details of all the present residents of the village from the Administration, as well as a complete history of Louise Lanoir. Farmer Jones will arrange for the residents of the farm to be available to be interviewed when we return tomorrow." I looked down at my hands and fiddled with the narrow lace edging the shirt cuff at my wrist. "I admit that I still hope there will be a voluntary confession when the person responsible has had time to fully realize the import of what he or she has done. This is a society where everyone is tested to ensure that they have an acceptable sense of morality as well as emotional stability. In theory, because of the guilt they would feel, such a moral person should not be able to remain silent for long about causing this woman's death."

"These things are good in theory, Count, but in reality people change, things happen, or a stranger who has not passed your wonderfully stringent tests is in the picture."

"What do you mean? Everyone here has been tested for emotional stability and morality at some time, by me or the previous counts."

The doctor leaned back in his chair again. "Many years ago when I lived in Ancient Greece—where I was a father of democracy," he added quickly, briefly placing his right hand on his heart and looking upward, "there was an elderly man who lived in the hills outside Athens. He worked sometimes as a shepherd and also traded wild game that he caught, rabbits and such. He was around for many years and no one thought anything of him until one day he was found unconscious and very badly injured at the bottom of a small ravine. Well, when the medical evacuation was done, we were amazed because they couldn't find any record of him on our files. DNA tests were done and showed he was, in fact, a man called Edward Kim, who had gone missing from some rough town about twenty years before."

"It was one of those hard-living, hard-drinking places where most of the men seem subhuman and the women are pretending to be men or are whores. Anyway, he had badly hurt another man in a drunken brawl and must have thought he'd killed him, because he ran off. He had wandered at least two hundred miles in the next few years before finally settling in the hills near the region of Athens.

"You may think we are very sophisticated and organized, Count, but you never really know who could be around."

"So I am to be reassured that there is an extremely remote chance that Louise Lanoir was killed by someone who has wandered hundreds of miles and should not be living here?"

"All I am saying is to keep an open mind. We have both lived long enough to know that life is full of the unexpected."

"Very true, Doctor." I sighed. "But whether I have an open mind or not, I am starting to fear that this crime may not be solved without the kind of extensive, diligent, and logically organized investigation that Lambert excels in keeping me on track with." And which I find exhausting, I added silently to myself.

Dr. Malwi told me no more then but only mentioned the important things as Lambert and I were leaving. He was a man who enjoyed being obstructive.

"Statistically, you know it's nearly always the husband, lover, or boyfriend who did it. I looked it up. Find one of them and you've probably solved it," the good doctor told me, as he stood ready to wave Lambert and me off from the front of the Jones farmhouse. Of course she had no husband in Madeleine and probably no lover or boyfriend in the accepted sense. "A pretty girl, but odd," he called out as we booted our horses on into the early-evening twilight.

CHAPTER 2

In which we make preparations for a full investigation

Lambert and I returned to the Chateau in growing darkness and were pleased when the golden glow of candlelight in its windows became visible ahead and welcomed us back. The ride home from St Clair had been slow and tense for both of us, each afraid of his horse missing its footing and falling in the failing light.

We rode around the Chateau into the torch-lit cobbled courtyard at the side of the building that led across to the stables. My little spaniel, Francis, was sitting at the side entrance waiting eagerly to greet me, accompanied by Cecile and Allen, and I was surprised that Leonardo was not there also. As soon as I had dismounted, I stepped over and picked up my little dog and cuddled my face into her neck as she wriggled her chubby body and wagged her tail furiously with pleasure. I greeted Cecile with a small kiss, uneasy about her presence, and Allen without one, and then Cecile left us to go about her duties, while Lambert, Allen, and I made our way up to my study.

As soon as we were actually inside the doors of the Chateau we were aware of numerous members of my household lounging about in the passages and rooms we passed through. I was surprised that I hadn't already realized they would be eager for any gossip or information about the girl's death, I should have known that such a shocking event in a small community like ours was going to cause considerable talk and speculation.

The candles had been lit in my study ready for our return, and a small fire was burning brightly in the fireplace, which pleased me, as there was a chill in the night air, which we could do without. Almost immediately Cecile and several helpers brought in supper for Lambert's clerks and us, setting a variety of hot and cold dishes out on the top of the cabinet against the wall near the door. When they had finished their preparations and gone, I made up a plate of food for Francis and placed it on the floor by my chair behind my desk. She leapt on it, completely losing interest in me as she scoffed it down.

Wonderful Dogs!
I have badly missed the company of dogs since I left there. Their easy and obliging ways, the feel of them. They were always about me when I lived on Earth, and I have found nothing to replace them since I left it.

Allen, Lambert, and I endeavored to briefly finalize the urgent trade matters we had been discussing earlier in the day, before the arrival of the news that had called me away.

"There is nothing else you can do here now, Allen," I finished. "In the morning Lambert and I shall be returning to St Clair as soon as we are able to."

"Of course, Count, I shall leave in the morning too," the young man said. "Do you have any idea of how long you will take to find the person responsible?" I was sure that he would have liked some inside gossip to take home to the court of Count David, but I didn't oblige him, aware that I had nothing to give anyway.

I asked him to let Count David know I might need assistance at some time if the matter dragged on. The talks we had been having earlier in the day could be continued at any time now that the urgent issues were settled.

"Of course I will pass on your message. What has happened is shocking, and I will tell David as much as I know when I return." He hesitated slightly. "I have no doubt, Count, that I speak for him if I say now that he will agree to provide you with any help you may require."

I thanked him, and after I had seen him out, I faced Cecile, who had returned to the room discreetly to rearrange the food and tidy the plates and cutlery. "Thank you for the supper, Cecile." It was said, I hoped, as a pleasant dismissal, but she didn't leave, instead making as if she had something else to move about. "Will you please ask Leonardo and Father Pierre to join me as soon as they can? I will keep Francis here and there is no need for you to return," I added, glancing down at the little dog, which having devoured her food was now asleep, curled up by my chair where my feet had been.

Then I looked directly at Cecile, then at the door. Lambert and the clerks were moving in and out of my study, and unless she wanted to have an argument in public, she had to leave. She gave me a curt nod as she left the room.

If I had not been so disturbed by the day's events I might have let her stay then, knowing that she was annoyed that I hadn't. But I knew I didn't want to discuss the murder with her. Not because the dead girl had been a woman or from squeamishness, but because I knew that she would never understand how I felt about what had happened. Cecile was very good at her job, beautiful and enjoyable in bed. But deep down I knew she was not a person I really liked or with whom I wanted to share significant personal feelings.

Unfortunately, easy enjoyable sex is so beguiling. At the Chateau she made it easier for me to spend my nights with her than with anybody else, and I knew that until that night I had been too complaisant to make the effort required to spend less time with her.

Cecile's Autobiography
She has written a fantasy novel about our time together that I found very imaginative and mildly amusing. But I would not recommend it to anyone as anything but clever fiction.

My study was very large and had an adjoining office and library, which was where the clerks were working, including Lambert, who generally worked at his desk in my own study.

This arrangement allowed all the administrative and legal work of the region that needed to be done outside the villages to be undertaken within the Chateau. As I have said, I traveled regularly throughout the region with my clerks, dealing with all the administrative matters and legal and social issues that arose.

The previous count had located his study elsewhere in the building, where he could look out on the formal garden on the southern side of the Chateau. It was a garden comprised of cleverly interlocking raked white gravel paths, which enclosed multicolored geometric plantings. The whole arrangement set within an immaculately clipped box hedge of great age. The formal garden was stunning, but with its brightly colored angular complexities, it overstimulated me and jarred my nerves.

In contrast, the side of the Chateau I had chosen overlooked an expanse of grass and mature trees, oaks, elms, beeches, and some magnificent pines. Almost my first act on taking up my position at the Chateau fifty years before had been to move the study there, and I had never regretted it. The seminatural park swept away from the Chateau into a slight valley before it merged in the distance with the wild native forest, which continued up into the low hills beyond. The view across the park to the forest always calmed and relaxed me, until the time when I felt I no longer belonged there. Then it was an ever-present reminder to me of the peace I had lost.

The library adjoining my study was not for purely recreational purposes; it was there to help me with the administration of the region. It contained a vast miscellaneous collection of books on everything from criminology and medicine to religion and the law, as well as an extensive collection of material relating to life in Europe, and particularly France, in the period from about 1720 to 1790—when the troubles overwhelmed France and the old order ended.

That was the historical period in which I lived, in which I tried to ensure the region of Madeleine lived. That was what we were and what Madeleine still is, an idyllic rural society based on an idealized eighteenth-century France.

Lambert had called his two senior clerks to join him there with the intention of working through to the early morning hours, and they had been instructed as to the documents they were to prepare for the investigation. I also wanted any legal and medical references that might be relevant to the girl's death to be noted and summarized.

Lambert had all our residents' applications filed alphabetically, according to the name people were known by in the region. The ones from those not accepted were filed elsewhere, by the name they had when they applied. When someone came to live in Madeleine, or left it permanently, they were interviewed personally by me, or, if I was unavailable, by a substitute. Going to the cupboard, I searched for Louise's application and found her completed questionnaire easily, wondering if in hindsight it would tell me something important about her.

But there was nothing particularly significant about it, and even with her papers before me, I had no recollection of ever having seen the dead girl before. The meeting would have been at the time of her arrival several years before, and I couldn't remember everyone I had ever welcomed, but it saddened me that if I had welcomed her, I remembered nothing about her or our conversation.

Discovering that Louise had changed her full name when she arrived was the only thing there to disturb me; she was previously Helen Farrow. Changing one's names completely was not an exceptional act; often it was merely done to fit the new society better. But it sometimes indicated a desire for a significant alteration in the resident's own life. The starting-over syndrome. Most of the time it didn't succeed unless the person got counseling. Otherwise the same problems would arise eventually, and I wondered if Louise had been running away from something and if it could have caught up with her in St Clare and killed her.

Lambert's first action on our return had been to request her complete life and medical history from the Administration. His clerks were now making up a list of all the residents of St Clare, detailing their positions, lengths of residence in the village and the region, and their previous residences. A further request was being submitted to the Administration for a cross match to be done to determine if any other residents of St Clair had lived in another society at the same time Louise had.

There was a knock at the door, and at my call for the visitors to enter, I was pleased to see Leonardo and Father Pierre come in.

Leonardo was my great friend. He was in charge of the foresters, the hunters, and the stables. He was a man I had always found to be down to earth and practical, but caring and thoughtful too, as anyone responsible for the life and death of living things should be. We hunted together when I could, fenced regularly, and shared a deep love of the forests and the countryside around us. Like Count David, he took his pleasure with men, which was unusual for a man living in Madeleine, and I often wondered if he wouldn't have been happier in St Louis.

I liked old Father Pierre for his humanity. I am not religious myself, as I have always lacked any belief in a god or a higher power, but I have no difficulty understanding the allure of a complete, all-embracing faith in a power beyond ourselves. A power that has a personal connection with us.

In fact, I envy those who can truly believe and embrace such a faith. They can't suffer from the same doubts as I have surely. And they often have no doubt about their role as the superior and ruling species in this part of the universe. Something I found quite unjustifiable then and now find ludicrous. But I can understand that for them it must be part of an acceptance of God's great design for man.

To me our Father Pierre always seemed to exhibit the tolerance, love, and forgiveness a true believer in a loving God should have.

Lambert I could rely on totally to organize the mechanics of the investigation, but I also wanted to talk to people I knew, who had common sense and an understanding of what makes people tick—to talk about why this awful crime may have been committed, if it was not an accident. I knew that Father Pierre and Leonardo were people who understood how men react—the feelings and emotions we have that could make us do something like taking a woman's life.

I also suspected Father Pierre of knowing everything that was going on, as he loved to talk. So I hoped I would also find out from them about any gossip going about concerning the girl herself, or a lover. Something that might help me find the guilty person.

They picked at the remains of the supper, and I poured us wine.

"I take it no one has come forward yet?" Father Pierre asked.

"No, Father. Unfortunately, we have not yet had a confession. I have done all I can to make sure that there was plenty of opportunity for one to be made discreetly. Lambert and I joined the farm's residents for part of their evening meal, and afterward I took a short walk alone, Dr. Malwi also walked about the village in the afternoon, making himself available. If anyone had approached him or Beryl Jones and confessed since, they would have found a way to let me know. Not strictly an approved purpose for emergency contact, I know, but I really don't care. What I would like to know is if either of you have heard any gossip about the girl and her death?"

"I'm sorry, I've heard nothing," Leonardo said.

"And you, Father?"

"I am in St Clair the first Sunday of every month, as you know, Count. I remember the dead woman well. She sometimes came to my mass, and she also spoke to me in private on several occasions, and each time it was about sin and God's punishment. She sounded as if she was blaming herself for something that had happened, but she never gave me the details, and I didn't press her. I thought it would all come out in time when she was ready to deal with it. I knew she would not have been here if she was emotionally unstable so even though she seemed . . ."

46

he paused to think, ". . . a bit obsessed by sin. What sins she never specified, but I was sure it was about sex. Which is odd for someone who has chosen to live here, but I didn't think there was any need for me to be intrusive or compel her to talk."

"If someone I have accepted into this society is capable of taking another persons life, then much as I want to believe that my questions and assessments are a guarantee of emotional stability and morality, I am forced to wonder about that, Father. And any resident connecting sin with sex, in a society that actively encourages open promiscuity, is certainly unusual."

"I disagree," Leonardo interjected, "No test will ever be perfect, but yours is such a long-winded rigmarole that it would be hard for anyone capable of murder to be accepted by you."

"Thank you for the vote of confidence, Leonardo," I replied, wanting to believe there was reassurance in what he said, but reassurance of what, I couldn't say.

"I must agree with Leonardo, Count. But I will qualify my confidence by saying that things can happen over many years to change people, and sometimes people and events from previous lives can come back to haunt us and drive us into a temporary madness. To return to your question, though, I have also heard in the past that Louise could be provocative at times, and misleading in romantic matters," the Father added.

"In plain language, Father, what do you mean?" I asked him. I had no desire for another entertaining tale of wandering strangers, such as Dr. Malwi's.

"I'm only passing on gossip, Count, most of which I heard several years ago. From what I gathered, she could be a tease, leading a man on to expect something from her but at the end of the evening not giving it. That can be very annoying for any man, and in this society is very out of character and not expected—of course some women

47

just say no in odd ways, and young women can change their minds quickly. But I have wondered if perhaps this time someone came back the next morning to take what he thought he deserved and got carried away forcing it from her."

"I am sorry, Father. But I can't see her being strangled in the morning because she didn't have sex with someone the night before. It's not impossible, but if he had done that I am sure he would have tried to have sex with her before, during, or after the event, which Dr. Malwi doesn't believe he did. Even I can't believe that I would have let someone that unstable in. It would be frightening too, because it would make the killing cold-blooded.

"You say there was no sex, Count?"

"No, Father, none with a man for at least for some hours before her death."

Father Pierre looked at Leonardo. "But I heard that she was tied up and raped."

"She was definitely not tied up," I said firmly, wondering how these lurid stories get about. "It may have looked as if she struggled, but she did not, and Dr. Malwi does not believe that there had been intercourse. This will, of course, be confirmed one way or another by the laboratory where her body has gone to be examined."

"How odd. I thought Cecile told us she was. I'm sorry, I must have been mistaken. If she wasn't raped, then I agree it is much harder to imagine it being a crime of revenge, or punishment for her behavior. Unless, perhaps, it was a woman who killed her?"

Leonardo made his apologies and left us then. He rose before dawn on most days and it was late. I had been so disturbed myself by events that I realized only then that it had been thoughtless of me to ask him to come and appreciated his attempt to reassure me.

48

When Leonardo had gone, Father Pierre and I talked for a while longer about various things, but I learned nothing more that I felt was helpful in finding the dead woman's killer. Finally, we discussed the arrangements for her funeral, after which Father Pierre left.

Details of the staff, horses, carriages, and wagons required for the following days were arranged by Lambert, and it was decided that as we had to make arrangement, we would plan for the investigation to take three days in the village. Lambert, a junior clerk, two grooms, two servants, a rider, and I would make up the group to go to St. Clair the following morning.

Finally, Lambert and I collected together the applications received from everyone now living in St Clair. I glanced through them all before retiring to have a few hours rest with only my little dog, Francis, for company.

CHAPTER 3

We begin our time at the inn in St Clare

Having so many aides de mémoire made available to me by the Administration's archivists, and having completely immersed myself in them for several weeks, it's astonishing how much came back to me. In particular, reading my own private journal of the time in conjunction with Lambert's let me see again, quite vividly, people and places I had thought completely forgotten.

Our arrival the following morning at the inn in St Clair was subdued, but we found about twenty of the villagers gathered in the road outside, awaiting us. After alighting from the carriage and straightening my coat, I had one of the wooden benches at the front of the tavern moved forward, and I stood on top of it, where I could be seen by everyone, and I made a short speech, as I knew I was expected to do.

"We are all deeply shocked by the death of Louise Lanoir," I said with gravity. "Her funeral is expected to be on Thursday, with Father Pierre officiating, and I shall be here to attend it. I hope to know the manner of her death by then, and who was responsible, so that we can lay the uncertainty caused by this matter to rest with her body." I avoided using the word fear. I had no idea if there was a madman loose among them or not, but I wasn't going to say anything that could encourage panic.

"I want nothing more than to find out how she died. Any help you can give me, any information you can provide, however trivial it may seem, will be appreciated. I will be interviewing all of you personally about Louise and what occurred yesterday. As soon as I know exactly what happened, I will ensure that you are all informed." Hardly an inspiring performance, but I was never a master of impromptu eloquence.

"Remember, anything at all you may know about Louise or anything odd that happened in the village yesterday morning or even in the previous few days could be important." In such a speech we should repeat a phrase like that with the aim of making everyone in our audience feel personally involved in some way, so I did.

Several people then called out questions, and hearing someone asking if the dead woman had been raped and beaten, I decided to answer a few of them, because I wanted as little wrong information as possible going about. I held up my hand for quiet.

"If you ask one question at a time, I will try to answer them," I said.

"Is it true that someone killed her deliberately?" a woman at the front of the crowd cried out.

"Someone else was certainly responsible for Louise's death. But there were no signs of any violence." Apart from strangulation, of course, I thought to myself. "She wasn't beaten or raped, I can assure you of that, as can everyone who saw her. At this stage we don't know who caused her death or exactly how. It could have been an unfortunate accident. And I know that, like me, you also hope that is what it was. I also trust that anyone here knowing anything about what happened will come forward as soon as possible. We can all do foolish and dangerous things, for harmless reasons. Again, I assure you she had not been beaten or raped."

"Was she strangled?" a man at the back called.

"I believe so," I said, "but exactly how we aren't yet sure." The crowd had now settled down and was losing interest. "You will be told what happened as soon as we know for certain. Thank you, ladies and gentlemen, I will be speaking to you all in the next couple of days," I reminded them. Then I quickly got down off the bench.

I also understood, though, that these people needed to feel that I was on top of the investigation, and I endeavored to look decisive and in control and made agreeable noises as I moved through the thinning crowd into the inn.

It was the first and only murder to occur in Madeleine during my time there. The region was a place where people went to live because they wanted to enjoy life and indulge themselves. And they were all selected and approved of before they arrived.

There had been sudden deaths before, of course, which I had to investigate. Accidents, unexpected illnesses, one accidental killing when a man was strangled in some odd erotic fantasy. But there was no doubt in any of them. What had happened was easily explained. All I was required to do was verify the details and prepare a report for the Administration. Louise's death was completely different.

Some of the staff members I had brought with me had remained to hear what was said rather than going about their work, and Lambert now hurried them off to the stables and into the inn, where they should have been. Almost immediately I called back the rider and instructed him to return to the Chateau and request Leonardo to come or to send an experienced gentleman of his staff to assist me. I had intended to have the servants help me in small ways but realized now that it was not going to work. I needed someone more disciplined and professional. The servants were generally young and came to Madeleine to enjoy the pleasures of youth rather than to do much else, and I sent back to the Chateau the ones I could spare, who were more interested in gossiping. They could return with the carriage to get on with their usual work instead of hanging about St Clair with time on their hands.

Inside the inn, Simon, the innkeeper, greeted us. He looked like a jovial host, portly and balding, with a red face, which normally had a smile on it, and he opened the first door in the entrance passage and showed us into the large room he had set aside for us. The chamber contained two large wooden tables, a couple of dressers, and a good many chairs.

"This parlor is usually used as an eating and sitting room by visiting merchants and tradesmen," he told us. "Somewhere they can receive their customers, spread out their wares, do business and afterward entertain them. I never expected it to be used by you for a murder investigation." He shook his head and sighed unhappily as he sat down with us.

Farmer Jones joined us there soon after, and I was shocked at how old and worn Beryl had become in just a day and at how tired her voice sounded.

"I have arranged a list and told them all what time you want to see them. Henrietta should be back soon." She sighed. "Since you left last night, I haven't heard or seen anything of any significance. The poor girl might have up and done it to herself for all the talk there is of anyone else being involved. No one on the farm is acting oddly either. I think they're all still in a state of shock. They are such a soft lot that they carry on for days when one of the big animals dies of old age," she said with sad affection.

I pulled out a chair and set it by one of the tables for her, and she thanked me, sitting down heavily and looking at her big, strong hands that rested in her lap. I took another chair, set it next to hers, and sat down to listen to her.

"I can't believe it's anyone at the farm," she said, looking and sounding even more worn and confused. "She used to talk to me, you know. She got very lonely sometimes and needed to talk. She was young and pretty, and . . . and I get a bit lonely myself sometimes.

"You work hard all day, and when you get a chance to relax, you haven't got the sort of friendship, relationship, I suppose you'd say, with anyone at the farm that gives you an excuse to spend time with them relaxing. You are always the boss when you deal with them, and it's so busy on the farm they don't see you any other way. They usually don't want you there anyway when they are 'off duty,' having fun. But because Louise sometimes used me for support, I could expect the same from her. She was a nice girl, in spite of being flighty. And I always knew there were good reasons for the way she was, I don't know exactly what they were, but I know she had them."

It was a long and personally revealing speech for Beryl to make. She was normally very brief and practical in her ways, not given to displays of emotion.

I knew yesterday's events would have put the farm work behind, and it still had to be done, so I let her go immediately as she had nothing more to tell us. When she had closed the door behind her, I turned to the innkeeper. "Well, Simon? Have you heard anything more informative?"

"It's getting her down terrible, isn't it? Like Farmer Jones said, though, for all that I've heard, she might have done it herself. That's not possible is it, Count?" Simon asked.

"No, unfortunately not." I paused, "There must be some talk. About her, about people she knew, men she was involved with, about what happened."

"There was talk of nothing else here last night. Plenty of talk. But nothing about who might have done it. The talk I'd expect about how she could be a silly young woman sometimes. But I knew that. Everyone did. And she was a nice young woman in other ways."

I focused on Simon. "People keep telling me she could be odd or flighty or silly, and I have let it go till now. But I find it a strange way to describe someone who lives here, so please tell me, what was she really like?" I was by now getting the distinct impression that because she was dead, everyone was being nice about whatever Louise's odd or silly behavior had been. "You weren't involved with her at any time yourself, were you?"

"Me? Never!" he blurted out. "She wasn't that bad, but I like a quiet life. You wouldn't know it, but I generally stay with enjoying myself with the staff, which is why I'm so particular about them. I'm careful who I get here, and they stay for years. Louise was pretty and young, so she always had men interested, and most of the time she wanted attention, and she knew how to flirt to get it, a great flirt. Get them going, encourage them to go after her. Usually that was fine and everyone had a good time, but then there were the times when she would change her mind . . ." He paused. "I don't want to speak ill of the dead, Count."

"I can understand that, Simon, but I want to find out who killed her, and it will probably help me to do that to know what she was really like, particularly if she had some sort of problem."

He looked unhappy. "Oh, well." He hesitated still, and I looked at him severely and he continued, "Occasionally she'd get very bitter about something. Then she'd drink more than she should and deliberately lead some fellow on all evening. You could see her do it; she'd deliberately pick someone she knew she could get a reaction out of. At the end of the night, you never knew what she'd do. Sometimes she'd just walk out—leaving him. If he went after her, which was a natural thing to do, she would like as not start screaming wild accusations at him. She knew some language, I can tell you. And she wasn't above taking a swing at him if he went too close.

"Then, next time she met him, she might flirt with him again, or she might completely ignore him. And if she did take a fancy to one of the boys and get together with him a few times, she was just as likely to be rude and insulting the next time he approached her. You couldn't win either way with her, it seemed. But everyone got an idea what she was like after a few months."

I was shocked by the details I had now heard of her behavior. It sounded completely unlike anything I would have expected from anyone accepted into the community of St Clare. She sounded extremely unstable, and I was concerned and mystified at how she had been able to successfully complete the application that had led me to accept her. Apparently I was not only letting murderers into Madeleine but mad women too, and I was horrified.

I had read through her application several times the previous night, and it gave no indication at all that she was not completely suitable. But then I corrected myself; all it showed was that the person who completed it was acceptable. "Was she ever bothered by anyone? Because of her behavior," I asked, sure that it must have caused difficulties.

"From what I have heard . . ." He hesitated slightly, but having already told me the worst, now wanted too much to show he knew everything. "It seems that Harry Bonato might have given her a hard time. Jacques Dupre's name came up and Fouquet too, which was a bit

56

of a surprise. But all the talk was about what they said a couple of years ago, nothing recent, and I think she had become less difficult over the last couple of years. I hear all about everything here—all the village gossip, as you can imagine. And I haven't heard much about her for a while now. Or seen it in here. It's a while since she behaved like that here."

I thanked Simon and told him I would talk to the three men he had mentioned. I also decided that Beryl and Dr. Malwi needed to be talked to seriously about what I had been told by Simon about Louise's behavior.

As the innkeeper left me, two servants came in, carrying a small chest, which they placed on the table, and Lambert followed them, bearing a smaller portable iron-bound writing desk, which opened out and held his pens and ink bottles inside. The rectangular room was quiet and cool. Its plastered walls had been recently whitewashed, and in the long outside wall, two leaded windows overlooked the road and the village pond. A large stone fireplace with an open hearth occupied one short end wall, and the heavy oak door we had entered by was set into the middle of the other long wall opposite the windows.

I knew that the inn was a comparatively new building, not original, as were most of the houses in the village, and I appreciated that it was built as it should be. Lambert and the servants moved one of the large wooden tables to one side of the room and then put a couple of chairs behind it so that I could sit in the center of the table with my back to the windows. Then they put a chair on the other side opposite mine. Lambert set up the other table near the door. We put a couple of chairs opposite his, and the room was ready.

The servants left, and we laid out the journals and pens and ink from the chest onto the tables and set upon them several candles. The windows were not large, and the light needed to be better for writing, particularly for

Lambert, who did not have the windows behind him. That done, we were now ready to commence the tedious part of the investigation, and it felt like embarking on some dreaded, put-off journey that can no longer be avoided. A hesitant knock at the door signaled to us that our first visitor was ready. I took my place, and Lambert opened the door and showed the man into the chair across the table from me.

The interviews were conducted by me and recorded by Lambert in his journal. Before leaving us, each of the interviewees had to read and sign the written record of interview that Lambert had made. During each interview, I would also make my own brief notes of any points I considered to be of particular importance and then make any other notes I wanted while I waited for the person to read and sign Lambert's record.

The first half dozen people we saw added nothing new to the information we had already obtained. Some of them hardly knew Louise, disturbingly only recognizing who she was with certainty when I mentioned she had sometimes been difficult. Then Simon came to tell us that Henrietta, the housekeeper from the Jones farm, was back, and that Beryl had sent her straight over to see us. We apologized to those who were already waiting for their arranged turn, and Lambert asked her in. I hoped to get something useful from her, because she was the person Louise had worked under since her arrival.

Henrietta walked in with her head held high and her graying hair tucked neatly into a lace edged cap framing her rather angular and fleshless face. Her plain dyed skirts hardly moved as she walked, her body lean and her chest almost flat under her tight bodice. She looked suspicious and defensive, and I sighed. Her replies to my questions were brief but to the point, and told almost everything I ever found out from the farm residents about the dead girl's life in St Clare. I have given her answers complete. You will be able to work out my questions I'm sure, and they do not need to be given. She told us very little really.

She did her work reasonably.

To me it seemed she got on all right with the men.

She arrived about four years ago. In July, I think, not long before the harvest. It was a time we had a couple of vacant places, and with the harvest, you know, we wanted help.

She settled in all right.

I have been here for nigh on thirty years, your lordship, and I reckon I'll stay as long again. Of course Madam Jones is a good mistress. Experienced in farming and used to having a large household. She knows how to deal with all sorts, so things run smooth. Unless people are difficult . . . then . . . then she can be too soft with them.

Who has been difficult, my lord? Well, I can't really say.

I've been running the house now for eight years. Before that I assisted the old housekeeper for over twenty-two years.

Yes, Count, I reckon the housekeeper knows most of what goes on in a big house like that, certainly more then the mistress does, her being busy outdoors so much.

Unless it was harvest time, Louise helped with the housework.

Yes, like yesterday. Most of the work in the mornings is in the bedrooms upstairs: changing linen, making up beds, collecting laundry and general tidying up.

I don't know what you mean, Count. What did I think of Louise? Yes of course I can understand your question. But a woman in my place learns to pay no mind to a lot of goings on, you know. And I have no wish to speak ill of the dead.

Well . . . she could be difficult. She could get on well with the men but didn't know her own mind. She would lead them on, you know, sometimes I reckon she just liked the drama. She was often running hot, then cold. You would have thought she was a teenager. But the men seemed to like her well enough. She was young and very pretty.

No. Um . . . Like I said, I don't wish to speak badly of her now she's gone, but I don't believe it were accidental, not entirely. In a way she were a woman you could see might come to a bad end.

Who did she spend most time with lately? I'd say with Raoul and Samuel. The last couple of months maybe it was Samuel. He's a quiet young man. Seemed to have a way of keeping her calmer too.

No. It weren't unknown she'd occasionally spend time with Beryl. Too tolerant and sympathetic of young people, is Beryl, I would say. But we all have a great respect for her . . . so did Louise.

After a hard day, her ifs and buts made Beryl laugh, I reckon. I know she didn't take the girl's moods serious. Even so, you could tell they annoyed her sometimes.

I never saw her angry with the girl.

At some time most all o' the men cept Jan and Ben. Those two avoided her they did.

She never spent much time with any o' the women. Me she saw about her duties and at meals. Many ways she kept to herself, not one to sit around with the girls and chatter.

Occasionally. It weren't often; she had no reason to be away but personal ones. It was rare for anyone to come to the farm asking after her. Only one stranger to my mind ever came. But she sent a lot of letters at the start. Hardly got any herself. I know, 'cause being housekeeper, I usually send out the mail and get it in and sort it.

Outside I wouldn't know. But like I said, she were probably less active than most, being changeable as she was.

There was no more to discover from Henrietta, and she left me to go and sit at Lambert's desk, waiting to sign his book. She looked worried, and I sighed again. She was someone who knew a lot about what went on in the farmhouse, and I wasn't sure if she had told me everything. She obviously felt very loyal to Beryl.

"Henrietta," I said, and she looked around from her seat at Lambert's table. "Farmer Jones has already told me about her relationship with Louise and that she had spent time with her the evening before she was killed."

She turned bright red, and I was fascinated to see the color spreading up her neck from her chest until it disappeared beneath the fabric of her cap. Then she dropped her head and turned quickly away.

I was more than ready for a break at midday when Simon brought in fresh bread, salad, smoked fish, fresh fruit, and wine for our lunch. I sent him back with the wine he had brought and asked for water and coffee instead. When I am involved in important work, I don't like taking alcohol or anything else that may dull my thinking or make me feel tired or out of control in even the slightest way.

Similarly, I long ago learned never to make any important decisions when I am in an emotional state, Unfortunately, that is something it is sometimes easy to forget when you are actually in an emotional state.

I know I said to Lambert then, "Do you realize, Lambert, that it's over twenty-four hours now since Louise died, but I feel no closer to knowing who caused her death than when you first informed me that her body had been found." I remember it specifically, because we had an odd conversation then.

Lambert looked up from his sandwich. "I think we now know of several people who did not kill her," he said in a critical tone of voice.

"I can't disagree with that. But what I really meant was that personally, apart from a sense that I probably need to find someone else as unstable as her, I have no feeling that I am getting closer. As far as evidence goes, the people on the scene know nothing and have told me nothing that gives me any direction. She had no serious relationships while she was here. Apart from Beryl, there doesn't appear to have been anyone who could be called a friend. We could interview everyone else in the village, and if they don't tell us anything more about her, then what have we achieved?" I asked him.

"I know you usually have good instincts about what is significant in these kinds of situations. If you aren't picking up any signals, then you may be frustrated. But I am sure that the killer will be found in the next couple of days. At the moment I see this investigation as a process of elimination. Eliminating the people who had the opportunity one by one, until we find the guilty party. I don't find it much different, in practice, to any of the other big investigation we have undertaken in search of a thief or fraudster." He chewed his food contemplatively. "In a way, taking a person's life is a kind of theft, isn't it?" he added.

It wasn't like Lambert to be profound, and I thought about what he had said. "I suppose it is, in a literal sense. But at the end, the thief has nothing, though he has taken something of inestimable value. The motivation must be very different. The result certainly is."

"Anyway, I think that looking for any criminal requires much the same procedure. We just have to do the same as we did when we investigated Michelle Trudot's death," Lambert continued.

It astounded me that he could compare the two events. "Michelle's death was waiting to happen, Lambert. It was a shock when she finally managed to kill herself, but not a surprise. What we had to do there was simply verify the obvious and leave no room for doubt. I'm sorry; I don't see any similarity between the two cases." Michelle had a death wish that was fundamental to her existence. It kept me from ever getting close to her, though I was very fond of her. She lived dangerously and rode like a maniac until one day she jumped her horse over an empty hay cart. Unfortunately, hidden from view on the other side of it were some large barrels, which were waiting to be loaded. Several witnesses saw rider and horse separate when they tried to land in the middle of them, and Michele broke her neck and was dead before anything could be done for her. Somehow her horse survived.

Lambert looked at me in surprise. "I didn't know you felt that way, my lord. I thought you were very worried about how Michelle's accident happened and took the investigation very seriously."

It was a pointless discussion. Of course I took it seriously. "From what you say, Lambert, you agree that none of the people we have interviewed so far killed Louise?"

"Yes. Probably."

While I ate, I went through the personal notes I had made during the mornings interviews. There was not much there. I always tended to deal with problems in an instinctive, but I believe logical way, if that makes sense. Lambert dealt with them in a pedantic step-by-step formulaic way. We complemented each other but could also irritate each other when we were working together for long periods without any results.

I was not bound by any rules of evidence or legality of procedure, and I was investigator, judge, and jury for Madeleine. So, instinct was just fine. But. There are always buts aren't there? Unfortunately, anyone I convicted for serious offences was free to appeal to the Administration outside the region. They could appeal my decision on their guilt, or they could appeal against the punishment I had imposed on them. Such an appeal involves a long-winded bureaucratic rigmarole, and the provision of all evidence and statements that led to the conviction or sentencing. This made good records of all significant investigations essential, and I was always very grateful to Lambert for ensuring that they existed.

A knock on the door signaled the arrival of our next interviewee, and before they came in, Simon returned and removed the remains of our lunch.

Shortly, all their answers began to blur together they were so uniform and insignificant. Henrietta and Beryl had essentially told me everything about the dead girl. All I learned during the rest of the day was that everyone who lived at the Jones farm had been where they were supposed to be on Monday morning when she was killed.

As they had worked in groups of two or more, their stories were all being neatly corroborated when we got around to interviewing their workmates. By late afternoon we had interviewed them all, and unless two or more were in collusion, it had become apparent that none of the residents of the farm could have killed Louise.

I wanted to hear a different view of the village and its inhabitants and decided not to put off what I knew would be a frustrating and unpleasant interview. I sent one of my servants to ask Fontenoy, the painter, if he would be able to join me after dinner. While we waited for his answer, I called Simon in and asked him to draw up a list of all Monday's visitors to the village that he knew of and sent another servant with a note requesting Beryl to provide me with the same list by morning.

Dusk had arrived, and because most of the villagers ate their evening meal at home and the tavern thus was quiet, I took the opportunity to sit outside undisturbed on one of the long wooden benches against the stone wall at the front of the inn.

It was a beautiful late summer evening, throbbing with the sounds of life. The air pleasantly mild, insects singing in the shadows, and the sky reflecting brokenly off the lake before me, the image disturbed by spreading ripples caused by fish feeding just below the surface and a family of ducks late in paddling home to the reed beds for the night.

The servant returned and informed me that Henri Fontenoy, our great artist in residence, would join me shortly.

While I awaited his arrival, I returned to the parlor and again read through the notes I had made during the day. Simon had brought a jug of hot fresh coffee and plates of cold food while I was out, and Lambert was having his dinner. I joined him, kept reading while I ate, and found no inspiration at all.

We had barely finished when Fontenoy made a noisy entrance carrying a bottle of dark red wine and waving two empty glasses.

"Join me in a drink, Count," he demanded loudly. "This is great wine."

I let him shakily pour me a large glass rather than argue. "How are you, Henri?"

"Fabulous as always, my lord, but it's time you got some new women living here." He waved his glass, spilling some wine across the table, and I regretted not making the invitation for the morning. The excess consumption of alcoholic beverages was an unfortunate habit of his. Considering his age, I frequently marveled at the stamina his brain exhibited by remaining in operation.

"The ones here are a bloody dull lot. I can't get them to pose for me more than a couple of times." He leaned forward and unfortunately breathed on me across the table.

"I am not appreciated here. There are societies, my lord, where my work is bloody well appreciated. Worth a fortune." He spat the last words out along with occasional droplets of wine.

"If you aren't happy here, Henri, you know that you are free to leave at any time," I said to him.

Once I used to be polite and say that I would be sorry to lose him, but later I didn't bother being nice. I would have loved to be rid of the old bastard. There were more complaints about him then anything, or anyone, else in the region. Now I look back, I still know he was an old bastard, but a part of me admires and envies his refusal to do anything except what it suited him to do, and with no regard for anyone else.

He stabbed a finger at me angrily, "You'd be sorry if I left, lord high and mighty. I give this place a bit of culture. My reputation puts you and your poxy Madeleine on the map." Then he slumped back in his chair and relaxed for a few moments. I was grateful that the preliminaries between us seemed to be over. "I assume you want to talk to me about this bloody woman's murder? I hardly knew her, you know."

I sipped the wine he had poured, and as always, it was excellent, and I wondered if he actually did appreciate the quality of what he drank. If he was able to taste it still.

"I am sure you had something to do with her. All I have heard so far is polite analysis of her unfortunate personality from nice considerate people. I thought that your vitriolic views of everyone around here might be more informative."

He laughed vigorously, ending with a bout of rough coughing. "You're a wicked man, Count. Don't you get sick of all these nice, boring subjects doing what they're told?"

"I like them just fine, Henri—certainly far more than I would a population of obnoxious old men like you."

He laughed again, and there was more coughing. "Before you choke yourself to death, you had better tell me what you know about the dead girl, Louise Lanoir, and any of her lovers." I could have said that I had heard she could be flighty, but I didn't want to encourage him to exaggerate her faults.

"She was a stupid little tart. I think I did a pretty good painting of her when she first got here. No problem getting her clothes off for that. She didn't do much for me, though. Fragile looking. When I did feel like a bit more, the stupid bitch thought she had the bloody true cross between her legs, started screeching filth at me. She did the same thing with other men, you know. God knows why she came to live here, or why you let her, but it was hardly enough reason to kill the slut. I've heard she was a lot of fun when she did deign to take the lid off her bloody box. There's nothing a woman's got that's worth killing her for, though."

He laughed again. "I've had so many knock backs in my time, I certainly wouldn't bother. Did he do it with her after she was dead? I heard a bit of talk about that. I've always thought that would be bloody dull, doing it with a corpse. But there's no accounting for taste."

I ignored his imaginings. "Did she have any lovers who might have got jealous?"

"Here? Bit against the rules having a regular lover, isn't it, Count? I think old Beryl, the boring sod, was about the closest thing she had to a lover. There was a brief passionate fling recently, if the stupid girl was capable of such a thing, with that gorgeous young Spanish boy, Raoul. A bit of cradle snatching there, my lord.

"I had a party one night to celebrate my latest show, elsewhere, where I am really appreciated as a great artistic talent." He got lost for a moment, blinded by his own starlight. "Anyway, what was I saying? Oh yes; a party. Well, she was quite appreciative of me kissing and fondling her tits during the evening, wanting to make Raoul jealous, I reckon. But when I wanted to get to bed for some serious sex, the tart put the lid on it again like before."

"Anyway, I did better than her. Stupid cow," he added, grinning.

"If a woman refuses to have sex with you, Henri, that is her right. I'm more surprised that any of them would actually want to do it. What about other people in the village? Are any of them into violence at all?" I already doubted it was worth spending any more time with him and wondered how I could get rid of him quickly.

"This dull lot," he laughed briefly and leant forward, "I think that Frank Lumiere ties Veronique to the bed when they do it. She has the most magnificent bloody breasts. Sometimes I paint them from memory when she won't pose for me. I . . ." He stopped suddenly and looked surprised.

"That was what I couldn't bloody remember." He looked at me with the expression of a brainless idiot, which on him looked appropriate. "I looked for Louise this morning, my paintings of her, when I heard she was dead. Wanted to remember what she looked like. I couldn't bloody find them. Didn't really care, though. There was something else important, though, that wasn't there, but I couldn't remember." He paused and then his lips started to tremble and his eyes opened wide. "Orlando," he wailed, tears forming in his eyes as the words escaped from his trembling lips. "They've stolen my beautiful paintings." He put a shaking hand on my arm. "My masterpieces, my children. God, Veronique's gone! Shit! shit! shit!" he yelled, his old eyes bulging in his red face. Then he leapt up and went to the door, throwing it open and staggering out much more quickly than I would have thought him capable.

I motioned Lambert to follow him and continued to sip the fine wine from my glass. I wondered if Henri would even know what pictures he had, and chastised myself for thinking like that, because I knew he was still surprisingly bright. However disgustingly drunk, vulgar, and arrogant he was, and considering the large amounts of wine he consumed regularly, he could still paint brilliantly.

At that time he still held shows all over the world on a regular basis and occasionally attended retrospective exhibitions of his work. I knew he probably was the most famous living artist there was and that somehow he painted women superbly.

Henri's Fate
Surprisingly, he is still alive, though I believe he has almost stopped painting, and the years of heavy drinking and wild living have finally begun to take their toll.

It took a few minutes, but I eventually also realized that his paintings were worth a fortune elsewhere, and that their theft could well be a reason for murder. "Damn," I said in an appropriate eighteenth-century French manner and emptied my glass. His house was conveniently near the inn, and I hurriedly walked over there myself.

It was a dark night outside, but the sky was clear and lit by a million points of starlight. Knowing the way, I took the path from the inn straight to the courtyard between Fontenoy's house and the old pale-stone stables, with their ancient tiled roof, that stood behind it.

The stables had been converted into storage for his paintings, and I could faintly hear the old man's voice coming from inside as I approached the large, partially open timber doors. He was moaning and yelling, and there was the sound of female voices also. Faint light was spilling out from the opening between the doors, and I went in, finding the place quite well lit by the flickering light of several lamps, which had been hung about. The voices were coming from upstairs, and I walked up the plain open-treaded old dark timber staircase, holding the handrail firmly.

I found Lambert standing on the landing at the top of the stairs and stood behind him, watching the old man going from rack to rack examining the canvases stacked there. Two young women hovered around him; one was slim, tall, raven-haired, and unfamiliar, the other blonde, petite, and far too familiar.

"Is anything really missing?" I asked Lambert quietly.

"Yes. I think so. The girls seem to agree that a couple of things are not here," He sighed with resignation. "I suppose I have to do an inventory, don't I?"

"Yes." We both knew that would be unpleasant. Spending much time with Henri always was. "This theft could be connected with Louise's death," I added.

"Oh." Lambert turned to me in surprise. "It could be, couldn't it? I'd only thought about the inconvenience."

"I only realized it myself after you'd gone. We forget that these pictures are very valuable and that there are people who would make you rich in return for a painting by Henri."

"I hadn't thought of that. I just think what a nuisance the man is. Anyone could have taken them, you know," Lambert added. "This building wasn't locked when we arrived."

At this point Henri let out another moan and wailed "Gone. Gone, my life's work . . .gone, gone, my beauties . . . bastards." The raven-haired girl was trying to console him, putting her hands on his shoulders, while the blonde one, I remembered then that her name was Maree, stood back, looking on, not really appearing concerned but seeming very irritated.

None of them appeared to have observed me there, so I quietly left and returned to the inn, promising to send a couple of people to help Lambert complete his inventory. I felt sorry for him being left there for the

70

night, to get little sleep and extract sensible information out of an emotional Henri.

I was fortunate to be able to retire to my room with Lambert's journal, to review his version of the day's interviews before going to sleep. With the discovery of the theft, I hoped that the dead girl's own strange behavior might become irrelevant in explaining why she had been killed and who by.

CHAPTER 4

The investigation continues

The following morning Vincent woke me at dawn, which was my normal time to wake, though at home I was usually dragged from sleep by one of my dogs or a woman. Perhaps it was because neither was there that I slept so soundly on my first night in the strange bed of the inn and was so deeply asleep that it gave me a shock to be woken suddenly.

I bathed in the common bathroom adjacent to my bedroom, and when I returned to my room, Vincent helped me dress. He had brought my official duty suits in a chest in the wagon, the garments I wore when undertaking my regular official travels about the region.

Aristocratic, muted but comfortable, today we had decided that I would wear soft gray silk with a tracery of pink and blue flowers, highlighted with silver mesh. The flowers were embroidered on the vest and trimmed the coat pockets and collar. Very elegant and sophisticated, but also very stressful to wear as I had to be so careful not to dirty my clothes.

It took four experienced embroiderers a fortnight to complete. Good embroiderers were difficult to find at that time, they probably weren't always easy to employ in the eighteen century either. Unfortunately, such garments only took so much cleaning before they began to look tired, then they were passed on to someone else in a less senior position or put into the common wardrobe, and I required new ones. At that time embroiderers were even scarcer than usual, which was causing serious delays with new clothing. So I felt even more relieved when I could return my garments to Vincent's care unsoiled.

Lambert joined us while Vincent was finishing with my hair, slightly powdered today, which blended in the gray in a very mature and sophisticated way I felt. Then I indulged myself in the search for perfection in tying the jabot about my neck. Poor Lambert looked tired, with deep shadows under his eyes, as he watched me.

There were always advantages in being a count. Don't let anyone tell you otherwise.

"It looks as if at least a dozen of Monsieur Fontenoy's paintings are missing." He sighed and was unable to stop a yawn. "He is a little hazy about which paintings should be in the storehouse, but the two women aren't quite as vague, and Maree actually has some records of what has been sent away to exhibitions and returned. They all agree that the Veronique series of six pictures is gone, Janet also described a few others, but Henri can't seem to remember them very well. It seems that as he is a 'true artist,'"—he said it with a good imitation of Henri's whining voice—"he doesn't remember paintings very well unless they are special to him. But at the moment I am satisfied that at least twelve pictures have been removed without his knowledge."

"What would they be worth?" I wondered out loud, still looking in the mirror but observing his reflection in the glass, rather than my own.

"A great deal, certainly several million. Do you want me to get a professional estimate in?" he was frowning, probably as unsure as I would be about how to do such a thing.

"It doesn't matter. Such a large figure would be meaningless to me." I sighed. "Are we to officially consider them stolen, Lambert?"

"Yes. I don't think we have choice. I did wonder if he remembers what he does when he's drunk, but he's never lost paintings before that I have heard. And he's surprisingly sharp about important things. I do not believe there is any alternative to theft, and I have already reported it to the Administration."

"The Administration already?" I was surprised and turned to look at him.

"The pictures could be on their way anywhere, Count. Even out to the Colonies. We don't want to seem to be lagging in such a matter."

He was right; we didn't want to look slow. "And how is the great artist in residence taking this?" I wondered.

"He's been sedated, and I hope he's still sleeping it off. He had drunk so much and was still ranting and yelling and drinking in the early hours, so I sent for Dr. Malwi, who thought it best he rested if we were to get any sense out of him today. I would also suggest, my lord, that Henri is the most obnoxious person I have ever met." He set his lips into a thin line of disapproval.

"You must have led a quiet, sheltered life, Lambert, if you think he is that bad." I turned and took a last look at myself in the mirror before leaving it, happy with my appearance. I took such things so seriously then and preened myself terribly. I still dress carefully for important occasions, but I have lost the pleasure in the clothes I wear that I had in those days. "So we have a murder and a major art theft to investigate now?"

"So it appears, my lord. It also seems that the dark-haired woman living with Henri, Janet is her name, is someone he just brought back here from New York, without asking anyone's permission."

"What?" I turned about angrily before remembering it was Henri we were talking about. "I suppose it shouldn't surprise me. You had better arrange for the residents who were kind enough to see us yesterday to return this evening. Just for a few minutes each. I will have to determine if there is anything they can add about this other matter."

"Will that be all?" Lambert asked, yawning again.

I paused to consider the situation. "Do you think that this theft could be connected to Louise's murder?"

"I cannot say, Count. It could be. It's certainly quite a coincidence, but then it may not be."

"Thank you for those words of guidance," I said, having no idea what he really thought once I had heard them, or what I did either. We proceeded downstairs and outside to a small wooden table and chairs set up under the shelter of the front wall of the Inn, which Simon had laid out for Lambert and me to breakfast at.

We were served by a pretty, full-bodied young woman I hadn't noticed before and now admired casually. She had fine large breasts very attractively swelling above a plain linen blouse, and she smiled seductively at me with her lovely dark eyes and full lips. But I had other concerns just then.

While I was cutting up a sweet apple, I held up a hand, stopping Lambert as soon as he started to talk. I needed a few minutes of peace and quiet to consider things. We ate together in silence, and I lingered over my coffee after Lambert had finished and gone about his duties. The reports had arrived on the examination of Louise's body, wherever it had been taken on the train, and also on the samples Dr. Malwi had been told to take from the scene. Lambert had already dispatched one of the servants to ask the doctor to join us when he could.

The principal question I had to consider that morning was—had Louise been killed because she knew something about the theft of Fontenoy's paintings? It sounded rather melodramatic and would be very ironic, given that the theft had not yet been discovered when she died. If she had not been killed, I had the impression that it may have been months before it was.

But if there was a connection between the two crimes then, why kill her on Monday if no one even knew a crime had been committed yet? Unless perhaps she'd witnessed the last paintings being removed from the village or the stables. Perhaps being picked up that very morning, or perhaps during the previous couple of days. Or perhaps she chose to say something to the person responsible for the theft. She could have spoken to them that morning, or more likely on Sunday, unless they too lived at the farm.

On Monday morning itself she should not have had the time to be able to leave the farmhouse for more than a few minutes before she was killed. She had been seen at breakfast, not leaving the table until nearly nine o'clock. Then no one had seen her leave the building. And she had removed the old sheets and made up the beds in several of the upstairs rooms before she died, which could not have occurred much before ten. So, it was extremely unlikely she had visited anyone outside the farmhouse before her death.

I decided I would have to revisit the Jones farm and see what could be observed from the first-floor windows, to determine if Fontenoy's house, or the stables, were overlooked from there. It was also possible that someone else living at the farm itself was involved, but from the interviews I had done already, I believed it was unlikely another resident could have killed her. With

Henrietta away, there had only been three people working in the kitchens, and they all swore that between nine and ten none of them had left the kitchen where they had all been busy washing up, drying, and putting away the breakfast dishes and beginning the preparation of the vegetables for lunch.

Another issue was Henri's unknown girl, Janet, I had no idea yet what to do about her.

But first I must visit Fontenoy's studio, then examine the medical reports and the lists of visitors Simon and Beryl had compiled all of which had just arrived. Though a lot of questions still confronted us, I thought I could easily find answers to some of them and I was ready to attack the investigation again with some enthusiasm.

When I reached the parlor we were using as our office, a large leather wallet and several sheets of notes were waiting on my table. The loose sheets contained the lists of names of visitors I had asked Simon and Beryl to provide. The wallet contained the results of the forensic medical tests that had been carried out on Louise's body as well as the findings from the samples taken from the room by Dr. Malwi. There was also a preliminary report from Lambert about the missing paintings. I sat down and skimmed through everything quickly while I waited for Lambert to join me.

The two lists of visitors were much longer than I had expected. I opened the wallet to find the test results and preliminary autopsy findings. A covering note explained that there were further tests that would take a couple more days to complete. They would advise me when I had everything. Apparently I could ask for more tests to be done or for tests to be repeated, but in this case the writer, one Damien Vagos, did not believe that any others should be necessary, because there was no doubt that the women's death was caused by strangulation with a piece of plain linen fabric. And her killer had worn soft leather gloves that had been around horses. Hardly helpful; everyone wore white linen shirts, scarves, blouses, petticoats; fewer people wore leather gloves often, but most people owned them for protection when outdoors in winter or when riding, which meant many people had gloves that had been around horses.

I was very much relieved that my ignorance of forensic medicine was unlikely to impair the investigation.

Unfortunately, the killer had been very careful by using gloves, not being observed, and being fortunate that it had taken so long to find the body. They had not found sufficient material that could be from the killer to do a DNA trace with. So, not only was I attempting to find the killer the old fashioned way as a matter of principle and historical correctness instead of relying on the laboratories. There apparently was no other way at that time.

After my earlier optimism it was not turning out to be a good day after all.

As soon as he came in, Lambert informed me that the young hunter Leonardo had sent me as requested to be my assistant was waiting outside. I had Lambert bring her in; her name was Josephine. I admit I was surprised, I had expected one of the men I knew, who had been with us for a few years, or Leonardo himself. This young woman had only recently arrived in the region, and I had met her briefly when she arrived, as I liked to do, but otherwise did not know her at all. She looked fit and athletic, with short, black, curly hair and tanned skin and was dressed in men's clothes such as Leonardo's occasional women hunters always wore when working. Underneath the severe clothing, she appeared slender and gave the impression she was soft and yielding.

I drew Josephine up a chair at my table and had her mark the lists, noting the names of visitors who were common to both. She did this very quickly while I finished with the reports and returned them to the wallet.

"Can you tell me a bit about yourself?" I asked, curious as to why she had been sent to assist me.

She smiled with humor in her dark eyes, and I experienced an unexpected flash of desire for her. "Leonardo sent me to assist you because I have worked in the Administration's crime service and have experience working on criminal investigations. That was a long time ago, though, and since then I have mainly worked with animals, which was how I came to be a forester. Working with criminals every day was making me far too cynical about people. With animals, things are much simpler. They don't answer back or lie to you."

"I am afraid that our investigation is not going to be like those the Administration would conduct," I warned her, wondering what she expected and whether her experience would be useful in a society without all the complex electronic aids the Administration presumably used.

"Then you probably have more success, Count. And you have the great advantage of only having to direct yourself to one crime at a time and not having to produce a mountain of paperwork to support every investigation even if it comes to nothing in the end."

Of course, little of what she said was really true, but I let it pass.

"Unfortunately, today I am not so fortunate. I also have a major art theft on my hands. It has only been exposed because of Louise's death, and events there are moving so quickly I can't keep up. It is also very distracting, because it may or may not be connected to the murder." I paused, unsure how much to tell her, then decided I might as well explain more to her if she was going to be assisting Lambert and me. "If the theft is connected, then I am dealing with one case with two

79

aspects; alternatively, it may not be connected at all. Which would make it two separate crimes. Until I know the answer, I cannot set aside the theft and concentrate on the murder or vice versa. So I have to devote sufficient energy to both crimes until I know if there is a connection."

I have always had great difficulty delegating the information-gathering process. I find that, for me, so many small things can tell so much. Casual conversations can lead to some casual remark that can change the way one thinks of a person. For me, gathering information is an art. If I rely on another person's notes, I am always frustrated by not knowing what has been left out. This was particularly true of Lambert's records, even though he tried to be so accurate and complete, he was such a precise, pedantic person—so unlike me. It sounds ridiculous, I know, but the way he recorded things was just not the way I would hear them.

But it was now no longer possible for me to pretend that under the new circumstances I could continue with the planned investigation of Louise's death and also give my attention to the theft. I was going to have to rationalize and delegate to allow myself time to read all the information that had come in. Primarily I wanted to determine who had really been in the village on Monday morning and on the day before. It had become obvious that the list Lambert had prepared at the Chateau of the residents of the village of St Clair, was only the largest part of the population, not all of it. I felt sure that I was probably more interested in the smaller parts of that population: visitors and unofficial residents. (Having found Janet at Henri's, I hoped there were no more such creatures.)

I asked Josephine to find out as much as possible about the visitors and extend the period out to two weeks. She could take someone to help her, one of the servants who had remained, and I thought of Vincent, who had plenty of time on his hands. They were also to check the official list of inhabitants and see who had or had not actually been in the village during the morning of Louise's death. It was a big job but one she could do without my help. I was glad to have her out of my way. I wasn't myself, she aroused me, and normally I would have wanted her company, at least for a night, if she was agreeable. But I felt constrained by everything I had to do, and I was deeply worried whether I had inadvertently let a killer loose among my people.

If I had a complete list of everyone who had been in the village during the last two weeks, I knew the murderer's name would definitely be included on it. I would have their name written down, fixed on paper, waiting to be reached at some time, even if I didn't know who or when. And I felt as if there was some achievement in that.

At last Dr. Malwi arrived, and I gave him the wallet full of medical reports.

"From the covering letter, I gather there is no doubt about the cause of death. The rest of the information is rather technical, so I have only glanced through it myself and I would like you to explain it to me," I said, pulling my small notebook in front of me and inking my pen in readiness for his explanation to start. Having refreshed my pen from the inkwell several times, I got tired of waiting.

"Surely it isn't that complicated?" I snapped.

Malwi jerked his head up from his reading, "Sorry, Count. There is just so much information here." Placing the reports on the table between us, he finally ran through them all with me.

In my notebook I noted that in summary Louise was a perfectly healthy young women, apart from being dead, of course, which was quite an unhealthy thing for her to be. She was not pregnant and had not had sexual intercourse for at least eighteen hours prior to her death. There was also no bruising or other signs of a struggle, which indicated that she knew or at least was not afraid of her killer.

He paused and looked up mumbling.

"Speak clearly," I demanded.

"It says here she gave birth in the last six years. I thought it was more recent than that."

"She had a child?" I was stunned.

"Yes, of course. Why?" He asked.

"Because her medical history, which I have here, doesn't say anything about her ever having a child." I rummaged through my own neatly arranged papers, and when I found the Administration's medical history, I pulled it out and waved it at him. "And where is it? The child."

He read directly from the forensic report in his hand. "'The deceased has previously carried a child to full term and a normal birth is indicated. The birth took place between five and six years ago.' I knew she'd had a child, but as I said, I thought it was more recently. Refreshing doesn't hide that after one treatment," he added.

"There was no husband and no child in her history," I snapped back at him and pounced on Lambert's neat desk, scattering notes and reports about until I found a copy of Louise's ordinary history as provided by the Administration. "Definitely no husband and no child," I said, confused, and waved it and her medical history at him. "Definitely no child. These are her official histories, Malwi, and there is no pregnancy." I dropped the Administration's histories on the table in front of him, but he had already dragged out his own journal.

I stuck my head out of the door of the parlor and called to Simon loudly to bring coffee.

It transpired that Lambert had received the wrong histories; one of his clerks had requested the Louise Lanoir history without giving her full details. It was ridiculously frustrating and stupid; apparently there had been two Louise Lanoirs living in Madeleine. Now there was only the one I knew all about, and she was happily alive and well in St. Evian about twenty miles away. The questionnaire we had for our Louise was fortunately the correct one, we hadn't confused everything.

If our dead Louise had indeed had a husband, almost no one has a child without a husband, then perhaps at last I might have something to work with. As Malwi had said on the first evening, just before we left, husbands do make good suspects. I had looked it up myself and found out it was true.

The most important thing now was to ensure that we obtained Louise Lanoir's correct details. Once these had been properly requested, we had to wait for their arrival. Then Dr. Malwi went through the rest of the reports with me, and finally it was time for me to voice my concerns.

"You knew the dead women, Doctor. Yet you still haven't told me she was emotionally unstable. And worse, you failed to advise us at the Chateau after she arrived that her behavior was unacceptable. It seems to have been obvious to everyone that she was too disturbed to be here. Several people have commented on it to me. So, why didn't you inform anyone?" I paused, giving him time to respond, but he just sat and looked at me.

"You also failed to advise us about the arrival of Janet. Henri brings a completely unknown outsider into this community, one who is very young and emotional, one who is living with a much older man, a drunk and a womanizer, and again you say nothing." I paused again, but all he did was to glare at me as if I had insulted him. "You are the most senior person in the village, Malwi.

You are the one with the communicator. Whether you like it or not, you are also part of the Administration. Part of my administration. It's part of your job to assist me in the proper management of the region. As far as I am concerned, you have failed to do that."

Malwi still glared at me. "What are you saying, Count? Do you want me to leave; are you threatening me? Henri brings strange women back here regularly, usually they only stay a few weeks. I had no idea when she arrived that Janet would stay longer." He spoke angrily but kept himself under control.

"And I should have been advised about each of them. What about Louise? What was your excuse there?" I asked.

"It's not my job to inform you of everyone's moods. I am a doctor, I cure the sick. I am not a spy." He put on his superior look and sat there, obviously furious.

"She has been murdered, Doctor. And if her death isn't connected to the theft of Henri's paintings, then the way she behaved may have been part of the cause—which to me implicates you in her death. But you sit here and say it is not your job to let me know if someone in the village behaves in a totally unsuitable way." I waited a moment for what I had said to sink in. "If someone goes insane and threatens to start murdering everyone here, then whose job will it be to tell me? His first victim's? As far as I am concerned, it's yours, the man with the communicator's job." He sat there silently, looking furious still.

"She was not insane, I didn't consider her a danger to anyone except . . ." he stopped, flustered and glaring.

"Except . . . to herself, I presume you were going to say." I needed a moment to settle my anger. "She was a danger to herself, and now she's dead. If you had advised us there was a problem, she would possibly still be alive. I am not at all pleased with your attitude, Doctor, and if you want to keep your position here, your attitude will change." I was rarely so forceful and wondered if I had been too easy on everyone lately and should remind them all of their responsibilities.

"Have you said the same to Beryl?" he responded angrily. "She was her employer; she should have let you know if the girl was unsuitable."

"I assure you I will be saying the same to Beryl as I have said to you. But you are still the most senior person here, Malwi, not Beryl. You are also a doctor of considerable experience, and you knew there was a problem. Did you ever ask Beryl if she had reported the girl's behavior?"

"No." He was losing his superior air. He'd finally realized that I really was annoyed and that I could ask him to leave immediately and could fill his position with any one of half a dozen other suitable applicants waiting eagerly for their chance to live in Madeleine.

I had the authority to ask anyone to leave if I had good reasons to do so, and if necessary, I could have someone forcibly removed from the region and prevented from returning. If anyone chose to question my decision, which in such cases they generally didn't, I merely had to provide my reasons to the Administration, and I knew that they were rarely interested in interfering in such matters.

"You will have a report on my desk in an hour giving all the details about Janet and anything else you need to advise me of. From now on I will expect a written report from you at the end of each month. If you have nothing to tell me at the time, you will still send me a report saying so." I paused and looked at him. "That will be all for now. Thank you for your help with these reports," I tried to finish in a more conciliatory tone.

He left stiffly, not saying anything until he got to the door, where he turned. "I'll have your report here on time, Count," he told me angrily. "By the way, Madame Colette would like to see you. This last week she has asked for you each time I have visited her. She has very little time left now."

"Colette. God, how old is she?" I exclaimed, completely thrown by his remark and by Colette's imminent death. "I've always felt as if they built this village around her, that she was here before anything else and would still be here when it crumbled into dust. I will see her, of course. Come for me next time you are going."

Losing Colette would be like losing history. Colette and her husband had lived in the village of St. Clare since they were born, since before it became a historical society. She had even been born in the cottage where she now lived.

Dr. Malwi left then, comforted by having been able to pass on bad news at the end. I turned to my clerk. "Lambert, make sure that everyone in Malwi's position in all the villages is written to. I want them all to provide me with monthly reports from now on, for a while anyway, to remind them that they have a job to do for me."

CHAPTER 5

In which I at last find a criminal

Following my conversation with Dr. Malwi, Lambert and I went to see Henri at his house. In daylight there was more to observe. Henri Fontenoy's home was set well back from the road, standing almost directly behind the inn, which was itself set right at the side of the road that skirted the lake as it ran through the village.

As we approached the inn along the front pathway, we could just see over the low stone wall surrounding the front of the house and into the wildly overgrown garden enclosed behind it. Lambert and I entered the garden through the wooden gate set between two urn-topped stone posts and made a limited inspection of it and the outside of the comfortable red brick house. We saw no obvious signs of any disturbance of the wilderness within the wall, which was interesting but of little significance as it was almost certain that the missing paintings had all been removed from the stables at the rear.

Having conducted our inspection of the garden, we moved around to the rear of the house, where a large glass-walled studio, which had not been obvious in the dark of my visit the previous evening, projected out from the back of the house into the cobbled yard between the house and the stables. The stable yard itself was surrounded by a high stone wall with a pair of large wooden gates let into one side of it. These stood open, revealing a grassy lane running along outside the wall. Walking out into it, Lambert and I found that it appeared to be screened completely from the neighbor's view. Looking away from the lake and the inn, the lane ran out of sight into the adjoining fields.

"Where does this go, Lambert?" I asked as we followed it for a short distance.

"I don't know, my lord," he replied, walking along with me until we reached the first fields. Here the lane ended at another track, which ran to the left and right along the back of the cottages and houses, following the edge of the fields.

"They must use it to collect grain during harvest; these are usually barley and wheat fields. This way," Lambert said, pointing to the left. "It probably joins up with the Du Lac road."

"So. Very easy for a careful thief to load the paintings on a small wagon, cover them to look like one carrying grain, then get on to the main road and out of the region. During harvest or planting no one would be likely to notice that it had come from Henri's house."

"Given the size of his paintings, I think it would have taken two or three trips," Lambert replied.

"I stand corrected, Lambert." I had momentarily forgotten that almost every painting Henri did was life sized. And as they all depicted at least one nude female, they were all fairly large. Thinking about it, I remembered at one time having seen an interesting picture with half a dozen female figures entwined, which would not have fitted on any standard wagon. But, of course, that probably hadn't been stolen.

I had no experience of how one stole paintings but had a vague thought that they could be cut out of their frames and rolled up. But there again, given the size of the canvases, if they were to arrive at their destination in good condition, they would have to travel in very long, rather fat tubes, which one could hardly carry away inconspicuously under one's arm.

We returned to the large wooden gates and reentered the cobbled yard between the stables and the house, where we found Henri and the two young women who I had seen with him the previous night, waiting for us outside the studio. Lambert introduced me to Maree and the raven-haired Janet while Henri ranted on.

This morning he smelt of stale, rough wine, oil, and garlic. His hair was an unkempt mess as if an old gray bird's nest had fallen on his head and got stuck there. He had a couple of days' growth of patchy stubble on a face that sagged, and tired watery eyes. The rough night had done his appearance no good at all, and I ignored his mumbled complaints.

Maree I knew well, as I had accepted her into the region as a student wanting to study painting with Henri and had also dealt with her when she had come to me soon after her arrival with complaints about her teacher's behavior toward her.

Unfortunately there was little I could do to remedy things for her. Father Pierre, Dr. Malwi, and I all spoke to Henri about his rudeness and inconsiderateness, but as she worked and lived in his house, it was difficult, and she refused to leave until she had completed two years training with him, so there was no more that we could do. The last time I had seen her I could remember telling her that if she didn't like it, she could leave at any time, but if she wanted to stay on as a pupil of his, then she had to understand she had no choice but to put up with him. She had left that last meeting angry, slamming the door behind her on her way out.

I had never seen the raven-haired young woman before last night. Then I had assumed that this other assistant was someone who had already been living in the region before moving into his house, presumably as a student. She looked extremely young, not physically, though she was young in that way too, but she had that aura of uncertainty and naiveté, which only the truly young in years have.

"How do you come to be living with Henri, Janet?" I asked bluntly.

The girl suddenly had the expression and posture of a frightened mouse, and she pressed herself against Henri at my question as if she required his physical support.

He put his arm around her protectively. "You should be looking for the animals who robbed me, not interrogating Janet. It's got nothing to do with her. I brought her here from New York, and she's the only bloody one round here who gives a shit about me."

He jerked her as he tightened his hold, and a couple of tears ran down his cheeks till they got lost in the stubble covering his chin.

"She really bloody cares about me. None of the bastards round here appreciate my great talent; I have to leave my bloody home to get any understanding. But this beautiful girl . . ." she was making soothing noises and smoothing his shirt while her eyes darted around uncertainly, and he ran some knobbly old fingers down her arm and squeezed a breast, ". . . appreciates me." The tears and patting started again.

"And now some bastard has stolen my greatest work." Then he yelled and waved his arms about, sending Janet reeling away a few steps. "Why aren't you out finding the assholes instead of hanging round here like an overdressed layabout?" He had made his face quite red.

As they say, there's no fool like an old fool, I thought. "I shall conduct an investigation appropriate to the seriousness of the crime, Monsieur Fontenoy," I told him coldly. "I now find that you have a person living in your house about whom the Administration, in this case my office, knows nothing. A person you have brought here to live without advising me." The girl shot me a terrified look, and I wondered if she was involved with the theft.

How convenient for me that would be, especially if she had an accomplice from outside Madeleine who had killed Louise. Any fault for the girl's death was then lifted almost entirely from my shoulders. A very satisfactory outcome for everyone.

I turned immediately to Maree, who had been standing off to one side observing our recent scene, and I was taken aback by the look of satisfaction on her face, which instantly disappeared. "Maree, show me around, please," I requested.

We proceeded immediately into the studio, and I wondered what the dynamics were between the three people living together in that house. Lambert followed right behind us, with Henri and his girlfriend at the rear of the procession.

It was much tidier inside than I had expected. There were several incomplete paintings about the studio on easels still being worked on, which were clearly by two different people, one of whom I felt had no natural artistic ability at all. I gazed at two pictures for a few moments, fascinated at the difference talent could make to the appearance of strokes of colored paint.

"This is the studio where Henri and I paint. As soon as a painting of Henri's is finished, it is moved into the house or out to the stables." Maree stopped. "I am

91

only allowed to keep mine in my room," she added bitterly and moved on into a passageway and through to a large, comfortably furnished sitting room overlooking the wild front garden and with a pleasant view to the lake.

"If Henri really likes a painting, he wants to be able to look at it regularly, so it will be hung in the house. When he's tired of a picture or if he doesn't like it enough to want it in the house at all, then it is removed and put into storage in the stables."

There were a dozen large paintings about the sitting room, filling all the available wall space. So much well-painted flesh in one place would have been overpowering but for one enormous canvas on the wall above the large fireplace, which was a magnificent landscape showing a group of people swimming in what was recognizable as the village lake on a bright, hot, sunny day. I also noted that all but one of the paintings hanging in the room were in the same style, Henri's style. The sole outsider was definitely not Maree's work. It was the landscape, which was slightly abstract and full of vibrant, moving color.

Maree led us back out through the studio to the stables, which we entered through the main doors as I had the previous night. Even in daylight it was still gloomy inside, but even so it was easier to see the wooden racks full of paintings, which formed rows on the stone floor, almost completely filling the space. I saw that there must have been at least a hundred paintings stored just on the ground floor, most nothing more than painted canvass stretched over a timber frame, only a few framed for hanging. Upstairs there were even more paintings with two or three leaning in each wooden rack, which here stood on the old smooth honey-colored timber floor— probably three times as many paintings as were in the ground floor racks.

"Are they stored in any order?" I asked, standing on the upper landing where I had stood the previous night with Lambert, looking about me and estimating that there were altogether probably three or four hundred finished paintings stored there in the old stables.

"The paintings that go out on display often are stored downstairs along with new ones he likes but not enough to keep hung inside," Maree replied. "Anything not taken out much goes upstairs eventually as do the paintings he doesn't like. Probably most of what's upstairs is stuff he doesn't like, because it goes straight up there." She stopped and we looked around.

Henri had followed us up and suddenly pushed forward past Maree. "She knows the special ones are up here too," he said belligerently. "My personal paintings, the one's I don't want everyone to see. They're up here. That's why I noticed that Veronique's painting was missing when I was looking for the dead one's." Louise's portrait apparently wasn't a painting he liked, but he had also kept it upstairs.

"There wasn't an inventory, I'm afraid. Lambert and I made up an inventory last night," Maree said, butting in.

"There could be a lot more than twelve paintings missing, couldn't there?" I asked, and Maree gave a noncommittal reply.

"Bastards!" hissed Henri, looking disconsolately about. "Bastards!"

"Has Janet spent a lot of time out here?" I asked.

"She would come out with Henri and get him to show her his favorite paintings. I have seen her out here alone at other times too, Henri often has a nap in the afternoons, and she sometimes disappears then. Also, Count, she has been away overnight a few times." Maree seemed pleased to be able to add this, and I realized that she strongly disliked Janet. Or was she jealous? Henri obviously didn't pretend to like her poor examples of pictures.

"Get out of my house," Henri yelled and went for her, trying to grab her but fumbling while she leapt nimbly out of his way. "You're not going to blame this on Janet, you stupid bitch. I never want to see you again." He yelled and swore angrily at her, while Lambert and I tried to hold him back and Janet joined in, trying to calm him.

"I haven't stolen anything," Janet was saying, looking at me with tears in her eyes as she tried to hold Henri." She hates me. "Ever since I got here she has been horrible."

I glanced up at Maree, who stood away from us, looking bored, as if she had seen too many of Henri's tantrums to be bothered by one more. Between the rest of us, we eventually got Henri back downstairs and into the house, where Janet forced him to lie down on a sofa and he seemed to calm down.

"I have taken nothing, I wouldn't hurt Henri. I love him," Janet cried. She was so intent the way she looked at me through teary eyes.

"How can you love him? He's an ancient drunk." I couldn't help myself from saying it, it was very improper of me.

"But to feel his magical hands touch me is, is . . ." she paused and gazed at the old man dotingly. "I was a cleaner in the hotel where he stayed, trying to paint when I had time. Now I can watch him all day. I can paint whenever I want, and he encourages me, he says I'm good. He is a god to me. How could I not be happy to be with him?" She was bent over him, patting his hand, and she still looked so intense that I had to believe her. I didn't know if worshipping him was somehow worse than her being a thief.

I asked Lambert to go out and find Maree, who hadn't followed us in. He ran back in a few minutes later."

She's got a horse and gone! I couldn't stop her," he said breathlessly and ran out again, with me behind him. We both ran to the gate at the side of the yard and looked up and down the lane, but there was no sign of her anymore. Lambert ran to the inn to arrange for riders to go after her and advise the train not to stop. I went back inside briefly and brusquely told Henri and Janet that Maree was gone and that I would be back later, and then I returned to the inn.

It was a warm day, and I was hot and sweating when I arrived back and found several people awaited me there also. But I left them where they were while I went to my room to remove my coat, waistcoat, and breeches before they were stained by sweat, annoyed that Vincent was off with Josephine and not available to see to the clothes immediately. I donned plain black breeches and a black waistcoat with a few small red flowers on it. It had become a very active day as well as a busy one.

Several of the people we had meant to interview that morning had arrived while we were absent, and I didn't want to send them away, which meant they had to wait for us. Lambert dislikes sudden changes in plans and, since he already was tired, the morning's events had made him short tempered and irritable as well. His mood was not helped by losing Maree the way we had, but now the riders had gone after her, and there was nothing else to be done about that.

It only took an hour to catch up with the morning's interviews, and the semblance of order calmed Lambert down. When we finished, I asked Simon to give the next people who came food and wine until I was ready for them, and I asked him what he thought about Henri's two women.

"That Janet is a mad one," he laughed. "I wish she would do for me what she does for that old bastard. How did he find her? Hey? But he was always lucky with women. Maree, she's a slave for him, keeps the place clean, cooks, and washes. But she's a cold one." His expression became serious. "I don't think she likes or respects him at all. Sometimes I even think she hates him, and I wonder why she stays, even if he is giving her lessons. He says she is no good all the time, and who can learn from someone who thinks like that about you?"

I wondered if I now knew what had made her stay.

Then Lambert and I visited the big farmhouse again.

We went around the large main building and upstairs, where we carefully studied the views. Together we confirmed that Henri's house was completely hidden from sight even from the first floor, and so was the left-hand section of the track running behind the village, the one that could lead to Du Lac. The right-hand end of the path was clearly visible where it joined up with a more used road, which ran along the side of the big farm's own yard. This road provided access for heavy carts to the outbuildings there, including the granary.

From inside the farmhouse, it was definitely not possible for Louise to have seen the paintings being removed or transported. She may have seen them from elsewhere, of course, or heard something incriminating about someone, but it made any connection between her death and the theft less obvious. With Maree's odd behavior and sudden escape, my own feeling was that there was no connection between the two crimes, only the coincidence of the discovery. We returned to the inn, and I sent someone to tell Henri to come and see me there.

Henri arrived still looking decrepit. He made his way unsteadily over to the chair meant for him and sat down carefully without being invited. "What do you want?" He snapped, then burst into tears "My Eritrea is gone. It's gone." He slapped the table between us with his hand to emphasize the fact that it had gone.

"Yes, well . . ." I had always thought of Henri as an arrogant inconsiderate and rude old man. Now it was difficult not to lean across the table and give him a good hard slap. "What we are all here for, Henri, is to find out where it, and the other missing paintings, have gone. I assume that Eritrea is one of the stolen paintings?" He glowered at me, a couple of tears still snaking their way down his face through the creases and hair growth.

"I have asked you here, Henri, because I need your assistance in my investigation into the theft of your paintings. I no longer think there is any connection between that theft and the murder of Louise Lanoir."

"I don't know anything; anyone could have taken the paintings. Any time."

Henri leant across the table and stabbed a wrinkly old finger at me while he whispered, "You be nice to Janet. I know she's not done anything wrong. And you remember they're my bloody paintings. Don't forget that. If she is involved in some way, I might just say that I gave her permission to take the paintings. Being old and forgetful, I didn't remember and I got confused when you came asking." He sat back smiling, his lined face slightly flushed. The cheeks and nose particularly, quite bright red, glowing with satisfaction, quite obviously pleased with himself for his craftiness. Though his blindness in not suspecting Maree, who I was sure he didn't like, of being the culprit surprised me. Until I realized that she had possibly become no more than a piece of useful furniture to him that he preferred to ignore.

"Janet has told me she thinks you are a god," I said calmly.

"I know. Wonderful isn't she, and she can paint too. The other painting inside, you saw it there on the wall, that's hers." He whispered it with pride, then cackled and choked together and coughed up several gobbets of phlegm.

Fortunately, he found an old crumpled handkerchief in one of his pockets and wiped the phlegm from the table where it had landed, so I didn't have to look at it or remove it myself. I can remember wondering which would have been worse.

"So how could the paintings have been removed, if we assume, of course, that Janet had no involvement, but perhaps Maree did?"

"How would I know? You're God; go figure it out for yourself. I'm the wronged party here, the aggrieved party." He paused then added, "We wouldn't hear anything if someone came stealing them from the barn at night. Not where we sleep. Usually I have a glass or two of wine with my dinner and sleep very soundly," he added primly. "Janet does too, and she does share my bed most nights you know, so she wouldn't hear anything either. God knows what Maree gets up to; probably hops into her coffin and grows fangs." He laughed again, this time without any mishap.

"She has no talent, you know, Count. Your little goody two shoes, God knows why she's bothered staying on. She'll never be a painter, and she doesn't even have enough of an eye to be able to teach. A bloody cold bitch too, but she's kept the whole house and the studio clean and tidy. Does the washing, cooks the food. Otherwise, I'd have kicked her out months ago. But she's gone now and good riddance." He finished with an angry growl.

I wondered how she had found time to paint at all and who his next slave would be. Janet, perhaps.

"I will be speaking to Maree again later." I thought again about her painting in the studio; it had been amateur and unattractive, I knew, but I couldn't remember what it looked like. Yet, I could easily visualize Fontenoy's own works, which had also been there, as well as the amazing painting of swimmers in the lake of Janet's, which was in the sitting room.

Maree was a fool to still be there, and it made no sense that she still was if she was the only one involved in the thefts.

"Who else knows the layout of your house? Who, for instance, would know how to find the War series of paintings, in particular? They appear to have been put away out of sight."

"I have had other assistants, you know. And other students." He leaned forward. "Other girlfriends too. The students come here regularly, and they've all been approved by you, Count. So, why don't you run through your bloody records and your little tests and find out. And of course there are the other people in this bloody village."

"Your short-term assistants and students do not have to satisfy the requirements of those wanting to come and live here, Henri. I expect most of them to only be here for several months, at the most three or four of them have stayed a year or two. And they spend most of their time in your house painting. So we don't go into much detail before accepting them."

"What about that bastard Avien?" he pouted and rolled his eyes. "He spent a few weeks prancing about with no intention of ever doing anything. He knew almost nothing about my work, either—that quickly became obvious. And he was arrogant. Maree liked him, so he has to be stupid. She was why I let him stay longer. Even so, he only lasted a few weeks; then I kicked him out. Can't remember his other name."

"When was he here?" I asked, realizing there could be literally dozens of his ex-students to be checked on.

"I don't know. A year ago, but it could be longer. I can't remember; they come and go so quick. At my age it can be hard remembering a lot of things," he reminded me. "You should know that, Count. You're no spring

99

chicken yourself." I felt annoyed at being compared to him in a specific feature.

"We will find out about him first then. But there is still the problem of removing the paintings. Do you have any idea at all when they could have gone missing?"

"No. If I knew that, I'd have known they were gone, wouldn't I? Isn't that your job to find out how? And to get the bloody things back too, I hope. I've lost valuable property, you know, very valuable property."

"When did you last see the War series paintings?" I asked patiently.

"I Can't remember," he snapped.

"I don't want an exact date, Henri, just an estimate," I said with resignation; things were getting painful. "Maree says she has seen them. As she has been with you for over eighteen months now, they were all in your stable at least eighteen months ago. Has Janet seen them?" I included Lambert in my question, because he had spoken to the woman in detail the previous night about the missing paintings. He was likely to give me a more useful answer than Henri was.

"No I don't remember showing them to her." Henri's face was screwed up with concentration.

"Do you remember showing them to Maree?" I asked the old man, who's face had remained frozen.

"Yes," he cried, and his eyes glowed with the light of revelation, indicating that his concentration had paid off at last. "Yes, Maree nagged me to see them. She had seen them in a book on my work. I am a very famous artist, you know, Count," he reminded me yet again. "I had to find the bloody things upstairs for her, and she saw them and stopped nagging me. It was a while after she arrived here."

I eventually discovered from Lambert and Henri that Janet had been living with Henri since he brought her back from New York, in the last week of April. He had been there for a couple of weeks as the guest of the Museum of Modern Art for a major retrospective of his work. Two paintings from the War series and three others of Henri's choosing had been borrowed for the event and hadn't been returned until the end of June. So, the theft had to have occurred after that.

Maree was brought back to the inn early in the afternoon. Two riders had caught up with her waiting at the station located beneath the little cottage about half way between St. Clare and the Chateau. She was angry and frightened, sticking her jaw out stubbornly and glaring at me with her pale eyes. She claimed she had no knowledge of Louise ever visiting Henri Fontenoy's house during the time she had been studying there. As he said, he had painted Louise about four years ago, several years before Maree arrived, and long before Janet.

"I knew her vaguely, but she wasn't the sort of women I am friends with. She seemed a bit silly," Maree said with that superior look less popular women often adopt. "She had no idea about art as far as I know, and certainly showed no interest in Henri's work while I have been living here. He has been able to get most of the women to pose for him when they first arrive in St. Clair. He can be very flattering when he wants something, and he can also manage to keep his hands to himself when he really wants to." The last was said with bitterness. His roaming hands had been a frequent cause of discomfort for her at the beginning.

I was finding Maree's stories very odd. She knew where everything was and pretended she didn't. She had seen two of the stolen paintings come back in late June and had seen the complete set when she arrived, but had not mentioned Henri kept them upstairs. She obviously disliked him and Janet, and must know by now that she had no talent and wouldn't learn anything in that house. "Why were you staying here, Maree?" I asked.

She looked away from me. "You don't have any talent; you must know that by now. All you have been lately is a domestic for Henri and his mistress, and you don't like either of them."

I paused, but she remained silently, looking away from me—I expected her to burst into tears, but she didn't. "Henri said you were very keen on another student he had here for a short time. Avien, I think that was his name. Did you like him?"

She turned on me, her face full of hate, and I watched it color, the red rising from her neck to her forehead like a wave rushing up sand. "That dirty, filthy, pig sent him away, treated him like dirt. He knew we got on together. That's why he did it. But I still see him!" She said it as a challenge. "Because we're in love. Maybe I don't have great talent, but I deserve something for the time I have had to be there in the same house as those two . . .animals." She almost spat out the words. "Hundreds of paintings sit there doing nothing; he doesn't even bother to sell them. He's an old fool. He doesn't deserve to have any talent. He should be dead, the selfish, filthy old man.

"All the time I've been with him and he wouldn't even give me one lousy painting, not one, not even the one I took my clothes off for. I let him paw me, and he wouldn't give me the one he'd painted of me that he didn't even bloody like." She was standing up, talking hysterically now, almost yelling. "I was entitled to everything. I've earned everything, everything we've taken." She stopped suddenly and after a pause sat down, slowly lowering herself back into the chair like some Methuselah, and the color drained out of her, leaving her face white as sand.

"So, you thought you deserved something in return for what you put up with from Henri. He's the pig, I assume?" I asked her quietly.

"Yes." It was almost a whisper. "Avien and I took them. We were going to live in luxury on what he got for them. I deserved it." She looked at me again, her expression one of loss. "I deserved it."

"Are the paintings with Avien, Maree?" I asked. "Can you tell me where Avien and the paintings are?"

"No," she replied quietly, as tears started to run down her face, "No. I don't know where he is. Something's happened to him. I don't know what. He was supposed to come back for me last week, but he didn't. I went to look for him, but he wasn't there. Something must have happened. I know he must be in trouble. I know he'd come for me if he could, but . . . but . . . I didn't dare tell anyone he's missing. Because of the paintings. I've been so worried, but I couldn't tell anyone." The tears ran down her cheeks, and she looked completely lost.

The silly fool, I thought sadly. Avien already had everything he wanted from her. He would not have come on Monday or any other day and murdered Louise for anything she saw or said. There was absolutely no connection.

I sent someone to fetch Veronique, the nurse with the wonderful breasts Henri so admired. She would see to the girl, and while we waited for her to arrive, Lambert and I got the details of Avien's last address from Maree, along with a full list of the stolen paintings. Of course she remembered them all. Twenty of them altogether, taken during the early mornings that summer. When she had gone, I requested Avien's details from the Administration and also that they try to locate him and detain him for us, in connection with the theft.

Lambert and I finished interviewing all the local people left waiting for us through the afternoon, while we had been occupied with Maree, but at least now we only had to ask them about the murder, nothing else.

When Veronique arrived, she told me Dr. Malwi was at Colette's cottage and asked if I was going to see her. "Of course," I replied, and making my apologies, immediately left. It was a pleasant walk along the road by the lake to the cottage, which was set back among century old pines near the junction where the road left the village in the direction of Du Lac.

I passed in through the broken-down gate, which was now almost unrecognizable as anything more than a small pile of rotten timbers. The path was a short clearing between grass that was too long and standard roses covered in buds and waiting impatiently to bloom. The front door opened to my touch, and as I entered, I could hear the heavy ticking of a clock inside. I passed its old timber case on the wall and noted it was fast, as I walked to the living room at the end of the short passage. At the entrance I paused for a moment, taking in the scene.

Colette lay on the old day bed against the far wall, where it caught the afternoon sun. She was wizened and shrunken, hardly making a visible shape under the bleached coverlet, her small head resting on an embroidered pillowcase, much faded, after how many years of laundering. Fake yellow flowers stood in a vase on the small table under the window, catching the sunlight.

She had lived here all her life, and some of the things in the house were older than her. Odd things, like the machine-embroidered cotton tablecloths and sheets she loved, the old aluminum saucepans she refused to give up, and the useless electric stove in the kitchen on which she kept dried flowers, as if, like an empty hearth, it would be used again when winter came, as if the electricity was expected to come back on some day soon. The power also needed to run the old brown Bakelite radio, silent now for well over a century, if it had worked at all after the century it was made in had ended. It was covered now with a lace-edged doily and rested in the center of the mantel over the wood stove.

Nothing in the house seemed to have ever changed. I had visited regularly to listen to her complaints. At the head of the daybed in a tiny space between the corner of the two walls sat her husband, Alfonse, the foreigner she found somewhere when she was young and dragged back to this isolated village and never allowed to leave it. She had spent her life instructing him in his duties. Last time I came she still ordered him about from where she lay, and the garden was immaculate, freshly dug and clipped. He would go about mumbling what one took to be curses at her under his breath, his head down, busy carrying out her orders. Now he sat there looking into space, and I knew he would be hardly any time behind her.

Malwi sat beside her and turned when I came in. "Count Orlando has come, Colette," he said, almost shouting. "You wanted him to visit you, and he's here now." He touched her hand and gave it a little shake. "Colette."

Alfonse looked at me vaguely; then forgot me. Colette's eyes seemed to flutter briefly. "A drink for the count," she croaked faintly, and Alfonse was alive again and mumbled as he went out to the kitchen and made a clatter.

"I haven't got long," she said while he was gone.

He returned with a glass of watered wine for me. Then he fussed briefly about Colette's coverlet before returning to his chair. I stood beside Malwi and looked down at her. What did I say? "How are you feeling, Colette?" I yelled at her. She partly opened her eyes and they rolled about as if to say, what a stupid question. "You wanted to see me," I said loudly, business like.

"Alfonse needs a job; he's a lazy bastard," she hissed.

"What sort of job?" I asked, realizing she was going to do her best to run his life from the grave too.

"At the Chateau, looking after the harness. He's good at cleaning leather." She had lifted herself up slightly to look at me while she said this. Now she lay back exhausted and waved a bony hand about, and Alfonse was instantly beside her, his ear to her mouth. I could hear mumbling, nothing more. Then he pulled away and returned to his place.

"He will go to the Chateau with you when you return there. I will be dead tomorrow. He knows; I have told him. Do not be soft on him. He is a lazy man." She said it in short bursts and gave a great sigh and seemed to relax and fall back in on herself at the end, and in spite of Malwi's shaking, didn't rouse again.

"Is that what you want to do?" I asked Alfonse.

I thought he wasn't going to answer. He stared at nothing for so long. " I always do what she tells me to," he said calmly. "I will be ready to go when you are, Count."

Malwi walked me to the front door, "She won't wake again, if I know her. She always had to be right." He smiled and shook his head.

"Someone will be here?" I asked.

"Of course, Veronique or I, or occasionally someone else has been here all the time for the last few weeks. I don't neglect my proper duties," he added with a hint of anger.

"I will be here for here for her funeral. Two in one week is rather depressing," I said as I left.

I returned to Lambert and the investigation. When we had finished the day's interviews I needed to get away for a while, so I left the inn and went for a walk along the edge of the village lake. Optimists usually called it a lake, and it really was very large. About 500 meters long and in several places a couple of hundred meters wide. The actual shoreline was about three kilometers long, because its shoreline wound around quite a bit.

There were small points jutting into the water where the twisted roots of old trees clung to steep banks, and there were small bays containing shallow swampy reed beds. A couple of deep inlets had small wooden boats pulled up on the bank to be used for fishing the deeper waters in the middle of the lake or collecting eggs from nests in the reeds and for pleasure in the summer months.

Pessimists and pedants tended to consider it a big pond. The animals, birds, and fish to whom it was home cared nothing for such names and lived quite contentedly in ignorance.

Here and there along the banks were wooden benches and I settled myself down onto one of them. I chose it because it gave me a wonderful view across the water toward the setting sun. Waterbirds were already leaving the lake for the night, coming out in family groups, settling into the reeds or wandering across to coops in the yards of nearby cottages. Some villagers were still returning slowly from their work in the fields and orchards, occasionally heading straight to the inn as they came in but most of them going home. Some waved to me as they passed, and a few came over to ask me how my investigation was progressing. I answered briefly but politely that it was slow but I was sure we would find whoever was responsible soon, and they moved on without pressing for more.

A young man in the clothes of a farm worker came over and, after introducing himself as Piers, asked if he could join me. So, I moved along toward one end of the bench to make room for him.

"How is your investigation going, Count?" he asked.

"Slowly, I am afraid," I replied quietly and then paused, waiting to see what else Piers had to say.

"I'm sorry I can't help you. I only knew Louise vaguely, and the day she died I was working in the cherry orchards." Piers paused. "It's a terrible thing to happen and it makes you think."

There was a long period of silence as we sat watching the light fade and the sun turn the surface of the water from pale pink to an almost red, orange glow as if the water itself were burning deep down.

"I am a mining engineer," Piers said, glancing at me. "I was working on the deep shafts of the Bre x gold mines in Indonesia when one collapsed in an earthquake. I don't know if you heard about it?"

"I have heard about it," I assured him, knowing now why his face looked vaguely familiar. When he had applied to come and live in Madeleine I'd been sent a full report of the disaster with his application.

Piers looked surprised and waited a moment before continuing. "Then you know that the mines were manually operated, not automated, sort of a historical mining society. There is something very masculine and satisfying about doing that kind of heavy, dangerous work, and a lot of men, and some women, like it. I loved it, the whole atmosphere, everything. Some people do, so we have those mines around and supposedly we know the risks."

"It was a shocking tragedy. But there was nothing that could have been done to prevent it, Piers," I responded. "Even in an automated mine it would have happened." I vaguely remembered what the details had been.

"But if it was automated, hardly anyone would have been down there to die, Count." He reminded me, "It was horrible. Forty people I knew died in the shaft I was in charge of. It just collapsed; they had almost no warning at all."

He paused again and I sensed that he was still holding back tears after a couple of years. "There was a few minutes' warning, but it was impossible to get anyone out before the movement struck the shaft. The rock in the deep levels just rose up and twisted sideways. The shaft collapsed. Everyone below the second level was crushed or drowned. Some died very slowly. Did you know that?" he looked across at me, and I nodded. They had brought in robots that had bored down to recover them, when it was too late.

"Some died instantly, but others died slowly. Alone, in pain and terror, but too quickly to be saved by anything we could use to reach those depths."

Piers continued. "There was nothing to be done, and as you say, Count, no way to predict such a disaster at that time. Now we have deep core sensors around those mines. But it's generally believed that there is still nothing that can tell you soon enough when such a thing is going to happen.

"I knew all those people who died—some only slightly and others very well. I lived with them, ate and drank and partied with them. When it was over and all the bodies were recovered, that could be, I needed to get away. So I looked for somewhere completely different, rural, relaxed, but where there was plenty of physical work to distract me—and beautiful women." He laughed. "So, I came here." He paused again. "And I have enjoyed it very much. Madeleine is a lovely place, Count. But Louise's murder has reminded me that even this is real life, not time out. And it's not the real life I want. I never intended to stay here long, but it's been too easy to drift along enjoying it, until now."

I wondered what he had thought we lived, if Madeleine wasn't real life, but I knew exactly what he meant. Life is always more real when we are doing what we really want to do. And when we are reminded of our own mortality . . .

"Louise's death has shaken me up. I've realized that I have a life to get on with, Count, I don't want to live a fantasy any longer. I know you don't want anyone leaving until your investigation is completed, but I shall be leaving as soon as I may, with your permission, of course."

"Back to the mines?" I asked, already knowing the answer.

The young man smiled and nodded, "I want to work in the really deep mines at Dreifontein. Suddenly, it's all I can think about."

"Are there many others who feel like you? Who want to get away from here quickly?"

"There are a few, but, like me, they will wait in case there is anything you require from them. We all want to find this killer, Count. And please don't take any offence at what I have said; Madeleine is a wonderful place to live. It's just not the kind of life I really want. Not long term. Not now anyway."

He was ready to leave, but I held him back, "You live here Piers. Have you heard anything, is there anyone you think could know more than they are admitting about the girl's death, anything at all?

"I'm sorry, I don't know anything. But I will ask around and see what I can find out."

"I would appreciate your efforts very much, Piers. Come and see me if you find out anything interesting. If you don't, we'll have a talk when you leave anyway."

"How long do you think your investigation is going to last?" He frowned.

"Don't worry. In a few days I will be willing to formally release anyone who requests to leave Madeleine, except those I think might be directly involved with my investigation. I will know where to get in touch with you all if I need to," I reminded him.

The sun had almost set when Piers left, and I remained alone as it died in a blaze of crimson clouds. The trees around the lake made an uneven horizon, and the light of lamps and candles coming from the village windows were now golden glowing spots breaking through the dark shadows of the night. The stars came out, and I stayed sitting there. Occasionally there was the bark of a dog, the faint sound of voices raised in laughter, or the call of an owl in the distance. For me Madeleine was no fantasy, it was my life and all I wanted.

CHAPTER 6

Telling how Cecile arrives at the inn
claiming to be something she never was

On Thursday morning Louise's body had still not been returned to St. Clare, though I had by then received all of the autopsy results.

Father Pierre called by early in the morning as I sat at breakfast. He assured me that he expected her return at any time and that he had put a notice up at the church giving details of the funeral service, which was set to start at 2 PM the following day, Friday.

I was annoyed, not with the funeral itself being delayed, but because it meant I had to remain in the village for another day. I wasn't annoyed because I had nothing to do, but because I needed to get away from the investigation. I was in a hole and my inability to make any progress was beginning to depress me. I knew I had reached that point where I had been looking at the same thing for so long I probably could no longer see it for what it really was.

Words, looks, voices, were all jumbled together in my tired brain like some lumpy soup, one with ingredients I did not have the energy to decipher.

The real Louise Lanoir's history, and the history of her ex-husband had arrived during the night. They were in the leather folder that lay on the table in front of me, and I had just opened it and was starting to read when Cecile arrived. I had only another five people to see and it was over; I would have finally spoken to everyone resident in the village individually. Josephine had provided me with what she considered to be a complete list of residents, and Simon, Dr. Malwi, and Beryl had gone through it and could see no one missing.

Dr. Malwi remained with us, having given me the details of another outsider in the report I had requested from him. Josephine had discovered the person was living there in the village, not someone likely to cause any problem, but that wasn't the point. I had spoken to Beryl about not notifying me herself or ensuring Malwi had notified my office of the problems with Louise when she first arrived, and she took it well, though I reminded her that her job meant she had to rise above her affections on occasion. Unlike Dr. Malwi, she understood that their failure to report Louise's behavior had probably contributed to the girl's death. If nothing else, a report from them when she had first arrived could have got her help.

Lambert had gone out for a short break to relieve the cramp he was getting in his hand from too much writing over the last three days, and I was alone when Cecile arrived. The sound of a carriage arriving and pulling up outside was unexpected, and curious, I got up from my chair to look out of one of the small windows of the parlor to see whose it was. I watched with growing annoyance as I saw Cecile alight from it and supervise the unloading of wicker picnic baskets, and it only added to my irritation that I could see her full breasts, pushed high by a tight pale blue bodice trimmed with pink ribbons and bows, above a wide ribbon trimmed pale blue skirt.

It was not a dress for traveling in, and I was sure it was the one she had referred to recently as my favorite. In fact, I didn't have enough feeling for her to have a favorite dress, I always thought she dressed in a way that suited her shape and nature, no more. I remained standing, brooding upon how quickly her presence, which had so recently been acceptably pleasurable, had become— dreaded, is too strong, but unwanted, lacks the unpleasantness of the feeling I now had for her.

Soon there was a tap on the door of the parlor, and before I responded, while I was still thinking about how best to deal with her arrival, she swept into the room, smiling at me with a swaying walk that emphasized her hips. Walking over to me, she embraced and kissed me. I pushed her away gently after only briefly returning her kiss from politeness. "Aren't you glad to see me, and my little gifts, my love?"

"Thank you for bringing us food, Cecile. It wasn't necessary, you know. We will be returning to the Chateau tomorrow evening. The days since we left have been hectic." I sat down at my place behind the table, wanting her to go. I wasn't in the mood for a scene, but from the moment I had seen her outside, there was no doubt in me at all that I didn't want her there. I didn't want her there so much that I was uncomfortably sure my annoyance must have been obvious. But she came around behind me anyway and began to massage my neck and shoulders.

"No, Orlando, it wasn't necessary. But I wanted to. I have missed your company at the Chateau. Though it has only been a couple of nights, I wanted to be with you."

"I have been too busy to even consider sharing my bed." And right now if I want someone, it will be someone else I want to have there, I nearly added. "If I want company, I will find it; there's no need for you to be concerned," I said, wishing she would hear what I was trying to say to her.

"But aren't I the one who gives you the most pleasure?" She nuzzled my neck. "Aren't I the one you most want to be with in the whole world?"

"No," it just came out. My only excuse for saying it so callously is that I had too much on my mind.

Once it was out I had to make a choice: either pretend the word was a joke and that what she said was really true or leave it there between us. I left it there and looked at her, wishing she would leave.

"What a silly man," she said, smiling at silly me. "Now tell me how pleased you are to see me," she coaxed.

"No," I said it again, I could not go back. "You are a beautiful woman, and I like having beautiful women around me. I enjoy sex, Cecile, and sex with you is always very good." I could have said, "You make it easy for me to sleep with you and more difficult for me to sleep with other women because you are always there, next to me at night, before I can retire." But I didn't. "That is all there is, Cecile. Madeleine is a place where nothing more is expected. There is nothing more than that between us." I just was not in the mood that day to keep her happy.

A hard note crept into her voice. "But for the last year there have been few nights that we have not spent together. In a place such as Madeleine that means a great deal. Don't you want us to be together as we have been?" she ran a hand down my chest, and I gently lifted it off and kissed it. I didn't hate her; I just didn't want to spend my time with her any more.

"There is no arrangement between us, Cecile, except convenience. I'm sorry. I have suspected that you may have wanted more, and I should have made it clear before now that I don't." I knew this was not what she wanted to hear. I knew I was at fault for having been lazy and allowing things to drift along for so long, even when I had suspicions that she expected more. It was turning into a scene after all and though it was a brutal way to do it I knew it was past time to be putting an end to her illusions.

Cecile's autobiography yet again!

Cecile has written a wonderfully fantastical book about her life at the Chateau and our time together, which tells how we were devoted lovers until I went on the first embassy to the Laurentians. As I have already said, I found it quite a fantasy. We slept together for the last time the night before Louise was murdered.

We barely spoke for the last year I was in Madeleine, and it was obvious her relationship with Valentine was well established within a couple of months of that day when she came to the inn at St Clare to be with me.

Fortunately, at that point Lambert entered the room. "I have Avien's details," he announced as if something great had been achieved, and Cecile smiled sweetly as if nothing unpleasant had been said between us and swayed out, momentarily bringing the feel of her hips into my hands. I hoped she would leave shortly and return to the Chateau, but I doubted it.

Finally I was able to read the reports before me, and as I finished each page, I handed it to Lambert for him to read. Louise's ex-husband was Edgar Holltense. He had been much older than her. For him it was a second marriage, the previous one having taken place about fifty years before. He favored frontier communities and had lived in four of them during his life so far, in between spending time living in Las Vegas and working as a barman or waiter. After Louise left him, he briefly went to an Indian community in New Mexico and then joined the monastery of Assisi, where he remained. A European monastery seemed rather out of character for him.

There was some detail attached regarding his first marriage, which I skipped over, and the medical report on Louise's dead child told me nothing significant. It still happens. It was stillborn, no one's fault.

"How do you think that may have affected her?" Lambert asked, but I had no idea.

"Everyone is different," I said and found I couldn't remember back far enough to know what I would have felt if my own daughter had been stillborn. It was so long ago I could easily believe I'd never even had a daughter.

Louise's report was as full of conflicting changes as her behavior in Madeleine had been. She was born and brought up in an Amish community. Both parents had been born and lived all their lives there; their extended family within the community was large. At seventeen she ran away and had never seen her family again.

She went wildly in the opposite direction, of course, heading to Las Vegas, where she had quickly ended up on the streets, but hadn't quite been a prostitute, though she got by providing a few day's company to lonely visitors who, in return, provided her with a bed and whatever else she needed.

She was only twenty-five when she met Edgar. To me it was so incredibly young. Six months later they left Las Vegas together and went to live in the Inuit community of Long Bay Island. There they married and immediately applied to have a child. Everything went well, and they raised a substitute child, a bear named White Snow (not a very imaginative name for a Polar bear I thought), and after he was released into the wild, it wasn't long before Louise was pregnant. She seemed to have been happy and stable at that time.

Then the baby was born dead. She could have had another straight away, but it didn't happen. She disintegrated instead. To put it briefly, rather than going into the technical details given in the reports by the social

117

workers and psychiatrists, she believed that the baby's death was a punishment God had sent her for the years she had spent living sinfully in Las Vegas, and less directly for having abandoned her Amish heritage.

Edgar stayed with her while she received treatment, though at times she seems to have been set against him too, perhaps because they had lived together before marrying. Eventually, she had begun to settle down, but she must have felt trapped, because she got up one morning and told everyone she was going back to Las Vegas and left Long Bay Island on the ferry. I gathered that after all that had happened, Edgar was a broken man, and he left the place himself not long after, going to New Mexico.

Louise never went near Las Vegas; she had come instead to Madeleine. No wonder her behavior was so odd. I had no doubt she could never have been accepted by me if she had completed all the applications herself. Presumably, she somehow got someone else to complete the tests for her or to give her proper answers. She apparently was on medication not long before she left Long Bay Island and appeared almost normal at our interview.

I immediately wrote a letter to the clerk at Long Bay Island to ask how she might have come to us, and sent it off.

Then I turned my attention to the papers Lambert had brought in. Maree's missing lover, Avien Portoux, was a sharp little character, whose picture showed a very good-looking young man with an engaging boyish smile. He had apparently displayed some artistic talent as a child and studied art for a time as a young man, but he was too interested in girls and too lazy to get very far with his studies, eventually drifting away from them. After that he'd worked briefly for several art dealers; then he'd come to Madeleine. After he left there, he worked for another dealer for a few months, and that was it. There was no record of what he had been doing for the previous six months.

Lambert drew up papers for the Administration requesting that the highest priority be given to locating Avien and taking him into custody. After he had dispatched them, we returned our attention to the murder investigation, deciding that I would question Edgar as soon as I had completed my interviews of the residents of St Clare and after Louise's funeral. Tomorrow we would bury her, and I was no closer to finding her killer than I had been the afternoon we first came and saw her body lying so horribly askew, in the small bedroom upstairs at the Jones farm.

"Do you want to go on and finish interviewing everyone in the village?" Lambert asked, and I was surprised he did.

"Of course, I must." I replied. "Why do you ask such an odd question? There are only five people left to see now anyway."

"If it were an outsider, how could they enter and leave this village without being seen? Can we be sure that no one came and went?" Lambert mused.

"Have you received some divine guidance in this matter, Lambert? Why do you suddenly feel it's not someone here?" he was not a man who trusted intuition so the remark he had made was odd for him.

"No, I wish I had. I just don't feel it was anyone who is living here. St Clare is too pretty and well ordered, and the people are all so nice," he finished in confusion. "Except Henri, of course." He added quickly.

"Ah, Lambert." I sat back and smiled at him in understanding. "What woman has caught your eye? Tell me. I am amazed you have had the time to even notice one." I enjoyed teasing Lambert about his women. He would be dazzled by them for a week or two, becoming very vague and useless for anything, then just forget them, completely and utterly—and it fascinated me.

"She is here at the inn, my Lord, or I would not have had the time." He admonished me, "Shall we continue with the interviews now? I believe we have people waiting on us." He went out before I could answer him and returned with another villager. These last few were people who didn't live at the Jones farm, ordinary villagers who knew little I hadn't already heard countless times. But they were the last, and once we had spoken to the last one, we labored on into the evening going over all our notes again.

Before the funeral took place, I wanted not only to have finished speaking to everyone living in the village, but I wanted also to have also spoken again to anyone I felt I could benefit from asking more.

Piers, my visitor at the lakeside, had visited briefly during the day to say that he had found out nothing new, and after the funeral, Lambert and I would return to the Chateau. The life of the village had to return to normal; it was summer and a busy time on the farms about. Once I had spoken to everyone and revisited the scene of the crime, there was no more to be gained by my remaining there.

Cecile finally believed what I said when I refused her entry to my room that night. Having to be firm then was difficult, and I would have liked company, but with her there and in a terrible mood, by then it was impossible to think of. I hoped she would storm off back to the Chateau then and there, but she remained until after the funeral, treating me as if I was temporarily deranged or impotent. I had nightmares in the night, broken up ones I couldn't remember—except that once I woke frightened, sure there was something malevolent in the room with me.

The time for the funeral arrived, and I dressed for my part in it. I would have preferred to be able to offer some real assurance to the villagers that the murderer was no longer among them but had to settle for appearing to be a man capable of protecting them if he was. The small church was full, and everyone from the village was squeezed inside, even Henri and Janet, who had somehow gained seats at the front, nearer me than I would have liked. Father Pierre spoke well, Beryl too, and when the service was over we moved out in procession, following Louise's coffin into the graveyard and to her freshly dug grave.

Once she had been lowered into it, I was the first to throw the dry dusty earth of summer onto her coffin, where it landed with the rattle of grit on the lid. Tears left my eyes as the soil left my hand, as it always does at such times, and then I moved sadly aside for Beryl to take her turn, and together we waited beside the grave while the rest who wanted to make that final offering of the earth did so.

Afterward there was a wake at the Jones farm, where the food Cecile had brought was much appreciated and she was thanked by Henrietta and Beryl before she finally left. Unfortunately, she didn't leave until she had taken the time to tell me sympathetically that she realized I was under pressure and she understood and would be waiting for me when I got home. Which only increased my determination to stop having any dealings with her apart from those that were unavoidable in the course of my work.

I spent the evening with Dr. Malwi and Beryl, going over everything we could think of to do with Louise's death. Dr. Malwi was still not entirely back to being his usual pompous irreverent self, which was a relief, and Lambert was absent, off enjoying his woman, which was the reason we had remained in the village for an extra night. In the morning we still had Lambert's things to pack, and by the time he had managed to organize himself, it was afternoon and we left hours later than I had planned.

CHAPTER 7

A crime remains unresolved

We eventually returned to the Chateau at dusk. I was tired, too tired to do more than acknowledge Cecile curtly when I found her waiting for us. I wanted to be free of her, and right then I wanted sleep, not negotiations.

She stormed off in a proud huff, and I berated myself for creating unpleasantness immediately on returning. But I also knew that if I were going to convince her of my sincerity, there was little else I could do, as she would certainly take advantage of any weakness I showed to her. Lambert and I needed a meal, and with Cecile gone, it was unlikely now that we would get it quickly. And I had no patience for emotional women just then.

"If we want to eat now, Lambert, I think we should go to the kitchens and get it for ourselves, Cecile is probably not going to feed us until she has to, now that I've upset her."

We took a back passageway and followed delicious aromas to the hot, steamy kitchens, where everyone was very surprised to see us and made quite a joke of it. The big cook with her round, flushed face pointed at me with her spoon.

"Ahh, Count, what are you here for? I know, don't tell me! I know!" she squealed laughingly.

She turned about and waved her spoon like a conductor with her orchestra, and her staff called out, "Tell us, tell us," laughing.

She raised her hands together for silence. "He has realized at last that I am the most desirable women in his Chateau. Yes, and he will beg me to show him again what love is all about." She whispered the wondrous secret loudly.

There was a roar of laughter from everyone, and I kissed her on the lips and laid a hand on one of her great breasts, because she was always fun. And once I had gone into her kitchen late at night to congratulate her about some dish. That done, I had, in drunken curiosity, gone between her massive thighs, her flesh and energy exhausting and strangely exciting me.

"I could not survive such ecstasy again, Deanne," I said, staggering back on weak knees. She laughed, and her body shook and she gave us food unstintingly. We carried a tray laden with the freshest and tastiest she could find up the servants' staircase to my study.

That visit improved my mood considerably, and Lambert and I ate in silence, glad to be home. I looked about me at the familiar room and the piles of papers waiting on my desk for me. Lambert and I both decided we would leave it all till morning and start early, refreshed by a good night's sleep in our own beds.

Unfortunately, the mystery of Louise's death hung in my mind like a weight, suspended, poised to fall, and I went to bed that first night back in my beloved Chateau and dreamed a nightmare there.

My oft-repeated nightmare.

124

There is a man's body, and I know it is I. I, Orlando. He carries the Chateau *upon his back along a dirt road set with patches of snow, and on either side he sees a dead and falling forest, deep in snow. Along the road there are other bodies, some living, grasping at him as he passes, trying to pull him and the Chateau down, down to a horrible end. Others are dead, decayed and desiccated, unable to endure the difficulties of the journey.*

His clothes are torn into rags, which hang about him, and his feet are bare and his skin is all the pale whiteness of cold.

Inside the Chateau he carries, he feels everyone living life as normal: candles burn, musicians play, they eat and drink as they laugh and embrace. It is full of safety, lust and warmth, confident of the future.

He is given strength and rewarded by the life of those within the Chateau. *That is his achievement. He is their protector and fights off the dangers that could bring them down.*

But it was not an eternal journey, merely a stage in his own journey, and he knows that one day he will set aside the load. Right now, though, in this dream, the journey and its difficulties seem almost unbearable, and he fears he may not be able to endure them.

It was a dream similar to others I'd had occasionally before then, and have had since, and when I woke, I felt weighed down with care, not refreshed, not ready to attack the new day with optimistic energy, which was what I needed to do. What I needed to find was a thread to begin unraveling the problems that beset me.

And I also knew that for the coming night I needed company, flesh, a warm, happy woman's flesh, moving against me, releasing me from dreams.

The morning sky was overcast and stayed that way with occasional drizzle throughout the day. Wet and dull—which was my mood as well when I arrived at my desk to find Lambert already busy at his. To see some downward movement in the week's accumulation of paper on my desk would give me some sense of achievement, and it was almost a pleasure to be dealing with the routine and mundane. To make decisions about the moving around of residents, the requests for extra craftsmen, the breeding of horses. After days of uncertainty and frustration, I was again confident in what I was deciding.

But I fearfully put aside the acceptance of new residents, unable to consider such a thing until I knew what had gone wrong in St Clare. And I was nervous about the five new residents who had already been accepted and would be arriving that day. They arrived from the train in mid morning, and I welcomed them and spoke to each one briefly as I always did when I was available.

Michelle Starr was a cheerful, plump woman of middle years with a great deal of nursing experience and obvious common sense. I had no doubt after our meeting that she was well suited to care for the health of the residents of La Bier.

The rather thin and dull Horace Runkerstein was very eager—but his ability to carry out the heavy laboring work given an inexperienced farmhand was dubious. Charles Hilary was a troubadour with dreams of traveling far and wide to serenade lovers and beautiful women. Not something we had much call for in Madeleine, but he was a tailor too, so he was more than welcome to help clothe us and join with my musicians in the evenings.

Helen Sharp was a big-eyed busty girl who wanted men and excitement, and I had no doubt that as a maid in the Chateau she would have plenty of both. John Paul wanted girls and didn't care what he did as long as there were plenty of women about. He was a big, but unenergetic, young man, and I thought he would make a good woodsman. Chopping timber all day long would leave him exhausted and more than satisfied with whatever female company he could find at the end of it.

We had no need for people who thought they would be able to do nothing but lounge around all day.

I was reassured that they all seemed normal, what I had been looking for that might have passed as abnormal, I wasn't sure. But after what I had found in St Clare, it reassured me that my selection methods hadn't delivered a batch of lunatics into our midst.

By the end of the day, the piles of papers on my desk were much reduced. I had achieved a great deal, and my mood was almost normal. I had hardly seen Lambert all day, and his clerks had been hard at work catching up too. They never seemed to be able to keep up when he was away.

When I finally left my office, I studied all the women I met as I walked about the Chateau, wondering who I would want to have tonight. Some I already knew well; others I had seldom even seen. Some appealed to me and others didn't, but what I most wanted was a happy, laughing one. Eventually, a plump, dark-haired maid ran by giggling, and I caught her by the arm, and after only a few words of admiration from me, we kissed hungrily and the arrangements were made. Then she ran away, laughing, telling her friends she was going to spend the night with me.

My future arranged, I joined most of my household in the main rooms for dinner, some music, and cards. Cecile made a point of caressing and kissing Valentine when I was in the room with them, and I made a point of smiling at them in encouragement, then ignoring them.

I left early and went to my room, where the happy maid, Elaine, had already made herself at home in my bed, and I was pleased that she laughed and giggled a lot, even if it was at times distracting.

Another day passed in much the same way. Then I knew I must return to the investigation into Louise's murder. Skimming through Lambert's journal and my own

127

brief notes got me nowhere, and rereading the medical reports provided little more inspiration. It was only Louis's history and her husband's that held real mysteries.

I decided that it was only by visiting Long Bay Island and the monastery at Assisi that I would be able to find answers, or failing that, at least some understanding of what those mysteries might mean. Lambert contacted both places for me to make the arrangements for us to visit. Long Bay Island was a very long way to go, but fortunately, the woman who had been Louise's counselor from after she lost the child until she left the community now lived in Brighton, in England. It would be very easy to go and speak to her there, and, if necessary, I could undertake the Long Bay Island trip after I had spoken to her and to Edgar Holltense.

I decided to speak to Edgar first, and a few days later the carriage delivered Lambert and me to the station, and we went into the small cottage, which was all that was visible on the surface and down the stairs through the floor to the platform underground. We didn't have long to wait before the train arrived, an incongruous-looking silver steel thing, with windows along each side and a mad assortment of passengers.

Most of them were traveling between the historical societies. They included ancient Egyptians, Romans, and Greeks, Celts, American Indians, medieval Europeans, Religious of many ages and orders, Renaissance men and women, even a few Chinese and Japanese in ancient costumes. Those in modern clothing looked just as odd, their garb being even more unfamiliar to us than many of the historical costumes we saw.

The journey took most of the rest of the day, and we arrived at Assissi in late afternoon. One of the monks was waiting for us on the platform there, standing apart from the one waiting for new arrivals interested in spending time serving God. We followed him up to the street and then up a winding cobbled road to the monastery itself.

I wondered vaguely if brooding in religious silence could have caused Edgar to change in his attitude to his ex-wife. I knew my attitude to my own wife had changed completely before we finally separated, just as her own feelings for me had apparently altered long before that.

When my wife and I first met, she thought I was wildly exciting I wanted a family and I thought I loved her; perhaps I did. She was an artist in ceramics, and her work fascinated me. In bed, I fascinated her. We quickly completed the preliminaries and soon had a daughter. I was a good husband and father, and I was faithful for twenty years, which I find hard to believe and know you probably do too. But I know it's true, and I swear it to you.

But gradually my wife changed, and to her I became demanding and oversexed, instead of exciting and fascinating. She had our child and her art, and I was demanding but dull. I was an administrator, who made uninteresting decisions about boring things and moved around bits of paper.

Strangely, that's all that I have ever done, all I do of importance, even now. I add my signature or a few notes to something and pass it to someone else—a yard away, a mile away, someone on another world. She never thought that, without dull people like me, no roads would be repaired, no books published, no planets explored, and no laws made.

When my daughter was fifteen, I thought she was wonderful. Then I saw my wife and daughter next to each other one day and I saw two clones, they were so alike. And as they stood there together, my wife said she didn't want me to go with them somewhere, because I would just be a nuisance. And my daughter agreed and laughed—as if I were what? Too dull, too conservative?

129

While they were gone wherever it was they went, I was unfaithful to them for the first time.

After that it just deteriorated, but I didn't want to lose my family, so I pretended nothing was wrong until eventually I became the center of a local scandal and it finished everything. We lived in a conservative community, suitable for raising a family, and I had worked my way through a lot of men's wives in five years. I left in disgrace after a terrible scene where my daughter was included and sided eagerly and vocally with my wife against me. They looked like two mad twin witches hurling abuse at me and accusing me of being a sex fiend. Whatever that is.

I tried to keep in touch with my daughter for a while, but we had nothing in common. She blamed me for everything and accused me of spoiling her mother's life, and she was so like her mother it was disconcerting.

Not an experience I ever wanted to go through again.

I had not thought of my marriage for many years and doing so then meant that I was quite depressed by the time we arrived at the gates to the Assissi Monastery. The monk who had escorted us there opened them for us to enter, and we walked through a cool and peaceful garden surrounded by stone colonnades two floors high, not unlike the monastery I had myself spent time in. In its center was a simple fountain, where water splashed gently into a large basin. At the far side we went through a door and were temporarily blinded by the change from bright light to deep shadow. When our eyes adjusted, the monk guiding us indicated the plain straight-backed chairs of the visitors' room. Then he left us there, and we sat down and waited.

A pleasant man of middle age entered, and we stood and shook hands. He introduced himself as Peter, the abbot, and we all sat down.

130

"I apologize for the change of venue," he said. "Brother Edgar has been with us for only a few years, but he has a true vocation. It is difficult for me to believe that he can help you in any way, but your visit has greatly disturbed him, and I would like to observe your interview with him, if I may?"

Originally we had been going to meet at the Administration's office near the station. Now I said that I would be pleased to have the abbot as an observer, if Edgar was. Shortly after, there was a knock on the door that the abbot had come through, and a small, thin brother with very little hair entered. I wondered vaguely why he was there.

After a while, the abbot coughed into his hand, and after a few more moments he leaned toward me. "What did you want to ask Brother Edgar about, Count?" he asked me quietly.

"I mainly want to talk to him about his last wife," I replied, and as we had now been sitting there for a while, I also enquired, "Will he be much longer?"

The abbot looked confused and looked toward the small, balding brother standing with his head bowed, near the door, then back to me and Lambert. "Then why don't you ask him, now he is here?" he asked.

I paused, trying to grasp what had happened. "This is not Edgar Holltense," I replied, confused myself by then.

The small brother dropped to his knees and began to sob. "Please forgive me, Father Abbot," he moaned.

The abbot himself looked very confused now. "This is not Edgar Holtense?" he asked, looking at us all vaguely.

"No!" Lambert and I replied in unison.

"Is this true?" the abbot asked the now-kneeling and weeping brother.

"Yes . . . Yes, please forgive me abbot," he replied with broken words.

"Why did you lie to us, my son?" the abbot asked with great compassion, after going to the man and resting a hand on his shoulder.

"I was afraid you would not accept me, Father." The little man spoke in quick shaky bursts. "I left my previous monastery in a fit of temper. It was many years ago, but I hit one of my fellow brothers and behaved in a dreadful way." He paused to sniff and wipe his tears. "I left without permission. And I had left another order before that. That was in very difficult circumstances too. When Edgar offered me his name, I was glad to accept. I had no fear of asking to come here with a new name." All of it came out in the same short bursts, and when he finally stopped talking, he shook and looked as if he was in fear of being evicted immediately.

"Why did Edgar wish to make such an exchange?" I asked. Asking the abbot about accepting into his community people he had not checked up on properly was best avoided, in case I gave vent to my rising anger about people's carelessness in such matters.

"He wanted to escape completely from his wife and the child they lost. He had wanted to continue the marriage, but she didn't, and he told me that sometimes she was violent and irrational. Eventually, she left him, but occasionally she still tried to make his life a misery." He looked embarrassed and avoided my eyes, "She wrote to him—awful abusive letters. I saw them. And she even tried to contact me here, twice," He said in obvious horror.

The abbot cleared his throat. "Well, I imagine that the question on everyone's lips now is what was your name before you took Edgar's?"

"Simon Williams, Abbott," he replied meekly.

The abbot stood. "It is a great relief to me, Brother, that you are not the man the count is here seeking to question. But I will see you about this other matter in my study when the count has finished with you," he said firmly to Simon. Then he wished us good day, and, apologizing for our wasted journey, he left, leaving the brother with us in case there was anything else we could extract from him about Edgar.

Simon knew little except where Edgar had lived when he last saw him, but we took all of Simon's details so Lambert could request another report in his name from the Administration. Simon Williams himself showed us out of the monastery and locked the gate into the courtyard behind us once we had assured him that finding our way back to the station was easy. But we didn't arrive back in Madeleine until very early in the morning and were both tired and irritable.

Fortunately, the carriage was there to meet us, and we were quickly home and in our beds. I had part of my nightmare again, and it didn't surprise me at all. As soon as I woke in the late morning, I knew it was nearly three weeks since Louise had died.

More routine work had piled up over the day we had been absent, and Lambert and I again felt relieved to be getting things we could deal with out of the way. I heard Lambert yelling at one of his clerks during the morning because he wasn't happy with the amount of work they were doing during his absences. The incident indicated that both of us being away so much was putting a strain on everyone, and I determined to go to Brighton alone.

I found the laughing maid, Elaine, and she joined me for another night. Then I came upon Flora, who was athletic as well as very merry, and I slept well for several nights before leaving.

The journey was tiring, and this time the train was full of noisy young people returning from a trip to the Mediterranean. Of course, Brighton was bitterly cold because of a gale blowing in off the ocean. Even the unusual bright autumn sunshine couldn't compete with it, and I had to get a ride from the station into the center of town because it was too cold to walk. My meeting with Elizabeth Hall took place in a red brick building erected for some worthy purpose by the Victorians and located not far from the seafront, known as the front in Brighton.

Elizabeth was a pretty young woman with auburn hair pulled back and curled and pinned neatly on top of her head but losing wisps here and there about her pleasant face, which made her appear to be slightly muddled. Fortunately, her records proved she was far from muddled. She remembered Louise well; she had spent a great amount of time with her after the loss of the child. Louise and Edgar had been well liked by most of the people in Long Bay Island, and many of them had been deeply affected by the tragedy that played itself out afterward.

"What would you like to know?" she asked.

"You know that Louise has been murdered, don't you?" I asked.

"Of course. Your clerk told me that when he contacted me and arranged for us to meet. It was awful to hear what had happened, and I still find it hard to accept that she's dead. I suppose you want to know if I have any idea who may have done it, or why," she replied.

"If you do have some idea of who might have killed her, please tell me. I will be more than grateful," I replied. Of course I was hoping she might be able to tell me something significant, but all she could tell me was what I had already read in the reports that she had written up at the time and that I had already been sent copies of. She didn't seem to have spent much time with Edgar, who had refused any more counseling after the first few weeks, but she considered him to be a reliable and steady man.

"I felt very sorry for Louise, but I also had great admiration for the way Edgar stayed by her. She did have some dreadful mood swings and was very abusive toward him at times, especially in the beginning."

I told her about the letters Simon had claimed Louise had sent to Edgar. "No! Poor man," she said with a pained expression. "Unfortunately, nothing would surprise me, Count. Louise was very unstable when I last spoke to her. She had been on medication for a while and seemed much better, but then she went off it and refused to take anything again. After that she was as moody as she had ever been and seemed to have decided to hate Edgar and blame him for everything. It was only a few weeks later that she left."

"Have you any idea how she managed to get accepted into Madeleine?" I asked her.

She looked away, flushed slightly, and took a long time to answer me. "I had completed all the papers to apply to go to Madeleine myself, but I changed my mind and put them aside. I have a habit of filling in the information on forms before I put in my personal details." She gave a little smile of embarrassment, which in other circumstances would have been endearing, "So if I get something wrong, I haven't wasted all that extra time.

"Much later, when I was packing to come here, I thought they had gone missing, but I really couldn't remember if I had thrown them away or not." She paused, and I felt angry, knowing what she was going to say next. "It was only when your clerk told me what had occurred that I realized Louise must have taken them. She was in and out of my house on an almost daily basis for several months, and she must have come across them and taken them, I may even have mentioned to her that I was thinking about making the move and had changed my mind. I'm afraid it's so long ago I really can't remember." She paused again, waiting for me to say something politely forgiving, the sort of thing an older man is expected to say to a pretty young woman who hasn't done anything but be foolish or careless.

Unfortunately, I was tired of people who hadn't done anything wrong, but who also hadn't bothered to be careful with a very disturbed young woman, and I must have looked angry.

"I'm sorry, I suppose this means what happened is partly my fault doesn't it?" she admitted finally, now wanting me to say no it wasn't.

But I couldn't forgive her. She should have known better; she was supposedly a professional dealing with an emotionally unstable young woman who was irrational and capable of doing anything. Leaving an invitation to escape lying about was completely thoughtless.

I didn't say anything, but she knew what I thought, and our meeting ended with her feeling guilty and annoyed at me for making her feel that way. I hated the dreariness of Brighton in winter and was glad to leave, having found nothing there to help me.

When I returned to Madeleine, it was over four weeks since Louise died. I couldn't see any reason for me to make the trip to Long Bay Island. All I wanted was to find Edgar Holltense and speak to him, but I knew he would tell me nothing important. I knew instinctively by then that Louise had stopped writing to him years ago. In Madeleine she would have been sinning all the time in her mind, and within a couple of years, the present sins would have far outweighed the past.

I wondered if, for her, being in a society where she was expected to live in a way that was sinful to her, might have been a punishment she forced on herself. And I wondered about that other person, the one who had killed her and what she had made him feel. If she was a danger to herself, how had she twisted his mind, and how unfair that they would both be paying for so many nice people's laziness.

CHAPTER 8

Journey to the monastery of the Knights Templars

When I lived in Madeleine, I seldom had reason to make long, fast journeys—no one had much cause to make a long, fast journey by road. Wagons full of grain would travel long distances on the gravel roads of the region, but they did it at a speed that was comfortable for man and beast. Wagonloads of garden produce moved about, needing to arrive fresh, but they rarely traveled far. A man or woman might need to be in a neighboring town or at the Chateau in a hurry if they had important business to undertake, but because of the size of the region, such a journey seldom took more than four or five hours on horseback.

But of course there was some provision for a long, fast journey that couldn't be done by the train.

When I ordered a coach to take me to the monastery of the Knights Templar as quickly as possible, the rider Sophie Hubert galloped ahead. After about an hour's riding, she stopped at the nearest farm or village or town to change her horse for a fresh one. Where enough horses were available, she requested them to be made ready for our approaching couch. And so it went on. When our carriage arrived, the horses would be changed. Lambert and I remaining seated inside while the coachmen did the work, rugged up in the chill air. Often someone would bring us out hot drinks, perhaps some wine and food, which we gladly accepted.

That night, as was previously arranged, we stopped to change horses and sit down for a hot meal at the village of Le Papilon. The innkeeper there welcomed us as we stepped down from the coach, but it took a few minutes to stretch our stiff and sore bodies before we entered the inn's warm main room. Sophie Hubert lay stretched out asleep on a bench that ran along the wall by the big fireplace, which was still full of ash and glowing coals from the day's burned wood, so we sat down to eat at a table as far away as possible from her so as not to disturb her rest.

After we ate we would return to our coach to sleep, if we could, in the carriage. It was a full moon and we had decided to continue the journey at a slow pace rather than stop for the night. But it was dangerous for any rider to travel at speed along dark roads even on a frost-free moonlit night, and to ride fast on horseback is a great deal harder on the body than sitting in a coach. I had the innkeeper send someone to rouse the most senior of the village's hunters, and the man who came quickly to the inn was known to me. After a quiet discussion about a replacement for Sophie, the man departed, returning soon after accompanied by a small, dark young man. He had a gypsy look about him, with a strong wiry body beneath his loose leather shirt and leather leggings. He smiled, and his eyes twinkled as his task was explained to him. He left us immediately to carry it out, directing a quick bob of his head to me as he went.

Sophie would be fuming when she awoke and found us gone, but after eight hours of hard riding, I knew she would be risking her life to go farther tonight. The young gypsy was fresh and had the advantage of local knowledge of the roads running through the forest ahead. I instructed the innkeeper to let the woman sleep and to only give her a horse after sunrise. I would have preferred for her to remain at Le Papilon till we returned.

My coach continued its journey throughout the night, moving at a moderate pace without incident. We were able to doze in spite of the rocking and bouncing. I was only fully awakened each time our coach stopped, when for a short time the surroundings were dimly lit by the sputtering light of torches, which were held aloft to illuminate the harnesses as the horses were changed. The animals being released snorted misty breath and pawed at the ground, made nervous by the flickering lights. The fresh horses would whinny with annoyance at being woken from their rest and harnessed up to work. Then the coach would move off again onto the road, which was illuminated only by the silver light of the moon.

As the gray light of a cold morning crept into the sky, we arrived at the gates of the monastery of the Knights Templar. They are massively constructed of huge oak planks; iron bound and studded with inch-thick hand forged nails. Above and on both sides rose the great dark stone walls of the rebuilt French fortress.

The gypsy boy had preceded us, and one of the two big gates swung open to admit our carriage as we approached, so that without stopping, we passed through the gate and the space behind, then into the arched stone tunnel, which gave access to the fortress, and we were deafened by the noise of the horses' steel shoes beating on the cobbles that paved the tunnel. The sound continued to echo loudly about the walls as we pulled up inside the central courtyard of the castle surrounded by its walls and enclosing buildings. Half a dozen grooms ran forward to meet us in the dim light, grabbing the horses' reigns as the steeds came to a halt. Several knights also came and helped us to alight from the carriage, which was quickly led away. We stretched tiredly, stiff and sore and grimy from the long journey. I looked about for Marius, but he had not come out to meet us.

An elderly man among the knights came forward and escorted us into the central keep, his white surplice glowing in the dawn light and the red cross on it luminous, as if drawn with the blood of the thousands of his brothers and their enemies who had died ten centuries before when the Knights Templar had real power. Even now, though they were an illusion like Madeleine, I knew that through Marius the Knights actually did exert a great deal of power in the Administration, and as there ever had been, there was uncertainty about their true objectives.

The elderly knight led Lambert and me up the wide stone steps into the great hall and across it to the far wall, where he lifted the edge of an ancient tapestry to reveal a narrow staircase built inside the thick stone wall that led up to Marius's private rooms.

There was a jug of hot coffee on the big oak table in the center of the room, accompanied by pale blue china cups and saucers and a blue and white glass plate with small pastries. I was never quite sure what historical period Marius had chosen to live in, as it seemed to vary depending on his mood. The knights themselves had ceased to exist in France in 1307, yet within this castle, they used weapons that were more at home in the seventeenth century, and Marius had beautiful eighteenth-century china and served nineteenth-century pastries to his guests.

The Abbot Marius himself was seated at the table already and rose as we entered. "I welcome you, Count, and you too, Clerk Lambert. Would you care for some refreshment?" He indicated vacant chairs around the table, and we seated ourselves opposite him. The elderly knight remained in the room and served us coffee and passed around the plate of pastries.

"I was quite surprised when a handsome young gypsy arrived on my doorstep in the early hours telling me you were coming to see me. I am flattered that you think I can be worth traveling all night to consult, and I'm curious about what can be so urgent as to bring you all this way without making prior arrangements?" I realized Marius was making it plain that he was annoyed at our impromptu arrival.

"It would be surprising, Abbot, if you haven't heard that a young woman was murdered in the village of St Clair. It happened nearly three months ago, and unfortunately we are getting nowhere with the investigation. No one knows if her killer is still in the village, living as if nothing has happened, or is roaming freely about the region. Everyone is frightened in case he kills again, and I can't do anything about it." Now that I was here it seemed childish to have come in such haste after so long. But I had come, and Marius was already annoyed.

"Of course I have heard about the murder. Hardly cause after so long for a nighttime dash through the countryside to wake me before dawn." He paused and emptied his cup. "Was it a sexual crime?"

That would always be Marius's first question. "I don't know what the murder was about, but she wasn't raped." I sat back and paused, my tiredness catching up. "Her clothing was in some disarray, but it was only minor and could have happened before or after she died." The old knight poured Marius another cup of coffee. "I interviewed everyone in the village and found out nothing, which gets me anywhere nearer to a solution. As soon as we began to investigate her death we found out that there

142

had been a large art theft in the same village. Some of Henri Fontenoy's paintings are missing. I don't know if you have seen any of his work; he does figure studies and portraits. Mainly nude women, some of them very erotic works. But the most famous pictures among those that are missing are a series of paintings he did many years ago representing the horrors of war."

"I do know his work vaguely. Not to my taste, but his paintings would be very valuable in the right place." He looked thoughtful as he said this. "Very valuable."

"Yes, they would. But we have the two people responsible for their theft, though we haven't recovered all of the paintings yet. At this stage there is nothing to tie the thefts to the girl's death."

"Regarding the girl's death, no one saw anything, heard anything, or knows anything about that crime," I finished.

"So, why have you rushed here to see me? Do you think that I, or one of my people, may be responsible?" The abbot smiled, "We have been accused of far worse. We were certainly guilty of far worse at one time. Now all we do is nurse the dying and pray for their souls."

"I am here because I need to talk the investigation through with someone who is not at all involved and can look at things with a fresh eye. I have discussed everything endlessly with Lambert and have gotten nowhere."

"Orlando, I have known you for a long time, a very long time, far longer than I care to remember actually, and I have always thought you were a boringly sensible man with a good natural understanding of how ordinary people behave. I think I can say much the same about Lambert's nature, so I doubt that there is anything I could add." He paused for a moment, looking at me. "But if you really want some lateral thinking to be applied to this, do you mind if I ask a couple of my brothers to join us? They will certainly have some novel comments to make, most of which I assure you now will be completely idiotic. But there might be something said that may help to give you ideas."

"As long as it is only a couple of people. I am sure you can understand, Marius, that I would like to keep some of the details about how the girl actually died confidential."

"Of course. I am an expert at discretion, as you know." He smiled wickedly and sent away the elderly knight to find the others he wanted to come and join us. We made small talk until the old man returned with two knights, one of whom was even older than he was and appeared to be a bit vague, and the other was a much younger man.

"May I introduce Brother Lee and Brother Damien," the abbot said, indicating the elderly man and then the young one.

The elderly man had sparse white hair and a distracted manner; the young man was tall, slender, and extremely beautiful—not handsome. From experience I imagined he was, had been, or would be, Marius's lover—if he were willing or persuadable.

We all drank coffee from the pale blue china cups, and I described the investigation so far. The knights listened quietly until I had finished my outline of the crime and our subsequent investigation.

"Do you believe the young man, Avien Poteau, is it? Such an exotic name for a small-minded, greedy young man," Brother Damien remarked, with a small laugh and a look of distaste.

"Yes. I think he has a very well-developed sense of self-preservation, and he isn't stupid. If he murdered anyone, I could only see it being a sudden act of violence, in a moment of desperation. If he had caught her watching them remove the paintings, for instance, he might have done it, but everything indicates that Louise did not die in a sudden desperate attack. So, yes, I do believe him."

"Is that the only thing that convinces you?" Brother Damien asked.

I sat back and considered this question for a few minutes, "No. Unfortunately, the dead woman should never have been allowed to enter Madeleine. I did not mention it before, but she was not the one who satisfied the requirements for entry. She replaced an acquaintance of hers, the woman who was her counselor. The dead woman's own behavior was . . ." I paused, unsure how to express what I felt about her. "She was a woman who made problems for herself. She was one of life's failures. That's a cruel thing to say, but it's the only way I can express how I feel about her. I can look at Avien's story again, though."

"I am not questioning your judgment, Count Orlando. But people can do quite unexpected things under extreme stress. You seem quite sure of your judgment, though, so I doubt there is any point pursuing the matter." Marius's lovers were often very intelligent; he didn't go in for dumb beauties.

"The only thing that I know disturbs me is the list I have of people who visited the village in the week before the murder took place. Whenever I read through it and put it down, I feel I have missed something that should be obvious," I added.

"Then, that is what you need to look into," Marius said decisively.

"Pardon me, Abbot, but most of what the count says is based only on his opinion of the people he has spoken to," the young man interrupted to say. "How can you accept his views so unquestioningly? I would think that you should be recommending serious scientific tests. His enquiries with the people in the village have got him nowhere."

"Like myself, the count is one of the first, of the first generation, Brother Damien, and much, much older than he looks. All his life he has been an excellent student of humanity. If he is sure about something people have told him, then unless it is someone he loves dearly, I would not bother to doubt his opinion," Marius said, in reprimanding the young man. "Now, if he loved them . . ." He let it hang in the air, ". . . he would believe anything they told him—however ludicrous."

I was annoyed by the remark, but I knew Marius too well to waste my energy saying anything.

"I must say I find that a very strange attitude, Abbot," Brother Damien replied with some fire in his voice, some personal difference between them obviously recalled.

"It sounds unlikely, I know, but I don't think it can be anyone in the village. According to both of you, they all seem to be accounted for except the girl. It's not possible she killed herself so it looked like murder, is it? I have known some very odd people in my time, and the buggers look so normal," Marius said, changing the subject.

"I don't believe it is possible to strangle oneself without some mechanical assistance," Lambert said in resignation, tired of this recurring suggestion everyone made.

"Shame. Looks like you are really going to have to turn over her whole life. The past holds so many secrets, Orlando." The abbot paused and toyed with his cup. "I think you will find it is someone totally unexpected. Tell us where he should look, Brother Lee," the abbot asked the previously silent old man.

"Among the aristocracy, of course. They have always been vicious and degenerate."

"So, good, honest laborers don't commit murder, Brother?" the abbot said, smiling.

"Of course they do," Brother Lee interrupted sharply. "But they get drunk and into fights, or they rape and murder women they know, usually ones they supposedly love." He gave a barking laugh. "They don't sneak round in the middle of the morning skiving off work to murder them in cold blood, unless they are insanely jealous. Your girl wasn't likely to be done in because of jealousy, because your peasants are encouraged to bonk themselves senseless in your den of free love."

"We don't have peasants, and there are no aristocrats," Lambert snapped back.

"Huh. Maybe. But those who pass as aristocrats move around a lot easier and a lot faster than the rest of them do."

Marius seemed to think the two men had helped enough, and I agreed completely—though help was not exactly the term I would have used—so they were sent away. When they were gone, he said, "There is someone here I want you to see, Orlando. She arrived a couple of months ago, coming to die in our infirmary, and I have wanted you to come. So, this visit is propitious. I wasn't sure how to get you here, and you saved me the trouble." The abbot rose and walked over to the door. "Are you coming?"

I remained seated for a moment, wondering who I would know well who would come here. "Who is it?" I asked him, but Marius opened the door without answering, and I had no alternative except to follow him.

The Knights' infirmary fills one side of the central courtyard of the monastery-castle and consists of two floors filled with the dying. It is the one thing about Marius that I have never understood; it is so much out of character. To me he had never seemed like a man who would give anything away. He had always liked pleasure too much, and power, as well as the trappings of wealth, and I had always seen a streak of evil in his character.

For him, most people were only means to pleasure, power, or wealth, and even his claims to religion seemed to me no more than another way to get more of those other things. Of what benefit comforting the dying was to him I was unsure, but he did it, and I had seen him doing it, with a generosity and gentleness alien to him in every other facet of his life.

Inside the hospice building it is always cool and dim, with floors of bare polished golden wood. The residents lie on single beds in small, curtained cubicles, and each space has its own cupboard, with a wash basin, a jug of fresh water, and a mug, and brother knights move about quietly ministering to their patients' needs.

I knew there was a doctor there, but everyone was past the need for sophisticated medical care. They weren't in pain, because they were given the best available pain relief. They were basically disintegrating until one of their vital organs collapsed and they died. Many were senile or well on the way to senility. The care was basic but clean, comfortable, and human, they were handled and talked to, and they didn't die alone.

Marius led the way to a curtained cubicle along the back wall, no different from any of the hundred others there. On the bed inside lay the gaunt figure of an old man whose wisps of coarse white hair were stretched neatly across his skull. His transparent skin showed lumpy, knotted blue veins on his hands and smudged blue snake veins just below its surface up his arms and across his chest. I was sure he was dead.

I studied the old man, but the features were unfamiliar. "Who is he?" I asked, confused, wondering what we were there for, as Marius had said he had a female acquaintance of mine there.

"She. It's Helene," he replied quietly.

"Who?" I asked shakily, sure that I had misheard him, frightened that I hadn't.

Marius looked me in the face across the withered shell, "Your beautiful Helene, Orlando." He said, then gently pulled back the sheet, which covered the body, and lifted the nightshirt to reveal two empty withered breasts stained with age.

They looked obscene. I stared at the body in silence for only a moment. "No," I spat out and backed away, before rushing out of the cubicle, blindly through the infirmary and out into the fresh air and sunlight of the courtyard. I fell back against the cold stone of the wall there and closed my eyes, feeling the weak morning sun on my face and my ragged breathing.

My beautiful Helene was there as vividly as if it were only yesterday. She was living in someone's luxury apartment in the center of Paris. Marius had taken me to visit her there, and she was making a display of herself. Bags and tissue paper and clothes littered the floor as she paraded her new wardrobe for us. She didn't wear a bra, just pretty underpants, and she stripped off in front of us to change, teasing us, teasing me. I could remember the intensity of my desire for her, remember wanting to reach out and feel her skin, hold the round flesh of her breasts with their hard little nipples. Wanting to posses her.

Whoever the someone had been who owned that apartment, he was obviously wealthy, and she had just done some modeling work, so there was plenty of money about. She was almost as tall as a model should be, and she had a willowy androgynous body that she made look taller. All the time Marius kept laughingly, telling her she looked like a tart, or a fat slut, in whatever she put on, and I could only tell her idiotically that she looked beautiful, hating Marius for being cruel to her. When I left Marius stayed at the apartment with her, and I knew he had sex with her while I rode home on the Metro, frustrated. Nothing changed for two months. I was obsessed with her.

Then one day when we were all in a café together and I was staring dumbly at her, Marius said, "Helene has a lovely dick, don't you slut?" She laughed at him.

"You should know," she replied then, "but you might frighten away my adoring little friend saying things like that."

Marius laughed and got up. "Maybe it's time for you to reward his devotion," he said, patting me on the back heartily before he left us.

We were alone for the first time, and she took my hand across the small table. "Do you love me?" she asked.

"Yes," I confessed helplessly. "Why do you let him say such awful things?" I asked her, my body on fire with my love for her. "You are so beautiful. I love you, Helene. Don't let him treat you like that."

"Would you like to treat me better?" she asked, and I was in total confusion as she led me away to her apartment and took me to bed.

It felt like my first time, what had gone before had been furtive and ignorant. She took off my clothes, we slid between the sheets, and the excitement was too much. I only had to feel her body next to me for it to be over. She laughed gaily, and soon she had me ready again, and she made me feel her, and Marius had told the truth, but I was so obsessed, so in love, and so exited, it didn't matter. "I love you; it doesn't matter," I said, panting and babbling about how I loved and wanted her.

She pushed me out of the flat as soon as it was over. It was only once, and it was the last time I ever saw her. I still loved her, but Marius no longer took me with him to see her, and when I went alone, the apartment was occupied by an elderly man who told me angrily the whore had left after spending all the money he had given him.

I shouted angrily at him that she wasn't a whore, because I knew she was. When I finally gave in and asked

Marius where she was, he told me to forget her, that knowing her would be no good for me.

"You didn't mind that she's not made like other women then?" he taunted me.

I blushed. "She is a woman," I said in defense and never mentioned her to him again.

Two months later I returned home to Australia. Somehow Marius kept track of me, and eighteen months later he appeared on my doorstep and invited himself to stay for a month. It was a strange month and sometimes frightening. He treated me like a younger brother to be protected but educated, exposing me to small doses of a world I'd never known existed and would never have visited without his dragging me along. Why, I was never sure. I had a steady girlfriend when he arrived, though I can't even remember her name now. But back then we were drifting into living together, not because I loved her wildly but because it was easy and convenient.

I knew without anything ever being said that within a couple of days of his arrival he had seduced her. She stopped calling me or visiting, and I never saw her again after about a week. By the time he left I knew he had done me a favor there, and I'd had half a dozen women, and developed a taste for self-indulgence.

Helene hadn't gone all the way with surgery when I last saw her. Apparently she never did. Along with the withered breasts, there had been a dick. I thought of the obscenity of the organs of lust in decay.

Once I left Paris Helene had disappeared from my life. I had consciously cut her out of my thoughts as if she had never existed, so that she had hung there like some all-seeing, all-knowing, perfect unaging being ever since. Now that I knew she was really gone, I suddenly felt alone and abandoned. I opened my eyes and tears ran slowly down my face while I watched a group of knights practicing their fencing skills over on a square of sand in a corner of the Templar's courtyard.

I had never really trusted or liked Marius, but he had somehow kept reappearing in my life, and our friendship, if it could be called that, had now lasted for centuries. He could be a very strange man, one whom I had no doubt had helped my career to advance, and deep down I was sure that he would someday ask for payment. I was afraid of what it might be that he wanted and of the power he had. And I wondered whether I would be able to refuse to pay when the time came.

He appeared in front of me suddenly. and I studied his features. "She always wanted to be with you, didn't she Marius? Even in death, apparently. Why was that? What did you have that I didn't?" I asked quietly, stopping the tears.

"I'd like to be able to say a bigger dick," he laughed, "but really? You couldn't help telling her she was beautiful, Orlando, every chance you got. Even when she had you in bed, you worshipped her. Unfortunately, she hated herself, so she didn't trust what you said. She knew you lied. I told her she had a fat ass and treated her badly, and it fitted her view of things. It was right for her. But she always thought you were better looking, you know."

It made a kind of sense, and the whole thing with her had been a late teenage infatuation that would never have gone anywhere anyway. Easy to know as an adult what we are blind to when we are naïve and young. Because I had been very innocent then. "I didn't know you'd kept in touch all these years. Why didn't you ever tell me?"

"What was the point, Orlando? She was still twisted and as self-abusing as ever, and you were getting on with living. And she only got in touch occasionally— usually when she was broke and needed drugs or had been beaten up by one of her friends. You didn't miss anything," he said gently.

"That really is him, her? You aren't playing some game?"

"I can be a bastard, Orlando, I admit it. I do it when I enjoy it. But that isn't something I would ever joke about to you. She's been going senile for a few years, and living the way she did hasn't helped, Helene was a transsexual, and you were infatuated with her. Centuries later she obviously still has a hold over you." He paused, and lifting his arms, he placed a hand on the stone wall at either side of my head. "If I had wanted to become a nice person, I would have grabbed you when I had the chance. But I didn't think I could live that way," he said, his eyes locked on mine and an expression on his face I didn't want to see.

"What are you talking about?" I asked, while trying to push him aside.

"We had great sex once, and I know how to push the right buttons with you. I think I could have hung onto you if I'd wanted to," he said matter-of-factly, still looking at me in that way.

"You made sure I drank too much, and I passed out on your bed. Nothing happened, except in your imagination," I replied angrily. He'd claimed there had been much more, and I resented it. Mainly because I knew that he was very good at manipulating people, and I couldn't remember anything of that night except waking up in his bed, stretched along his body, both of us naked.

I turned away from him. I had been watching the knights fencing without really seeing them until then and vaguely thought that one of them looked and moved very like Leonardo did when he was practicing the foil. Usually once or twice a week, early in the morning, Leonardo and I fenced together, sometimes with the foil, usually with sabers, and generally he beat me. I lacked the killer instinct required to be a great fencer. Something bothered me about the fencing, and I missed what Marius was saying.

"I'm sorry, what did you say?" I asked as he dropped his arms.

"Nothing important. What were you thinking about?"

"The fencing." But I looked at Marius and saw someone who had always been a friend to me, if not one I always wanted to have, or one who always acted the way I thought a friend should. He might play games with me, but I knew he also respected me and had prevented others from using me in their games. I knew he was very high up in the Administration. Exactly what he was he would never say. Apart from routine paperwork, he was the person I always dealt with whatever the matter was, which wasn't normal. It was because he had the power to have it so. I was in some way his creature. When you deal with the Administration regularly, that is a valuable if frightening sort of friend to have.

Fifty years before it was time for me to leave my monastery. I knew any religious zeal I had ever imagined I'd possessed was long gone and that I was far more interested in the flesh. I had applied to go to Madeleine, willing to take almost any position to get there, and knowing I would probably have to wait some time. But within a couple of weeks, I was the count. The previous count had not been planning on leaving but had suddenly been offered a position he could not refuse, and there I was. I knew Marius had arranged it that way for me.

"Thank you for showing her to me. Did you ever love her?" I asked out of curiosity, because I didn't know if he was truly capable of it, or if he gave it out casually.

He thought for a moment, which was surprising, because he always had an answer ready to anything. "I honestly can't remember. I think I knew the first time I met her that she would be fun to play with but was too

154

flawed to get attached to. We had played the same game before with other students, you know. There was a stream of naïve young men who stayed at my parents' pension like you did. You weren't the first, or the last. But you were different for both of us."

Now I had things on my mind and no desire to talk any more. I left immediately, not spending the night as I had expected to. Glad to get away from the secretive brooding fortress, which I now saw as full of dead illusions and unknown threats.

CHAPTER 9

In which I make my final choices

We returned to the Chateau in the middle of the next day. I was tired and slept for most of the afternoon, and when I finally awoke, it was already evening. I rose and slowly washed myself and dressed carefully, as if preparing for some ritual ceremony of great importance. When I was done, I went to my study. Lambert, and his clerks, had gone for the day. It was silent, and I was alone.

In the silence I organized my desk with unusual care. And when it could be avoided no longer, I took all the journals and papers, which composed the product of my investigation into Louise's death, and I set them down before me, upon my desk. And with dread I went back over the list of visitors to the village on the day she died and immediately saw clearly what it was that had been bothering me subconsciously for so long.

Then I sat alone there at my desk, thinking for a long time. I sat past the sputtering death of the candles, one by one, and on into the dark night. I felt old and lonely, but it was too many people betraying me and my faith in my world, in small ways, that had brought me to this point. And now I didn't want to see them again until I had to. I had no doubt I knew the truth, but I had to ask the question. And having decided that, I finally went to bed, alone and lonely, and didn't sleep.

In the morning I sent someone to ask Leonardo to dine with me that night.

Lambert wanted to get some of his real work done; as usual it had been collecting on his desk while we were away, and I let him. I left him alone and stayed away all day, doing things that kept me moving about, kept my body busy, and my mind occupied. The room where I could get the most privacy was my study, and I arranged to have my dinner served there, which, Cecile gave the impression, was like asking for a ridiculous favor.

Cecile was making it obvious that she had moved her affections to Valentine and was annoyed that I gave no indication that I was jealous. As I wasn't. I was relieved and hoped she had a good time with him. She might even have a chance of getting him to settle down, if that was what she really wanted. He was much, much younger than me and hadn't already been married, and he had no children.

Again, that evening I washed and dressed with unusual care and was ready and waiting in my study for some time before Leonardo came.

We ate alone and talked of the work he and the foresters had done during the last couple of weeks and of the last hunt we were on together. Then he asked me about my trip to the monastery. Far too soon. I wanted to keep talking about other ordinary, pleasant things. I wanted to talk of them forever.

"I watched the Knights practicing their fencing," I replied.

He laughed, "What? That's a long way to go to watch fencing practice."

"Yes, it is." I waited before I began to say what I dreaded saying. "There was a man there who worked with the foil much like you do." I paused, uncertain how to continue, "You had visited St Clair a few days before Louise was killed. And I had forgotten it completely, until I saw the man who resembled you, there, at the monastery. But weren't we supposed to practice fencing the morning she died?" I spoke quietly as I watched him.

He had turned to the fire and sat motionless as he watched whatever he saw in the flames.

"We were supposed to fence on the morning Louise was killed, but you sent one of your hunters to tell me you had to go away unexpectedly. He woke me up, but I went back to sleep and I forgot about it."

He smiled sadly at the fire, "I knew you would work it out eventually." He sipped his wine again before getting up and taking his glass with him and leaning against the mantelpiece with his back to me.

I waited patiently for him to tell me what had happened, extinguishing most of the candles in the room for something to do, while I waited. Finally, we were lit only by the intimate flickering light of the small fire. And then I sat in one of the chairs close to the hearth.

"I was there a few days before and met her. We had a good time, and I drank more than I ever usually do. She teased me, and I wanted to have sex with her. A bit of a change for me, and it was OK. I actually enjoyed it. And it was good to be normal, to feel normal like you are, like most of my friends. I was excited." He stopped. "I felt like seeing her again a couple of days later, so I rode over there early and found her alone in the house. She teased me again and took me upstairs, but then she changed. She started telling me she wasn't going to do it with a fairy, and who did I think I was that she would want to do it with me? She was vicious. Ugly and hissing filth and wouldn't stop." He paused again, and I felt as if the world

158

had stopped when he continued, "I wrapped my scarf around her face to shut her up. But she started pulling off her blouse and telling me I wasn't man enough to have her. She kept going on, and on. And the more I tried to shut her up, the more she seemed to want me to keep stopping her. Until the scarf slipped down around her neck and I pulled it so tight she stopped talking. But I couldn't stop pulling it tighter."

He hesitated again, seeing it all, I imagined.

"I just went back because I thought I had found a woman I could have a normal relationship with. Like everyone else. And she turned on me. It was almost as if she wanted me to stop her, stop her being a woman."

I had never before heard him say so much at once. What Dr. Malwi and the counselor had said about her came back to me, and I had no doubt that she had wanted him to stop her.

"I'm sorry I didn't tell you earlier, Orlando, but in a way I couldn't really believe it happened. I couldn't believe I had done such a thing. I hoped it would just go away and I could forget about it."

He was still standing there, standing but leaning forward on the mantelpiece, looking into the fire.

"I'm sorry," I said quietly, sorry for both of us, for what we'd both lose, as sorry as I was for the lost girl's life, already gone.

"So what happens now?" he asked quietly, standing up straight and facing me. Serious and waiting for me to tell him, not expecting anything but what was right.

"Just go on as usual," I said with resignation. "But don't go away from the Chateau without telling me first." I said it even though I knew there was nothing he would do.

When he had left, I sat on alone for some time, thinking about all the coincidences that had led to this. About a silly disturbed young woman who wouldn't be

159

helped, but who was helped to cheat so she could escape. About what it was like to be wiped. He was my best friend and I was going to miss him badly.

I wanted to find out how I could go about reporting that Leonardo was the murderer with as few people as possible knowing. Marius always seemed to know about everything that required discretion, so I sent him a sealed letter asking for his advice.

Two days later Marius himself arrived at my Chateau, on his way to visit the Knights' German castle on the other side of St Louis. He brought a large and impressive retinue with him, and it was a major performance to accommodate them. Finding beds for all the men inside the Chateau and for all their horses in the stables. There was a rushed, formal dinner that night, and because of the numbers, I had no chance to speak to him alone. To see if he had received my letter. Though I assumed he must have, as if it had not arrived before he departed, he would have passed the rider carrying it to him on the way to the Chateau.

After the meal Marius avoided me and retired early. In the morning I accompanied him out onto the square, where his men waited for him, mounted and ready. He turned to me, taking my hand and holding it hard, and I felt something pressed into it and then he embraced me.

"I have destroyed your letter without anyone seeing it. Read what I have written and destroy it too. Do what you choose and tell me nothing." He released me and made the sign of the cross before me as I stood transfixed. "I have made this journey for you alone. Now act like a count should," he whispered, as if it were a blessing. I pulled myself together and made the proper farewells and smiled as I went inside. But once I could get to my study I closed the door and locked it.

I unfolded the fine, thin paper Marius had pressed on me and read his spidery scrawl. Leonardo had already been wiped once. Which was not necessarily a problem, I thought. People had their minds partly wiped and rebuilt for a variety of reasons, sometimes several times when they had certain mental disorders or behaviors. Then I read further, and what I read stunned me. Leonardo had been totally wiped once already, because he had killed a young man he worked with.

If you are wiped for a crime like murder and you do it again, they don't bother to wipe you and rebuild you again. Not just because they don't want to; retraining a person who is totally wiped is time consuming and very expensive. So they are very careful to get it right.

Wiping

Totally wiping a mind a second time usually leads to severe impairment in one or more areas of the brain. This is because the total wipe they do for very serious crimes or behavioral problems alters the way the brain functions, which makes retraining a second time much more difficult. When it was tried, it usually resulted in someone who had difficulty functioning at all in society. So, for people who had murdered more than once, they stopped trying that very early on. And of course there was the fear that if they got the retraining wrong once, it was likely they would fail again.

Leonardo wasn't going to be wiped, the Administration would automatically require him to be executed for having killed again.

I could issue a judgment of self-defense if I dared, and it might do him some good. But it would be hard to make it believable. The small young woman, unarmed, against the tall, wiry hunter. I would have laughed at it, if it weren't so tragic. I sat alone and tried to find a way out. I could tell him to run away. But if he killed again, if the circumstances were right, then I would be guilty of murder too. And I doubted he would run; he wasn't a man who had ever run to protect himself.

I had to know more, and I had to be sure that there was no doubt about what Marius had written. I waited two days and reviewed all the notes Lambert and I had made during our investigation. Then I announced that I thought I might have a theory and would be going to see Marius again. I waited a few more days to be sure he'd had time to return to his fortress. This time I didn't take the carriage. I left very early on horseback, with one of the hunters to accompany me. The journey was exhausting, but I was there that night.

"I'm sorry I had to give you such bad news," Marius said as soon as we were alone. "I have already told you I will go along with whatever you decide to do. The decisions are yours alone, and I don't want to know about them."

"Do you have the details of what occurred the first time?" I asked. "I need to know before I can decide. And I need to be absolutely sure that he did do it. I need to know that. And I want to know how it happened, what sort of person Leonardo was then."

Marius pulled a thin folder out of a drawer in his desk and put it on the table for me. "He was much the same kind of man he is now, I imagine—too much the same."

He sat back watching, while I read the few pages inside. There wasn't much detail. Leonardo had been working in a game reserve, and I was angry he had been allowed to go back to the same kind of work. I thought they didn't allow that, because it tended to encourage people to develop the same kind of behaviors that they had before.

At the time he was happily married with one son, which surprised me. Then a young man started working under him who he was obviously attracted to. According to what Leonardo said afterward, they were camping in the bush, alone, for several days, and one night they got drunk and the young man encouraged him, and they had sex. Leonardo obviously liked it, because it happened again, and then the boy claimed to be in love with him. Reading between the lines, because he said little during the investigation, Leonardo had been greatly distressed by what happened and by his own feelings for the other man, but was unable to control them.

He was happy with his life and kept saying that he just wanted to be normal and despised what he saw as his weakness in not being able to refuse to see the young man. One night they met again, and there must have been some kind of argument, because Leonardo strangled him with his bare hands. In the morning he went and reported the crime himself.

Leonardo said it again in the transcript of later interviews. "I just wanted to be normal; I hated being attracted to men. Then suddenly I couldn't control it any more." So they had wiped him and rebuilt him so that he was able to live comfortably with his homosexuality.

Then a silly girl came along, and he thought he could be normal again. Whatever that may be. To him it was obviously something to be desired; and everything fell apart when she wouldn't let him be.

"What a mess," I said, filled with the pointless futility of everything. "What a stupid, hopeless mess."

Marius had sat quietly while I read everything in the folder. "I'm sorry. Orlando. He's a fine man, and I know he's a great friend of yours." He got up and, taking two small crystal glasses from a cupboard, poured us each a dark drink.

"I realized it was him while you and I were talking in the courtyard. Talking about Helene. When I was here last. I watched your men at their fencing practice with the foils. We'd been going to have a fencing match that morning, but he had to go away unexpectedly. Someone must have said something about him going in that direction. But his name was on the list as a visitor a few days earlier and not for that day. It might have been nothing, but it was what had been bothering me all along.

"He never told me that he had been to St Clair only a couple of days before she died, which was odd, because he always tells me what he has been doing. Where he's been in similar, less serious circumstances. And if he canceled an arrangement we had, he would normally tell me the details of why, next time I saw him. But on this occasion he hadn't said anything about either incident." I paused and wished I hadn't solved the puzzle. "Silly little things, I wish I hadn't remembered."

Marius sat silently waiting for me, and I thought about him for a moment. Why did he treat me with so much consideration when it really mattered? "Is there any alternative?" I asked. "The girl had serious mental problems herself, which were probably what really led to this happening,"

"It's a murder, Orlando, not self-defense. You do what you want, but I can't change the law on this, even for you. Especially not right now. For a price I might be able to soon. But there are maneuverings going on in the Administration at the moment that tie my hands. So there is no point talking about it. I'm sorry. If I could do more, I would."

"I wouldn't want to inconvenience you, Marius. In your rise to greater power and influence," I snapped angrily, but then recovered myself. Marius was not to blame for any of it. "I'm sorry. That was uncalled for. But there are always alternatives of one sort or another available. Can you keep this quiet until I decide what I am going to do?"

"Of course," he replied.

"Who gets my final report?" I asked, wondering if it mattered.

"The Administration. Where I have some influence, but not enough to get him off. I can't have your report ignored if you try to claim self-defense, which could keep him alive. You will have to justify it yourself, and it could cost you Madeleine and your career, and Leonardo might die anyway."

"I'll send you my report as soon as I can," were my final words, as I left him there, in his room.

It was a long ride back, but I wanted to be on my way. Preferring to stop along the road to sleep rather than delay leaving the monastery until the following morning. Before I left the Knight's castle I had already decided what I would do.

Back at the I sat down with Lambert for the next couple of days and prepared my official report on the investigation. Then I made time for myself. In the mornings I fenced with Leonardo, and I joined the hunters in the field as often as I could.

Leonardo was his usual self, perhaps quieter and staying closer to the Chateau. I had feared that perhaps he was not the man I had always thought him to be, and that knowing what I did, I would see another sort of person now, when I spent time with him. And before I could finish my report, I needed the time to rediscover with certainty what sort of man he was.

The last of winter was passing away when the Administration sent me a letter regarding the investigation. They were asking if I required expert assistance to conclude what was a serious matter. I replied that I still had avenues to investigate.

One day Leonardo said, "I will not run, Orlando," and I believed him.

Spring came, and the Administration sent another letter. I wrote to Marius, who replied that things were such that he still could not interfere with individual departments at that time.

165

Soon after that Leonardo and I were riding together one day when he reined his horse in for no reason. When I pulled up beside him, he said quietly, "You must do what must be done, Orlando. This delay is painful for me. And you must remember too, that a young woman is dead, because of me. And I know what I have done."

A few days later I arranged for Leonardo and me to go on a short hunting trip alone. As we often did. The other hunters would join us the following day to do a sweep through the nearby woods for sick or injured animals.

Lambert wondered what I was doing when I added to Report 509, bringing it up to the point we had been at in the investigation before he and I went to the monastery together. He knew I had been to see Marius again on my own, but I had told him nothing about that visit. There was only so much that could be kept completely private, and I would make the best of it by saying nothing.

CHAPTER 10

The ending of many things, including illusions

Leonardo and I left early the next morning, riding out into the beginnings of a warm, beautiful April day. The ground was firm beneath us, but not hard, and the horses were glad to be out, as were we. We checked the places where the deer fed in the forests near the Chateau and found the small herds we came upon to be all fit and healthy. So we moved deeper into the forest and farther from the Chateau and its surrounding farms.

It was perfect weather for riding, and the health and liveliness of all the wildlife we came upon fitted the atmosphere of the day. We walked the horses frequently, stopping for lunch and letting them graze for an hour or so. Then later in the afternoon heat we walked them through a fresh running stream to cool down.

It wasn't until very, very late in the afternoon, when we were passing through a stand of young trees close to our planned campsite, that we found anything amiss. There we found a young deer with a badly injured leg trying to keep up with the herd, which had bounded off as we approached, leaving it staggering painfully after them, shaking and frightened. Even from a distance one leg appeared broken, and though the injury was very recent, the young animal's coat already looked dull and its body thin. Leonardo felled it cleanly with one bolt from his crossbow, and we dismounted and set to skinning and butchering the carcass.

"Had I done it before?" he asked, as he cut the meat cleanly from the bones.

I took a while to answer, confused at first about what he was asking, but finally saying, "Something similar."

When I had cleaned as much of the flesh from the deer's hide as I could, I rolled it up and wrapped it neatly in a piece of heavy, waxed linen, to take back for proper cleaning and tanning.

"I thought so." There was a pause. "I've never been able to remember back before a certain place, so I always knew there was something," he explained, packing the meat into his saddlebags and leaving the bones for the forest to clear away.

We moved on a way, leading the horses, the meat he'd cut split into two bags, one slung on each side of his horse.

There was a sheltered clearing by the river ahead where the Chateau residents would sometimes come to picnic and swim in summer, and where the hunters camped only occasionally. Only if they were too busy in the local area to return to the Chateau for the night. A place too close to home to stop and camp in normally.

Once there, we unsaddled the horses and rubbed them down before hobbling them loosely and setting them to graze for the night on long lines. It was still warm, and Leonardo started a small fire while I got water from the river. While the fire gained heat, we spread our blankets by it and arranged our saddles and saddlebags where they would be safe from damp and insects. And then we went down to the river to wash off the dust and sweat of the day.

The forest was quiet as night set in, and I watched him strip off in the shadowy moonlight. A lean, hard man, whose body showed the first signs of the looseness of age in his skin in daylight. But those signs of age were hidden there in the gentle moonlight, and he could have been a young man still.

We both entered the cold water naked, shivering until we were under and moving. I could feel the water moving along my body, sensual and seductive, as it weaved about me. Then we raced across the river, and he won as he always had. A natural athlete whose body I had always envied. Winning again, as we raced back to where we had entered the water.

He rose up out of the water to claim success at the end of the race and it ran from his body. Silver glistening streams in the moonlight, the water sparkling as he dived into it again. Smoothly and effortlessly arching his body like a fish and breaking the surface. I dived under too and caught his ankle, twisting him off balance, both of us coming up spluttering, and diving off again. Play fighting in the dark. Pulling him under, I felt the rough scars on his hip from last winter's boar—the one we all thought was dead until Leonardo went to make sure and it rose up in a death throe, savagely goring him with a tusk.

We both surfaced, and the water ran from the coarse hair on his arms and chest. "I love you," he said.

I knew it. We were in the middle of the river, now treading water, but I moved closer and gripped his shoulders and hugged him hard to me for a brief moment, then pulled away so I could kick properly and stop sinking. "In my own way I've always loved you too," I said, "but not . . . in that way, I'm sorry," and turned and swam back to the shore before I said any more.

We left the water flowing in the warm night air, and I dried myself and put on a linen shirt and long pants and we walked silently back to the fire. The fire was hot coals now, and Leonardo took out strips of the meat he had butchered earlier, and set them to cook. We discussed the day's ride and the kill while we ate, and I poured us both a mug of wine, a rich, dark wine. We drank it as we watched the fire die down. The noises of insects, which had surrounded us, faded and a lonely owl hooted in the distance. "Thank you," he said when we had finished.

I said, "There's nothing to thank me for." And he laughed quietly.

We lay down on our blankets and told each other a few old stories. Then we said goodnight, and I waited until I heard his breathing become regular and shallow. Then I waited until the night was still, and I moved over and cradled his body in mine and he moved slightly against me. Eventually, I went to sleep.

I woke in the early dawn, my hip and thigh cold and wet from the pool of chilled urine that had soaked the blanket beneath us. There were any number of ways it could have been done. A hunting accident would have been convenient, but I couldn't bring myself to deface him. His kind, angular face, his lean muscular body, the pale milky torso attached to weathered brown arms and neck showing a lifetime spent outdoors. And I couldn't take the risk of failing at the first attempt. I think he knew I had put it in the wine we drank after we ate.

There was still warmth in his back, and I briefly hugged his lifeless flesh to me one last time. Then I got up and pulled my rug over him and went to the river, where I stripped off, washed, and dressed in clean clothes and waited for the hunters to come as I had asked them to. But when they did arrive, I remained by the water, unable to leave. Several of them came to ask me if I was all right, and I said I was, and eventually they all left, taking his body with them.

When there was nothing but the noise of the forest, I went back to the clearing and began to obsessively clear away every sign of our being there. I removed the coals from the fire and threw them in the river; I dragged branches across the ground to remove our footprints and the impression of our bodies and the wet patch he had left there. And I spread fresh, dry soil and leaves about so that when I finally left, there was no sign of us at all.

I have no regrets. I could feel no grief, no guilt, no remorse, because I knew I could never regret what I had done. But I could take no satisfaction in it either. I could feel nothing.

I could have no regrets and I never have.

Leonardo had done it twice, the first time he lost his past and became a child again. A new child, in a grown man's body, but still with a fatal flaw that hadn't been removed. Such a small thing. The second time you go into a white room naked on your trolley ready for the morgue and have a stranger stick a needle in you. Or you can go to sleep in a place you love with someone you love. I gave him everything I could and lost the person closest to me.

I wonder what the flaw is in me that has caused me to have loved such flawed people. Helene, Leonardo. Or perhaps they just seem to have been special because I lost them before I stopped loving them. I must have loved my wife once. We made love, we had a child, but I never think of her. I fell out of love with her long before I left her. And my child? I love her still, but she is so distant from me it is like a fading, remembered dream of love.

I rode back to the Chateau alone and left the young deer's hide with the tanners. Then I went up to my study and called Lambert in and finished Report 509, telling

171

how Leonardo had confessed to the murder of Louise Lanoir and then taken his own life before I could stop him.

That was when I realized that I had lost myself, utterly.

The report was signed and dated the 17th of April.

And it was sealed and taken directly to Marius and put directly into his own hands.

Afterward people looked at me strangely, and I knew why. Secrets like that can't be truly kept in a small place. They kept their distance, and I felt absent and adrift. I went through the motions of my life for the following months, and they looked at me oddly less often, but we all knew I no longer belonged in Madeleine.

Unfortunately, there was nowhere else I wanted to go.

Then Marius decided he had just the job for me. The deer's hide was tanned by then, and I had Rebecca make me a small bag up out of it. When it was done, I thought for a long time what to put inside it, and when it was filled, I closed it, and I took it away with me when I left.

I still have it with me now.

CHAPTER 11

I pause briefly between the stages of my life

I doubt you will be surprised if I tell you it is a while since I have written anything here.

Sometimes things are remembered too well, things that we might better never be able to recall again. The intensely sweet, sad memories of what is gone and lost forever.

Because naturally I recalled the happy times, which seemed endless, along with the painful. Wonderful evenings of music and opera, which I miss so much now. The perfect sound of the human voice—the most wonderful instrument of them all. Beautiful works of art, though we were not able to have the originals of any except those painted upon the Chateau walls. Brilliant plays we would perform ourselves, Moliere was perhaps my favorite. And amusing conversations. Ah, human conversations. How I miss them.

And of course the countryside, which was always such a great pleasure to me. I remember the wonder of the seasons, how they changed my world. From the lush, green growth and abundance of spring, to the brilliant orange and red landscape of high autumn. And I miss the wonder of riding out in a hunting party into the misty chill of dawn, and feeling the living day arrive about me.

I miss it all. And the people—who I imagine are still there, though many aren't, of course. I visited once when I was doing my research at the Administration's archives, and it was a mistake, as such visits always are. What I had wanted to find there was gone. As I was. Never to return.

And I can admit now that I also feared for myself after Leonardo's death—not terribly, I was too empty. But I still had no desire to be found out and have my mind cleaned away and rebuilt as Leonardo's had been that first time. To lose the memories of my life.

Anyway, as I have said, Marius had a job for me. Before my already-maudlin humor was forced to face the anniversary of that day in April, he ordered me away. The letter came in early March, and I obeyed.

I left my Chateau in a fine dark suit of pewter gray silk with blue forget-me-nots embroidered upon it. My beautiful, talented Rebecca's kind thought to make me such a thing, to sew a pattern of affection and fond memories upon the garments that would cover me as I embarked upon my new life.

It was a period of almost a year, that time when I lived in the "present." What people like to call the "real world." Something I had not done for well near two centuries. And it was in some ways a restful time for me, as I was emotionally empty. But it was mentally very busy, with many things to learn and see, and even more to inspect.

I still inspect things. It seems to be what I was made for—inspections. Buildings, farms, hospitals, housing precincts, libraries, forests, planets, ships, armies.

I have inspected them all. Then I have written reports, made brief speeches, or faced the media about them. So it was a very normal time in many ways, that time between my past on Earth and my precipitate plunge into humanity's future.

The people I met and worked with during that year considered much of Earth to be a museum. One where the planets flora and fauna, and mankind's past were preserved. A place where their history was frozen for them to admire, or perhaps visit, when they thought of it. Which I suppose is partially true, though it's not the way I had ever thought of my world.

As I came to them from Earth and had retained the dress and manners of the place where I had lived for so long (because when I left, I didn't want to admit even to myself that I might never return to my position there), I was also regarded as a relic. Something wonderful, preserved from a bygone age, and then kept in a museum for them. Perhaps like a Tutenkahmun mask, which has suddenly been taken on tour for them to see. And wherever such a relic goes on display it has crowds queuing eagerly for a chance to glimpse it.

So in their "real world" I was also greeted by crowds, like any other famous relic. I was watched avidly as I went about the rather dull but demanding job I had been given to do when I had lost myself, but had no idea where else to go, what else to do, but what I had loved doing for so long. The one Marius gave me no choice but to accept when he believed it was time for me to leave Madeleine, although I still retained the title of Count of Madeleine (as I still do to this day).

I was the temporary assistant governor of the Southern Quadrant. A job much the same as being Count of Madeleine, but in an ugly place in transition from one thing to another. Its large colonies were no longer outposts where people went to work for brief periods. It had become well populated and established, and it was a place where people now lived, raised families, and stayed.

Many things needed to change; the residents were eager for it, and Marius would have been satisfied by whatever sort of job I did there. If I annoyed everyone with my recommendations and ideas for change, then he could move me on and my replacement would be welcomed gladly and have an easier time continuing the work. If I proved satisfactory in the position, then that was convenient for him also.

I traveled about and worked and remained dressed as I had dressed on Earth for so long—a fashion I clung to also because I was too lonely to dress as a stranger when I was forced into the unknown "real" world.

And so "real" people came and stared at me as I did my job. And they trampled their fellows in the squash to see me plant a small shrub or unveil a plaque somewhere, on Senatus 5 or Carr's Iron Rock, or a dozen other ugly places.

Those places, those colonies, which their inhabitants knew were totally in the present, in the real modern world, whose populations enjoyed the spectacle of a museum piece among them. Before I lived in their present, their real world, I had lived where? What made those colonists think they lived somewhere more real than any other, more now? Having pointy toes on their shoes, while last year they had round ones, that they had seen certain things, knew certain modern things, traveled about, went to new entertainments or talked to each other using certain pieces of equipment instead of other ones, as they used to.

None of those things make the world "real," or a life "real," or one person more important or progressive than another. All that matters is what is happening and the choices we make, and those things that happen however one dresses, or thinks, or wherever one lives. That

176

someone dies, that someone is born, that a world has been discovered, that a race hangs on the threshold of the future, or of its annihilation. That is what makes the now; that is all that's truly real.

Whether or not one ever hears about it, or how one hears about it, is irrelevant. Whether I lived the illusion of the past that was my life in Madeleine, examined a new housing development on Senatus 5, or plunged humanity into a dangerous future by being selfish, I have always lived in the present. Like everyone, I have never had a choice. None of us does more than occupy a small space for a moment of time. While we strive to do the best we can, to achieve what we wish to achieve. While the universe turns, time marches proverbially on, civilizations rise and fall, people love, people laugh, and people cry.

What else is there?

Nothing.

CHAPTER 12

*In which I play a part in the first embassy
to the Laurentians, until I discover my
own virgin land to ravish*

Now I have to talk of things that are well
documented in many ways. The records of the first
embassy to the Laurentians are, of course, extensive, if
boring and ridiculous. They are, naturally, held at the
Academy of Extraterrestrial Science and Anthropology
(commonly known as AcExsa). The academy was the
organization that provided most of the personnel for that
embassy, but I am pleased to say that it has improved
considerably in its academic standards over the succeeding
fifty years.

I wouldn't recommend that anyone waste their
time studying the original written reports of Dr. Lee and
Admiral Malouf, unless they are interested in material for
some comedy act. In fact, I believe that they, along with
most of the other records, are usually conveniently
discovered to have been "lost" when they are requested.
Marius was able to have them "found" for me, and I

reluctantly admit that those I consulted were surprisingly useful to me in remembering those days. I thank the "finder" for their efforts.

But I did not seriously watch anything of the recordings of those meetings apart from briefly flickering through the first two days. I had learned my lesson already, in the Administration's archives, when I saw myself in the record of the scene of Louise's death. I could not have borne to see myself, and another one who was also present at those meetings on later days, as we were then.

Yes, I have become a coward. I do not deny it.

I also kept a journal of my own at that time. I had anticipated being part of a major historical event when I joined the embassy. And I was, but not in the way I expected. Anyway I have a journal, which I kept properly at the beginning.

The first embassy begins—at last! No more of my ramblings.

It wasn't long after we arrived that I became quite sure that the building in which they had housed our delegation was deliberately built for that purpose. Dr. Lee and the admiral were quite satisfied that it was some sort of college used by our simple hosts, presumably to educate their young in the joys of manure and the simple life down home on the farm. But to me there were odd anomalies that made me suspect that the whole simple, rural, agricultural community image might be just that. An image. A performance created for our benefit, put on for some reason of their own.

Michael, our clerk on the embassy, one of Lambert's assistants who I stole from him when I left Madeleine, and I both found the rural concept difficult to accept. But, of course, as Count of Madeleine, I was an

179

expert in facsimile societies, while the good Dr. Lee and the admiral lived in the "real world," where everything was supposedly just as it was.

During the evening of our first day there I had annoyed the others on the delegation by telling them my thoughts and voicing doubts about our host's legitimacy. I had made my views known again in front of the Laurentians themselves during the afternoon session on the second day, hoping for some reaction from them I admit, but getting nothing but polite disavowals.

I had also made it clear that my view was that we should be trying to discover their motives and learn first about their political and social behavior. Surprisingly, Dr. Margaret Zigaron, our anthropologist, supported the majority view that it was more important for our delegation to establish a formal dialogue on future trade than to understand them. This made me wonder who she was in bed with. By the third day I was sure that it was Admiral Malouf.

On the morning of that third day our leader, Dr. Chin Lee, was not in a good mood. "Do you always have to go on about understanding each other, Count? They're low tech, digitally unsophisticated. The Laurentians have an agriculturally based society and a simple culture to match. What we should be doing is finding out what we have to offer each other. Trade. . .," he paused for a moment, "my work at the academy is at the forefront of this field, Count. And everyone else working in my field agrees that the indications are clear. Trade is the best way to bring alien races together. New technologies, improved communications; we've got it all to offer them. Everything else comes from trading with each other. We've only got another two and a half weeks here, and that's what we've got to keep on the agenda."

I couldn't help myself from thinking that in Earth's own past, unknown diseases, economic dependency, and the collapse of traditional social structures had been the handmaidens of unbridled trade with newly discovered races. Not to mention the problems with introduced drugs such as alcohol, which generally seemed to have preempted any other benefits of commercial colonization by many years.

Religious conversion had also been big when we went out and colonized the "simpler" people on Earth, causing even more dreadful problems on top of the ones physical contact and exploitation caused. Of course everything has two aspects, and I do believe that there is sense in the concept of trading with people as a way to get to know them. But it needs to occur against a background of cultural understanding and consideration.

I wasn't against anything in principal. On a personal level I was there because I wanted to discover the unknown. And I would have been more than a bit annoyed if someone tried to stop me, just because the Laurentians were supposedly simple people who should be left alone. For them and us, everything changes all the time. Nothing is ever static; sometimes things just change a lot quicker than we are used to, or want them to.

"We know you don't agree with what we're saying here, Count. If you want to write up your bizarre theories in a report of your own, that's your prerogative. But can you let us get on with our discussions with the Laurentians without expressing them out loud?" The admiral added, "This is a serious business, and Dr. Lee and Dr. Zigaron are the experts here, Count. OK?"

Our party had arrived at the staircase, and conversation ceased, as we ascended into what the admiral must have considered enemy territory. Reaching the top in silence, we entered a bland hallway, just like the one we had left downstairs, both of which ran the length of the low, two-storied, rectangular building.

The upper floor was taken up with their offices, accommodation for some of their staff, and meeting rooms. Our accommodation and facilities took up most of the ground floor, with the remaining space downstairs presumably being put to some other useful purpose I was unaware of. The accommodation provided for us was surprisingly human, with normal-looking taps and beds, and what surprised me most, normal toilets—ones that looked and flushed just like our European-style ones. If it was all done for our benefit, I wondered where the sewerage went—presumably somewhere that it could be collected, dissected, and analyzed by a team of specialists, which was rather an amusing thought.

I also wondered what our hosts thought of us after the meetings we'd already had in the two days that had passed since our arrival. Those who paid attention during their school history lessons, or followed the news at the time, will already be familiar with the basic details of our embassy and its members. But you won't have the benefit of my personal opinion of the nine people on the mission, which I give you now. Of course, there were others involved in getting us there, people who remained in orbit, and I have ignored them, as history generally has also.

If Earth's embassies had continued as this one began I doubt humanities position would be as secure as it is now. Yet for many years the senior members of this embassy did all they could to discredit me, and Marius's support of me, so I will be completely honest about my view of them.

Admiral Malouf looked about my age and had years of experience at fleet administration. He was very senior, so senior that I think that alone, and a natural desire to take charge, were the reasons he was theoretically second in charge, but effectively leader of our embassy.

Dr. Chin Lee was there because he was head of alien studies at the academy. Not that there had actually been any aliens to study before then. But he had built an illustrious career on his theoretical expertise in dealing with prospective alien races. This had made him an obvious choice to head a hastily thrown-together contact group. Janine Edwards had been his devoted research assistant for many years, which in the eyes of the academy made her indispensable to the delegation.

Lieutenant Patrice Magombe was an engineer, with good shipboard experience and time at the academy lecturing in alien technology.

I was amazed at how many people were making a living teaching others about things they had no actual knowledge of themselves. Her father was chancellor of the academy and an ex-commander of the fleet; more helpful for this posting, I was sure, than any academic alien talent she might have.

Dr. Margaret Zigaron's area of expertise was anthropology, as I have already mentioned, specializing in, what else, but alien social structures. She was also the trading-inclined anthropologist, in bed with the admiral.

Captain Anne Jefferson was a woman on a mission in the service. She was already the most rapidly promoted woman ever, and time spent as assistant to the fleet commander headed her credentials. She also had a brief, but never mentioned, stint as a first officer on the Mars run. And according to Val, rumor had it the posting was brief or there would have been a mutiny. At the academy she had done doctorate research in alien archaeology. I was curious to know what that research had involved her in studying, suspecting it might have been the writings of our associates Lee, Zigaron, and Edwards. After all, up until now, there was nothing else for her to dig into.

Val had considerable shipboard experience as a navigator, medical officer, and second in charge. In his early days he had spent time preparing sociological analysis of the crews of ships in the service and manning fixed stations and ports. He wrote reports, particularly about the people involved when things weren't going right. Val himself suspected that a long-term friendship with Cliff Reynolds in corporate management at the fleet was what really counted in getting him chosen for the delegation. Cliff had luckily contacted him before the selection, telling him to get on to anyone he knew who could put in a word for him.

The fleet always thought the academy had too much pull. The academy, of course, found the fleet intransigent, old-fashioned and unwilling to accept their superior knowledge. The fleet was going to have at least one of their real ship boys on board the delegation. Val's qualifications were ideal for the practical end of the job, which was getting the doctors on and off the Laurentian planet and keeping them healthy.

Michael was, and probably still is, an agreeable and diligent young man trained in administrative and secretarial duties by my wonderful clerk, Lambert. And he is also a generous man to whom I still owe a wardrobe of good plain clothes.

And myself. Why was I there among this illustrious and highly qualified team of spacemen and alien specialists? Because the Administration also wanted one of their men on the team, and like Val, I also did actually have some real qualifications for my position. And I had wanted to be there, and more important, I had good contacts.

I was acting as the Administration's Governor of the Southern Quadrant when I heard that we had at last encountered an alien race, out there in space. That was the job Marius had sent me to do to get me out of Madeleine. Going around as usual inspecting things, only these things were not the attractive and living things of Madeleine. Instead they were mines and domed residential complexes, sewerage recycling plants, underground complexes, schools and hospitals, ports, food growth systems, and orbiting stations. The everyday working reality of the colonies in the near Earth Southern Quadrant.

I was the funny man from history that the shadowy Administration had sent to visit. It was the cause of some humor, occasionally ruined when I showed I actually knew my job and had the full power of the often-resented Administration, behind me.

Anyway, this new species, race, whatever, was intelligent, very humanlike in appearance and its members wanted to meet with us formally. I immediately got onto anyone I knew who might be able to help me to get a spot on the first contact mission. My efforts had also included literally begging Marius for a place, which was probably the real reason I was there, though I was reluctant to admit it.

Things couldn't go on the way they were, either Dr. Chin Lee or I would have to pull back, and I knew there was no reason for Dr. Lee to. A running battle between us wasn't going to impress the Laurentians or the others on the team, who disagreed with me anyway. And that wasn't the sort of disharmony I wanted to show the aliens. I had come on the embassy full of enthusiasm and a burning desire to achieve something for humanity and our new companions in the universe, but instead I found myself caught up in academic and military politics. Unfortunately, I knew I was not a political animal and now wished someone more like Marius were there instead, knowing it was an environment he would have thrived in and come out on top of.

We arrived early at the meeting room to find a sign directing us to another room down the hall. This was larger than the room we had used during the previous two days for our meetings, and Dr. Lee and Admiral Malouf preened themselves, taking this as an indication that the status of their embassy was on the rise. Dr. Lee showed only a flicker of irritation when he found that our new room had two large windows along one wall.

"I would prefer not to have any distractions if we are going to get down to serious business," he said when he saw them.

Sometimes I think he was a man who just liked to be difficult. Personally, I liked being able to see the world outside and went over to look at it through the glass. We had seen nothing outside the walls of our building since we had arrived, in the dark, from the large open field where our shuttle had landed. Below me was the wall surrounding the building we were in, and just inside the wall was a narrow strip of neat garden. Beyond the wall I could glimpse parts of low, brown, tile roofs among trees, and, of course, sky. Lots of sky. Brilliantly clear and blue that day. Part of the road running along outside the wall was just visible if I pressed my face to the glass and stood on tiptoe.

I was so intent on my peering at the real Laurentian world that I was only vaguely aware of the noise of shifting furniture behind me.

"Perhaps you would like to join us, Count," the admiral barked.

I turned, to find that the Laurentians' party had arrived and everyone was standing waiting for me to go to my place. I disliked the admiral's attitude, so I deliberately took my time getting to my seat while I examined the Laurentian party and smiled pleasantly at them.

There were nine of them and nine of us as usual. The old Sarolan was still there, along with several younger ones, who may or may not have been the same ones as yesterday—they did all look the same in their gray uniforms and large turban-like hats. And the younger ones all looked beautifully soft and smooth and delicately pale, with beautiful round, dark, liquid eyes. And from the first time I saw them I had I wanted to reach out and stroke them and see if they felt as soft as they looked.

But standing out from among the rest of today's group was a young person I definitely knew I hadn't seen before. It looked as if it were some artist's dream of angelic perfection. It was formed of an even softer, paler translucent fabric than the others, and even as it stood patiently, waiting for me to get to the table and sit, I knew it moved with elegance and flowing grace.

When both our parties had taken their places at opposite sides of the table, the new one was seated with old Haj Sarolan at the center of the long rectangular table and was introduced as Han Dellier. He looked too young and far too beautiful and delicate to be anyone senior on their embassy, so I took him to be some sort of secretary, or assistant to old Mr. Sarolan. I was reminded of Marius string of beautiful young brothers and vaguely wondered if the old Sarolan and he were together in any such way.

I had decided to be discreet and well behaved from now on, so I seated myself at the end of the table next to Val. He wasn't really considered by anyone else to be a proper part of the delegation, and it was a quiet position to sit in.

There was another member of their delegation called Dellier, an older Laurentian, and I wondered if there was a relationship between the beautiful marble angel and the older man.

As I had decided to do nothing that day to upset anyone, I observed the meeting almost as an outsider, more interested in what I saw than what I heard. Mr. Sarolan was more formally in command of the meeting today. And in his perfect, modern, English discreetly directed the discussion this way and that, in such a flattering way that Dr. Lee, the admiral, and the others were soon overflowing with the eloquence of self-satisfaction. Mr. Sarolan and all his compatriots had supposedly learned our language from a set of disks and a reader, which the first contact ship had left with them only six months before. We, in return, still had no more than half a dozen words of their language, which they were reluctant to speak at all in front of us.

At dinner the first evening Dr. Zigaron claimed this was a common happening, as the primitive race sought to imitate those they saw as vastly superior to them. I almost choked on my food, thinking there might be some truth in the theory but that to apply it in this case was ludicrous.

Han Dellier moved paperwork around precisely, and when the old man spoke to him, consulted the notes he had and murmured his responses quietly. Whether in our language or theirs, I couldn't tell and was irritated that I couldn't hear his voice, though the whisper of it sounded melodious.

I was disoriented when I heard my name mentioned.

"Admiral. I'm sorry, you asked me to call you Tony. Tony." The old man was saying, "If it's agreeable to you, Jaia here is available to help Count Orlando and provide him with information on our social customs. We are most flattered that he is interested in the ways of a simple people such as we. We can also arrange for him to visit some of our farms and meet some of our ordinary people, if he would like to."

"That is very generous of you." The admiral replied before I could speak for myself. "It will be an ideal opportunity for him to see what your people are really like. He thinks it's very important for us to understand each other," he added, smiling down the table at me. The smile of a man who thinks he's won.

"Good. We are very proud to have one of you so interested in how we live. Jaia can arrange a program with him now, if you like. After all there is not endless time for this to happen in."

"That sounds good, doesn't it, Count?" Tony looked at me happily, quickly adding, "He'll be glad to do that right away."

I could do no more than politely leave the room behind Jaia, a slightly ivory-tinged young Laurentian person, of rapid movements and nervous hands. Finding myself removed safely from the serious business going on inside. Jaia led me to a small office along the corridor, where we both sat down at a tiny desk, and I remember thinking that it was a shame that the angelic Han Dellier hadn't been given the job. And annoyed at having to end my study of that alien.

Jaia was not particularly attractive, having an ivory tinge to his skin and uneven features. He was also so organized it was obvious that this apparently new duty had not come as any surprise to him. He had a diary already drawn up, and all I had to do was make the appropriate noises and agree to his suggestions, and my days were to be full for the rest of the visit. I firmly declined several of his offers. I did not want to make trouble, but I did want to keep in touch with what was going on in the meetings. Apart from my own interest, I was also there to oversee what went on for the Administration and to report back to them.

The diary showed that the next day we would be going for a trip out past the forests of the blue lake to a place that sounded like a tikta farm. We'd have to leave before dawn. By the time we were finished with the diary and Jaia's long-winded explanations of where we were going, which involved going through all the routes on a large map, the official meeting was just finishing for the day.

When I left Jaia's office and headed off to join the others for lunch, I was able to watch the Laurentians disappearing down the hall ahead of me. And I couldn't miss Han Dellier gliding along elegantly and gracefully among them, inclining his head to listen to what the slightly shorter old Haj Sarolan was saying. I stood and watched until he disappeared around the end of the passageway.

As everyone now knows, the younger Laurentian males particularly have a physical appearance that to us, appears to have many attractive feminine attributes, and of course some have a more feminine and beautiful demeanor than others. For me, then, they were a new race, unknown and exciting. And I was lonely and isolated, and I admit that I was ready to be fascinated by them.

In the afternoon I was eager for the meeting to start and preceded the others to the meeting room. But while they went in and seated themselves, I waited outside until the Laurentians arrived and watched Han Dellier walking gracefully along the corridor toward me. He looked at me briefly, as he passed very close to me when going through the doorway. He was even more angelic close up.

I followed their delegation in and took my seat at the end of the table beside Val, again. I knew already that I wanted to touch it, feel the fine, pale, soft flesh of my angel, and taste it, and caress it. Unless we were alone I doubted I could do any of those things, and I began to think of how it could be arranged. I knew I had been lonely for too long, and the angel, sitting and moving so gracefully before me that day, became an obsession.

Jaia took his duties seriously, and from the moment I entered our vehicle the following morning, he carried on an endless lecture on where we were going. He told me the names of the streets we went along, which were invisible in the dark of predawn, and then went into the anatomy and economics of the tikta, and tikta farming in great detail. Also the tikta products, again in great detail, and the lives of the people who raised the tikta. Because it was still dark, I saw nothing of the town as we passed through it. The windows on the vehicle I was in, I realized later, were also darkened.

The sun rose just as the road we were traveling on reached the shore of the blue lake, by which time we were well out of the town. That blue lake is the most beautiful lake I have ever seen. At dawn the water is an unearthly lapis lazuli blue, around it the forests rise and fall as they climb the surrounding hills, and the sunrise sweeps across it like a golden curtain being lifted. Jaia stopped the vehicle and, taking out a box and a mat, laid them down on a patch of grassy flat lakeshore, where we ate breakfast while watching the sun come up, quite a magnificent backdrop for any meal. In full daylight the water is a paler luminous pearlescent blue.

As we resumed our journey, Jaia was feeling the strain of his duties. Even his father, who had apparently farmed the tikta all his life and loved them greatly, would have wanted a change of subject by now. But unfortunately it was quickly apparent that most other topics were not suitable for discussion with an alien stranger.

Jaia concentrated on our surroundings for a while and then, to break the silence and keep me occupied, began to name the trees we passed, in his own language, of course. I recited these back to him until I could pick most of them out for myself. We were passing through a forest that comprised trees of only six or seven main varieties, which made learning their names easy, but the lesson rather short. Then we covered the flowers, which were visible along the roadside, and then any animals and birds we saw.

I was just glad to be out in the fresh air after being confined in domes and ships and buildings for so long, and after a while let him go on without bothering to ask anything or even listening properly.

The road we traveled on through the countryside was smooth and topped with white gravel, and the wheels of the vehicle caused a constant crunching noise as we rode along. The vehicle seemed to require little effort to drive, and though Jaia talked and pointed things out, we stayed in the center of the road and even more surprisingly we saw no other vehicles. When I asked him why the roads were so quiet, he told me that it was a holiday and everyone was sleeping in that morning. From what I knew of country life and farming, that sounded very odd, but he probably assumed that, like the others on our embassy, I had lived a technologically sophisticated life far from the routines of the countryside.

We arrived at the tikta farm, coming up the winding track, out of the forest and into fenced fields of lush green and yellow, before stopping before a large two-floored timber house with equally large outbuildings behind it. The family were coming out to meet us as we arrived, obviously expecting us and dressed in brightly colored robes and the large turban-like hats, which appeared quite odd on everyone.

For the first time I saw several females of different ages together. There were twelve members of the farming family, both males and females, and it was interesting to compare them. The young boys and girls looked quite similar, the boys taller and slimmer, the girls thicker, but not that different. Then at puberty, presumably, something serious happened. The girls' legs stayed short and they became thick and elongated around the middle, while the boys grew taller and more slender. As they age the females' torsos get thicker and can become distended from bearing young. I have never found a female attractive and believe that few humans do.

The tikta are a valuable beast. They are moderate-sized grazing animals that produce a coat of fine hair of extreme softness and shine. The meat is tasty, and they are easy to maintain. This family raised these animals, removing their hair in spring for weaving and spinning, and in autumn they slaughtered and butchered excess animals, smoking and preserving the meat, which is regarded as a delicacy.

The outbuildings were used for housing the equipment used to spin and weave the tikta hair, and there was a slaughterhouse I did not enter. At first glance the spinning and weaving equipment looked simple, but it was all powered by small motors, which appeared to be electric, and I had seen no power cables on our journey. I asked how they powered the looms and was told that they used a water wheel to provide the energy. No one offered to show me the wheel in question, and I was led out of the shed quickly to see the young tikta and to select some pieces made of tikta fabric for myself and the other members of Earth's embassy.

The display of tikta products was laid out in a small room in the house. There were hats and gloves and other small articles, collars and odd-shaped things I didn't ask about, and small pillows. I would have liked a small rug or shawl and asked if they made such things, but I was told that Tikta work is very valuable and highly prized, so only small objects were generally made, large ones being too expensive. I did not say that Jaia had implied that tikta farming was one of the major activities on the planet. This would mean an abundant supply of the fiber, but I had also noticed that the family themselves wore only a few small items of clothing made from the fiber, though it is quite luxurious and soft to wear. At lunchtime Jaia and I ate with the family, though only the special food and drink, which Jaia had brought was offered to me.

It was a fascinating day for me, but the journey home was long, and we arrived back in the town after dusk. It was totally dark when Jaia delivered me inside the walls, and right to the doors, of the building where the embassy was housed.

My compatriots were in our eating area still, and I delivered the gifts I had brought for them. For myself I had chosen a small pillow in natural shades of hair that seemed to glow and shimmer, like water in sunlight, and I had a fancy that if I slept on it, then only sweet dreams would come to me. And I actually did sleep on it that night, but I didn't remember anything about any dreams, good or bad, in the morning.

Jaia had set the next day aside for a study of the seasons. For this we did not need to go out, and I had insisted on sitting in on the meeting in the afternoon. The day after was to be a predawn trip, again, to the sea fishers' harbor.

At that afternoon's meeting Han Dellier again assisted Mr. Sarolan, and I sat at the end of the table and observed him. He still looked beautiful. He had not become ugly or ordinary, as some people seem to do between viewings. The meeting talked of the wonders of modern communication methods, a subject subtly introduced by Zan Dellier. I was sure that he and Han must be related but saw no real resemblance between the young man and the middle-aged Zan. I admit though that most Laurentians still looked indistinguishable to me at that time.

My own people seemed to be oblivious to how they were being led on to give detailed descriptions of the scientific marvels of our time. And fortunately I didn't think they were giving away anything the Laurentians did not already know or guess, or I would have been in a very difficult predicament. But the meeting decided me that it was time I put my thoughts together formally and sent them to Marius and the Administration.

That night I wrote out a short report in which I tried to explain, reasonably, what my instincts were telling me about the aliens. And before I went to sleep I quietly talked to Val and arranged for him to send it directly from the shuttle the following day. Val was too junior not to follow any reasonable order from someone as senior as myself. And it was a routine that each evening just after dusk he was escorted back to the landing site to check the status of our transportation.

I was tired in the morning when Jaia arrived to get me, and in the predawn dark I fell asleep in the vehicle and slept through most of the journey to the sea fishers' harbor. I confess I love the sea. My one regret at Madeleine was that there was no border with the ocean. And though the Laurentians' sea air wasn't like our sea air, otherwise the expanse of choppy wind swept water reaching to the horizon was much the same.

The boats were also similar in shape to those on Earth, as all sea craft must be. These were about fifteen meters long, or just over forty-five feet, with nets falling from the booms extending out from the sides of each vessel, and they rode at anchor in the harbor looking like a flock of dark seabirds eager to fly away.

A small, motorized boat appeared and pulled into a pontoon from where I easily embarked, and it took us out to one of the vessels.

As we rode out I was thinking of this and that. And I was reminded that there was just two weeks left for me there and that if I wanted to observe him more closely, I had to do something about the Han Dellier.

I knew they were people.

The Laurentians

They appear to be so like us, but when you look closely, you realize they are very different. Their skin looks like velvet and is not like our skin, it seems to be without pores and is very even. Their eyes are dark liquid pools, and they are not like our eyes. They really are dark liquid pools, with no iris or visible pupil, just that dark, bottomless, reflective mass. Their hands resemble ours, but they are more bone and less flesh and elegantly longer. Artistic hands, but ones that grip like steel. In a way they were humans to be respected and treated as equals. In a way, I confess, they were beautiful animals I felt should be tamed and stroked till they purred.

That evening I also arranged that Michael would pass an invitation to Han Dellier when he arrived for the next morning's meeting, not wanting to think he mightn't be there. I was due to attend an information session on farming methods somewhere that required us to leave before dawn again. I was getting rather tired with such early mornings and active days.

As usual, I returned late that evening and found Michael immediately, to see what reply he had for me from Han Dellier. I was ridiculously nervous and excited and wanted every detail of their meeting.

Michael said, "I was able to draw him aside, alone, as you asked, and I said, 'I have been sent to the honorable Han Dellier by the Count Orlando. He wishes to invite you to join him at dinner tomorrow evening. As he has limited facilities at his disposal here and is unfamiliar with the city, he would like you to select a suitable eating place for such a meeting. One offering excellent food. He will be honored by your acceptance of his invitation.'"

That was what Michael had said to him, as I had instructed. Apparently Han had looked blank and blinked his large dark eyes several times. "What reply shall I have the honor of giving the count?" Michael had prompted him, after waiting some time for a reply.

There was more blankness, but before Michael dared to prompt him again, Han Dellier finally spoke.

"'Tell Count Orlando that I shall be honored to dine with him. But it shall not be tomorrow, or the following night. It shall be the one after that. Shall six be a suitable time for transport to be sent?' I told him Yes. And that is everything," Michael said. "Are you sure you know what you are doing?"

"I have no idea what I am doing," I replied, filled with my nervous excitement and hating the delay. "But I must do it."

Michael understood that it was my private business and not to be passed on to the others. He was from my home, from Madeleine, and still thought of me as answerable to no one but the Administration. As indeed was the case—legally.

The next day I was to attend the meetings and was surprised at the first one of the day to have Mr. Sarolan convince our delegation that it was time for them to get out and see some of the country. The trip was set for the next day, and my fellow delegates needed some expert coaxing to convince them it was a wonderful idea of their own. I was even more surprised when Mr. Sarolan turned to me and said, "I'm sure, Count, that you will be pleased to be able to travel with your own people for a change."

Then I remembered that Val would have sent my report the night before, and I wondered if they had intercepted it, then realized it was coded, and didn't believe they would have been able to decipher it even if they had intercepted it.

So, I politely acknowledged his considerate comment and looked at my angel, who was there again. I wondered then if the young Han had passed the details of my invitation on to his older associate and worried what that might mean. I was fixed briefly in his gaze and smiled at him before his eyes slid away.

After lunch my angel was not there. The seat next to Mr. Sarolan was empty. I was devastated.

Admiral Malouf made a point of telling me in the evening how pleased he was that I had settled down and was being a useful part of the delegation instead of behaving badly.

Are you surprised that I gave him no reply?

The following morning we all left early, as usual, after I had spent a long time deciding what to wear and ending up in the same plain clothes I had worn on my other rural excursions. We were all called and assembled in the entry to the building, where four vehicles waited. To my disappointment Admiral Malouf, Dr Chin Lee, and Janine went in the first vehicle with Haj Sarolan and Han Dellier, who had reappeared. Somehow I got maneuvered into the fourth vehicle with Val, the other Dellier, and two other Laurentians.

"You have been very quiet since the first couple of days, Count. We have never had a chance to talk about your role in these meetings. What is your main area of responsibility?" Zan Dellier asked me as we moved quietly through the half-dark streets.

"I have no responsibility for anything in particular, Zan. My only role is to observe what occurs for the Administration." I didn't want to be interrogated for the entire ride, but I realized that I had done two things to make them suspicious of me. "Where are we going today?" I asked to move the conversation away from myself.

"For a cruise on the Blue Lake. I believe you have been there already, and to a tikta farm. When you spoke about yourself on the first day you made no mention of your qualifications. The others on your delegation were very forthcoming about their expertise. We are honored to have such a highly qualified group of humans sent to us.

198

So, I am also interested to know why you were so well qualified as to be sent."

"The lake was quite magnificent when I saw it early in the morning with a light haze coming off it as the sun rose over the hills," I replied.

I continued to extol its beauties and then began a monologue on the trees, plants, and flowers I had seen that day and since, and then went on to describe the animals and birds. I remembered roughly how long it took us to get to the lake, and I filled the time with my chatter, being sure to talk down Zan whenever he tried to interrupt me. He gave up after only six tries, by which time I had made it plain I was not going to allow him to ask anything else. Even I was fed up with the sound of my own voice when we finally arrived at the lake and I could escape from the vehicle. As I got out I turned to Zan. "Are you a relation of Han Dellier?" I asked.

The way he looked at me I didn't think he was going to answer, but he did eventually, simply say, "Yes." If he'd been his father, I thought he would have said so.

"What was that about?" Val asked.

"I think they know I got you to send something for me. I am sure they know that and have it, but I doubt if they have decoded it. So, now I don't want to answer any questions that will tell them any more about what I think." As I wanted as few people as possible to know about my arrangement with Han Dellier, I did not tell him of that other possible reason for an interrogation.

A large flat-bottomed boat awaited us at the lake, and we all walked up a ramp and on board. Once we cast off, Han Dellier seemed to have disappeared. Tony and Chin were talking loudly as usual, telling Mr. Sarolan about the wonders of modern transport, I think. I didn't bother to listen. I found a quiet spot out of sight of everyone and settled back in the warm sun for a nap. No one bothered me, and as far as I knew Han Dellier didn't appear again.

Occasionally, I heard Tony booming at Haj. "Hey, you know we've got blah, blah, or we can do blah, blah." We traveled home in different arrangements, and no one bothered trying to find out any more about me.

I had already told Jaia that I might not be able to go with him as planned the following day, as I knew he wouldn't have me back in time to get ready for my dinner. In the morning when he arrived I was waiting to tell him that I definitely wasn't going as I had already warned him might happen. He didn't seem at all surprised or concerned, going off immediately, though he had been obviously put out the previous day when I first warned him. I decided that between times he had probably thought of a lot more things he would rather be doing as well.

I joined the others at the day's meetings but paid little attention to what went on, which all seemed like ridiculous self-aggrandizement on behalf of our supposed experts. Admiral Malouf seemed to be brainwashed by both sides, and oblivious to what was going on. Val was now too involved with Patrice to care, and Michael took notes impartially as always. The Laurentians were quite different to watch. I thought they were becoming tired of playing with Doctors Lee and Zigaron, the way they listened to their theories, and agreed with everything they suggested, but gave no real information about themselves.

While dashing about the countryside with Jaia, I had learned more about what the Laurentians already had and were capable of than did my fellows who had remained inside. I had seen small electric motors, good winches, machine-made stainless steel cables and synthetic machine-made nets, that had not been knocked up in a hay shed. My compatriots still seemed to think the aliens did nothing but raise the Laurentian equivalent of pigs.

The Laurentians themselves seemed to be bored with the meeting, and Han Dellier wasn't there, so I was bored too.

That evening I fussed about with what I would wear, like a teenager on a first date. And all I wanted to do was see my angel up close and touch it. The fact that I had arranged something with one of them all by myself and without the knowledge of the others on my embassy added to the clandestine excitement of the evening ahead.

I had to sneak out while no one else was about, and then wait to be collected. I hid just inside the main entrance door for about fifteen minutes like a criminal. I had been feeling isolated and cut off from my own kind, I had lost my roots since Leonardo's death, and now I felt reckless. Now I was full of curiosity. I had a passion and it exited me.

CHAPTER 13

I seek to explore the unknown and gain the rewards and pleasures of flesh and desire

Of course caution intensified my desire. I was a man used to getting what I wanted quickly and easily. Now though, for the first time in centuries, I had no idea what it was that I wanted. Because I had so little knowledge of the flesh that was the object of my desire.

I had spent a very long time being promiscuous, including a lot of time living in Madeleine, a society where it was almost obligatory. It was how I wanted to be. Now I was out of my own environment and confronted by an alien society with unknown social mores. This was a vague concern. But I was too interested in the Laurentian angel to let it hinder me and had proceeded cautiously because of a desire to succeed rather than any sense of wrongdoing or danger.

And I was in an odd isolated state at the time; I had slept alone since I left Madeleine. And also for some time before I left. I was lost after Leonardo's death, afraid in case the truth came out and I was sent away to be wiped, and angry with the world for what had happened, and my own inability to feel anything about what I had done. One day, not many months afterward, I had almost hurt a woman I found myself making love with in a dark hallway. Suddenly, I was directing the rage I felt at the world against her, and my behavior frightened me badly. I apologized profusely, and she did not make a complaint, but I knew I had best keep to myself until I had gotten over the anger and frustration I felt for what had happened.

When I looked upon her, Han Dellier was certainly not a male to me. For me she was a beautiful androgynous girl, and I lusted for her flesh, for the sensual pleasure of her touch. But I had no great expectation of the sex of a man and woman. I had no notion what organs she might possess, though I knew she had two hands and a mouth, which was quite adequate equipment to be going on with if it was appropriate. Unless, of course, my touch, or hers, was somehow fatal or dangerous. Since we arrived, we had been living there as if we were completely compatible, which at the time should have seemed more odd, I suppose.

Now I sometimes wonder if I also wanted to possess her body in some way as much to revolt against the others in my embassy as for myself. To physically possess that beautiful angel in any way was so much more than sitting talking all day.

And for me the Han was the undiscovered land sighted on the horizon, lying virgin, waiting to be explored. And I was the alien who had come by ship as all explorers do, passionate to discover and ravish it.

I was thinking in poetry, I was so nervous I was being ridiculous, I knew.

The vehicle that collected me from the meeting house had dark windows, as usual, and in the fading light I saw little of the town and wondered if I would ever see more of it in daylight than I could from the windows of the meeting house. It was fully dark when we came to a stop in the courtyard of a rather plain white house. There was an upper story, and the whole building appeared large, but much smaller in size than the one our embassy was housed in.

A covered way ran across the far side of the courtyard, and the house was entered via a doorway in the center of it, directly opposite the large arched gateway through which the vehicle had brought me. The only lighting was from ornate lamps set out from the white plastered wall on each side of the door. My driver helped me to disembark from the vehicle, and we walked up to the entrance where I stood behind him while he knocked on the dark timber door. Almost immediately it was opened by a mature Laurentian female, and my driver stood aside for me to pass. The female led me inside and down a short hallway into a large, comfortable dining room, where Han and six other Laurentians were standing about.

I was disappointed at the number of people present. In my vision I always imagined Han and me alone. And the room was disappointingly familiar in its similarity to those in a hundred other country houses I had seen at home. There was a large old timber dresser along one wall displaying a collection of brightly patterned ceramic platters and bowls, and in the center of the room a round low table was surrounded by eight stools with large, square padded seats.

The female who had led me there announced my arrival, saying, "Your visitor has arrived, Han Dellier." In the bright light of the room, she looked older than she had in the dim light at the entrance. Then, obviously having completed her task, she left us.

Han and two other males wore the same uniforms as they did for our meetings. If they hadn't been, I would never have recognized his companion, Zan, the fourth man. The females wore long, finely pleated robes of various dull colors. But I noticed that several of them also wore very fine delicate slippers of a velvet-looking or shiny fabric. Of course I had envisaged a private tête-à-tête, somewhere discreet, and was irritated at being included in what appeared to be a family gathering. I wondered what Han and the others thought was the purpose of this meeting, which I had attempted to discreetly arrange with him.

Perhaps they expected a bit of personal lobbying by me for some Earth based company. Powerstations United perhaps? Or Global Entertainment—the distraction of the colonies masses. Or perhaps they were going to take this apparently golden opportunity, which had come their way, to try and sell me something that Earth could not do without. Tikta droppings—the ultimate manure?

I hoped not.

Han Dellier performed the introductions, and not having noted them down, I forget the names. But I greeted each one in the way Jaia had told me was appropriate when meeting a Laurentian for the first time. Then Han took me to one side of the room, near the dresser, where we were joined by Zan. I noticed that all the decoration on the items in the dresser appeared to be abstract. There was no Laurentian equivalent of the old Willow pattern plates we would have on such a dresser on Earth, showing stylized scenes from their world.

"I do not believe that the others in your embassy are aware of this visit?" Han asked, looking directly at me. His voice was melodiously, sweet, and cool, as I had imagined it would be.

I looked about the room, "Does that concern you?" I asked, turning back to him. "I asked for a private meeting with you because I wanted it, not for any other reason." I was as close to him as I had ever been before, and I looked at him directly and examined him in detail.

He was more ethereal and so much more female close up than at a distance, and to me the flesh before me became entirely she, and I desired her even more.

"As we are unfamiliar with your methods of getting to the point, I hope you will not be offended if I ask you directly, why you wished to meet us on your own?" Zan asked.

"It was actually my wish to have a meeting alone with Han Dellier, just the two of us." I smiled at the Han, her. "I do not want to sell you anything, nor do I wish to buy anything. My purpose, is solely of a personal nature."

"And what do you and I have to meet about?" Han, her, replied. Returning my gaze steadily, with bottomless black eyes, which showed no white, seeming like pools of night set in marble.

"About my fascination with your beauty and the sensuality of flesh, about my desire for discovery." I wondered if any of it made sense to her or her companion. I doubted there would be a second chance of a meeting unless I changed my story, which I did not intend to do.

If I made a fool of myself and was sent home in disgrace, what did it matter? The embassy was a joke, and I knew that there was nothing I had to return to that it would bother me to lose. Marius would have been annoyed, true, and could have made my life quite uncomfortable, but that thought was far away then.

Sensuality is not at all the same thing as sexuality. We associate the two things often, but that is a narrow view. There is a tendency to discount pleasure as only a component of sexuality rather than the reverse. It is both a part and greater. Far more appropriate to accept it as a principle component of all pleasure.

The Laurentian's opaque, unblemished, marble-like skin was an unknown universe crying out to me to caress it, to feel its texture, its warmth or coldness, its density. Is it as soft as it looks? Is it hard like leather or the stone it mimics? How does it smell and taste?

I imagined I could experience a living body of flesh for the pleasure of discovering its mysteries. Whether or not I would want to extend that exploration to a sexual act was a matter of choice, depending on many things. But sometimes, back then, I was an explorer who could set out and wonder at what he found without having to perform. I am also not someone who needed to have an alien sex story to amuse his guests with during dinner.

A million mysteries waited. Could I stop being one part of the seething mass of humanity by exploring this one person? "For me your flesh, your body is the undiscovered land, appearing on the horizon, lying virgin, waiting to be explored." I said to Han, I was in an odd poetic mood I know, and the line had seeped into me as perfectly descriptive of my mood.

She looked steadily at me. "Are you asking me to provide you with a live body to examine? It may be difficult to find anyone who is willing to allow . . ."

"Thank you," I replied sadly, "But it's you alone that I am interested in."

There was a sudden cessation of movement in the room. I never break these moments and I outlast everyone, but we must all have read the same article, because it seemed to last forever.

Finally, Han went to the table and sat down and everyone joined her and took their places, leaving me to sit on a stool opposite her. She took a drink from her cup, "I believe that you are questioning our honesty. That you don't believe we are the simple farming people we say we are. I am curious to know why you would think such a thing?" she had changed the subject completely.

I had been waiting for some ax to descend, to be thrown from the house; instead she had walked away from what I had said as if it had never been spoken. I sat there and drank from my own cup and made the huge switch in my mind that was necessary to answer him sensibly, "You are all accomplished professionals, you are never shocked, you are never frightened, never violent, whatever we say or imply.

"Everyone here is healthy and well fed, your English is exceptional, your bathrooms perfect. The roads are well kept but empty. The menu is varied, the food always fresh, the water pure and plentiful." I stopped to see what reaction I got.

"So, all simple rural societies should be intolerant, incompetent, and illiterate?" someone asked.

"No. But I have spent fifty years living in a community that is very sophisticated, but primarily rural." I spread my hands out, palm up, on the table in front of me and looked down at them. "I haven't yet seen anyone except your quaint Tikta farmers with hands as rough as mine, and I have spent two months in a space ship getting here. No lady in my court in Madeleine would get even a day's wear out of the dainty slippers your ladies are wearing tonight." I looked up, "And your light bulbs in the meeting house are cold, and the fittings are just for show. Take the bulb out, and it keeps going on and off when I press the switch even if it's in my hand," I folded my palms up. "It lights instantly, has no warming time, and never gets hot; we can't do that yet."

Han shot one of the other men at the table the most eloquent glance I had yet seen on a Laurentian face.

"I have spent fifty years running a pseudo-historical, rural community, and everyone, including myself, has to work. With the population you supposedly have here, you couldn't afford to support a large unproductive elite without serious sacrifices elsewhere. Yet, you appear to. And when we arrived in orbit and could see the whole planet, I could see no signs of heavy industry to account for your obvious wealth or the manufacture of the light bulbs. Does that answer your question?" I finished.

There was a long silence about the table.

"You surprise me with your honesty," Han replied and paused for some time. Everyone else took the opportunity to chat and drink, but stopped when he spoke again. "I am curious about the living myself. Perhaps it would be interesting to study a living human, perhaps after that, I will consider your request."

"The decision is yours," I said, not knowing what he meant.

Han looked about the table. "Yes, it would be interesting to see what you are like under those garments. We would like you to take them off so we can examine you."

I was surprised; "I would prefer to show my body to you alone, in private." I replied, not keen to be the only exhibit in a communal show and tell. "I did not ask you to show yourself to my embassy, just to me."

"I will consider your request if we may examine your body first," Han said, and what her expression was I had no idea.

Did it matter, I thought, if she would consider what I had asked for? I stood up and began to remove my clothes, placing them neatly on my stool after I had folded them. I could have said I wasn't a particularly fine example, but why should I? Finally, I stood there, naked, holding myself as straight and firm as I could manage. Han got up and walked about me, then the others joined him, and then they all felt me and prodded and pulled.

"I would rather you didn't pull on that," I said as one of the females tried to ring me like a bell.

She dropped me instantly, "I'm sorry. Does it hurt?" she asked.

"It could hurt or it could be an embarrassment," I replied diplomatically, not quite sure how much to say and very aware of the Han, her, standing close by, watching.

Han walked around me several times more, and they made some joke about me in their own language before losing interest. "Thank you, we have seen enough." Han said.

I dressed myself carefully, trying not to fall over or flap about, and returned to my seat. I said nothing more about my request. Food was brought out on large platters, and I was given an individual plate of the same sort of stuff we had at the meeting house. A conversation began about flowers, and I was relieved to be able to join in, having gained some knowledge of flora during my trips with Jaia.

Then they asked about the roses embroidered in pink and white on the soft blue of my vest and jacket, and I removed the jacket again so that I could better explain the design to them.

"This is the rose as a new bud, when it is deep pink. Here, as it opens, its color begins to fade, so that here," and I indicated a nearly burst flower, "here it is white, with a thick rim of delicate blush about the edges of the petals." The work on the coat was superb, the product of Rebecca's artistic eye. "And here, finally, in full bloom, it is almost totally white." Here I showed the false pockets on the jacket, each of which had a full-blown bloom at its center." I was pleased by their admiration of the work, which I believed was genuine appreciation, not just polite. I didn't put the jacket back on and finished the meal without it.

When we had eaten, everyone but Han rose and said polite good-byes to him and me. I was obviously not expected to go, so I remained seated.

"Have you considered my request?" I asked, looking Han her squarely in the face.

"Yes," she replied, and I waited.

The house was silent. Wherever the others had gone, they were being very quiet or the walls were extremely thick. Han, she, got up, moving gracefully and began removing her uniform, I couldn't help myself going to her.

"I want to reveal your flesh myself," I said, trembling as I took hold of the fabric. And she let me.

The jacket came away as one piece and revealed a smooth, rounded, marble torso which I ran my hands over gently. The flesh was soft and cool, and I closed my eyes and leaned close and breathed in the delicate sweet scent of it. The Han, she, breathed deeply and stood still for me, and I touched the flesh with my lips and tasted it gently before I opened my eyes. She was still there, looking at me, and I wanted to drown in her eyes. Instead, I touched the delicate mouth with my fingers and pressed the tiniest part of one between her lips.

I will not say more here. I know this part greatly offends another and the pleasures of the flesh are best experienced, not described. They can lose their magic when you try to turn them into words.

But what can I say to give you some idea of what I felt? No more than that—I could not have imagined it better.

"I have to leave," I said some time afterward. "I want to be back before the others wake."

I had explored the undiscovered land and taken its virgin beauty for my own. Now I sat on the edge of the low, padded bed and gazed down at her, putting out a hand and gently pushing aside a thread of heavy mane that lay across Han's face. The mane was a wondrous thing of heavy silver fur that covered her head and ran halfway down her back before it stopped. It draped about her shoulders, and I could lose my face in it, breathing its heavy scent of aromatic oils.

"Would you like to meet again?" I asked, hearing my voice break into a fragile whisper.

The silence continued, and I knew I had no way of knowing what she felt now. Had she allowed me to do what I had done because she was too young and dispensable and it had been someone else's choice? My body said otherwise, why ever it may have started, she had continued it eagerly.

The marble of her eyelids parted to reveal those bottomless black pools. "I want you to stay here with me," she said.

I smiled. "Han, I'm tired, too tired to do anything else now, and we both have duties to perform. My behavior may seem irresponsible and foolish but . . ."

"I have already sent two of my delegates to apologize for your absence. They have a story for your people about a long trip, which explains why you cannot return to them for several days."

I got up, and, finding my clothes, I began to dress. "I have been honest with you, Han, about whatever you have asked. As honest as I can be. I want to meet you again. You can have every night from now until I leave, if you want it. But I am not completely irresponsible; I take my job here seriously. Whatever I may think about what is being discussed by them, my delegation has a meeting at 10 o'clock, and I will be there. The next day I will go with Jaia, which is why I am here. I'm sorry," I explained.

I went to the door and let myself out, but I could go no further, the door of the room beyond was locked. When I turned, Han stood in the doorway behind me. "Now I must explain the situation to you," she said.

I remembered what I had told them the night before, and wondered if I would leave this house before my delegation was gone or never leave it. "I have already sent a report to the Administration saying what I told you last night. There is no point keeping me locked up here, if that was sent." I blanked out the fear and frustration I felt, and waited.

"Laurentian females come into heat every two years. Their heat gives off odors, which drive everything but the need to mate out of our male minds. Once a male mates, he goes into heat too, and for the next three or four days is totally obsessed with keeping his female with him and mating with her until the heat passes. It seems you have brought me into heat."

"I am not a Laurentian female," I replied, confused. "It can't be the same."

"It amazes me too. But you have a pleasant scent and what we have done together has been to mate in many different ways. The result is the same for me, so now I cannot bear to be separated from you, and I must be alone with you until the heat passes." She came closer. "It will pass," she said, standing in front of me. "I will care for you while you remain with me, and when it's over you can return to your people."

"You are serious about this?" I asked, touching Han's face. If she was, then the situation was difficult— but I would not unnecessarily antagonize our hosts. "What about your people?" I asked, "Mr. Sarolan, the rest of your delegation. What will they think about this? Your family may be willing for you to keep me here with you, but will the others understand?"

"They understand what I must do, I have sent the messengers to your delegation with their agreement."

There was no more I could say. I didn't know if all she said was true or not. When I first touched Han in private, I knew I was the first person of any race to do it that way, and I had been humbled at the wonder of being granted such a privilege.

If I had been given such a gift to remove me from the delegation for some reason, or if it had happened because I had asked for it and seduced her, it was no less rare. The passion I found in her was that of a passionate uninhibited woman discovering what she has been longing for, and wanting every pleasure revealed to her at once. And now I wanted to protect her from frustration and disappointment, so I could not deny her anything so important. I wanted this first time to be the best it could for her.

Should I have beat on the door demanding to be let out? As you all know, the biology of the Laurentians means that it was better for me physically than with a human woman. Not that biology is everything, or even very much, but I also found her beautiful, obliging, and eager, everything a lonely infatuated man could wish for.

Sensible thoughts passed briefly through my mind but found nowhere to rest. Who would beat the door demanding to escape from bliss? And anyway, even my fleeting sensible thoughts told me that if her people were truly willing to leave Han with me, then there was no point in resisting. My own people would have no objection to my absence, and much as my recent travels had interested and informed me, they were nothing compared to the pleasures of the previous night.

"I am hungry," I said, carefully removing my clothes again and hanging them neatly over a stool.

"I shall have food brought for you," she replied.

"Thank you," I said, and reached out to stroke the smooth flesh, "but it's you I have a hunger for."

CHAPTER 14

In which I fall from the heights of pleasure into the emptiness of the undesired

Again I am uncertain what to say here. Han Dellier and I shared a mutual, overwhelming pleasure for the days of her heat. When I felt it wane, I had become so attuned to her body that it felt like a loss. But she said she needed me still, and I was helpless, too caught up with her to know what to say.

Then she left me, and I found that I was still a prisoner there, but one who was tired and with stale clothes. I washed and found a robe in one of the cupboards and slept a while. Then she returned briefly, and left me again, dazed, as all she did was to kiss me and then slap my face, hard. I slept, the sleep of the tired and confused.

Finally, they came for me, and I was taken away.

* * * *

The building I was taken to was in the countryside and built like a fortress. Huge Flat slabs of dark gray material, which could have been cut stone or else were some material cast by the Laurentians, lay on their sides at odd angles to each other, spreading for hundreds of yards in either direction. The only thing to show the structure wasn't unoccupied was a square inserted into its center to form a courtyard, which our vehicle entered, stopping in front of massive white stone doors. It was far from welcoming and reminded me of nothing more than some forgotten bunker from a cataclysmic war, or a prison for the damned.

I had no choice but to enter it. Collo Dell, who was one of those who had taken me away was some sort of secretary or minder for Han. He was courteous and opened one of the white doors for me, and I went in with the others. We immediately walked down several steps, which took us below ground level to an open hall where the temperature was icy. But once inside the building I saw it was obviously a house, and right before us was a large square frame inside which lights of different colors formed patterns, with the small white lights being brightest.

Patterned tiles were inlaid into the floor, and the walls were covered here and there with hangings and objects. Laurentians walked about in fine robes and the lighting was gentle. We walked for some distance along different corridors until we arrived at another door made of some glossy white material, and I was shown inside and left there.

The door was locked, and I appeared to be alone in a huge room. Opposite me was a wall of glass, which was partly opened, revealing an enclosed courtyard containing a large pool and nothing else. The walls of the court were at least thirty feet high and constructed of the same dark gray material as the rest of the house. The floor I recognized as being of cream sandstone, and the pool was lined with the dark gray material and full of clean water that tasted fresh. The room itself was walled in the same dark gray material as the rest of the building and contained an odd collection of furniture; decorations; what was clearly a library; a large, raised sleeping or sitting platform; and various cupboards and chests for storage. In one corner was a small array of totally unfamiliar but obviously sophisticated equipment.

I had completed my inspection and was wondering what to do next when Han came in. "Who are you, Han, and why have you had me brought here?" I asked angrily as she came toward me.

"We are joined, Orlando; it is unheard of, but it has happened. This is my house, and this is my room. I have brought you here to live with me while I think about what to do with you. It may be that you can be joined to me also, or perhaps the connection I feel can be broken." Han sounded angry too and reached out for me, "I need you," she said, taking physical hold, and it was an order from my angel who suddenly looked more he than she.

Afterward she left me there, and I had to find a way to release the anger pent up inside me. I stripped off the robes I'd been given to wear, dived into the icy pool, and swam furiously up and down while my mind went around in circles. Eventually, I started to tire, and my mind began to relax. When I was nearly exhausted and the skin on my hands and feet had gone white and wrinkled, I stopped and levered myself out of the water up onto the sandstone floor.

I found her watching me from just inside the room, and I stood there, dripping water, too tired to think of what to say, surprised that she still looked so beautiful. I walked over to her and stopped, getting my breath back, not knowing what to say or do, and she reached out and grazed a finger over the few course hairs on my chest, The

217

drops of water caught there ran down her finger, and I grasped her face in my hands and crushed her mouth with mine. We staggered in a confusion of panting and clinging, finding ourselves lovers again.

I didn't understand it properly then, but she was joined to me as if we were a Laurentian husband and wife. She explained to me that she had a sense of me, which was a constant part of her unless I was taken too far away, and then she would feel a terrible loss, as if part of her was gone and the grief and confusion would be unbearable for weeks, even months. At the time, of course, I understood little of the significance of what she was telling me, and I was confused and angry and frightened by my situation.

"I can understand that you don't want to go through that, but I don't belong here, and you should have asked me if I would stay, not made me a prisoner," I said gently after she had finished her explanation.

"There are things you don't know, Orlando. I cannot go through that sort of grief now. I have duties and I cannot leave them. If you left with your people, I would grieve for you, unable to do anything else. Now is not the time for that." She became hard again, and I realized her decision about what happened to me was final. I would not be going home. I was surprised to be able to accept it calmly, and I wondered if I loved her.

"On the way here Collo Dell said that you were the head of your embassy. Is that true?" I asked.

She looked at me, resting her wonderful eyes on mine. "I am the Han Dellier, and this is my world, as you are mine, now. The meeting with your race was my doing. Han is not a name, as you think it is, it's what I am. I am the first among the Dellier. I am their Han. As you are Count Orlando, and count is not a name."

I had begun to think she was someone's overindulged child, and what I found out then still seemed odd. She looked so young, and perfect, and beautiful. "Why was what happened between us, the first night, allowed to happen then? Shouldn't someone have been protecting you from something that might have been dangerous?"

"No one thought anything that happened could possibly occur. You had been forthright with me when you came. You seemed to want to make a bargain. You did what I asked, and I assumed if I did as you had done, I would have made the bargain. I could ask you anything I wanted to know and get answers. But when you stood close by me and touched me with your hands and mouth, your scent became overpowering. We know now, when it's too late, that it has part of the smell of a female's heat in it."

So, he was my she angel, and I seduced him with the odor of a Laurentian female in heat. I had to laugh at the ridiculousness of it all. "And what was it you wanted to ask me that made the bargain worth making?" I asked, curious, because she hadn't yet asked me anything about the delegation, or about humans, or where we came from.

"The bargain was never made, and what has happened has made our situation difficult enough. Whatever I want to know, I will find out anyway. But I think it would be good if I joined you to me." She explained no more then.

The next day there was a hunt, and I was taken along by Han, I was so used to calling her Han that I decided I would continue to. For the hunt we left the great, dark house and joined half a dozen other members of Han's family, or household, in the hills, where there was a pack of hairy, thick-skinned animals with four legs and large bodies, which were to be ridden. They were ugly and they were called vergin. The Laurentians were helped to mount them and looked ungainly on top. I had a choice to ride or not, but having ridden horses for so long, I was confident I could manage the beast and joined them.

They were much more uncomfortable then a horse, but similar enough for me to settle down quickly, and I began to race anyone who wanted to put on a spurt of speed. When the vergin were forced to move fast, they were very quick indeed. Han began to call out encouragement to me when I raced a challenger, and when I won, I heard pride in her cries at my success.

She was at home outdoors on the hunt, and Han rode with strength and confidence, if not with great speed. Soon I was acknowledged as the fastest rider and had no one to race but myself, and I wondered how Han saw me. Was it as an ugly female playing at man's games? The party joked among themselves in their own language as we rode along, and I wondered what they said, as they often seemed to be looking at the two of us. But Han laughed sometimes, so it seemed to be good humored.

Eventually we came to rocky hilly ground, and the party became serious. We stopped briefly, and weapons were removed from the pack animal we'd brought along and were handed out. They were vicious, archaic crossbow-like weapons, but in place of a bolt resembling an arrow, there was a short, wide, barbed, steel blade, which would rip most Earth animals in half. We all dismounted and the weapons were handed around and each hunter tested and practiced with his own. Han pulled her's back first and aimed at a thick stumpy tree and released the blade and it thudded deep into the middle of the trunk. The others fired and before they had all had two shots the tree broke in half through the target area, where the blades had cut deep, close together.

I was embarrassed that I was barely able to draw back the bow. I struggled to lock it, ready to fire. And I was almost knocked over by the power of the release when I fired it, which sent my aim wildly out. Everyone laughed and watched as my blade spiraled up to the left, barely missed our tethered vergin, and landed in a cloud of dust on a nearby slope.

"I think you will be safer if I am unarmed." I handed the weapon back, and Han laughed at my inability to do something that she did so easily and proficiently, after my showing off my skill as a vergin rider.

Then everyone took a long knife from the pack animals bags, and I felt safe using one of those. Though I had no idea what I might use it on.

The party remounted, and we moved slowly and carefully into the hills, spreading out in a long line when we came to a large depression. It was probably half a mile wide, and a couple of miles long, and was full of enormous weathered boulders ten to twenty feet in diameter, surrounded by thick, stunted vegetation. Being unarmed except for the long knife, I rode close behind Han, having no desire to meet alone, with nothing but a knife, whatever creature it was they sought to kill with the vicious crossbow blades. By now the hunting party was spread out in a well-spaced, line beating the game out in front of them.

From the backs of the vergin, we overlooked the vegetation, and I wondered what everyone was scanning the ground ahead for. The party moved forward quietly and steadily, keeping the line through the bushes straight, and I knew this was a serious hunt, which they had undertaken often before.

We forced out half a dozen fast, little animals from behind a rock, and the line halted briefly while they disappeared into the vegetation ahead. Then the line moved on again, slowly but steadily forward for an hour or more, before there was a cry from our left. Suddenly, there was the noise of some large animal moving through the bushes and making loud noises, not growls or grunts, but in between. Han and everyone else was suddenly driving their mounts faster, and I knew that at last we were chasing our quarry.

It was easy to follow the noise it made as it ran from us and we came closer to it. Han and a couple of others had their crossbows ready and rode without their hands, holding the weapons steady ready to fire, then suddenly there was the beast, directly ahead. It was ten feet high, standing on all fours and covered in a bright reddish hair. Han fired, and the great beast lost its footing and half slid until it landed against the base of a large boulder, where it lay still. The bolt protruded from its skull, and Han jumped down from his vergin and moved toward it with the empty crossbow still in his hand. The rest of the party were coming up to join us, and I moved forward meaning to look at the creature when I saw one of its eyes move. I grabbed my knife and dropped from the vergin's back to the ground in panic, seeing Han only feet away from the thing and unarmed.

I had visions of the day Leonardo went to the wild boar we assumed was dead, and it reared up and gored him. But my arm, which was holding the knife, was grabbed violently by one of the party nearby and nearly pulled off, and I struggled as I watched Han. She had dropped her empty weapon and with the long knife in her hand instead dived forward and sliced into the animal's neck as it started to move. It fell back as huge quantities of black blood gushed out of it. I relaxed and the Laurentian who had held me back let me go, but not until he had taken my knife. Han had moved and sliced open the beast's belly and put her hand in and grasped some organ and pulled it out as the rest of the party moved to join her where she stood, like some avenging and bloodied Greek goddess.

I hadn't moved, unsure why I had been stopped from going to Han's aid and seeing more he than she as she bit into the dripping mass she had extracted from the

222

beast. Then she waved me forward. "Orlando, come here," she called, and I went over to join him and the others by the carcass. "I know you can't eat this," she said, holding the raw mass toward me, "but I give you second turn at it." She motioned me closer and when I was a foot in front of her she symbolically pressed the raw and bloody mass against my mouth. "I saw its eye move only because you did, but I think they feared you had the knife for me. It is the first Hergender I have ever slain alone, and perhaps I owe such a clean kill to you." She left the blood on my mouth and handed the flesh to another one of the party who bit into it eagerly and passed it on. When it was gone, they all fell on the raw carcass, cutting strips from inside it and sitting on the ground, eating the raw and bloody flesh and laughing.

My angel was a blood-covered primitive killer feeding. Gone were the cool, graceful Laurentians of the meeting house.

When the party had eaten their fill, two remained to skin and dissect what was left, and the rest of us returned to the place where we had first gathered. We dismounted, the vergin were returned to their pens, and Han and I returned to her fortress, entering it from an underground area where the vehicle we traveled in was parked.

She was still elated by her success at the hunt, and we went immediately to her room. Outside we found a small, worried-looking Laurentian male waiting with a wooden case. "The bands," she said eagerly and pulled the man inside, "Put one on him; join him to me," Han immediately ordered the man, pointing at me and obviously wanting it done so we could continue our other activities.

The man hurriedly opened his box and, selecting an innocuous-looking gold bracelet with some small stones set in a mesh panel, slid it onto my wrist.

I fell over hard. I could see the man twice and myself and Han and the room from at least two angles. I didn't realize that at the time, of course. All I felt then was complete disorientation and overwhelming dizziness and nausea. I fell about painfully and that penetrated slightly, and I vomited everywhere.

"Leave it longer; he is not one of us; he may need time to adjust," I could hear her saying. Then it was gone and I lay on the floor panting and shaking in shock.

"It can be done; it needs adjusting," Han was saying angrily.

"There is no adjusting, Han. You must know that," the small man replied.

Han helped me onto the sleeping platform, and I lay there, recovering.

"Was it the bracelet that made me feel like that?" I asked shakily.

"Yes, but it proves it can be done, and they often need adjusting." She looked at me closely. "It was strange being able to feel you sense me, even though it didn't work properly. It can be done."

The little man came over, and I hesitated before Han held my hand for him to slip another bracelet on me. This time Han held me down for five or ten minutes, but I was just as ill. The disorientation was not as bad when I couldn't move, but seeing and feeling several versions of the world overlaid in my mind at once gave me a shocking headache, and I was shaking and in tears when Han finally decided the experiment was a failure and let the man remove the band.

I staggered to the bathroom and refused to let them try again. The little man ran off clutching his case. It had spoiled the afternoon, I knew, and I tried to make it up to her. She told me the band should have given me the same sense of her that she had of me after the heat.

I went to sleep afterward and woke at some time to find her at the equipment, which was in one corner of the room, talking to someone. She spoke her own language, and I had no idea what was being said, just a sense that she was not pleased.

She decided I had to join the rest of the family in the morning because she wanted to relive the previous day's hunt with the others and because I had been there and seen her kill the beast, so it was my day too. That night she spent some more time at the equipment she had in her room, and I heard voices again, Han's obviously annoyed.

Looking back, those seven or eight days from that first night we spent together were the best ones. From there on things deteriorated, suddenly at first, then slowly.

My presence had become an inconvenience. Han had work to do, and the time she had to give to me because of her need was an unfamiliar distraction. When a couple of weeks later it was realized Han really was bound to me and that I had to accompany them to the homeworld, there were arguments among the people about her that even I knew about, though I couldn't understand what was said.

Han began to resent the problems I was causing her and became increasingly uncommunicative and occasionally brutal when she needed me. This was particularly so if she had put off satisfying her need, or if there had been an argument with the people around him. I soon discovered that my delicate-looking angel was wiry and gave a slap like a wooden club.

When I finally spoke to her angrily about her behavior, I was shocked at how far things had deteriorated.

"You are not one of us. Why do I feel the way I do about you? Why am I joined to you? It's not natural, it's

225

not normal. Have you been sent to destroy me? To destroy my family?" she yelled back at me.

I was speechless.

"At first it seemed wonderful, but now there are so many problems," she said more calmly and left me.

After that, I only really saw her at night in the dark when we shared the sleeping platform together. I was isolated from everyone else as well, but she coped much better and things between us were at least physically enjoyable again.

But I began to fear for my life if she found some way to dispense with me, and the business with the joining that had failed was forgotten about.

Then it was time to leave Heinget, and I saw a starship like nothing I had seen before. But that was almost all I saw, the outside of it. Once on board I was again a prisoner, now in her cabin. She was becoming my fallen angel, but never falling so far in my eyes that she became less desirable physically. I had an idea the little usefulness I retained for her might end after the council meeting we traveled to was over. What would happen then was not something I dwelt on.

I was only allowed out of her cabin again once we had landed.

We were down. And the first people to come on board must have been the equivalent of customs or quarantine officers. Han got very angry when I was required to stand for inspection. Presumably, this was so that they could check whether I was diseased or dutiable. I proved to be neither, to their great disappointment. So they waved documents about, which Han Dellier ended up signing, after some protest, and then they departed.

Immediately after they left us several others, who were obviously Han's people, came on board, bringing with them a large, ornate wooden chest and several bags of clothing. I had been told that the worst of the winter was over on the homeworld, but it was apparently still cold enough outside for everyone to require several more layers of special clothing before they left the ship. Much of this was in the bags. The chest contained furs. Black and glossy, deep red, gold and white, all very thick and long haired. Han pulled out a deep red fur robe after already putting several layers of clothing over his uniform. The fur was a plain straight coat crossing over at the front with a large hood and full sleeves. With what she had already put on over her uniform, I thought she would swelter in the Arctic.

So, I thought I had better put on another layer of synthetic wear also, and then Han told me to select a fur from the chest for myself.

There were occasional times when she was extremely considerate of me. Her attitude toward me wasn't personal; the situation for her was just extremely difficult. I had no idea what I would do myself in her position.

Several other crewmembers had already selected furs for themselves. What remained was a long, black coat like Han's, a gold coat fuller but with small sleeves, almost a cape with hand holes rather then a coat. The white fur that remained was probably the largest. A great hooded cape with no sleeves. Something so thick I imagined you could roll up in it then lie down in the snow and sleep comfortably.

I put it on and found that the hood had long white tails like a scarf. I pulled another pair of black pants on over my already well-covered legs as an extra layer there and hoped that my boots would keep my feet warm.

We lined up at the door like a herd of chubby and furry, multicolored Teddy bears, passing out through the airlock just as if we were in space. As the doors slid open on the other side, we were hit by a wall of ice. I buried my face in the fur and gasped for warm air. My exposed skin was almost instantly on fire with pain, the cold was so intense. All I could do was to pull the fur tight around me and concentrate on trying to find unfrozen air to breathe, and I was vaguely aware of bending over, staggering, and nearly falling.

I was bundled back into the ship, where I gasped and shivered uncontrollably. "God, nothing can be so cold," I stuttered, through shaking teeth.

A major discussion was going on around me; then someone gave me a mask and there was breathable warm air, and then they put some ointment on my face where the skin had been briefly exposed. This was a big improvement. When I was alive again, I was installed in a space helmet with an insulated container of air, unfrozen, and with another layer of clothing on, I was presented to the world again. With the helmet on, it was a breeze, except that carrying the air, and all the clothes I wore, made walking rather difficult.

When we had reassembled outside the ship, I observed that we were in an open space near a row of buildings with a few brightly lit windows. The sky was clear and black, with a million stars feebly showing in competition with the landing field lights. We moved ponderously across the shiny, ice-covered ground toward a group of people who, by the way they were lined up, were obviously waiting for us. Han led our group, and a fur shrouded figure, presumably their leader, waited slightly out in front of the other group. He wore a magnificent black fur cape and a small fleet of closed vehicles waited, invitingly, off to one side of his party.

Han stopped when he, I found I was now thinking of Han as he, not she, was about three yards in front of the waiting man, and I could just make out that the other man's lips were moving now and then. They seemed to be having quite a long conversation considering the weather. Then someone led me forward to where I could be easily seen by the other party, not that they could see much of me, except for a bit of my face through the helmet.

Unfortunately, the reception committee behind the black-coated man didn't seem impressed, and suddenly our party became quite agitated. The family guards moved forward to flank Han. Several members of their reception committee fanned out and cleared clothing away from what had to be weapons.

"And I thought this was going to be another one of those boring formal reception parties," I murmured and found everyone looking at me.

Everything going on outside my helmet was so quiet I hadn't even thought that they could hear me. But apparently the helmet was still turned on and had broadcast my remark out loud and live. I was hustled back into the main body of our group, but my comment seemed to have broken the tension, and the black coats reception committee stomped about briefly and then left in its vehicles, which looked comfortable and warm.

"What was that about?" I asked hesitantly, and everyone ignored me.

I must have been turned off now, I decided, but shortly two guards came and checked my helmet and air.

Han and his advisers were in a compact circle. Guards stood around them, watching the surrounding area intently. Reinforcements had arrived from somewhere, and now there were twenty, or thirty, retainers standing about openly showing devices that had to be weapons. Obviously our arrival hadn't gone according to plan. But I had no idea what had gone wrong, just a feeling that my presence hadn't pleased someone. My presence, I thought unhappily, pleased no one nowadays.

A vehicle came up, and after further discussion, an old man and Hans's secretary got in and were driven off. I would have liked to get in too but was being ignored by everyone. And in spite of everything I was wearing, the cold was starting to creep in to me.

There was a bit of snow falling then, and standing round in it wasn't going to make things any better. I started flapping my arms and waddling round in circles to keep warm, fed up with being told nothing about what was going on. I could see our ship not far off and decided to head back inside, unfortunately, our guards were not going to let me wander off. They also weren't letting me near Han. Shortly, my feet and hands were starting to go numb. I endeavored to get to Han again. I yelled, but yelling was obviously useless. When a guard tried stopping me from approaching Han again, I swung my air supply at him, and it landed with a thud. Everyone, including Han, turned around and I pushed on toward him, finally getting his attention.

"Can't your bloody bond tell you I'm freezing to death out here," I yelled at him when I was close enough.

He peered at me, so I shouted at him again, and then he reached out and touched something on my helmet.

"Don't you know I'm going to freeze to death if I stand here much longer. My feet are nearly numb already," I repeated more quietly.

He pushed back his hood and removed the fine gem-studded net covering his skull, which he had been wearing for some days. "With this on, I can only feel you enough to know you're alive," he said angrily "You should have gone with the others in the car." He sounded as he obviously felt, angry with this new situation they were in, and also best pleased if I shut up and disappeared.

"It's a bit late for that now," I said, stamping my feet and flapping my arms. "I would like to return to the ship."

"We cannot return to the ship, or they will think I am leaving. It's time we moved on anyway, so the guards will have to carry you."

Han took off the fur coat he wore, handing it to a couple of guards, who spread it out on the ground fur side up. The Dellier turned and everyone started to walk away from the ship.

"Lie down on it," one of the guards instructed, and feeling like an idiot, I did.

Three guards lined up each side and lifted the coat like a stretcher. I adjusted my fur cape to cover my body as well as it could and settled back, trying to relax. We moved off at a good pace, and I can honestly say that my ride was surprisingly smooth. I didn't really get any warmer, but the cold didn't penetrate any deeper either.

The whole episode seems so comical now. It wasn't at the time, though.

I tried to see things in a positive light but was uncomfortably aware of my growing rejection. I was kept removed from the family; I was being ignored by everyone. And I knew that I was alive only because my death would have been a greater inconvenience. Han still felt something for me, but it was nothing that could survive in his real world.

I was carried right into the main entrance of the public accommodation center we then went to. Being bundled up as I was, with a bottle of air and a helmet on, I felt like some mad invalid, and was embarrassed, but relieved, when I was tipped out onto the floor in the main entry, rather than laid down, as I would have had difficulty getting myself up. My helmet was removed for the further amusement of the audience. There were a lot of people standing around the open foyer, and our group was obviously the focus of everyone's attention.

Several people in bright uniforms were about, and when some senior person appeared, we were whisked over to the lifts and up to a set of rooms. I was led off, away from the others, to a room with what looked like a small pool full of hot steamy water and helped off with my many layers of clothing. It appeared that someone was thinking of my welfare still. My feet and hands were massaged by an attendant, and in the hot steamy atmosphere they soon stopped tingling. I was relieved when the feeling in them and my feet returned to normal, and I was able to get into the pool and lie back in the hot, scented water.

I still didn't know what was going on and was feeling very insecure and frightened. I didn't speak the language, I had no money, I couldn't get in touch with anyone I knew—except Han. And he was probably thinking, with relief, that soon he could dispense with me. I was a damned long way from home, with no transport.

When I had finished my soak, I was given a large robe to wrap myself in and left in an adjoining bedroom. I was happy to be warm and able to relax in comfort, but with nothing to occupy my thoughts except worrying about my future, time dragged. And my anxiety increased.

CHAPTER 15

*In which I change hands and first meet
the one my life is bound to*

Eventually, someone came and got me and. I was taken back to the main room where three strangers, in traditional dress, were standing with Han and his advisers. They all fixed their eyes on me the moment I entered the room. The new arrivals were mature male Laurentians with full gold striped manes and ivory skin. The one standing right next to Han wore a bracelet like Han's, but the stones were green, not white, and he had on fine green robes. The other two wore black robes with patterns of deep green and had several plain bracelets on each wrist.

The newcomer who wore the simple robes of a deep green color appeared to be in command—Han and the other senior members of our party who were present were treating all three with deference. One of the black-clad strangers came over and led me off to a seat on one side of the room, and I noted when he came close that his robe's black appearance was deceptive, it was, in fact, a complex swirling pattern of very dark green and black.

"Sit down," he said, and I sat down facing away from everyone else while he stood behind me. It flitted briefly through my mind that they might be executioners, probably because of the black, or interrogators. And I wondered again what the problem had been that Han had encountered with the black, fur-coated man on our arrival.

The other black-robed man joined us and, pulling two stools in beside me, sat on the one closest to my right side and laid the wooden case he had been carrying down on the other.

"Can you tell me what is going on?" I asked nervously, wary of what his case contained.

He paused for a moment and looked directly at me. Few of the aliens did that, so I expected him to say something, but instead he looked briefly away behind me to where everyone else was, before opening the case. It contained trays, neatly divided into compartments, which were filled with cut stones of every color and size and a number of openwork metal bracelets. I recognized its contents, with horror, and tried to get away, but the man standing behind me held me down firmly.

"What are you going to do?" I asked as the man behind me pushed down hard on my shoulders, somehow stopping me from moving away from the box of bands, one of which the seated stranger was fitting with small gems.

"Han, what's going on?" I shouted in fright, struggling and twisting about as far as I could, but only seeing the man in green off to one side behind me, and realizing the room was quiet.

The man with the green robes and bracelet came over. "I know what happened before," he said. "We need to check something for ourselves. I am assured by

234

Hoonan that this time you will feel almost no discomfort."

"Can you tell me what is going on?" I asked him.

He ignored me, indicating to Hoonan, the man who sat beside me, to continue. I pulled my arms in and fought them. Then I seemed to lose my strength, the hands on my shoulders taking on tremendous weight and my own arms going weak.

"You will just stay still so that Hoonan can be comfortable while he works," the man with the green bracelet said sternly.

The man behind me still held my shoulders, and if Han was going to let them force me to do what they wanted, then I knew I had no choice. I relaxed, and my strength seemed to partially return, and I held my arm out so that my wrist was free and then closed my eyes and turned away.

I felt something slipped briefly onto my wrist and felt nothing. Cautiously I looked at what they were doing. I wondered, with little conviction, if Han was still seeing if he could bond me successfully after all. Hoonan attached a stone onto the plain band he held and slipped it on me. This time I could feel a faint hum, but he slipped the band off almost immediately and the hum was gone. The three men were silent, the other two concentrating on watching Hoonan as he tried several other combinations of stones. Always briefly, and with nearly each combination I was conscious of something different in my mind that was not mine, but each time it was so light, it was quite bearable.

"That is enough," Hoonan said, putting the last band and stones back neatly in the case.

"Yes. Not quite what we expected," the man in green said, as he sighed and seemed to visibly relax.

He left us then, leaving his two companions with me, and I could hear voices behind me. The man standing behind me put his hands over my face, which I didn't like but I accepted, and suddenly I felt considerably more relaxed and completely calm. Then he helped me stand, and I felt light-headed and was taken by the arm and led to the door where the green man joined us, and I was led out.

I caught only a brief glimpse of Han and the old man, Zan Dellier, disagreeing about something as I left. I knew I should cry out something to Han, but I lacked the physical will or energy to. Outside the room were several of Han's family guards, who accompanied us down to the foyer. Then the green man waved them away, and we moved quickly outside to waiting vehicles. I was hit momentarily by the cold outside, but the entrance was sheltered and warmed air from the building followed me out and into the nearest vehicle.

"Are you going to kill me?" I surprised myself by asking once we were all inside the vehicle. I knew that the calm I felt was unnatural. "I was told that Han was bonded to me and that we couldn't be separated." But I knew now that Han Dellier had somehow been able to cast me off after all. "Was that lies?"

"Why would I kill something I have given a great deal to acquire? I have paid the Dellier for you," the green man said and seemed to be laughing.

"You have bought me?" I asked, stunned even in my calmness. "He said that he needed me to be with him because of the bond. Why would he sell me now? I could have gone home with the others if he didn't need me."

I almost cried, confusedly convinced I had been lied to all along but unable to feel angry. I wanted to be angry. I should have felt angry. But I said the words as if half asleep, "Is there any authority I can appeal to about being sold like a slave? I am a representative on an official embassy from Earth. Do you know that?" I wondered if the man did know.

"I know that you have been left behind by your own people, and that you are no longer needed, or wanted, by the one who kept you. And there is no one in authority who wants to know about you," he said it bluntly, and I knew he was right.

"Who are you?" I asked, peering at the green man.

"I am the Han Kirkillian, and Hoonan is one of my seers and also my personal adviser."

"And why do you want me?" I asked.

"We are amazed by you, and I want you so that we can study you. Fortunately, you had become most inconvenient for the Dellier, and I can take away the pain he feels at losing you. It is difficult and time consuming, but worth it, because now I have you."

"But why?"

"Ah now, because you are such a curious thing. When I was first called on by the Dellier, I wondered if he had the madness after all. Someone who cannot wear a band, he says. So ridiculous. I put it out of my mind. Then my people receive a message from the little man who puts together the simple bands for some small planet no one's heard of. A message that he has found a person of great strength, very great. And this is my passion, strength, so what did I say?" He kept looking at me as if I were a laboratory animal, but it was Hoonan who answered him.

"'Where is this place Hoonan?' and I told you it was the Dellier's wintering planet of Heinget," Hoonan replied.

"Yes. And I said 'Ah how odd. I have had a strange call from the Dellier about someone he cannot bond because the bands send that person mad. And now another from one of my own people about the same thing. So, perhaps the Dellier isn't mad.' So, I ask the Dellier for more details, which was quite difficult after the way I had dismissed him originally. And what do I find?" he sat back and continued staring at me. I was something under glass. "The Dellier's person and the little band makers are the same, but both are oddly reluctant to tell me any more. And this is most, most curious. So, I say to the Dellier, 'Hoonan and I can do anything you wish. Bring this person with you when you come to council. I will do whatever you want us to in return for him if he interests me.' He says he may do so, so Hoonan and I look forward eagerly to the Dellier coming. But when the Dellier is still on his way, what strange story do we hear?"

"That the Han Dellier is bound to one of the humans he had arranged to meet in isolation and is bringing him to the creation homeworld." Hoonan said.

They obviously did this double act often, because Hoonan knew what questions he was supposed to answer and which ones the Han Kirkillian would answer himself.

"I wondered again if some new madness has taken hold of his family. Do you know that the current Han Dellier holds his position as Han because nearly all of the first twenty of the Dellier were culled when he was a very young child?"

I shook my head. "No. I don't know anything about that."

"No, he wouldn't tell anyone who didn't know. Unfortunately, they carried a madness, which would take years to appear. Such a history makes claims of instability a dangerous thing for our Dellier.

"Anyway, the Dellier comes at last, and we rush to meet him and see what he has brought us. And before we reach the visitors' resting place, Hoonan can sense something different is inside, and the closer we get to the Dellier the stronger it becomes. Then we enter the room he occupies and what do we see brought in, an ugly stunted creature, which the Dellier has seemingly bonded to, and I know he is mad. But then I must be too, because even I feel the creature's mind now I am in the same room. So we test it, and what do we find?"

"The Han Dellier and the little band maker tell the truth. You have a very strong mind," Hoonan said, actually talking to me.

"I am ecstatic, and the Dellier has problems with the Metjhan because of this ugly thing, so I can acquire it easily from him. So now you are mine and it will be wonderful to bond you and for my seers to discover what such an ugly human can do."

I resented his description of me very much. I was hardly stunted; he was only a head taller than me himself. Unfortunately, ugly was a matter of opinion. But he was certainly no Greek god.

But worse than that, he obviously had no real interest in me and hardly saw me as a person, which worried me. The Han Kirkillian himself was obviously old. His mane was full and long but had turned dark, streaked with pewter and gold and with none of the silver of youth left in it. His skin was the dark gold of old ivory, but he must have been a fine specimen in his youth, as he was still lean and carried himself straight. I had to admit that his mane shone with luxuriant health. He also gave off maleness as if he were the only male there. The three of them with me in the vehicle were middle aged, with little of the ethereal beauty, and none of the sensual grace and obliging temperament, the Dellier had exhibited at the beginning, and that had been so alluring to me. But I was still reeling from the suddenness with which that relationship had soured and left me trapped in misery.

"The Dellier's beauty made him so desirable to me that I wanted to be with him. After a night together, I had caused him to come into heat, and he formed a bond to me, as if we were male and female. I believe that is how the bond forms." The Kirkillian tried to interrupt, but I kept talking, too calm to feel bad about doing so. "I find you and these seers very ugly; if you wish me to mate one and bond it, you will have to find a much more beautiful

239

and younger one for me." Knowing what it was like, I knew I could probably have had sex with any Laurentian male at least once, if I was lonely enough, but I wasn't going to tell him that.

The Han Kirkillian looked as expressionless as ever, but Hoonan's head moved about between us as did the head of the other seer, who had been silent up to then.

"You do not expect us to do that?" both seers said.

"There are other ways of forming a bond," the Kirkillian replied, unconcerned.

"I thought it was formed during the first matings?" I said.

"Normally it is, between us. But how could you mate the Dellier?" the Kirkillian asked.

"We mated many times," I replied, feeling less calm now and annoyed by his disbelief. "How else would he have been bonded to me?"

"You may have some trick to fool the inexperienced such as him, but you would not be able to fool anyone else."

"Actually, his organ is much like that of our females and my own is, I believe, much like that of your females. Physically, we were wonderfully compatible." I might have lacked the ability to become angry, but I was obstinate still, and annoyed at being called a liar.

"You can touch its mind," he said to Hoonan. "Tell me the ugly thing lies."

Hoonan seemed to enter a trance for several minutes, and I tried to imagine myself with Han Dellier again. Then his eyes snapped open and he looked at me. "It is true, what he says. I have no doubts, and the biological bond is always superior."

"Curiouser and curiouser. I understand now why the Metjhan was so dangerous for the Dellier, and why he knew he would be," the Kirkillian said. Then they began to talk between themselves in their own language, staring at me occasionally.

The Kirkillian was a man who obviously had power and liked to have things as he pleased. If I became inconvenient to him, I had no doubt he would not hesitate to dispose of me cleanly, and if he thought I was useful, he would use me however he wanted to. He was not a man I wanted to belong to.

"I am a member of an embassy from Earth, and I demand to be taken to someone in authority." It was stupid to repeat it, but I wanted to escape and had no other way to.

"You are nothing here. I have already told you this. The Dellier was forbidden to allow any of your kind to know more than Heinget," he said. "No-one but the Dellier has any interest in your species. I can take you to the Prime, but then I would request you back to use in my experiments, and I could get three votes of five without any negotiation, and I will have you back. Don't put me to the trouble, dwarf."

Hoonan looked at me with what I thought was pity, but was probably not, and I ignored them. I would have to make myself useful to my new master; it seemed I had no other choice.

Even between themselves they now continued to talk in English so I could understand them, and in their private conversation, the Kirkillian asked how strong the bond would be between a mate and me. Hoonan replied that its strength always depended on the mate.

"Is it strong enough to bother with?" the Kirkillian asked, "What about with me. If we bonded somehow, would I be able to see as you do Hoonan, using its mind?"

"I can't be sure what an alien I know nothing about can do when it is bonded, Kio. I only know what I sensed between it and the Dellier. I might know more if I did more tests."

"Then do some now." The Kirkillian ordered. "We have enough with us for you to get some idea surely?"

I had no desire to be bonded to the Kirkillian as well as owned by him. He was dangerous. I held out my hands for Hoonan, and he and his fellow seer played with their mesh and gems. The Kirkillian kept up a sporadic dialogue with them in his own language until they finished.

"It would be stronger than anything you have been able to share with me through the bands," Hoonan said quietly as he put his things away. "I think it would be immensely stronger in some ways but weak in others and not at all stable, without assistance."

Then they both stared at me. "It's so ugly, and it's male! It was easy to acquire, but now everything about it is difficult and unpleasant."

"There are other ways," said Hoonan.

"If you can find a better one, wonderful. But at this time the biological bond is always better. And I tire of this ugly way of talking; it shall be made to speak properly immediately."

Soon after, we arrived at our destination.

The building's outline was softened by a heavy covering of snow, and I was wrapped in something thick and pulled quickly from the vehicle and through the door, gasping again for breathable air when I entered the room inside. There were several people about who were bright and helpful, removing the rug I was wrapped in and talking to the Kirkillian and his companions cheerfully in their own language.

We moved into the house further, passing quite a few other people, mainly young, with wonderful silver-white manes. Some of their manes were decorated with colored streaks, and all were wearing bright-colored clothes, moving about busily and seeming cheerful. The somberness I had found in the Dellier's house was obviously his families' own, and not Laurentian in general.

Someone had taken hold of my arm, and I was almost running to keep up as the others strode gracefully through the cool halls.

A door was opened, and I was helped to follow the Kirkillian and Hoonan through it, into a short, shadowed passage, then through another door, and on the threshold, I stopped dead, my body frozen in fear.

We were in what could only be an operating theater. There were two people in simple green robes; there was shiny equipment, vessels with tubes going in and out of them and a brightly lit soft white table. My stomach knotted up as I wondered what they intended to do to me.

The Kirkillian turned around and was suddenly face to face with me, and I was afraid but determined not to show it in front of him, in spite of which determination I nevertheless felt my body shake.

"If you are going to be able to communicate properly, you must have a converter implanted," he said and surprised me by attempting to reassure me. "It is only a minor procedure; if I wanted to know how your body functions, we already have human corpses available to study. It would be a waste to use one as expensive as yours."

I wasn't sure I believed him. "Where did you get human bodies from?" I had to ask, suddenly terrified it might be the rest of my embassy.

"I don't know. They were not of any interest to me before now, but I assure you they were already dead when we acquired them," he replied.

"I'm not a Laurentian. How can you know that whatever you are going to do is safe. Have you tried it out on the bodies?" I wanted to get out of there—alive and sane.

"It would be useless to implant a converter in a dead body. You can be reassured that I won't let it be done unless I am sure it will be safe. You are still worth something to me, dwarf. But I need to study you, and I find your language inadequate." He indicated the table, and I got myself onto it alone, ignoring my walker's attempt to aid me. Whatever was going to happen there, I couldn't run away from it, and I had no real reason to doubt him.

"Then we put this net over your head," someone explained as a frame was placed around my head and one of the gem-studded nets was supported on it. "Your head must be still." I felt a restraint tighten firmly around my forehead, which did my nerves no good at all. "I will not stay here," the Kirkillian said. "I shall return when you have finished."

He moved out of my sight, and I heard the door close. Then someone asked me a lot of silly questions. I had trouble thinking of what to answer to many of them. Then, when I was able to talk eloquently about something, they would quickly interrupt me with another totally unrelated question. I also had to move my arms, legs, toes, etc., etc. on request and listen to odd noises and look at objects they placed in front of my eyes. Meanwhile, I occasionally felt things placed on my wrist and removed.

Whatever they were doing to me now, I was reassured by the amount of effort that was being put into it. The time seemed to drag on, and I heard the door open and close several times, so I knew there were more comings and goings, and eventually the Kirkillian's face reappeared above me with a younger man beside him.

"I think it is quite safe to install it," the younger man said. "But it may not work perfectly."

"If it can work in the others as well as it does, I would expect it to be easy for him to use it," The

244

Kirkillian replied, with a hint of annoyance, and the two men disappeared from sight.

"It will be easy, but the language center is not as clearly defined as it has been before. The physical range may cause anomalies. Even if we created something with a bigger range, we wouldn't get an improvement. It might even be worse, because the edges of the area we want are not clear," I could hear someone saying, and it didn't sound very reassuring to me.

"If you are sure it is safe to go on, then do it," the Kirkillian said.

"It is as safe as it ever can be," someone replied.

They started asking questions again, and the Kirkillian remained. I was annoyed at the meaninglessness of the whole thing. Then I started to have trouble understanding what was being said to me and had to ask for things to be repeated. It got worse, and I was apologizing for still not understanding when things had been repeated two or three times. They had been working for some hours, and I was worried about what would happen if I failed to perform as expected with this new thing.

Then I had trouble getting my words out and had to really concentrate for a while to speak clearly. Concentrating seemed to help me understand them, though, which was a relief, as I was getting frightened. Whatever they were doing to my brain was not working well, and I tried to tell them this.

The Kirkillian appeared. "How do you feel?" he asked, and I noticed that there was something odd about his mouth.

"I think I'm hallucinating, and I am having trouble understanding what is being said, and I can't control my speech properly." It came out jumbled and slurred, and I closed my eyes. "Whatever you have done is making me mad," I stammered, and suddenly my head started to hurt terribly. "Now my head is hurting."

I opened my eyes to try and find something to fix my mind on, to hold it steady as I was near terror.

"It seems to be working quite well," a voice said.

"Yes." agreed the Kirkillian. "He has an odd accent and a stiff mouth now, but that will improve. Most Laurentians wouldn't have any trouble understanding him."

"It's not working well," I cried out in panic, gasping for air as a shocking pain pounded in my head. Then something warm was wrapped around my skull, and there was silence for a few minutes, and I felt myself relaxing mentally and physically. My breathing slowed, and my head stopped hurting, and finally I opened my eyes and could see clearly.

"Is that better now?" the Kirkillian asked quietly.

I nodded slightly but didn't dare speak.

"He has no understanding of what has happened," a voice said, and I thought it was Hoonan sitting by my head. Someone tapped me on the shoulder lightly. "You are calmer now. Has the pain gone?" the voice asked. "If it has, it will be all right to speak now, but just a few words. Don't try to say anything complicated."

"Yes," I said and paused, flooded with relief that the word had been clear. "I feel much better now." I spoke slowly and carefully, still feeling all right. "What happened? What went wrong?" I asked, exhausted but calm.

The Kirkillian leaned over me, "Nothing went wrong. You are just highly strung. As I have already said, everything with you except your acquisition seems difficult. I am talking your language now," he said and paused, then went into weird lip twitch mode, "and now I am speaking mine." His lips were really odd to watch. "You will soon get used to it."

It was a relief to hear him say it, because I wanted to believe him. "So, now I understand your language? But how do I learn to speak like you?"

"You are speaking Laurentian now. You will automatically change to whichever language is being spoken to you. If you haven't heard a language for a while, it may take a couple of attempts before you switch over properly. You are doing quite satisfactorily," the Kirkillian said briskly.

"Soon you can rest; it has been more difficult for you than we expected," the voice by my head said.

It all sounded quite unbelievable to me. The band around my head was removed, along with the cage and the net. I sat up on the table and saw that Hoonan had been the one sitting beside me, and ignoring the case of bands and stones he had beside him, I said, "Thank you," grateful for his help. When I had rested briefly, my walker took my arm again, and with Hoonan and his fellow seer and the Han Kirkillian, I was walked further into the building.

Finally, we stopped, Hoonan placed his hands about my head, and I remember no more till I woke in my cage.

A cage. That is the only way I can describe it. It was a room inside a room. It was comfortable, or I should say it had a bed that was comfortable, a seat, a table for me to sit at, and a basin and place to go to the toilet. Three sides of the place were solid, and the other was made of a strong mesh—as if they were afraid I might try to chew my way out—with a strong double door in it.

Outside, aliens, Laurentians, they suddenly seemed more alien than they had been since I first met them when the mission arrived on Heignet, walked about and peered in at me. Otherwise, I was ignored; I occupied a space, that was all. When I felt properly awake, I tried to catch the attention of the people outside, calling out, talking to them. They would look around briefly then return to whatever they were doing, and I caught only snatches of their conversations, which meant nothing to me. They were so full of unknown words. Food was passed through a slot. Eventually, everyone left, and the lights were turned out, and I went to sleep that first night fearful of what I had become.

When the lights went on again, I woke and cleaned myself as best I could. Then someone came to open my door, and I went forward to meet them. But I was ordered to get back like some wild animal. They were afraid to open the door with me close by it. But then they came in and grabbed me by the arm and led me out to a seat by a table. A variety of people in everyday robes of various colors and patterns repeatedly tested my mind in some way with different bands. With some, it was as it had been the first times, and they were annoyed by the mess I made in their room, but they ignored me when I begged them to stop. I was soon fighting them, and someone put their hands over my face, and I became completely calm and relaxed. This seemed to suit them, and they continued their experiments, and if I started to become frustrated or tried to talk too much, someone would put their hands over my face to calm me, and soon I was in a half daze more than I was myself.

After ten days, the green man came again, I had forgotten his name. I was completely dazed now. He looked at me and touched the metal bands they had on my wrists, while he talked to the people with him about things I didn't understand. Then he left. Their equipment was removed, and I was led to my door.

The Laurentians have strong fingers, and my arm was bruised from being held firmly by one of them as I was made to wait, looking at the floor. I did that the whole time then, so as not to annoy anyone. When the door was opened, I only entered my cage when I was told

248

to. They held me firmly and had shaken me when I originally tried to go in as soon as the door was opened. Inside I went to my bed and sat down. Later I found my journal was gone, and I had nothing to do with my time, but I was too calmed to worry about it.

I lost track of the days then, and in the moments I was aware of myself, I grew afraid I would completely lose my mind there; often I had no idea where I was. The green man returned again after a while, but only ever briefly, until one day he spoke to me. I didn't realize he was talking to me until he had said my name several times, and I was afraid to move or look at him, frightened of what they would do if I did.

"Answer me, Orlando," he said angrily.

"Yes, Yes" I mumbled, confused, not having heard his question and still looking at the floor. "What do you want me to do?" I asked hesitantly.

"I am not happy with the testing. There is almost nothing to sense from you now. Why is that?" he asked, obviously displeased with me in some way.

I had no idea what he was talking about. I tried to think of an answer, afraid he might want to get rid of me if I failed to satisfy him. "I don't know. I've done whatever I've been told to do." I was terrified and angry but not as dazed as I usually was, because I had been behaving so well that they had been calming me less.

He turned away to talk to others who were there, the ones who had been doing the testing. I could hear them saying I was unintelligent and uncooperative and no longer showed any ability though there had been some indication of it during the first days. Someone took me to my cage, and the door was opened, and I entered it as I should and sat on my bed, looking at the floor.

"I acquired this creature because I thought it would be interesting to study. Now instead of something with an unknown ability, I find this, which as well as being ugly is now hardly able to be sensed." He turned and gestured at me. "What is the problem?" I thought he was speaking to me. He spoke loudly and stood near the front of my cage half turned to me, half to the others standing in a group behind him.

Suddenly, I hated him for what he had done to me. I hated them all. I became enraged at myself for being so obedient and subservient, and enraged at them all for demanding it.

In a fury I flung myself at the mesh of the cage in front of the Kirkillian and I tore at it with my hands and screamed at him, "I am a man, not an animal. A man. Not something to lock in a cage and study like an animal." I saw I frightened them and was pleased, repeating it over and over, shaking the mesh and shouting until I was hoarse. Finally, I staggered back, breathing hard, and glared a them like some enraged gorilla in his pen, before sitting on my bed and looking at the floor again, helplessly weeping, because I knew I had annoyed them and all I wanted to do was live.

I looked up finally, and nearly everyone had gone. Part of me felt some pride that I had exploded, imagining I might prefer to die rather than continue to live like that. But most of me was terrified by what I'd done, because if I didn't survive I would never go home. Home. I longed to go home, to Earth.

Shortly, there was a noise, and looking up again, I saw that though it was still light there was no one left in the room outside my cage.

CHAPTER 16

I begin a life with windows, where the bars of my prison are invisible to all but me

You thought my story would be all romance and the wonders of science, didn't you?

That is what I have read about my life at odd times, written by people who have never asked me anything about it, or even met me. You thought I was complaining like a spoilt child when I said I would rather not have had this life.

And you have no idea what it is to be so alone. Because when people so resemble humans, it is hardest to understand that there is nothing that is common or shared in your lives, before you met them.

I was taken from my cage. I do not remember it happening, and I never asked why. It was enough that the wire mesh and the observers were gone. Now I entered the cage of invisible bars.

The room had a large window that looked onto falling snow and heavy drifts. All was whiteness. I was no longer caged on public view. Now I was a specimen frozen inside a block of ice. Like those mammoths they used to find preserved in the arctic wastes of Siberia.

I had awoken there and had no knowledge of how I had got there. They must have waited till I was asleep and then ensured I remained so while they moved me.

The room was comfortable. Of course the door was locked, but on the second day, one of the people who looked after me—I had learned to tell them apart sometimes by then—brought in a trolley, and there it was. On it were my things from my life before, those possessions I had taken to the meeting house that had later gone to the Dellier's house, and the plain, daily clothes Michael had so thoughtfully left behind for me— the only one of my embassy to consider me when they departed.

When I realized what had been brought to me, I couldn't help crying, and my hands shook as I went through what was there.

I was overcome to have my four books, two unread and waiting to carry me away from where I was to worlds created from images of home. Seeing and touching my own clothes, clothes that all came from Earth and Madeleine, made me cry more, reminding me of the life I used to have when I was free. More than anything else, they were filled with memories of the man I used to be— when I was still a man—and I held them over my face to hide my pain from everyone, and the world from myself.

However long I was alone with those things of mine, it was long enough to leave me exhausted and soul-destroyingly depressed. I put myself to bed knowing that sleep would lighten my mind more than anything I could do awake. I planned to begin to read one of my unread books the next day but was depressed even by that thought, knowing that in a couple of days I would have read both and drawn from them most of their magic of escape, with only a little left waiting in them for me to call on in the future.

I didn't remember having any nightmares that night; they had haunted my sleep many nights and woke me in a sweat, fearing for my life or my sanity, sometimes crying for the lost feel of loving, warm, living flesh.

The following morning I delayed opening my book and beginning its journey, I found many excuses to occupy me. I went through my clothes again and refolded them and put them neatly into the cupboards and drawers in my new room. I went through the few papers I found among my possessions and stopped because they made me want to weep again, they were so full of the world I had left behind. I put them into a drawer for another time when I felt stronger. Then I found the small deer hide wallet, and I couldn't go on. I put it in a drawer on its own and closed it. Then I sat on my bed and wept again until I was exhausted. But I wasn't tired enough to sleep, and I just sat there emptily gazing into the past.

A knock on my door pulled me out of my reverie, it was so unexpected, I waited and the knock came again, I felt foolish, realizing I was out of the habit of being in my own place but confused that they did not enter. "Come in," I said finally.

"I thought having your own possessions back would please you," Han Kirkillian said as he came in. "Would you rather they were taken away again?"

"No." I gasped involuntarily, "No. But they brought back too many memories of what I was, of what my life was, before."

"Ah," he said and walked the few steps about the room slowly.

"My journal is not among them," I said hesitantly, then fell silent, amazed that I had already said so much to him and afraid to ask for it.

"No, it is not, but you shall have it soon. Would you like to walk?"

"Leave this room?" I asked confused by such an unexpected choice.

"With me. Yes. We can take a sort walk about."

I was frightened of what this might mean but torn by wanting to get out and move. I didn't look at him. "If that is what you want."

"No, I want you to decide. Would you like to stay in here or walk outside?"

It took me a while to say it. "Walk outside." I stood up and went to the door and waited for him to let us out.

"You can open it," he said quietly.

I breathed deeply before I could reach out and take the handle and was still surprised when the door actually opened.

"I'm sorry, I shouldn't go out before you," I stammered, having learned my lessons in the cage so well.

"No, it would be better if you didn't, but I would not be so bothered."

We walked together along the wide corridors, and he pointed out this and that and tried to explain, but there were too many things for which there was no equivalent thing in my past, and the strange foreign names were forgotten by me almost as soon as they had been spoken and left behind. When we returned to my room, I looked at him as I stood outside the door, and he nodded slightly. I tried the door hesitantly and was able to open it myself, and I went in, leaving it open behind me, expecting him to follow, but he stayed there, outside.

"What happened was unfortunate. You are difficult, but I do not know what I would be like if I were in a similar situation," he said, standing there, looking in at me. "Tomorrow we shall walk again. If you want to be more the man you were before, then perhaps you should wear your own clothes, not the robes we have provided."

"But do you want me to be more of a man?" I almost whispered, but he heard me.

"I am curious about you, as you know, but a cowed prisoner is never interesting to spend time talking to, and apparently also loses what I am most interested in," he said, standing there with his head slightly to one side. I was surprised enough to look right at him, and our eyes met if only fleetingly. "Until tomorrow at the same time then."

"I have no clock to tell me what time it was you came," I said quickly, as he turned to go, afraid of not being ready for him when he came again.

"I shall arrange one for you," he said, remaining by the door but looking quickly around my room before he turned and left.

I was almost shaking as I closed the door, afraid of doing something stupid if it wasn't locked and fearful and elated at having been briefly treated like a human being. I could put it no other way. I went to the cupboard and drawers and inspected my clothes and began to try them all on, wondering what I would wear tomorrow and finding that I had shrunk and they all hung loosely on me.

Later there was another knock on my door, and I hesitated before opening it, afraid it might be locked now. I called my visitor to come in, which they did. I was to be moved and for a moment could see myself returning to a cell after a torturous glimpse of the world. But instead I was taken, along with all my possessions, to a small suite of rooms some distance away in a more populated, spacious, and colorful part of the building. Now I had a sleeping room, a bathing place, and another room for sitting and eating and a small place where there was water for drinking and some items of food. And there was a clock, not like anything I was familiar with, which was

255

pointed out and explained to me, and I was told the time that the Han Kirkillian would come for me on the following day.

When the people who had moved my things were gone, I tried to open the main door to the apartment and found I could open it and step outside. I couldn't help doing this several times like a child's game, skipping in and out of the wide corridor until someone passed by. I wanted to ask if I was allowed to leave my rooms on my own, but there was no one there to ask. I spread my things about in the space and drank my water and ate a piece of my food and almost laughed and cried together with the sense of wonder at being able to do such simple things again.

My sitting room had a large window, like the one in my previous room, and outside the same snow fell steadily and lay in drifts. But occasionally I could see Laurentians moving across the outside world off to one side and watched, fascinated, these people moving about their lives. The different sizes and shapes of them and the variety of their clothing and the way they moved individually. When it was dark, I slept and was hardly troubled by nightmares.

The next day we walked again, and I wore clothes I had brought with me, but plain ones, I didn't want to delude myself that my position had risen above the most tenuous level of acceptability. And I asked how far I was allowed to go if I left my rooms alone.

"As far as you like. I know there is nowhere for you to go. But I would recommend you do not leave this building, Metjhan land surrounds it, and he has forgotten you for now, but if you appear in front of him I think that would change."

"Who is the Metjhan?" I asked.

He looked at me. "You know little of our society. I forget that. Now is not the time for a long lesson in our politics. But I will tell you this . . ." He moved next to me.

". . . If you are taken by the Metjhan, and he discovers all that has occurred and presents it to the council, I will get you back, but your race may cease to be anything but a memory." His face was close to mine as he said the words, and for the first time I had the scent of his mane, which reminded me of the Dellier.

"I will make the time to tell you more soon," he said before he left me.

After that I walked about the house myself, and the Han Kirkillian came for me each day at the same time for the next few days. Then as we were parting after our walk, he said to me, "It's time you learned about our politics, so tomorrow I shall come for you early."

He came early as he said he would and returned my journal to me. I took it and couldn't help saying, "It's private."

"Nothing in this house that I want to know is private," he said. "Put it away, and we will walk. Then I shall tell you what I think you need to know to understand some of what has happened."

I did as he said, not saying anything for a while, reminded again of his power over me, something his recent friendliness had enabled me to forget.

We joined Hoonan in a small room, where food was set out, some for them and the usual plate of safe yellow and dirty green mush for me. We sat down on stools as usual, and the Kirkillian began his lesson.

"The Kirkillian are the second of the five families in council. The Dellier are the third. The one who refused to accept you as a guest in his residence when you arrived with the Dellier is the Han Metjhan. He is the fifth in the council but deludes himself that this is because no one sees his true merit."

"What did happen at the space port when we arrived?" I asked cautiously, genuinely interested to know, but wary of interrupting him.

"This city is where the council meets, but it's Metjhan land. The Metjhan should have formally welcomed the Dellier and his party when they arrived. Then he should have taken you all to his house, which is where the council members and their attendants are accommodated when the council is in session. It is his families' duty to do that. Of course he can refuse to accept an attendant, not a Han or his dragar, but anyone else, if he has a very good reason to do so. It has rarely happened."

"A previous Metjhan refused to accept Hanorer Proctor because he carried out the siege at Menare. And he killed the Metjhan's dragar there," Hoonan interrupted.

"Yes, so it was justifiable for him to refuse Hanorer accommodation in his home. And he killed him after he gave his refusal. Our Han Metjhan refused to accept you, calling you an alien wizard and whore, who had corrupted the Han Dellier. He also claimed that you had turned the Dellier's mind to favor you by somehow deluding him to believe there was a bond between you. And that you had done that in order to be brought to the homeworld, against the council's orders. These are very serious accusations."

"But they are false," I exclaimed. "How could I have known about the bond, and the homeworld? And why would I want to come here as a virtual prisoner anyway?" But I could see that it was all dangerously plausible to a Laurentian.

The Kirkillian shrugged. "True or not, those were the claims he made to the Dellier. They threw the Han Dellier and his family into confusion. If the Dellier abandoned you and joined the other councilors at the Metjhan's house, he would be unable to function properly because of the effect of the bond. They knew the Metjhan would immediately kill you. It would also be admitting that you were an aberration, which would give credence to the Metjhan claim that the Dellier is mad."

"But," I stammered, "you said you knew he wasn't mad. Couldn't . . ." But the Kirkillian ignored me and continued with his lesson in politics.

"Alternatively, if the Han Dellier held to you, he could not go to the Metjhan's house. He would also have to risk his entire future and bind you as dragar. At council the Metjhan would charge him with disobeying the council instruction to restrict your race's knowledge of us. Even with you bound, he would be in direct conflict with the Metjhan in council. If he couldn't bind you, then you would have no legal status and unless he could have you accepted as his dragar another way—impossible I'd say—you could still be removed. In each case the Han Dellier would again be unable to function properly for some months. Which would make him very unlikely to be selected Prime."

"So, you removed me from the equation, thwarted the Metjhan's plans, and assured the Dellier's accession to the position of Prime?" I said slowly, taking it all in. It was frightening to think that my presence could have such an effect on Laurentian politics.

The Kirkillian nodded.

"But what happens to you on the council now? And to me? Am I still here illegally?" I asked, suddenly realizing my position had been even more tenuous than I had thought.

"I sit second on the council, and the Dellier wanted my favor, which they now have. They will not tell anyone about you, or they will lose it. Few in my house know what you are, and those few will also not tell anyone outside."

"If Han can let go of me to you, then why couldn't he let me go home with my own people," I asked. It was what had really confused me.

"Even if he had known that I could free him of his bond to you, he would have had no reason to expect me to do it for him. Unfortunately, you joined with an emotional child and created a situation that the Dellier would need to be an experienced man to deal with."

"So, why did you free him?" I asked, knowing he wanted me to study, but thinking he was taking quite a risk.

"As I have already said, there are a few things about our society you need to know." He paused. "The Prime is old. This council meeting or the next one will be his last. The next Prime will then be selected, theoretically from the five Hans on the council. In fact, a new Han is almost never in consideration, so it will be from the four remaining Hans on council that the successor will be chosen. The Dellier have worked hard to have the next Prime. They know that I do not like their Han particularly for the job. The Han Metjhan and the Prime's successor, the Han Riag, are old friends and do not want the Dellier to be Prime."

"The Sarolan are agreeable to the Dellier, so the current situation on the council is that there are two votes for the Dellier and two against. I have held the casting vote for some time now, and to be sure that I would acquire you, I have promised the Dellier to vote as they direct me on all matters relating to the succession at all council meetings for the next year. So I have given them the Prime in exchange for you. But, in fact, I gave nothing there. I like the Metjhan less than the Dellier. But I have also given them the services of my seers to replace the bond holding the Han Dellier to you. That will occupy most of the time of several seers for several months. There you have been very expensive, but I did not want to haggle over something unique."

He was telling me things I had no knowledge of before and found I badly wanted to know. I was going to say something, but he leaned closer and held up a hand to stop me.

"He has a pleasant scent, Hoonan." He said still looking at me. He was a great starer.

"One day soon we must do something about bonding you. Hoonan and some in my own family will know if we are bound, but it will mean nothing."

"I was told that mating normally takes three or four days," I reminded him.

"I don't believe that I will actually go into heat." He almost laughed. "You are ugly, and whatever your scent may remind me of, I am no longer young and was well joined for many years. It may be difficult for me to do anything. But fortunately all that is necessary is to do enough to establish the bond."

I certainly knew the basics of their high politics after that and was quite astonished by what serious complications my desire for the angelic Han Dellier had caused.

Kio came for three more days, and we walked together without any more being said about bonding. Then, on the fourth day, he said, "There are serious things I wish to discuss with you tomorrow. Will I come to your apartment, or would you rather come to me?"

"How serious?" I asked. I had again begun to think of him as a friend. I so badly needed one. But I was now reminded yet again that he was instead my what? My owner, my jailer, perhaps my protector? All of those together, and I didn't want any serious talk to be in my new home, the place where I was rediscovering myself.

He shrugged, "There are things I want to know about you and your race."

"Your rooms," I said, not feeling like talking any more, and we hardly spoke till he left me at my door.

"I will send someone to collect you at the same time tomorrow."

I cursed myself for having been a fool, not to anticipate that there would be a price to pay for my comfort and freedom. I hoped he wouldn't be too disappointed when he discovered that I knew nothing of any importance about anything. I even laughed at how little I knew of the politics of Earth.

I was sitting nervously waiting for the knock when it came the next day. I answered the door and immediately stepped out into the passage, out of my private place, and followed the young female who had come for me. I had dressed as if I were going to my own execution. I knew I wouldn't survive another round of bad treatment such as the Dellier had given me after those first happy days. Or the treatment that I had experienced in the Kirkillian's cage. I had no doubt the Han Kirkillian was quite capable of equaling either, or of removing me completely if I ceased to be of interest to him.

CHAPTER 17

In which I am interrogated about my true motives

The room I entered was magnificent, but of moderate size, and I found the Han Kirkillian there, dressed in fine gossamer layers of green robes appropriate for his position—not those serviceable ones he wore when he walked with me—and the soft velvet-like slippers. Hoonan was there also with another two Lurentians in fine yellow robes. It was very formal, and I was glad I looked like myself, the Count Orlando, for my visit.

The Kirkillian greeted me courteously and introduced the two in yellow as the Haj Sarolan and the Zan Sarolan. Then he accompanied them to the door and farewelled them before returning, and only Hoonan remained with us. The Kirkillian had shown me to a brightly patterned padded seat, and once the others had left us, he sat on the one next to me with a small table holding food and drinks between us while Hoonan sat opposite.

I tried to be relaxed and make myself comfortable.

"Tell me about yourself, Orlando," he asked.

In spite of my efforts not to be, I was still afraid, "There isn't anything for you to know about me. I've led a very dull life." I didn't want to talk about things that were gone. My own personal, ancient history, that to me was covered in dust and stale cobwebs, buried in some cellar and forgotten, on another world.

He took some papers up from beside his seat where I had not noticed them and then rearranged the documents upon his lap. "Why were you chosen to be part of your human embassy?" he asked, looking directly at me over the small distance between us. "What skills did you have to qualify you to be part of such a significant group?"

It was the same question asked so long ago on Heinget by the older Dellier, as if there was some secret about me. "I wanted to be there," I said. There was no other reason for me. "I am, I was, a competent and experienced administrator, and I was determined to be part of the first embassy. It excited me to think of being among the first to meet an alien race. I used whatever contacts I could to help me to be considered. I didn't have any other particular specific skills."

"What did you know about us before you arrived?"

Nothing that was true, I thought, but I did not say it. "What you had wanted us to think. What everyone was told. That you were a race of simple farming people. That you resembled us in general appearance and wanted to meet with us officially. Why do you want to know this now?" I asked him, curious why he wanted to discuss such things now when it seemed irrelevant.

"There was nothing else you knew? You didn't think that your physical tastes and mental strength were going to give you an advantage?"

I almost laughed. "I have no idea if I have any more mental strength than anyone else on my embassy, and as far as physical tastes go, well I obviously let my sensuality control me." I paused to think of how foolish and self-indulgent I had been, "But I think that a lot of my people would find you, as a race, physically appealing. I am sure that I am not unique in that way, though I am more used than most to indulging myself in the kind of behavior that followed."

He moved some of the documents about. " You sent a report to the Administration?"

I was more than surprised by this statement.

"Yes, I did."

I wondered idly what might have been different for me if I hadn't sent it, whether it had had any influence on what had happened after. "I'm surprised you know about it, but I made no secret of my suspicions. I told the Dellier the night I . . . the first night I visited him." I wondered what he was looking for. "You seem to know everything. Do you also have a copy of the official report?" I asked. "I have been curious to know what they said in it."

"Yes, only the preliminary one, though," he replied and immediately returned to his line of questioning. "Some interesting things seem to have happened as a result of your report. You appear to have much influence for someone your own embassy treated as a nuisance and our embassy therefore regarded as an unimportant observer. Apparently we couldn't ever understand why you and your personal attendant dressed so differently from everyone else on the embassy. And apparently the leaders of your group wanted you out of the way so they could talk seriously without supposedly stupid interruptions from you. Did you know that they asked for you to be kept occupied elsewhere?"

"I suspected that, but it could also have been your delegation's idea. The Dellier's delegation I should say," I replied, mildly surprised. I looked over at him, wondering at his sudden knowledge of something he had professed to care nothing about recently.

"No. But it appears that the ones who wanted to have serious talks were actually of no importance at all. Their reports seem to have been dismissed by your Administration, while yours was accepted without question. Why was that?" He stared at me with his black eyes, like something hunting.

"I had no idea anyone had taken any notice of it at all. You forget that once I mated the Dellier I was not allowed to see my people again. I had no discussion about any reports with them or anyone else, though they knew I had sent a preliminary report of my personal opinions. I made no secret of it." I looked directly ahead sitting erect, proud in having done my duty and in the way I carried myself under difficulties being the only sort I had left.

"Their preliminary report wasn't sent until the day after they left the planet. But soon after that a person called Marius and the Fleet Commander both ordered your delegation to cease transmitting anything that related to their discussions. Even though those were finished. Dr. Chin Lee sent a reply to them both immediately. Would you like to see it?"

"I would be fascinated to see the report they sent," I said, but he ignored me, and I had no choice but to ask for the message, though I was becoming nervous and couldn't understand what about it could make him consider it so important.

The Kirkillian handed over two of the documents and I saw they were identical except for the addressees.

"Associates in my field are desperate for any information about the historic meetings we have been attending with the Laurentian. Withholding that information from the Academic and Defense communities at this time is unconscionable, and I wish to lodge a strong formal protest."

One was addressed to Marius for the Administration, the other to the Fleet Commander.

"Of more interest," said the Kirkillian, "was the response from the Fleet Commander. He ordered the captain of the ship not to allow any of the delegates to send any transmissions off the ship or to store any more information in the ship's own systems."

"If anyone attempts to do any of these things they are to be confined to their quarters, by force, if necessary, until your return. Only transmissions of a routine nature essential for the safe handling of your ship are to be made," he read out from a document before him.

"The captain was also ordered to obtain statements from each person about your movements and conversations with anyone in your own group and with anyone in ours." He read the next part, *"These reports are not to be entered in the ship's systems. Repeat none of this information is to be entered into the ship's systems.""*

I found it all quite surprising, and I said so.

"Really? You were very quick to decide that the situation on Heinget was a sham. Now tell me who Marius is, and why he accepted your report and not the one signed by everyone else."

I had no doubt that the Kirkillian had access to many methods of making me talk, which I had no desire to experience unnecessarily, as there was nothing I could tell him that wasn't conjecture. Even much of what I knew about Marius was no more than guesses.

"Marius is a man I have known for a very long time, most of my life, to be precise. He has a senior position in the Administration, but I don't know what it is, and I am surprised that he would take my small report to him so seriously. There is nothing else I can say about the matter." I filled a cup with water and drank it slowly to hide my nervous tremor.

"You were a highly regarded member of your delegation. You present a cautionary report saying we are liars back to your associates on Earth. Then you are taken away from the meetings much of the time and finally removed altogether and kept isolated and stopped from leaving with the rest of your embassy. If I was an associate of yours who was back on your home world, I would be very suspicious."

"You make it sound like a plot to silence me. It was nothing like that at all," I responded, completely thrown by his comments.

"Still, it would be very easy to see it that way. We have no desire to make enemies of your race. Unfortunately, it's not possible now to give you back to them."

I looked at him. "That was never going to happen even after the first night, was it?" I said bitterly.

He paused a while before he spoke again. "I still want to know why you were chosen. The whole scenario could be read as a plot against us too. That scenario would go: you are deliberately represented to us as a minor member of your embassy because it is known that you are physically and mentally capable of interesting us. You send a report that is designed to threaten or intrigue us, so that we separate you from your companions, inadvertently giving you more access to us.

"Alternatively, as you did, you find a member of our embassy who you believe you can seduce and do so knowing that the joining will make it likely you will remain and find out whatever it is you want to know about us. Those are both versions the Metjhan would like to be able to put to the council. It would make the Dellier, and even me, seem to be tools of yours, and perhaps discredit us."

He was disturbing me with his wild but plausible theories. "I've already told you I asked to go on the embassy. I knew that the Administration would want one of their people there. I've known Marius for a long time, and I begged him to send me. He spoke to whoever he needed to speak to, and I was on the team." I could say that quite honestly because it was the truth, and I looked him in the eye as I said it but shook slightly, knowing it wasn't what he wanted to hear, and I needed to know I could still go home to my nice apartment afterward, not to some cell somewhere. "There is no conspiracy. I wanted to go and I begged to be included. I am hiding nothing from you. And hiding things from them—from us, won't work," I added. "In the long run, it will only cause them to mistrust you and everything you say."

"It is not our place to make those decisions," the Kirkillian said.

"I didn't imagine it was. I am just giving you my opinion. And perhaps one day it will be partly your decision." I almost whispered, too tired to fight whatever happened, knowing I was no one of any importance.

He moved about the documents on his lap and then set them aside. "What are you thinking?"

I was a stranger in a strange land. Alone. No one but me here knew the smell of fresh cut grass in the park outside my study window. No one had smelled the scent of the soft skin between a woman's breasts or the rich odor of hunters after the chase. I wanted to cry for a lost world, for being alone.

In his place I had no idea at all what I would do with me.

"I'm lonely," I said tears, tightening my throat. I seemed to be crying like a teenaged girl. I was never before so emotional as I was in those days. "I want to feel human warmth, have someone to hold," I said quietly to him. "that's all I am thinking." I looked at the water in the cup shaking slightly in my hand and the room was silent for a along time.

"I would still like to read the delegation's official report," I finally added, too depressed to be more than vaguely interested and having no idea if anything had been resolved.

He shuffled about until he found several pages he wanted and handed them to me.

"What happened between you and Han Dellier?" he asked unexpectedly.

"I seduced him. We mated, and he claimed he came into heat and when his heat was over we were joined. Whatever has happened since that night I have brought on myself."

"I know more than that already," he said, reaching over and taking the cup out of my hand where I still held it, with the pages he had given me in the other, and touching me when he did it more than he needed to. I looked at him briefly. "Tell me about the first time you were together. You have mentioned it several times, so tell me."

"I became obsessed by her, the Han Dellier's physical beauty. To me he was . . . was female, a beautiful young woman. I wanted to touch her and feel her flesh. I arranged to meet her, and I was taken to a house where there was a group of your people, including her, and I said what I wanted to do." I stopped and tried to remember the feeling. To discover her physically. She changed the subject, and I told them effectively what I had already sent in my report. That I didn't believe what was being said about their world.

"Then she said she would consider my request to see her body if I showed them mine, which I did. Later the others left, and she started to show me and I seduced her." I stopped and there was silence for so long that I was forced to continue. "We made love together half a dozen different ways that night, and she seemed to want it as much as I did. I thought it had been a pleasure for both of us." I was almost whispering, remembering it. "But in the morning she wouldn't let me leave the room. She said she was in heat, and I had to stay. I stayed willingly for four days; then her heat was over.

"Even though she had promised she would release me, she still wouldn't let me leave. She left me for a while, and when she came back, she stroked my face, then slapped it hard and left. Then I was taken to her house and stayed there till I came here, to the homeworld. She claimed we were joined, and she couldn't have me away from her." I wondered what might have happened if she hadn't joined me. Would I have been allowed to leave, I wondered.

"Soon she began to resent me for being necessary to her and for being what I am, and I knew she wanted to be rid of me, but she said she couldn't because she had important things to do and my loss would be a nuisance for her." The humiliation and anger of it surfaced briefly.

As soon as I stopped talking, Hoonan came over and laid his hands over my face, and I began to feel the same calmness I had when I had been taken away from the Dellier. I relaxed and thought of nothing, and he removed his hands and sat down.

"I would like to see your body too. Would you show it to me now?" the Han Kirkillian asked me quietly.

I was too relaxed to care and too fatalistic to object to repeating a scenario that had gone so wrong before. I stood up and removed my nice black Jacket with the small red flowers embroidered on it, my vest embellished with the same delicate work, and the soft white linen shirt I wore and folded them neatly on my seat. But before I removed anything else, the Kirkillian stopped me. I hadn't moved from in front of my seat, and he was only a couple of feet from me when he stood up and in a step he touched the old bruises, almost gone now, left on my arm from my time in the cage.

"Is that damage?" he asked.

"It doesn't hurt now." I touched it briefly myself to confirm the pain wasn't still there, wondering vaguely if he thought I was too ugly to see more of.

"I can understand you are lonely," he said and handed me my shirt and helped me dress. "I will take Orlando back now," he told Hoonan.

We walked all the way in silence, and when we arrived at the door to my rooms he asked if he could come in. Even though I didn't want to talk, and I was calmed to feel little, I didn't want to be alone, and I said he could. Once inside he poured me water, and I removed my jacket and vest from habit before I drank it, feeling silly doing so there, and explaining it to him. How I had to keep my clothes clean because they had taken so long to make. We were still standing and I moved over to the window.

"I would like to see all your body now, Orlando, and I want to know what you did to the Dellier that first night."

I hesitated. "Why all these questions suddenly? You had no interest in my embassy before. What's happened?"

"When I acquired you, it was on a whim. My hobby is of little interest to anyone else. It was only when I had a translation made and read your writing in the thing you call a journal that I began to be curious about what had gone before. Then we talked of politics, and as you said, because of you important things have happened, and you are still dangerous for others to have about.

"So you have become more than you were, more than another toy for me. So now I need to know more about you and what you have been involved in. I received the information about your embassy from the Dellier, and you became more curious still. Now I need to know what is true and what isn't. Because I now need to know if you

272

are actually worth the risk I may be taking keeping you here."

It was plainly put; I was no longer a minor thing. "I don't want to be alone. Will you stay a while," I asked, trying to make some bargain, knowing that even then when my fate was under consideration, he was still the closest thing I had to a friend in that place.

"I will stay a while after you have told me what I want to know. Then Hoonan can come and help you sleep if you want him to."

I moved to the bedroom away from the window, and he followed me in there. Then I carefully removed and folded the rest of my clothes and stood sideways to him, naked, not wanting to look at him, this powerful old man who owned me now. He walked about me and looked at my belly button and touched it. "You don't improve," he said. "So, what did you do to the Dellier?"

"I removed his jacket and . . ." what wild, yet wonderful, things I'd done I thought, embarrassed at talking about what had happened, to him, ". . . I stroked her, sorry, his, chest and kissed him. Then I removed his skirt and did the same to the rest of his body and discovered his organ, and I made love to him."

The Kirkillian stood there for a while, as expressionless as ever. "Unfortunately, that doesn't really explain to me why anything ever happened between you. And how anything happened is what I really need to understand." He began to remove his robes, "I do not understand this stroke and kiss. You will need to demonstrate at least part of what you did," he added, with what I felt was a trace of annoyance in his voice.

What Hoonan had done to calm me earlier was the sort of mild hypnosis I had been given often before, that he did better than most, and I was still dull from it. I vaguely helped the Kirkillian to undress, seeing smooth marble skin, ivory yellow with age, but still surprisingly smooth. I began to caress him as instructed. And closing my eyes I caught the scent of his mane, which for me was the scent of sex. Then I was half dreaming what I had done to the Dellier that first evening. I hadn't touched anyone since, and it was easy to like the feel of the Kirkillian's cool soft flesh.

Unlike the Dellier, he knew what he was expecting, and what normally happened. But he kept rubbing my belly button, and I ignored it, having no idea why he continued and waited till he was ready.

"How could you enter him with this?" he finally grunted, squeezing and pushing at my belly button again and again. Finally I understood what he was thinking.

I took his hand down to where I was ready, and he felt it. And suddenly I was too far along, and after so long, needed it too much to stop. He was confused by what happened next. He was both trying to keep me away, and wanting it. Too aroused himself, so that while trying to avoid my touch, he was not actually wanting me to stop.

We staggered about, in what must have been a ridiculously comic way, trying to achieve two things at once. My mouth locked to his as I moved my body rhythmically against, and inside, his. We almost fell several times, and my moaning and his grunts made a wild background to our writhings. When I was spent and we moved apart, I saw the shocked look on his face.

"I'm sorry," I said, suddenly dull again after the heat of sex. But alert enough to be afraid of the consequences of what I'd done. I took a robe from one of the drawers and wrapped it around myself and wrapped another about him, and sat on the bed. "I couldn't go through what the Dellier did to me afterward again."

The Kirkillian stood there for a few more moments as if stunned, then appeared to jerk himself awake.

"The Dellier is a fool. We all knew he was strange. I didn't realize how much until now." He threw off the

274

robe I'd given him and began to dress himself. I got up to help him, the long robes tangling as he tried to put them on, obviously not concentrating properly on what he was doing. "It's so long since I mated last. I can't even dress myself," he joked, then pulled open my robe and looked down my stomach and poked at my navel. "I was waiting for this to distend like a females," he said with a laugh. "If it had, I would probably not have let you get me so aroused. The Dellier is a fool."

He sat down on the bed beside me, and I lay back and must have gone to sleep almost immediately because the room was dark and I was alone when I woke, and I couldn't remember him saying anything. I washed and got into bed and read for a while, having slept too long to be really tired and feeling refreshed and alive, as one does after any kind of reasonable sex following a drought.

It was an interesting book, though I had read it before, and I read for some hours, well into the night, according to my clock. The next day Hoonan came and placed a band about my wrist and left it there.

"Am I going to be bound to him?" I asked.

"No, this is only for his benefit, so he has some use of you," he replied, and left in a rush.

Later I was moved again to other rooms, these larger and more elaborate, being full of bright colored patterns made in stone on the floors, and painted upon the walls. I again put my possessions away and was joined by an elderly female who introduced herself as Kapjhan and said she had been given the job of teaching me history and customs so I would know how to behave. Her first lesson was almost all about the hierarchy within the house and how I held no proper position there and must come behind everyone else.

The Kirkillian was so business-like and self-assured about everything that after the romance and magic and drama of the Dellier, sex with him was disconcerting. He

275

visited from his adjoining rooms each night, staying briefly and requiring that I not touch him. What we did was the least that could be done to still count as anything, and it surprised me that we managed anything. And for me it often felt little different to accomplishing what I could do alone.

"I mated the Dellier because he was beautiful. For me he was more like a woman of my own race. He was angelic, and I was obsessed with him," I said to the Kirkillian the first night in my new rooms. "I don't know if I can mate you as much as you will want." I would rather say it immediately, than have to tell him I couldn't do it, when I wasn't so desperate for any company. "Why don't you mate another female, take another wife?"

"Since my dragar died, I have had the pretty daughters, and even beautiful granddaughters, of old friends and allies paraded before me. Some smelling so close to their first heat they should not have been out of their homes. And sometimes I wondered if I should take one. But you may have noticed how boring very young people are after the novelty of their looks wears off, and then all I would be left with is a dragar carrying a litter, and her family and relatives who think I should pay for the mating with favors, and who come around constantly seeking advancement.

"I want no more offspring. I have sufficient already, and those of a late mating usually cause problems. So, instead, I have made do with those odd females who don't come into heat properly and aren't really very good to be with. But you, Orlando, have no relations, have an ability I want to gain access to, and are satisfactory to mate with. And if the Dellier still mated you when you arrived here, then you are better than any female I can ever have apart from a dragar.

"For your part whatever happens now you will not be allowed to return to your world, for many years at least.

276

Perhaps I am not beautiful, but you aren't either. I acquired you because you have a strength I want to study, and use, and the bond created during mating is far stronger than anything that could be created any other way. Now I find I need not settle for less. When the matter was first raised, the thought of mating you horrified me. But now I find it can be satisfactorily agreeable.

"While it pleases me, my ugly alien pet shall have the best of everything, and no one will think more than that I have odd whims in my old age. Do you understand me?"

"Yes," I said. I understood.

"Let there be no confusion that you are anything but what I choose to say you are," he added unnecessarily.

CHAPTER 18

*In which I get a real job and become a
useful member of society again*

Finally I was settled sufficiently to not be
wondering each time I woke if the new day might be my
last, if I might be returned to a cage, or if some other
unfortunate event might be in store for me. I had arrived
in some position, with a comfortable private home of my
own, and however unofficial my place was, and however
discomforting I found it at times; it had the illusion of
safety and security. But I badly needed distractions. It was
time I got my own personal life into some sort of order.
Time I made a routine to shape it about and used my
mind.

"I need to have work to do," I said to the
Kirkillian.

"Pardon?" he said, confused.

"I need to constructively occupy my time. I'm
settled now, but there is little routine in my life, and for
much of the day I have nothing to do. I can't leave this
house alone, I don't know how to cross the city, I know

no one who doesn't live here, I can't even make myself a meal. At home I would have found too many things to do with my time, but here I don't even know what can be done. I need to learn to read what you write, and I need to get out among other people so I can learn what else I can do."

"Kapjhan can teach you to read and write. Someone can show you anything you need to know about living here. There is no need for you to leave my house. Everything you need is here. If you need to go across the city for some reason, though I can think of none, someone can take you there," he told me.

He was right, but that didn't change my desire. "I am grateful for my teacher, but I still need to know that I can do something for myself, something that is more than a child could do. I know I can wash and dress myself. I know that if I ask I will probably be taken wherever I want to go. But I am an adult, and I want to have a part of my life that reminds me I am."

"If you want work," he paused, not obviously happy with the idea. "I will arrange for you to go to study in the Cargo House. It's part of this house, so you will be able to go there alone. Will that satisfy you?" he asked.

"Thank You, I'll let you know if it doesn't. I want to start tomorrow."

He wasn't pleased about that either, but I wanted to start without people having too much time to get ready for me. And I was ridiculously excited about learning something new by my choice, of having something of my own. I didn't ask any more; I would enjoy finding something out for myself whatever it was. In the morning Celina, who had become my personal attendant, took me on a long trek through the house to places I had never been before, and eventually we passed through a door and entered the Cargo House.

On rooms, and the houses about them.

A house within a house. "Room" translates as that because their concept of a house is as something that holds people inside it, no matter how big it is, or what they do inside. The Kirkillian's house was enormous, as you would have gathered by now, and it was part residence, part school, part laboratory, and part offices. It was built low, being only two or three floors high, but it meandered about in every direction. Obviously built over many years and going wherever the builders had been told to take it or found it easiest to go. There is really no word for a room in their language, and because I found it quite confusing, I began to use my word for one, and it seems to have taken on now, certainly in the larger houses.

So the Cargo House was an enormous room three floors high but open from floor to ceiling in the center, and we entered it half way up, walking onto a projecting gallery floor, which overhung the room below by about thirty feet all around three sides. Against the outside walls private offices lined this projection, and an open walkway with just a railing along the open side ran around the inside edge. The floor below was full of people, mostly males, but a large number of older females too. Many sat at what were obviously desks, and others were walking about. I saw at once more Laurentians in one place than I had ever been close to before. I saw some glance up at me as I hung over the railing looking down at them and their busy world below.

It was a surprise to realize that I was an oddity to them. I had been living with Laurentians for so long and I'd been so sheltered that I'd forgotten what I was. I was the alien here, not them. I wondered if they knew I was their Han's thing and was uncomfortable from the thought, wondering if they did know what they thought about it. I would find out, I knew, if I stayed here any time at all and spoke to many of them.

"So many strangers," I mused.

"They share the river with you; they are not strangers." Celina said.

The river
I had little idea of what she meant by "the river," though I had heard of the river before, and gathered it was a term for the whole of the Kirkillian family in its widest sense. All those who lived and worked on the family land and for the family seemed to be included.

In fact, it is more; it is also the faint buzz I am always aware of now and it is why I no longer feel so alone, because I too am part of it, as she said. It is best described as the faint sense of the family, of all those related to them. The ability to sense a mate, which is enhanced by the bands they wear from the first mating or just before, sometimes detects this faintly heard echo of the larger world because of the way their minds work. Because of the bands nearly everyone has some faint sense of the river, and those who are strong, such as the seers and the Kirkillian also sense the rest of their race even more faintly and are said to know the ocean.

I was introduced to Karlos, the manager of the Cargo House, who occupied one of the offices opening off the balcony. He seemed to have no idea what to do with me but diligently explained what he did, until I was completely lost. Finally, I realized that he seemed to spend a lot of his time dealing with what sounded like insurance and contracts. As I couldn't read or write, I saw no place for me with him and I quickly said so.

He was then lost again and looked blankly at me, the unwanted intrusion into this busy world.

"What if I start at the bottom?" I said, rather deflated, "something simple. Something I don't need to be able to read very much to do, and I don't need to know a lot of other things to learn."

He looked about and hesitated a while longer before he spoke again. "Assisting in loading cargo is the first job we usually give learners, but I would not offer you such work without saying that I am willing to take you on at whatever level you choose."

"I would like to see if I can learn to load cargo," I replied, not entirely sure this wouldn't have me rolling up my sleeves to physically do it, which I thought might be better for me than remaining in the Cargo House, as I knew I was not doing enough physically.

He was unsure if my starting at the bottom was a good idea, but I think he took me down to the lower floor because he was too afraid to argue with me and really had no idea what to do with me otherwise. He spoke to several people among the sea of desks and industry and eventually left me in the care of an elderly female called Shasa. As he left, I sensed the manager's relief that I was out of his way and somewhere I couldn't get into too much trouble.

Shasa was very old and claimed she knew everything about cargo loading. "They always send you learners to me," she said. "I have taught them all, and everyone here now, even him in the corner." She indicated a male in a far corner of the room less cluttered than the rest. "So, have you seen one of these before?" She had a large, clear panel in front of her.

"Similar," I said.

"Really, so they got glass where you come from have they?" she said, and laughed. "Bet they think they're real sophisticated, being able to see out without the rain coming in." She laughed again.

I ignored her slur to my ancestry.

"Well, this bit o' fancy glass here shows loading space," she explained. The screen came alive with four views of something rectangular with a dome at the front and a string of colored shapes and numbers and symbols down one side. "And it shows the cargo that's got to be loaded. My job is to put the two things together and show you how to. So you primitive farmers can have those big metal things in the sky come bring you primitive aliens all sorts of miracles." And she laughed again.

"You have never given us anything, Shasa," I said coldly. "None of you have ever been to the place I come from. You don't seem to be surprised to find me here, though. Do you have many different aliens coming to learn cargo loading?"

"So, you can't take a joke. So, just learn the job, ugly. Then you can go home."

I got the impression she wasn't keen on visitors. But I had discovered something amazing now. It was not just us and the Laurentians in the universe. I wanted to know what others she had seen there. "What other aliens are there?" I asked.

"None," she said sharply. "You are the first one I've ever seen, and you're so ugly I hope I never see another one."

I knew she lied, certainly about the others anyway; everyone seemed to think I was ugly, and I was getting used to it and had accepted that to them I was.

Then she indicated the four views on the panel before her. "This here's the ship that's to be loaded." There was an overhead view at the top of the screen, a view from below at the bottom, and a view of each side in the middle. The cargo was color coded by consignment. The legend and net numbers were displayed down each side of the screen in a long trail of colored shapes and numbers. Fortunately, I knew how to count already and I wasn't color blind. The writing was nothing but squiggles and dashes to me.

"So, as each consignment's loaded, the nets that color go into the loading space," she said, illustrating how it was done with lightning-quick movements of her hands across the screen standing on her desk.

On the usage of words

I write "desk" here, but it was a small, low, flat thing she sat in front of on one of the ubiquitous stools. I have used ordinary words for extraordinary things. I use the words the converter gives me or that most simply explain the function or appearance *of things, though the thing itself may be quite alien in appearance and use. So a clock may look like no clock ever seen on Earth, but it remains a clock. You probably see a very familiar world as you read this, but in fact it is quite alien in its appearance in too many ways to even begin to describe. I have avoided being very descriptive partly for this reason. If you live somewhere, it doesn't matter that things look odd to others, and it is irrelevant to the important things, or to my story.*

As she worked I saw how the little colored shapes representing nets neatly slotted into the space available until it was filled. She made loading look very simple. Then she gave me the vacant desk and screen beside hers, turned it all on, and sat me down in front of it. It was straightforward to use. A cargo ship came up on the screen, and above it was the legend, equivalent to KG5S, meaning Kirkillian general cargo ship no. 5 standard load. A standard load, I learned, was 100 nets long, 10 wide, and 10 deep. A net, she explained, was about an eighth the size of the Cargo House. I was stunned, as it was a huge quantity, and there were at least a dozen other loaders at work in the room nearby.

Down the side of the screen appeared a legend 7,100 pink triangular nets, 350 round green ones, 28 square red, 17 strange-shaped purple, 63 starlike yellow, 617 triangular light blue, etc. etc., and I needed 1,000 nets per layer, 10 layers to a full load.

I went up and down the legend looking for cargo that would total as near as possible to 10,000 nets. When I had put together a package that was only a few short I stacked them in. It was dead easy. I filled up the space with layers of nets, watching the colors flashing in the top

284

view of the cargo space as the nets were positioned layer by layer. When I had finished loading, I finally looked down at the side views to see how the colors looked all stacked up.

But something odd was happening in the bottom screen. At the front end, a patch of squares, representing nets, was alive. They flickered and flashed and occasionally changed color. I watched for a few seconds and couldn't make sense of it.

I turned to Shasa. "I've loaded the cargo, but something's wrong with the bottom screen," I said to her and turned back to see a few flickers on the other three screens, "Now they're all playing up!" I was watching helpless as three images of the ship flickered and flashed incomprehensibly, with only the top view remaining unchanged.

Shasa leaned over and peered at my screen. "Looks like you may have a problem there, boy," she looked me in the eye. "Your load's evaporating." She paused and gazed back at my screen. There was flickering everywhere now, even in the front end of the top view.

"How can it evaporate?" It was stuff in nets, in space. "It can't possibly evaporate!"

There was a gap appearing at the top of the load in the left-hand side view and there were now a couple of green nets in what should have been a layer of pink. It dawned on me at last that the cargo was slipping down to the bottom of the cargo space, and as a large patch at the bottom flickered and changed color, I realized there was a big hole in the bottom of it.

"There's a hole at the bottom!" I said, stating the obvious with disbelief.

I turned to see that Shasa was laughing her head off and so were the two male loaders sitting behind us. I closed my eyes and rested my forehead in my hands as the rest of the nets escaped and drifted off into space. I couldn't make up my mind whether to laugh or to cry. I didn't need to be reminded of how ignorant I was. But another part of me knew that this was what they did to everyone when they first arrived in the Cargo House. It was a simple joke even ignorant me could understand, and finally I let myself laugh too.

It was patently obvious that aliens weren't a rarity for Shasa and the others working there, and I wondered what the other races they were familiar with were like, and what those races relationship with them was.

I picked up my stool and set it down behind Shasa and smiled at her and said, "You are going to explain to me everything you are doing, and at the end of today, I am going to be able to do by myself the simplest loading job there is. No missing walls or floors, no other tricks, all right?"

"I've got my own work, you know," she grumbled.

"I know you have. And if you don't start explaining things to me properly, and stop moaning, you won't get it done."

I made myself comfortable and watched her screen. She was not happy, but by the end of the day, I was able to load a standard ship with a uniform cargo. Most of the job was about checking everything. Check the ship, what sort it was supposed to be, which for me meant comparing unintelligible symbols. Check that it is rated in good condition, check the cargo is all ready, check the insurance, check departure time, check delivery and projected arrival times. Sort the available cargo and take out what's unsuitable—you don't ship wastes with high-grade equipment, especially liquid waste. Some of the job I was unable to do, of course, not being able to read. I had to get Shasa to check the insurance details before I began, but the other things all involved only four or five alternatives, and she wrote out the words for me well enough so I could compare them to the symbols on the screen myself, and I wrote down my own explanation of what they meant.

When it was time to go, I had to wait while the Cargo House emptied out at the end of the day. Wait for someone to come and take me back to my rooms. While I waited I wondered what sort of homes the other loaders went back to and what they did when they got there. And for the first time I wondered about the size of their civilization. I had been too preoccupied with my own problems before to do so properly.

The Cargo House held fifty-two loaders, including the isolated one in the corner with several screens, and I estimated Shasa had loaded five ships that day, which meant about 250 ships a day were loaded there, and the house worked almost every day. Ships took anywhere from a few days to several months to arrive at their destination. Putting all that together, it meant that there was an almost incomprehensible amount of cargo and a huge number of Laurentian ships traveling about.

I made a point of telling the Kirkillian that my first day had been satisfactory and I would stay there. Then I ate with everyone and returned to my rooms and wrote in my journal till quite late, because it had been an eventful day.

The next morning I found my own way to the Cargo House and, in spite of a couple of wrong turns, arrived on time, to find an empty office. A couple of others were drifting in and looking around when someone stuck their head out of the manager's office and waved them inside, and I made to follow them.

"There is no need for you to come . . . count. The manager is having a meeting for the . . . for the other staff," he said, waving me away.

I took the opportunity to wander around the room looking at all the live screens. They were all like mine except the ones in the back corner. Ours all showed rectangular boxes pulled from in front. The screens in the corner were far bigger and showed a circular space, which was driven from behind by a curved ship shaped like a new moon. There were four views, as usual, and all showed the cargo space as a ball. There was no legend down the side of the screen, just one line, something in alien letters then the number 28. I had the impression these ships cargos were huge and was still contemplating this and trying to think of what the cargo might be, when the loaders came out of the manager's office.

I returned to my desk and prepared to start work with Shasa, but I had to wait a while as she was the last one to appear.

"I hope you didn't think me disrespectful yesterday, Count," she said when she arrived and was nervously twisting her robe about in her hands. "It's an honor for an old woman like me to be asked to teach you the little bit I know." She paused, "about the wonderful Kirkillian cargo business."

"What has caused you to speak like this?" I asked. "The manager? Yesterday you were rude and treating me like any other ignorant new boy you'd just been lumbered with."

"No, I wasn't!" she exclaimed, "Well . . . well, that's what I thought you were, though."

"And what am I today?" I asked

"Someone under the most personal guidance of our Han."

"I thought the manager had told you that yesterday." I was getting confused, or she was?

"They'll tell you foreigners anything, if it suits them. How was I to know you really were someone important, you don't look like it. Oh . . .uh. . . I am sure you are quite a fine specimen of . . ."

288

"Why would anybody want to pretend I was important?" I may not have looked like I was somebody, why I had no idea, but it was all very odd.

"The Twenty are always playing games like that. Anyway, I'd better teach you to load properly now."

I was getting annoyed, "So what did you show me yesterday? Rubbish."

"Of course not, I showed you how to load a space." She paused to stare at her screen intently. "Only, um . . .it was a liquid waste carrier, and you filled it with rock. I'm sorry, forgive me."

I was surprised she didn't burst out laughing again, and now I really was annoyed. "So everything I did was wrong?"

"No. I just didn't tell you a couple of things."

"A couple of things! You said the ship was a standard one and the nets were full of processed foods."

"All right, I lied a bit. If you don't want me to be your teacher, I'll understand. I am sure . . ."

She wasn't going to slide out of it that easily. I was quite sure she was good at her job. Also, and, more important, she liked to talk and gossip about everything. I didn't see my future in cargo perhaps, but I did want to get the satisfaction of learning to do something practical in this alien place. And I wanted to know about other "foreigners," and the real Laurentian world.

"I'm sorry to disappoint you, but you're stuck with me. I can't imagine a better teacher than you are going to be from now on, Shasa. And you are also going to tell me about foreigners and the games the Twenty play. I'm rather curious about them too."

"How'd you get to be a favorite, anyway, when you're short and damned uglier than a Locite? And rude too," she grumbled, then laughed, and I let the comment lie.

She taught me properly afterward. To be sure she did, I went and spoke to the other loaders, asking them questions when I wasn't sure if what she was telling me was right, and it was then I discovered that the moon shaped ships, the loader in the corner loaded, trapped ice asteroids and pushed them to dry planets. I had thought them big but discovered that when loaded they could be the size of small moons. They were the pride of the cargo fleet. After a couple of weeks, I was left to do simple loads myself, which Shasa would check before the instructions were released out to the real world where the physical loading took place. There was a lot to learn, and in the beginning I went home each day I worked with some sense of achievement and mental stimulation.

And I gained the briefest explanation of the foreigners. "We're part of the Empire. Your kind aren't, but the other four are." Then she shut up and refused to ever say more.

I was astonished, and in spite of my own experiences, excited to know there were four more intelligent species to be met. And it wasn't many years before I did meet them.

Having gained some idea of the size of the house, I began to explore it on my way to and from work. I found the rooms where the seer's students were taught. Where they lived. And I liked the look of one of the students too much. He reminded me so of the Dellier. Whatever the band I wore did, it had shown the Kirkillian what I had felt for this young male, and that same evening I was forbidden to enter that part of the house again.

But I also saw offices and grand rooms, and one day asked for and found the Han Kirkillian at his desk. It was strange to see him like that, in such a mundane role.

"Is something wrong?" He asked, standing up and coming to me. The others in the room looked at me and then hurriedly returned to their work.

"No, I have been exploring the house, and I wondered where you worked, that's all," I replied, suddenly uncomfortable at invading that place.

"Why did you want to know?" he asked coolly.

"There is no reason but my own," I replied, feeling that he was never entirely sure even then why I was there. Still not completely convinced I wasn't a spy. I was intruding where I was not wanted and left quickly.

In bed, in the dark, we had an accommodation. I assumed gender was malleable for us both, and I easily imagined I was with some unseen, unknown woman. One not particularly interested in me, only in what we did with our bodies and that we both happened to need. Our only real connection was extremely brief and physical. But there in his office I saw a man much like I had been, and I was unexpectedly bitter that he had everything I had lost, and that he was a man still, while I had been reduced to some sort of female subservience and use.

I saw little of the Kirkillian. We shared little except the physical need for each other, yet I had more in common with him than with anyone else. Because in my past, my life had been much like his. The Cargo House was work, but it was not my kind of work. I knew there was a problem, but I had little idea of how to resolve it or even define it clearly.

The weeks passed and became months. I was still not bound to the Kirkillian, but he had the band on me, which gave him some access to whatever it was he had acquired me for.

I began to feel depressed and constantly tired. I had become pared back to a minimalist version of myself. I was reduced to a shadow, and everything I did was done as unobtrusively as possible. Sex was almost a memory briefly recalled, it was so minimal. It involved only the absolute unavoidable contact between us, no segment of my body not absolutely essential to the process touched the Kirkillian's. It still had that moment of intense difference about it, but it was rather an uncomfortable exercise, though I'd got used to his requirements. It was part of my daily routine, like getting up and dressing each day, or going to the Cargo House.

He no longer walked with me. There was almost no conversation between us any more, as much because of my discomfort with the situation I was now in, as with his ambivalent attitude to me.

My work filled a portion of my time, but once it was learned, it became repetitive. Learning to read was going to be terribly time consuming and difficult, and other things did no more than fill my days. I spoke mainly to old women, to Shasa at the Cargo House and to Celina, who took care of my practical needs: cleaned my clothes, made sure I woke. And to Kapjhan, who was struggling to teach me now to read and write as well as about the Laurentians and their ways.

Each night I ate at the main table, but my position there was hazy. No one was quite sure how to rank me. Position in the hierarchy, be it of the house, of the family, or of the race, are all matters of great importance to the Laurentians. I sat at the main table, but at its end, and had no ranking among the hundred, and no recognized relationships within the house. I think none but Hoonan and Celina even knew the truth of why I was now accommodated in the rooms adjoining the Kirkillian's.

But everyone saw the band about my wrist, which enabled him to have some use of whatever it was I had in my head that fascinated him, and knew I had some role to play in the Kirkillians' studies, so they did not actually ignore me.

I was discouraged from associating with other males I felt a liking for. Jealousy or possessiveness run strong in them, understandably. The creation homeworld has an incredibly harsh climate. They mate for life, and their young, like ours, take several years to reach independence, and they live a long time. They evolved to survive the harsh winters and prosper and did it by being fiercely protective of their own and totally committed to their mates, which is the origin of the bond they acquire with mating. It allowed them to always know where their mate was when they ventured out to hunt in the winter. It enabled the males to find their way home again with their kill in the winter dark and through falling snow. And it enabled a female to know when her mate was gone and wouldn't return. While the males feel terrible grief and would, I suppose, effectively hibernate for some months after a loss, the females either hibernate and miss that winter's heat, if it is due, or if they have feeding young and are in need of food, know immediately that they must go out to find it for themselves. I believe it was a brutal world outside, and a totally committed and loving one inside the family cave.

In the evenings I wrote in my journal, and I became very poetic at this time, my only passionate outlet.

I have been reduced, shaved away by how I live,
I am raw flesh, aching for a skin thick enough to cover my
pain.

I am alone among cool pale ghosts who do not recognize me
Who generally pass me by as if I were not here at all,

Each time they pass they take another part of me, so I
become less real
I fade, I am reduced by them to a dry shell holding the feint
flicker of life.

My memories are hidden, dangerous temptations to me
They are full of the food of life that makes me want to burn
brightly once more

But I am surrounded by a world of snow and ice
and burning brightly would melt the ground on which I
stand, and drown me.

Apart from my own emotional unhappiness, I still knew too little about where I was to always feel truly safe, and in the end that wears you down as much as anything else.

I began to sleep a lot and to do each day no more than was required of me. Then one day I went in to the Kirkillian's room in the evening. Hoonan was there with him, working on something, but as I had discovered, he was seldom alone, and as I needed to say what I had gone there to say, I remained. I told him I could not go on any more as I had been, that I needed more.

He looked at me blankly. "What do you need?"

"I don't know, but I can't continue to live like this, alone and not as myself. I need real company, I need affection, I need to not be reduced so much in everything I am. I also need to belong, not to be a shadow here, no one knows what my position in this house is, and few people talk to me. Either you will not allow it, or they are unsure if it is acceptable. Even Kapjhan thinks she may lower her status by spending so much time with me."

Those were not really the things I wanted to say, but how do you explain the loss of identity, your sense of self, the feeling of being knowledgeable, cultured, loving, and involved with everything about you, everything I was before. And of wanting to go home, when you know you can't.

"If you are the only person I can ever share anything with here, then there must be more. I cannot go on being so alone."

I left then. If he had an answer, I knew it would come later, when we were briefly together.

But he gave nothing. He would not allow more than the absolute minimum between us physically, he said, and I should be grateful I ate with them. I had the work I had asked for, and if it no longer suited me I could be given another job in the house, if I wanted it.

"Hoonan thinks he can now make a band suitable for you, so it will be done tomorrow; then you will no longer be lonely."

It was not what I needed.

The next evening I was caught unprepared when in a few moments the band that had been talked of so often in the past was placed around my neck. Not my wrist, as was everyone else's, or the one I already wore for his benefit, but about my neck. And I did not like it. If I had been a possession before, then having a metal thing I could not remove placed about my neck suggested slavery.

"I do not feel less lonely," I said, "all I now feel is that I have finally become your slave." And I left the room angrily and walked aimlessly about the house depressed and even more alone.

That night was like any other until he had been near me for a few minutes, then I had a strange dizziness, which came and went. The next night it was worse, and on the third night I seemed to become lost and could not recover myself. As I moved inside him my whole being was drowning in his flesh, and I had to grasp him to stop my falling. Then my hands seemed to sink into his body and I was overcome and mindless. We blended like two thick liquids poured into a glass together, to become one. I thought I would die of so much pleasure when the nervous shock from him ran through me and mine engulfed me. It was a fire seeping out into my flesh until I burned with it.

Only after I recovered, did I realize I clung to him and had my face buried in his thick mane. He said nothing about my behavior before he left, which was odd, as he was so against our touching. But for the first time, I felt released from everything afterward and slept so deeply I woke late.

Nothing changed apart from that, and I could not understand that he did not complain about my holding him, which I was unable to stop myself from doing and preferred not to think of after. But I saw no indication that having me bound to him made any difference. To me it made none apart from that one thing, which overpowered me briefly each night. I perhaps had a buzzing in my mind and was oddly aware of it at times I knew he was further away from me. It was a nuisance buzzing, like something you have forgotten but can't quite remember, nothing more. It told me nothing about what the Kirkillian was thinking or feeling. But I was now woken occasionally by the oddest vivid dreams.

Bonding
I still do not understand what it is for them. Hoonan occasionally says that I feel as a person should, and when I try to think of those moments, it seems little different from normal to me. They, in turn, generally only seem to have a faint sense of their mate and their own young children. Only the seers have more. The training they receive and the bands they wear to assist them give it to them, along with a greater inherent natural ability, which they are born with and chosen for.

In the Cargo House they often asked me about the gossip that was on the streets. About what happened in the Han Kirkillian's section of the house. It fascinated them that I might see him regularly there, because though most of them had worked in his house for many years, some of them had never seen him in person.

At about this time they began to ask me when the Kirkillian's mate would be acknowledged and what she was like. I had no idea what they meant, but I saw so little

296

of him, except in the dark, that it was not surprising. The rumors became more prevalent and stronger over the next week, and finally I became concerned. If I was in the way, I wanted to get out of it. Whatever we now experienced briefly at night would be gone if he took a female as his mate, and if I no longer filled that need of his, I couldn't see myself as anything but a nuisance. I had no desire to be discarded and sent back to a cage as no more than an item of study and hoped there was something I could say to stop that.

Again I went to his room in the evening, and as before Hoonan was there. "They are saying in the Cargo House that you are taking a mate. Is it true?" I asked.

"They say many things when they gossip there," he replied.

"If you do, then I will not be welcome here, so I would like to know if it is true? If other arrangements are to be made for me, I would like to talk of them," I said firmly but quietly.

"What are you talking about?" he asked and looked at Hoonan, who shrugged.

"There has been talk in the Cargo House for over a week now that you are taking a mate, a dragar. Every day there is more talk. And as I live in this house, people ask me what I know. I tell them I know nothing, but they are certain that the announcement will be made any day. You have said nothing of this to me, and I want to know, what will happen to me when you do?" I was becoming frustrated. It was hardly a complicated question.

They both looked at me blankly, and I was very angry at them for playing games. "I have asked you a simple question politely. What will happen to me when you take this female as your dragar. Why can't you be courteous enough to answer me?"

"He doesn't know," Hoonan said, "he has no understanding of what has happened."

"Who doesn't know what?" I replied, becoming angry, annoyed now that they were talking in riddles.

"If the Cargo House know, then everyone knows," the Kirkillian said.

"Yes," Hoonan replied.

The Kirkillian came close to me. "Count Orlando of Earth, I acknowledge you my dragar, here in front of Hoonan. It is done, the Metjhan will know any day now what has been happening. Then he will move."

"What is going on?" I asked, still confused.

"I should have removed the collar after it happened the first time, but I believed it could be shielded. Apparently we didn't do it completely. This town loves gossip, and there are those who are more sensitive to such things. Now it is too late. Once the Cargo House has been talking of something for a few days, everyone knows it. The Metjhan seers may not be as strong as mine, but they are not incompetent."

I finally realized he was telling me that he had felt what I had after he put the collar on me, and that he had deliberately let it continue. "Why? Why didn't you stop it?" It was an incomprehensible action on his part.

"I have acknowledged you as my dragar. Now go and do whatever you usually would," was all he would reply.

I left more confused than when I had gone in, and angry too, not sure that I was relieved that I was not to be replaced. I'd had pleasant visions of having my own independent quiet small life there if he released me.

CHAPTER 19

I attend on the Laurentian Council, and a surprise awaits

The Metjhan made his move the day after the Han Kirkillian acknowledged me as his dragar. He sent a formal request to the Prime desiring that he convene the council to urgently discuss the danger posed by an alien allowed to move amongst them at the highest levels. The Han Dellier and the Han Sarolan were not present on the creation homeworld, so the meeting was called to begin in a month when everyone could be there.

There was some fear in the first days that the Metjhan might move before then and enter the Kirkillian house, as he could if he had good cause, because it stood on Metjhan land.

In the Cargo House there was much curiosity about less-important things. They seemed to know a dragar had been acknowledged, but none of the usual announcements had been made, and there was no holiday declared and no gifts or feasting. There was much complaining and grumbling among them, because there was no fun in a wedding without a party, and it was universally agreed that it "wasn't proper for a Han to behave so."

Naturally I made no comment to them about any of it, though I was often accosted by those who thought that, living in the main house, I must know everything that went on there, even though I never did.

At this time I also gradually found that I did not feel so alone as I had before. There was a feeling of something present in the constant hum that faintly filled my mind, which was oddly comforting. I continued working in the Cargo House and with my lessons, and again nothing seemed to have changed apart from the companionable hum arriving. I remained tired, and sometimes I felt like a body whose flesh has been frozen on its bones and then shattered, leaving empty spaces.

A couple of weeks later I returned to my rooms from the Cargo House in the afternoon to find an old female there.

"What are you here to do?" I asked her, as she seemed to be doing nothing.

The other old females who came there were always busy about their tasks, Celine with her tidying and cleaning, Kapjhan arranging her books for my lessons.

"I am Amee and have been called here to watch over you, Dragar Han, to protect you if the Han Metjhan or anyone else sends someone for you."

I was surprised. "Is that likely now?" I asked, knowing it had been thought of in the beginning and wondering what this old female could do if anything did happen.

"Who knows what a Han seeking greater power may do?"

It was a strange answer. "So, what will you do to protect me?" I asked, rather annoyed by the whole thing, assuming she would be hanging about there all the time.

"I shall be with you all the time, Dragar Han, except when the Han Kirkillian is with you. I am highly regarded and would not have been placed with you if I was not. I was chosen to watch his first offspring when he was born. When the Han himself was a child, I was also a child and the offspring of one of his watchers. I was there to take a knife that was meant for him when my father had already died trying to stop it. You need have no fear that I shall not do the same for you. My Han has taken you and asked me to be here for you. There is no more I need to know. You are second to me now, as you are to him and all the family."

I had never been addressed so formally by one of them or had my place there made out to be so high, and I was rather taken aback by it.

"I think you mistake my standing here, Amee. I am in no high position; my place is very low. I have no idea why I am bound to the Kirkillian and acknowledged by him, but I know it still leaves me far lower than second. And you will have little sleep if you only leave when the Kirkillian is here. His visits are very brief," I said to her and went to change out of the robes I wore to the Cargo House into the lighter ones I wore in my rooms, which were heated warmer than the rest of the house for me.

"These are your rooms, but you no longer sleep here. I have spoken to him about this. it is unsatisfactory for you and makes a distance between you. You sleep on his platform from tonight. It is the proper place for you."

I was stunned.

"I do not want to sleep all night with him. There is a distance between us because we both want it that way," I said, annoyed that this female was trying to push me and the Han about.

"Only he and I can be completely trusted to protect you, and I must rest. You shall be with him when I do. You sleep longer, and his sleeping platform has been replaced. You can sleep quite apart from him as you do now, if that is what you wish. You worry me more than one of my own race would. You are not much shorter, but you are much more delicate and thin skinned and fragile than we are. It is a great concern, and it makes your danger more extreme."

Without having an argument I was sure to lose, and too tired to be bothered with one, I saw no way other than to do what she wanted me to, for a time at least. I went to his room that night and found it changed. It was no longer more office than personal room; it was now all office, and a smaller room beyond had become his sleeping place with, as Amee had said, a large and very comfortable sleeping platform, which would have easily accommodated five or six people.

I was glad I had not wasted my energy on an argument.

I went to the side that was not his and lay down and was instantly asleep. It was little different to being in my own room, because I went to bed alone and got up alone, the Kirkillian sleeping less than me, as all Laurentians do in warm places. The last and first person I saw each night was Amee.

Amee was with me everywhere, but discreetly. She followed me to the Cargo House but remained up in the gallery watching the room below, so no one but those in the offices there really noticed her. She accompanied me to dinner, on the second night stopping me from going to my usual place and making me go instead to sit beside the Kirkillian, and then she sat behind me to eat her own meal.

"Amee has lived always in the first house. She knows the way things are properly done better than most, and she has reminded me what your place now is." He looked at me and spoke quietly, and I saw the rest of those there looking away, obviously confused that I was being seated next to him.

"I am not bothered where I sit, Kio," I replied, not wanting to cause difficulties or to be with him so much.

"I know that, Orlando. But I have acknowledged you, and I will not go back on it." He paused, and made me sit down. "So, it is time I did what is right." He stood up and announced to those gathered, "I have taken a dragar, and acknowledged it in front of Hoonan. Now I acknowledge my dragar to you all." He said it loudly, and there was a great deal of confusion further down the table.

I was required to do nothing in response; I was seated beside him in the second place. That was enough.

"The council meets in a few days. You will be with me, and we will see what the Metjhan plans to try. You know nothing of what is required of a dragar, and I know little myself. My first dragar was well trained before she entered my cave. Amee and the other females shall advise you," he added, then seemed unsure what to do, not being used to having me there. "It is a long time since we said more than a few words to each other; yet I remember a time when we talked every day."

"That was when you walked with me, before we mated and you had what you wanted from me," I replied coolly, remembering that I had enjoyed those walks I had taken with a man I had often thought of as a friend.

"Yes, for a short time it was difficult for both of us," he said, which seemed like an idiotic remark. It was still difficult.

For the rest of the meal our conversation was strained, until we suddenly seemed to find a subject we both had an opinion on, which was Amee, and he told me about her and I complained about how she was pushing me about. He amusingly told the story of how he had enjoyed playing with her when they were young and, being very sensitive to the scent of a female in heat even in his youth, had been extremely interested in her when her first heat approached. He had chased her about his family's house in the weeks before, eager to get to her. His mother had been outraged by his behavior, and Amee had been quickly sent away.

Amee listened in from where she sat behind me and made rude comments about his manners. It was obvious they had a long and close friendship. By the end we were almost friends, ones who should have been happily returning to our own homes after a pleasant evening, but instead I went to his bed.

The next day, which was only a few days before the council meeting, the public announcement was finally made that there was now a dragar Han Kirkillian. It was vague in detail, but a holiday was declared. The "wedding" gifts were distributed the following day and the feasting was arranged and everyone in the Cargo House was satisfied. Everyone there, but me, received some sort of voucher, which they could exchange for something—I could never quite work out what, but it seemed to make them all happy. And everyone seemed to be going to a string of feasts on my account, while for me the Kirkillian's house remained quiet, and I was fed in my room for a couple of days. The first time that had occurred. I spent the evening alone writing in my journal, and the nights unaccustomedly in uninterrupted sleep. The Kirkillian was attending public feasts, which I was not expected to appear at and which apparently continued late into the night.

The bride has missed the wedding celebration,
while everyone else feasts she is confined to her room unseen,
knowing she was never truly married.

The bride is flesh, and has been taken and bound
Brief pleasure is all she is required for

Lusting for another's flesh has brought her here
Where she is no more than the requiter of a stranger's lust

She wants to become the groom again, one who may choose
his own Bride
taste her flesh, then release her so he can choose again

Then the council was to meet the next day, and I was to be made ready to be there.

"You have to attend the first day to be welcomed. What happens then, I have no idea. The Metjhan will try to cause some trouble, of course, but I doubt he will have much support. He is not a particularly good speaker or arguer," The Kirkillian told me.

I wanted to wear one of my own suits again, which still appeared to be in good condition. As Amee and Celine both regarded me as terribly ugly, they felt that for me to dress in an outlandish, but obviously finely worked and unique costume was probably appropriate. The one I chose was in a pale gold silken satin, a very formal and rather splendid thing I had rarely worn, with only a narrow pattern of decoration, but that was everywhere on it, all about the edges and along each seam. But I could not wear that alone. As such a recent bride, I would have to go veiled in such a crowded place. A male could still be slightly feverish so close to mating, and it was accepted he would not want others looking too closely at his dragar. The women were sad to admit, however, that was unlikely in my case, because I was so ugly and not a bride anyway, and so strange to think of in such a way. In these sentiments I agreed with them entirely, finding the whole business quite bizarre.

In the very early morning on the day the council meeting began, with Amee standing near, but at my request politely not looking on, I washed and began the laborious process of making myself splendid. I shaved close and removed stray hairs. Then I put on my underclothes, my shirt, then my short, pale gold stockings, the garters, and my britches. After this I sat down before my mirror and, with a thick cloth draped about my shoulders, began the process of waxing and powdering my hair with the help of Celina. When it was done, it was pulled back neatly and tied at my neck in a small black satin bag with ribbon. Then I whitened my face, though it needed very little powder, being already very pale from the lack of sun, and I darkened my eyes. I looked like a corpse until I put pink on my cheeks, which made me look like a doll. I was going overboard a bit. I seldom did so much in Madeleine, taking the trouble only at Christmas and Easter and for very occasional other spectacularly grand occasions. But I knew that the powder would come off as I moved about, so the effect would not last long, I finished with my nails, which I had forgotten, and they were buffed until they gleamed. Then I put on my vest and coat and gold shoes with heels and finally tied the lace jabot at my neck.

All of this seemed like wasted effort when they placed a black garment made of a stiff opaque fabric, which covered me like a massive tent, over my head. I was a walking blob in it, and I tried to complain, but they ignored me. Then I found out the tent opened at the front as if to let the happy campers out. I felt absurd. Having satisfied themselves that I looked almost invisible in it, I was able to remove it and they brought out boxes of jewels, which Amee told me were mine now, because they had been the Kirkillian's late dragar's.

In that house and given my relationship with him, I had, of course, been made very well aware of his complete power over me. But his wealth and high position themselves had been of only limited interest to me. They were abstract concepts of little importance compared to the rest. But part of his wealth was now laid out for my use, and there were pieces there that were almost incomprehensible in their size and design. And I was taken aback to suddenly have the reality of the other aspects of his immense wealth and elevated position forced on me. But there was no time to do more than register it, and what did it matter anyway? It changed nothing. The women wanted me to wear as much of the jewelry as I could fit on myself, as if to make up for being so ugly myself, and there were difficulties about how much I was to wear of it, and I had the Kirkillian called in.

He paused when he entered. "I would not recognize you by your appearance alone," he said, and walked around me like a valuer assessing an unusual, but not very attractive, piece of furniture. Then he surprised me by saying, "The sudden way I acquired you, and the difficulties with you, have often left me feeling you are someone unsuitable I found in heat at the back of a cave. And I forget that you are a person of high position yourself." Amee made a protest, which he ignored. "They cannot see you clearly," he continued, obviously pleased with the tent. "That is important, and as it should be. What else you wear is your choice, but I do not wish you to display too much today."

He left, and the women fussed about, tempting me only with what they claimed were the finest or most valuable pieces, and saying I looked surprisingly impressive. I was stuck with the tent, but I wore only a few small pieces of jewelry that would be appropriate with all the gold I already wore.

"What did his remark about the cave mean?" I asked, curious.

"Hiding young females in their first heat in caves or other similar places where hunters may take shelter is an old game in the countryside, if the unmated high member of a family is nearby. It has led to some most unsuitable matings, and often the females have been killed afterward by the male's family. It is not something he should have said in front of you, Dragar Han. He made his choice. I know you did not want it and it was not forced on him."

"How do you know so much about it, Amee?" I asked, even more curious about that now than his remark.

"Because it is important I know such things. I must know how things stand with you, so I know what behavior is likely. With an alien it is, of course, impossible to know, even with much experience. But I ask, and I see with my intelligence, and my knowledge of him. Kio is unsteady about you, but unfortunately for all his family, I believe he will not give you up, whatever he imagines."

She seemed to know a lot, and he was certainly unsteady about me. She stayed by me on the journey to the council meeting, her seated on one side of me in the vehicle and the Kirkillian on the other.

I have never seen the outside of the Meeting Cave when it is not covered in snow. Whether the covering is heavy or light, it always gives the building the appearance of being a small hill. Inside it is high ceilinged, and the walls, ceiling and floor are all brightly colored and elaborately patterned—so much so that one's first sight of them is briefly overpowering, coming as it does immediately one arrives after the journey made through the endless whites and grays of the snow-covered city outside.

No one in our party was stopped by anyone as we entered the building from our vehicles, which halted under the huge, ice-covered porch. From there we made our way down a wide gallery through several open rooms before arriving at a pair of dark, elaborately fashioned doors, which were closed. To either side of them stood a robed guard.

"Who asks to join the high families in the Meeting Cave?" one asked.

One of our party, an old man with a mane streaked with gray and red gold, and skin the color of polished oak, stepped forward, "The Han Kirkillian comes to sit with the most revered of the families in negotiation. He sits for all of his family, the Kirkillian."

The answer was obviously satisfactory. The guards immediately opened the doors, one to each door, and they appeared to be as heavy to move as they looked. We passed through them into the anteroom of the council chamber, or Meeting Cave.

It is narrow, elaborately decorated, and holds no furniture. Beyond it and through a small archway is the Meeting Cave itself, which is hardly a cave in appearance. Its size is astonishing, its height being so extreme that the ceiling has always been invisible to me in the dim light of the place.

Inside the Meeting Cave

There are no windows there, but the walls glisten and flash with the abstract bright mosaics of flat cut, polished crystals, which are set into them. The floor appears ancient, being also set with mosaics of cut crystals, but these ones are so worn down in places that the hard gray layer of material beneath them shows through.

The lighting is hidden subtly so that there is only a dim glow, brighter about the center than at the edges, and in the middle of the room is an hexagonal-shaped table, with one side longer than the other four (the long side being always turned to the place of the family whose Han is currently Prime). The floor beneath it bears the colors of the five families, and above this the table appears to be plain dark polished wood. There is one large, deeply padded stool set on each side, covered in the family's color and sitting above the same colored floor, and behind that are arranged smaller stools, also colored, and set in rows.

The Meeting Cave still remains accessible to none but those members of the five families who sit there, and the invited. And there is no available representation or visual record of it that I can recommend you to if you wish to know more of it. Though I would be fascinated to see its elaborate interior in good light and examine its detail myself, it has never been possible even for me. Whatever my position I remain an outsider, admitted there, but not belonging there.

No one was going to have trouble knowing where to sit, I could see, though how the hierarchy of seating in the rows of stools behind the Hans was determined, I was sure would be immensely complex, but, in fact, wasn't.

There were already a large number of people milling about in the chamber when we entered it, but no one yet sat at the central table.

"Are you the first Han to arrive?" I asked the Kirkillian.

"No, the Sarolan is here already." He pointed out an older male in yellow on the other side of the room, who was talking with several other people in white and blue. "No one will sit to share food and drink until we are all here, or accounted for, and the Prime will then ask us to sit with him."

Our party made its way to a group of seats and a table behind the green section of the council table. There the clerks began to unpack their bags.

"The mother of the Sarolan is here," an adviser came over and told the Kirkillian.

"I know, and his sister too, come to see what sort of victory there will be here today."

"It would be advisable to show her the dragar now, Han."

"I know, I know." Kio said, but did nothing but continue to stare across the room for some time. "Come, we must do this. She could push the Sarolan against us if

310

she is determined to, and I doubt she will approve of you in any way."

We went over with the elderly attendant who had announced us at the great doors. "The Han Kirkillian and his dragar greet you, mother of the Sarolan, and the family honor you and wish your family warmth and good hunting," he announced.

The Sarolan's mother was a large, elderly woman, probably Shasa's age, her mane a rusty red gold and thinning, but she almost bounced forward to meet me, full of energy.

"And who is this fancy girl you have with you? (I think her actual words, in fact, meant something much less respectable, but the converter always tends toward polite translations) Turn around so I can see you, girl," She croaked loudly at me.

I was, in fact, only faintly visible through the fabric of the tent and was aware that I was now conscious of something—the hum in my mind had become more than the usual faint buzz. Which could only be some warning of something particular in the situation, as it was the first time I had ever felt that. So, I remained where I was and looked past her. One thing I had learned well in my lessons was that the Laurentian Hans are extremely formal with the senior members of other families.

"You haven't introduced me," I said quietly, looking at the elderly man who was apparently performing this task.

The old man coughed and stepped forward quickly. "The Dragar Han Kirkillian greets you, lady."

The old crow then stepped back, and if it's possible for one of them to have such an expression, I would say she glowered at me. Then she waved her aged hand at one of the yellow-robed clerks standing around watching, and he immediately moved forward and said, "The mother of the Sarolan greets you, dragar of the Kirkillian."

"I am honored to meet you, mother," I said, and I looked right at her and tried to look blank, though none can do that as well as a Laurentian, and inside my tent it was probably pointless anyway.

She returned my look and chewed her lips noisily, a dreadful sound some of them make, particularly the females, as I have discovered since that first time I heard it. It's some sort of insult, implying you have fed them bad food, something no person of any status would ever do. So, it implies the person it is directed at—in this case myself—is lower in ranking than they are claiming to be. But at the time I didn't know such things and merely thought it an awful noise.

The Han Sarolan and the others of her party looked on in silence. "I was looking forward to seeing the female who could manage to mate two Hans in as many months. You wouldn't know it, creature, but only Avien Sule ever managed it before, and that was in the time of eight families, so she had it easier. And she waited decently till her first mate died." She paused while she looked me up and down. "Now I discover you are an ugly, stunted alien male and I'm afraid what this means, finding the Kirkillian's actions in taking you disgusting and obscene. The Dellier I might understand, as he is known to be odd and possibly mad. But the Kirkillian never showed signs of such madness before."

I had no idea what to say. She was being incredibly insulting, not just to me, but also to the Kirkillian. My lessons with Kapjhan would have had me believe such words could start wars between them. But obviously this wasn't so, as everyone else remained standing about and looking on in silence. Then, against the faint buzz of him, I was reminded that he had warned me to say nothing if I was unsure what was going on. That was most definitely the situation then, so I looked past her and stayed silent, as did everyone else.

Eventually, she spoke again. "You may be the first male to mate two Hans, but I don't like you. Your dragar is ugly and arrogant, Kirkillian, and it has the feel and scent of mating, though the heat is over. Are all these primitive creatures like that?" She asked.

"Whatever you feel, mother, my dragar is my choice, and if there are difficulties coming from it, I shall deal with them. The world changes, and we have found another race, one that can join with us. What this will mean for us I do not know. We shall talk again later, mother," the Kirkillian said coolly, ending the meeting and immediately guiding me away from her.

He found Hoonan in the growing crowd and spoke to him in a low, angry growl. "She oversteps herself badly, Hoonan, far more than is acceptable. I must know if it is only her anger at my not taking a mate from her family that is making her so bold with an ally, or if the Sarolan thinks to serve the Metjhan."

"I warned you that what you have done is dangerous and that no one will understand it," Hoonan hissed back.

"It is done, it is my dragar, and I will need more than that old female's insults to make me give it up."

The two of them stood close, face to face, and Hoonan looked at him steadily before he spoke again. "This thing has become more to you than it is worth, Kio. You cause dangers for no reason."

"I have said what I want you to discover for me, Hoonan," Kio replied in a low, growling voice. "I know your words now are those of an old and loyal member of my house."

I knew that Hoonan moved off unhappily, and I stood by uneasily, Amee close by me and alert. It was not in my own interests or humanities, if my presence severely undermined the Kirkillian's position within his own house, or alienated his allies.

313

"Do I really need to be here?" I asked.

"Yes," was all he replied before he left me in Amee's care and moved off to speak to his own party, and to those of high rank in other houses who came to him.

Amee, who was usually talkative, said nothing to me, but concentrated intently on the comings and goings about us. I had assumed Kio knew what he was doing when he acknowledged me, and that it was appropriate. Now I knew it was not, and was not a decision even Hoonan, his closest adviser and friend, supported.

The Han Dellier arrived, and I couldn't stop myself from watching him, finding I had lost none of my appreciation for his feminine grace and beauty. And though I had no wish to do more than watch from a distance, I found that in spite of the pain and fear I had suffered with him, I was now able to understand much of the reasons for that, and I could not regret what had happened between us. Amee suddenly realized where my eyes rested and pulled me about so I looked away, her fingers biting painfully into my flesh she was so insistent.

Shortly after that, the Han Metjhan and his party entered, just ahead of the Prime (who was also the Han Riag) and his people. Every Han was present then, and the Prime moved immediately to his stool. The other Hans took their seats, and Amee led me to a stool just behind and off to one side of the Kirkillian's before she disappeared into the gloom away from the table.

There was a brief ceremony where baskets of some fresh leaf and greasy lumps of brown stuff were brought in and placed before the Hans along with pitchers of liquid and small, elaborate mugs. Presumably with their delivery, the ceremonial food and drink had been served and taken, because immediately that was done, the Prime welcomed everyone formally. Then he singled out the Kirkillian.

314

"We congratulate you on taking a dragar for the house, Kirkillian. I believe she is here and welcome her."

"My dragar accepts your welcome as do I and all my family," Kio replied.

"I see no female behind you Kirkillian, and I ask you to show your dragar to end my confusion," the Han Metjhan said immediately.

"My dragar sits behind me in the proper place, Metjhan."

"I still see no female there."

"Our custom does not require a dragar to be female, Metjhan."

"Perhaps not, if one reads legends as history or listens to madmen, Kirkillian, but I think our law still requires it to be one of us, to be Laurentian."

"Our law does not require that either, Metjhan."

"Then I think you must have found some new law unknown to us. Prime, can you request the Kirkillian to show plainly to us the thing he brings into this cave and calls his dragar," the Metjhan spoke slowly and clearly and didn't seem at all uncertain.

"Kirkillian, show us your dragar so we may consider it," the Prime said then, and it was obvious they must have arranged the scene beforehand.

Kio had obviously expected at least some of what was happening, as he remained calm and casual as he replied. "It sits here by me, as you see. Is there no more important business for us to consider but this? A dragar should be of no interest to anyone but a mate."

"I think if you pretend to us that you are bound to this ugly, odd-looking thing we have cause to worry about you, Kirkillian," the Metjhan said and paused briefly for effect, and to me he appeared to know he was a good speaker, or to be very well rehearsed. "And of what race is it? I have never seen any like it before."

"It is my dragar; you need know no more."

315

"I think I know of what kind it is. I believe it may be one of the primitives the Dellier gained our permission to meet with in isolation, on Heinget," he said, laying obvious stress on the last words.

The Kirkillian said nothing, which concerned me.

"The Dellier himself was deluded by one of the primitive's wizards to believe that he had mated with it, so he would keep it and bring it here to our precious homeworld of creation. But with my help he was able to throw off the madness it caused in him and get free of it."

"Do you say I am mad, Metjhan?" the Kirkillian finally spoke, "Or no longer control my own thoughts?"

"I am very concerned, Kirkillian. This creature is obviously dangerous and evilly clever. It seems to have strong magic if it can delude even strong men and their seers. I fear the madness, which numbers of its kind could cause. And I believe there are millions of its evil fellows on its worlds. What could so many do to harm us, if just one alone can get among the Hans of our families so easily?" He spoke now with a full resonant voice, and great confidence, and I had no idea why the Kirkillian had claimed the Metjhan was a poor arguer, as I thought him very competent.

The Kirkillian said nothing and the cave was worryingly quiet. I could see where the Metjhan was going, I was frightened of it, and I was sure the Kirkillian had not expected things to go so far.

"I believe it would be best to destroy all its ugly misshapen kind now, before this one can find a way to get many of them among us and make us all believe its lies. If we remove it, and its kind, the Kirkillian shall recover himself I am sure, and all will be well again."

If I had not already believed it, the continuing silence in that vast chamber would have made me believe his threat of annihilation.

"I am not tainted with any madness, as you well know. I control it, and I say it is my dragar. There is no more for you to know. Prime, I ask that you set this matter aside. You have welcomed my dragar; there is nothing more to be said."

"It was agreed by the Council that the primitives would know no more than Heinget, Kirkillian. I understand the Metjhan's concern, and for myself, I find it unlikely an alien creature could ever be truly bound," the Prime replied.

It was an escape for Kio, and the Prime was not sitting on the fence; he was preparing to jump. The Kirkillian might have the Sarolan support him if it went to a vote, but not the Metjhan, and probably not the Dellier, and now apparently not the Prime. I felt frozen by this knowledge.

"I do not believe such a thing is possible either," the Metjhan continued, "the bond of mating is unique to us. It is what let us prosper in the harshness of the homeworld, and no other species has it. You are deluded, Kirkillian. You must be saved from this ugly deformed thing, and its kind must be stopped from ever coming among us again. If you do not give it up, it must be taken from you," the Metjhan said. He was speaking loudly and getting quite excited from seeing victory in sight.

And I was even more frightened at finding that the destruction of humanity was again talked of seriously as if it were a minor act, and that there was no one to support my race and me other than the now-silent Kirkillian.

There was finally some murmuring, which broke the silence, but it seemed to come from the Metjhan and Riag parties. And it indicated they approved of what was being said. The Kirkillian was silent, and I understood how fatal almost anything he might say in favor of me or my species could be. But if the fate of humanity was

317

seriously in question, I could not stay quiet for his sake or my own.

"I think you are jealous, Metjhan," I said, standing up slowly. "The Kirkillian has bound me, Metjhan, but still you wish to separate us as you succeeded in separating me from the Dellier. Do you wish to have me for yourself?" I asked, as I removed the enormous cape I wore, opening the front of it and stepping out, and moving toward him.

"You are filth. I am not a mad man to be drawn into your net of delusion," the Mtejhan responded, rising up and eagerly pointing to me and crying out, "See how it is trying to use its evil powers even here?"

"You are obviously more powerful than this one I have now, who says nothing. Perhaps I should let you have me." My jacket was removed by then also, and in my fitted short eighteenth-century aristocratic breeches, with the hard on I had worked up, I knew I was an obscene sight to them all, and I moved closer to him.

"You are vile and obscene. You cannot delude me with your magic," he cried but with less confidence in his voice.

I was then close to the Metjhan, and I thought of the act of mating, concentrating on it and trying to put his features on my partner. If I had any of the Kirkillian's and Hoonan's claimed strength, then I hoped he would get some disgusting image from that. I have no idea what I hoped for, except to stop him being so self-satisfied and assured.

He was obviously genuinely repelled by me, because he was pulling back and his mouth was partly open, and his nostrils flared, a sign of definite discomfort.

His own people were obviously also convinced that his claims for my evil intent were true and were too busy moving away themselves to stop me reaching him.

"I would like to mate with you, I think, knowing you want me badly." I was reaching out my arms and had come almost close enough to touch him when he finally jumped up from his stool and stepped back.

"Get away from me. I know what you want; you want my body and my mind. I know it, I know it, I have been told. Others know what you are," he shouted, losing his clearly spoken assurance.

I moved quickly after him, knowing I had to be stopped by someone soon. "I know you want me more than the others did. I know it. I will let you have me." I was talking excitedly now and still trying to keep a picture of him mating with me in my mind.

"Never, you shall never have me. I have been warned. The Yan Riag knows of your vileness and says I'm safe. I have a true mate."

I could have told him that a wife may be a protection from many things, but an amorous pursuer isn't always one of them.

"I know you want me," I repeated fervently, making a leap at him.

"The Yan Riag said I am safe. He said I am safe. If you touch me, he will destroy you when he is Prime," he yelled, holding his arms out in front as if to force me back as he backed away from the table. "He will destroy you and all your kind!"

I was reluctant to chase him and was aware the room had gone quiet again. I looked about and found everyone but him and me seated and unmoving. Shaking from the stress of my actions, I meekly returned to my own stool after replacing my jacket and the cape, and then I tried to pretend I was a harmless and mild alien. I also realized the soon-to-be, new Han Riag, could not also become Prime. Whatever was going on, the true object of it was something other than the elimination of my race and me. We were possibly merely a tool.

The silence continued for a few moments before the Kirkillian made a formal request for his dragar to be allowed to leave and rest after the awful experience it had just suffered. He was formally granted permission to do so, which didn't make much sense to me, after the earlier animosity, but I was certainly shaken by events and wanting to know what would happen next. We left the table slowly, with Amee coming to "help" me, and left the cave and returned to our house. Nothing was said at all on the journey. I had many questions but was also uneasy about what Kio and Hoonan thought of what I had done and not keen to be reprimanded or lectured and have an argument just then. But when we got to the house, I had to ask him.

"Why did you choose to acknowledge me? You must have known everyone was against it and that it could cause terrible problems for my whole race, as well as you."

"I had to acknowledge you or give you up, and I was not able to give you up."

"It was you who enabled the Dellier to give me up, so why couldn't you?" I asked

He stared at me before he answered. "You have answered your own question, Orlando, I did not give you up because I do not want to be without you."

"Why not?" I asked.

"Today went well, but now I have work to do," was all he said, and he turned to go.

"Have you destroyed other races?" I asked, having to know.

He turned back, but waited before answering. "Yes, but they were a violation upon creation."

Then it was my turn to have to wait before I could speak, "So, for now humans are safe? I want the truth."

"I can guarantee nothing. But for now, yes, I think they are, and I see no reason for them not to remain so, if you have been honest with me, and the Council continues to think that you obey me."

In my opinion I had always been honest with him. "And what do you mean when you say I obey you?"

"I made it obvious to all that it was my encouragement and Hoonan's that made you go after the Metjhan."

"I felt nothing," I said, stunned by his claim and trying to remember if there had been anything odd about how I felt. I remembered nothing but did know that I had been very calm when I first spoke. "Have you done that to me before?"

"No, there have been times I would have liked to stop you doing something, but I was never able to affect you in any way and now waste little time trying. What they felt in the Meeting Cave was a lie, but it is important they believe it."

I looked at him uncertainly. I understood nothing about the things he and the seers did. "I do not like to wonder if my thoughts are not my own, Kio. They are the only things left to me," I said angrily, and left him, not wanting to think he might make me feel anything I did not feel myself.

I returned to my rooms and removed my clothes and lay down, finding I was quite tired.

I have no idea how long I slept for, but I was awakened by Amee and Celine, who brought me food, and once I was awake and had eaten, they began to carry in garments from an adjoining room.

I ignored them, but then the women were getting impatient with me and finally explained that they were there to help me decide what I would wear tomorrow for the Council meeting. Apparently it would be an occasion of great formality, for which I would have to be prepared carefully. I was confused, momentarily wondering if I had dreamed the meeting where the Metjhan had incriminated the Yan Riag. The two females were not impressed by me, in any way, but whatever sort of inadequate creature I might be, they would again ensure that I at least looked as much like the Dragar Han Kirkillian as they could manage.

"He did not want you to appear as too highly regarded today. Tomorrow you shall be accepted as you should have been today, and he will have you showing what great wealth you are second in, and what regard he has for you," Amee explained, obviously happy about things. "Today was unexpected. You are safe now and a serious conspiracy has been revealed. Things go well."

I was dressed carefully again the next day, in the formal black suit with small red flowers, and allowed to go without the tent. But I was required to wear a great fur cape of black-tipped, gold Segedee, which dragged along behind me, and a large amount of gaudy jewelry, which weighed me down and created the effect of some tasteless dilettante.

The preliminaries were much as on the previous day, but we did not speak to the Sarolan mother, and I was annoyed when I saw her sitting behind her son this time, hoping she didn't want to make trouble still.

After the food and drink was brought, the Prime stood and announced that he would pass on the duty of first of the first, which suddenly weighed too heavily on him. Apparently it was a surprise to everyone that the first item for the day would be the election of the new Prime. There was a noisy stir, and the Kirkillian turned to look at those behind him, who lent forward and whispered rapidly to him.

It was a normal vote, taken quickly, and then the Han Dellier was Prime. Everyone stood back for a few seconds while the large table was lifted and turned, so that the long side sat above the white part of the floor, which was the Dellier's place. Then everyone sat down again, and after he was formally congratulated, in a very brief way, it was done. Then unexpectedly the Sarolan stood and formally asked the Hans to hear his mother speak.

She rose and looked briefly at me before she started. "You know that I have three times had true visions of our future. To be able to read the river's dreams is a gift some of the females in my family have. Last night I sought to do this because of the turmoil I saw caused by this ugly alien who has been brought among us." She waved her yellow hand at me but didn't look. "I had my weak seers join me, and together we sought the peace of the river."

"This morning I told the Prime of what I saw there. Now he is gone and my son has stood by the Dellier. And now I stand by the Kirkillian and his dragar." She paused, "Why, you wonder, should I stand by a creature I find ugly, and who frightens me?"

"A vision is true in what it shows. It does not show us what we would want to see in the future. And my vision was as strong as any I have had, and it tells me to accept this creature and its kind. In my vision I see a young arrogant changeling, and I see an old man. But the old are enlivened by the young and regain some of their youth by the association. I now see these creatures are not evil things to be quickly destroyed, but I see they are dangerous. They are young and arrogant and ambitious."

She paused, leaving me surprised by how much she could see from just the one example before her and a bit disappointed that she saw me personally as ambitious and arrogant. Young was nice.

"In my vision I see the likes of this blending with us and making us, the Laurentian, who are an ancient and great race, more as we were when we were young. And I see us clearly together, standing strong about the whole galaxy."

"I have spoken; that is my vision. Now I leave this place for my homeworld, for I am old and have no taste for this new future where we must bend and change ourselves."

She left her place and disappeared into the shadows, seeming tired and slow, and I wondered what power her unexpected words would have.

There was a subdued silence as she walked away, which continued until the Kirkillian formally asked if he could arrange for an embassy from the humans to visit Hienget again, and if he could take over the Laurentian embassy. It was agreed to by all but the Han Metjhan, who had sat silent and bent over throughout the whole meeting.

It was done. Their world and humanities had changed in a morning.

When we returned to the house and I undressed, I sought some privacy and inspected the huge bruise on my arm where Amee had gripped it the day before. I seldom bruised, and those bruises I had gained from my supervisors when I was caged had never been so large.

In the midst of my relief that things were now going well for my species, I felt a stab of fear for myself.

CHAPTER 20

*In which I see death, but recover, and the
second conference with humanity occurs*

When death approaches gradually, you often do
not see it until near the end. You feel unwell, you may
have a general ache and tenderness, you have less energy.
But it is a slowly arriving state, and you discount it as the
weather, the wrong sort of food, too many late nights, a
busy job, and getting older.

The world about you shrinks; as you become less
well, it becomes less, so that eventually you do one thing
at a time and are glad to get it done. Your ideas and
thoughts become reduced. You put one foot before the
other, and it occupies your whole attention, so you have
nothing left to think about the change with. You live less,
that is all, until all of the life in you is gone.

I returned to the Cargo House after the two
council meetings, and no one there had any idea of what I
had become. The Han's dragar was not generally a public
figure, and the affairs of the Meeting Cave were not made
public. To them I remained the same odd alien I had

always been, but inside I was not. I found the days long, the evenings seeming gone before I did anything, and the mornings coming too quickly. I was tired but didn't seem to sleep more. I was just too tired to have the energy for life.

Then one night, when the Kirkillian was done, I knew. I had felt him not as the brief consuming passion he always was when we were together in the dark after I was bound to him, but as a distant dream, and afterward I just lay there, because I knew.

I went to the Cargo House the following day but drifted off and got almost nothing done as I brooded about how things were and all the things I would have liked to have done. When I was leaving at the end of the day, I told Shasa I would not be there for a few days and ignored her when she wanted to know why. I walked home slowly like an old man, passing through an unseen world of shadows. In my own room I sat my aching shell down in the dark of evening to rest, but it seemed like only minutes till someone came to see why I was not at dinner. Life had become too complicated for me, and I ignored them, and to escape the cold, crawled into my bed, imagining I would never again leave it.

But they made a fuss, and my room was suddenly full of people asking loud, pointless questions when I just wanted to be warm and quiet and sleep. The Kirkillian and Hoonan were there, and he asked me what was wrong, and I knew he deserved an answer and that I'd have to make the effort to give it.

"I'm sorry, Kio, I'm dying. I can't cope with all these people. I want to be left alone. I'm sorry."

I would never have remembered what I said, finding later that I had already stopped writing in my journal a couple of weeks before then, without realizing it. Afterward I had only vague images to make note of when I wrote of that time.

But he, of course, remembers every word, as you do after times like that.

The doctors were able to do little; mine was a physiology and chemistry with which they had no experience. But they had some test details from when I had first arrived and had the converter implanted and had gone into the cage. Of course there were a lot of things that were no longer as they had been then, but I had been living on their food, their water, their air, shared the space of their small creatures. And of course I would have absorbed anything that frequent intimate contact with them could pass to me. They did what they felt was safe to try to remedy the differences they saw, and they did it conscientiously, being very careful to try to get things into me in a lot of small doses rather than large ones. And I survived and actually felt a bit more alert after a couple of days. Feeling better, I felt guilty about being so defeatist.

But they really had no idea what they were doing and also didn't know what might be wrong that they had done no tests for. I needed a human doctor and human facilities, but those were far away.

Another meeting had already been arranged for Heinget, and this time Marius would be there. It was only weeks away, but it was still weeks I might not have to spare and no one had any idea of how long I would survive.

The Kirkillian went to the Prime, now the Dellier, and asked if he might meet Marius's embassy early, while it was still on its way, because I was ill. This was a serious matter, as it would mean revealing to the humans some part of the Laurentians' true technology and equipment, because whatever Marius might suspect and despite my own wishes, they had intended to continue with the simple rural society that had been the fiction of Heinget. The Dellier asked how ill I was, and when he heard, he gave his permission.

I think the Kirkillian might have done it anyway, but to have permission to do it and to know he would have three votes on the council if it came to that afterward, was a great relief for him, I know.

After briefly getting better, I gradually got worse, and I remember little of the journey there and none of my treatment. I might have vague thoughts, but I slept much of the time, often with Hoonan's help, as I remember I ached terribly all over at that time.

At some time I began to recover and woke up to the world again. Then I found myself possessed of loving parents who fussed about me as if I were a precious ailing child. The Kirkillian and Amee always seemed to be about, and he himself gave me my medicines regularly throughout the day and night and stayed near, most of the time. Amee watched me and called him at the appropriate time, if he was elsewhere. She made sure I was always warm enough and she fed me real food too, food from Earth, and I improved quickly.

It sounds foolish now, but it was only then that I realized he loved me. Now I have written all this and looked back, I see he loved me long before. He had tried to tell me that he would never have bound me to him if he hadn't loved me, so he must have started to even earlier. I have never asked him.

Life would be much easier if we could love those who were worthy of our love and not have it confused by other things that seem to be less important, but aren't.

We had moved away from Marius's ship once it was determined what was wrong with me and my treatment had begun to show good results. I was deeply upset that I never saw a human there; the doctor was a woman and the Kirkillian was frightened of me seeing her. Which sounds so paranoid, I know, but they are intensely possessive of their mates during the heat, which is always there for us, if only faintly in my scent. So Hoonan put me to sleep each time she saw me and ensured I stayed that way.

Then we stayed close to them nearly all the way to Heinget, in case I needed the doctor again. Finally, we arrived only a couple of days before Marius was due to arrive, the day before the next round of meetings were to begin.

Humanity's future was so closely bound up with the coming meetings that as I improved and took more interest in things about me, I tried not to think too much of what was involved. My great fear always was that Marius and the Kirkillian were too alike. I knew Marius's desire to be in control, his almost obsessive need to achieve it, and his great ability to manipulate others. What use that ability would be against the Laurentian I was unsure, but I was secretly glad that he had seen the ship we were on.

I now knew it was an asteroid ship, one of those huge things I had seen being loaded in a corner of the Cargo House, where the cargo space was circular and trapped and held commercially useful asteroids; driven from behind by a curved ship shaped like a new moon. I knew it was so huge he would have been overwhelmed by its size alone. Otherwise I would have been fearful of him believing he was on the vastly superior side.

The Kirkillian always assumed he was in command of everything, or could, at the least, influence it strongly and knew the superiority of his race and its capabilities. I was afraid Marius's behavior and attitude could arouse his anger and that they would instantly dislike each other. That would be a disaster. Especially if the two of them spent the time trying to take control of what was going on.

When we had arrived, I was pleased, and then relieved to be back on the surface of Heinget; the advisability of my being allowed to do so had been debated till the last minute. My health was supposedly the reason, but as I was explicitly forbidden to go near the meeting house if I went down, I think concerns about my contacting the human embassy may have been more the cause. Finally, the decision was made as much because we would not be leaving on the same ship we had arrived on, which had been the best thing available on the creation homeworld when my health made a hasty departure imperative. Now it was required elsewhere and would be replaced by something better on which we would depart.

It was odd to see the pretty Earth-like world of the Dellier again, their place of escape from the winter cold and dark of the creation homeworld and presumably from their own family homeworld. What that was like I had no idea, but either it was not as pleasant in its climate as Heinget, or it was his own memories of the culling that had occurred there which kept the Dellier away from it, and made him winter on Heinget instead.

And as soon as we arrived there, it was as if the fresh air alone were medicinal for me, and I found I had reached that point in my recovery where the flesh decides celibacy is no longer acceptable. I can never imagine Kio celibate any more than I can myself. But he had not come near me in that way since the day I let my illness take me. And while I was physically ready, I was reluctant to have such intimacy, while I wanted to know what was happening in the meetings and was spending so much of my time in his company. And I disliked knowing he loved me and brooded on it.

A great quantity of Earth-grown food and several well-packed boxes of clothing were delivered for me when Marius's party arrived.

I feel guilty sometimes about how expensive I am to keep. Wherever I am now I eat the food of Earth, transported across the galaxy in huge quantities for me alone. I have seen it packed into a freezer in the Kirkillian house, one set aside entirely for it, and I am astonished by how much I eat. If we go anywhere, then an appropriate amount is packed and taken. And all my clothes come from Earth. My beautiful Rebecca—I always annoy Kio when I say that—still makes them for me, though she now does strange designs at times. I have a suit of stars and moons, which was made especially for the emperor's inauguration.

Amee fussed about as much as ever, and after the first few days on Heignet, I began to get restless. I did my exercises, ate regular and balanced meals, and took my medicines. And I remembered that first embassy and had my first thoughts about writing down some details of what had happened then so I would not completely forget it.

And oddly, I also remembered pleasantly my trip to the tikta farm, my first journey into the outside world on that first visit. And I remembered the pillow I had acquired there. More than a year and a half later I could almost imagine that what had occurred since was no more than a bad dream brought on by sleeping on a pillow covered in the lustrous soft hair of the tikta. I wondered where that small pillow I had selected for myself on the farm had gone, knowing it had not been among my possessions, which had been taken from there, and had followed me around the galaxy.

"When I was here before I visited a tikta farm and was offered a choice of items they had there, made from the woven hair of the Tikta. I wanted to be able to take home a rug or blanket of the fabric, but they didn't have anything that large, and I had to settle for a small pillow instead. I slept on it that night, with some imaginative idea that it would bring me sweet dreams," I told the Kirkillian one evening while we ate together, with Amee in discreet attendance, so familiar now I often hardly noticed her presence.

"Did it?" he asked.

"No. I remembered nothing in the morning. And I have never seen the pillow since."

I paused, remembering that had been the day after I had first seen the Dellier, and only days before I ceased to be part of the human world. Now I wondered if perhaps that small pillow had instead captured my sweet dreams and taken them from me. But perhaps coming back had partly returned them. My position was certainly very different from what it had been when I left there. It was difficult, but I felt safe, I was not the fearful and isolated man I had been then.

"Marius can be a difficult man, Kio. Like you, he is used to having his own way and wielding considerable power."

"It is not your concern," he replied.

"It is my concern as much as anyone's," I said with consternation.

"You are removed from it, Orlando. I am Laurentian, and that is my first duty always. The Sarolan mother has spoken, and all the delegation and I will work to see that the future is as it should be. You are now part of the Kirkillian river and may not take their side. So, it is best you say nothing."

I was denied my humanity.

There was nothing I could say to him then that would have served any purpose. My position has always been difficult. You ask why I didn't simply leave and return to Earth with Marius and his party? I could not leave the house where we were accommodated without being escorted. And if I could evade my escort, I would still have had to enter the meeting house or their shuttle, and then make contact with the human delegation without being observed.

And then what? They would never have been allowed to leave with me if he did not want them to, and I knew he would not want them to.

And I also knew that the Sarolan mother's prophecy could happen in a multitude of ways. I am the Dragar Han Kirkillian. I am bound to the Kirkillian, and yet I still only live because he wants it so. He reminded me of it in odd indirect ways in those days and even now does not see me as I do.

I did not want all of humanity to be made less, as I was, in a union of inequality. My presence was in humanity's favor while he looked well on me.

Perhaps I could have forced him to release me then, but I knew that if I did, I would always fear that I had set myself above mankind. Remember that I knew how powerful they were, and I knew they were not alone.

I requested to be taken to a tikta farm because I wished to order a rug of the fiber to be made for me. And as I have said, it was a journey that lived in my mind as a very pleasant one, and one that would keep me occupied for most of the day. But in the end it was more. The trip was rapidly organized for the next day, and we set out early, stopping at the blue lake again, but too late to see the beauty of the early morning. When we arrived at our destination, it was to find myself back at the same farm I had been to that first time. My driver was not Jaia, and the vehicle I traveled in the second time floated noiselessly above the track, which now showed only faint traces of the white gravel it had worn on my first visit.

At the farm I asked them, "I came here over a year ago. Do visitors always come to this farm?"

"Important visitors do; we are a large farm and closest to the main town."

I unexpectedly sensed there was more, "There is more."

"My brother is the town manager for the family, and we are paid for our hospitality," the elder male said grudgingly, "But we are also one of the closest farms and have a bigger range of equipment than the others have."

"When I came before I was disappointed not to be able to have a rug, so now I have come to order one and another pillow. The one I chose here last time was lost before I left."

"Whatever you wish to order you shall have, Dragar Han, but your pillow was not lost; it was found at the laundry amongst the bedding after you were gone to the family home. When someone sought to return it to you, they were . . . unsure what to do. In the end it was returned to us, but as it had been used, we were reluctant to sell it again and put it aside. My dragar will find it for you now."

It was said calmly, as if nothing out of the ordinary had happened between then and now. I was simply a visitor who had mislaid a small pillow, and now I was there to collect it, nothing more. But the hesitation and a feeling behind it told me more; it said that my fate inside the Dellier's dark house had been unknown and that perhaps the pillow's only user was therefore suspect, and the pillow they had rested on best put aside in case it was a bringer of bad luck.

I was worried, though, as to why I had such strong instincts about what they felt. I never had before, apart from those I had of Kio at the council meeting, before the Sarolan mother. But then I realized that I had probably been unwell for some time. Certainly I was already tired when he finally bound me to him.

When the pillow was returned to me, I found it as attractive as I remembered, and I held on to it, keeping it by me when lunch was served. I had the wish to pretend that now it was returned to me, all the sweet dreams of my life would come back to me if I slept on it again in the same place as I had so many difficulties ago. I ordered my rug in matching colors and was told it would be begun that afternoon and, if woven by hand, should be ready in four weeks time. I preferred it to be made by hand rather than by machine, and I asked if the woman who had brought my pillow back to me could weave it for me herself. It was agreed, and I left there feeling calmer and somehow more settled, as if something long left undone had finally been finished.

When I returned to the town, I asked that I could sleep again in the room at the meeting house where I had slept on that first visit. There was some consternation at this, but I was firm, the Kirkillian was occupied with more important thoughts, and I stressed that it was only for one night. He was annoyed at my demand but seemed to accept my reasons, though they sounded quite foolish, and he is a great pragmatist. But I was told that I had to wait until the meetings were finished and the humans had gone.

"Has anything been discussed yet that is important?" I asked him.

"Everything that is said is important, Orlando. Marius understands that; he knows he is working in the dark and doesn't want to move any further than he feels confident in going."

"What does that mean?"

"I can't explain it to you." He looked at me. "The less that happens the better; right now all we want to do is let things settle and show that we have no trouble dealing with each other. That is going to leave the council with nothing to annoy them, and they will forget about the excitement you have caused."

"Are you saying that it was only my behavior that almost had the council consider wiping us out?" I asked, knowing it might be, and wondering how much of the way I bent myself to fit in with the Kirkillian's requirements was my way of atoning for that, of getting his support. I left the room uncomfortable at being so close to him.

Then to fill my days I walked about the town aimlessly, noting the many things that it would have been so inconvenient for them to hide from the first embassy. The things that had required all our trips to occur in the dark. And I wondered what would have been the outcome of that visit if I had not been there.

It was the question that had been hanging over my head unadmitted, for too long. I had nearly brought about the destruction of humanity because of what I had done, because of my selfishness and arrogance. And in the position I was in, there was little I could do for the human delegation. But I was the greatest danger still to them. More dangerous than the Metjhan, or the Riag, or any other Laurentian, because I was the only human the Laurentians had to judge from, and I had no idea what I was doing.

The less the Laurentians saw of me in future the better, I decided, leaving me there on Heinget out of the way was the best option. Understanding the situation, I was no longer able to deal with it, and I walked about the town wondering how I could convince the Kirkillian to do that.

That evening when I returned I sought him out and I said I wished to speak to him.

"What do you wish to talk about?" he said, sounding tired and unhappy.

"I wanted to see you because I needed someone to talk to about serious things," I replied, knowing I didn't want to think about his difficulties with me or the embassy, I had enough of my own.

"I am here now, so talk to me."

I walked to the window and looked out at the pretty garden beyond. "What would have happened if my embassy had been dull and I had never done what I did?" I asked.

"It would have happened eventually, Orlando."

"Perhaps, but would anyone have been seriously thinking about destroying us then? Would the Metjhan hate me and my race? What would have happened if I hadn't gone after the Dellier?"

"Who knows? Once a meeting like that has occurred, it is difficult to end contact, but it can be kept minimal until something is decided." He paused and stood next to me, which I would rather he hadn't.

"You were right about Marius; he sees himself as a Han or Prime. Now he has some idea that we are more than we seem, he is far more cautious than he would have been. The Sarolan mother said your kind was ambitious and arrogant, and I had difficulty seeing that in you. But I see clearly now how right she was. It could be that if things had happened differently, then one day we would have grown tired of you and your ambition and decided to remove you, for the peace of the galaxy, before you could threaten us. Who can know all the possibilities that are there?"

"You talk easily about removing another race, as the Metjhan does, and it frightens me," I replied, taken aback to know that leaving things to drag on for years may have led to a situation that was as bad or worse, than the one I had created.

"It is not a decision we would take lightly, but we give nothing away, and there is only room for so many around these stars. Once there were a dozen Hans, but the strong who could live amicably with others have survived. Constant fights for more land and power eventually do more harm than good. Now we work together and present a united face to the rest. And we are stronger for it. If we can destroy our own families for peace and prosperity, we would not hesitate at destroying a difficult alien race, if we thought it necessary." He stopped, and I turned to him, knowing he was a truthful man.

"Thank you. It may sound foolish, but it concerned me."

"I know it did, and with understandable reason," he said quietly.

It was time for the evening meal, and I went with him to the small dining room we used there and felt uncomfortable, because I knew that my obviously improved health must soon raise the question of when we would again be together in the dark.

In the following days, I returned several times to the sea and walked along the shore with Amee, who was the perfect companion, as she was very silent at this time and it was easy for me to forget she was there.

My health had improved hugely in the weeks since I had seen the doctor.

Then they had gone, Marius and his companions, without me ever seeing any of them, and arrangements were made for me to go to the deserted human rooms of the meeting house with my pillow. And it was a more important thing to me than any meeting. I knew it was a foolish whim, but I also knew it was not. It was something else. We are what we believe, and I had become too convinced of my own discontent, and that now I had a charm returned from the past, which could somehow fix it.

Amee accompanied me as I was taken to my old room in the building, and I was surprised to find it was small and that with its high bed and pale walls and its human furnishings, it appeared very alien to me after so long in their accommodation. I set my pillow on the bed and turned out the lights and lay down to sleep. But of course I couldn't for a long time, and instead I turned my mind to what I had been when I first lay upon that pillow in that room.

I had been lonely and isolated, and I had just begun a passion, which was to lead me to the heights of pleasure and to a cage from which I had made the painful and isolated crawl back up to where I was. And I had been lost back then, I remembered, still bent under the weight of taking Leonardo's life. There had been no sweet dreams in my life except the Dellier, just disillusion, and I had made my choices.

But I also turned my mind to many things that I had not taken the time to turn it to before. I looked at what I was and how I lived with it. And I discovered that I truly wanted no more than to be free to return to a human life, to be able to love by my choice, to love women and to feel the warmth of human flesh, not the coolness of his.

Which of course made me wonder how he lived with me, how he loved me, what accommodations he had made with himself to make that possible.

I am his dragar; I am part of him; there are moments when he is part of me. I do not claim that this is not the life I would have chosen because of only one or two things. But I have made the choices, I acknowledge that, and I can have no regrets. But don't tell me I would not have preferred another life.

Finally, I drifted to sleep and I dreamed a long, sweet, strangely comforting dream. I entered a flowing river of gentle water, and I swam in it. It was the dark river pool where Leonardo and I had swum that last evening; it was the water of the blue lake at dawn; it was the strange ocean I'd walked by the day before; it was full of the memories of all the water I had ever entered or ridden upon and of the water that was inside me to. I swam gently in it through its myriad bright, flowing threads, twisting my body through the caress of it, cool and soft against my skin. Nothing much apart from that happened, but it seemed to be a long dream as I swam effortlessly and dived slowly down to the water's depths and floated back up to its surface.

In the morning I woke up calm and with the companionable hum more a part of me than it had been before. Then within moments Amee was there hurrying me into my clothes in a panic and others came, and I was hurried out and into a vehicle, which sped away at a frightening speed to where our shuttle was.

"What is going on?" I asked Amee, annoyed that my calm was being spoiled.

"The Han Metjhan may make claims against you, Dragar Han. We take you to our homeworld, the homeworld of the Laurentian."

"But the council has voted. What can the Metjhan do?" I was frightened suddenly, feeling lost in an unknown sea of dangers.

"Things change, Dragar Han. You change them. The Han Kirkillian changes them because he is bound to you. The Han Metjhan watches everything about you now, and we cannot know what he sees. But we shall not give you up." She said it angrily, and I wondered what had really happened, knowing it was something that had frightened even her.

Everyone else was already aboard the shuttle when we arrived, and as soon as I entered it, the door was sealed and the departure began. Hoonan came and placed one of the jeweled nets over my head as Amee led me through to my small cabin. Inside the Kirkillian waited, and immediately he stepped close and pulled my face into his mane. The scent of it meant sex to me. I had buried my face in the Dellier's and breathed its scent in like a drug. Now I buried my face in the Kirkillian's in the dark. But not in the light.

I pulled back, not wanting such an intimacy forced on me.

"Everything with you is difficult. Then suddenly I find something about you so perfect it is worth all the rest," he said gently, letting me go.

"I can't do this," I said and left the room. I was tired, feeling my morning's equilibrium spoiled by the rush, and completely ruined by what he had done.

Amee ran after me. "You stupid child," she cried harshly.

The only place I could get away from her on that small shuttle was in the bathroom. So I went there, wishing I could lock the door and keep them all outside forever but no door of mine ever had a lock now, which worked two ways.

Perhaps I was being childish.

There was a knock on the door, and I briefly thought of refusing to see anyone, but Amee's remark had stung me so I opened it.

I was surprised it was the Kirkillian.

"I'm sorry. You never know what you do. You do wonderful things that touch me and others, and for you they are nothing," he said. "What you worry about has become a minor thing now. As you recover you become stronger and drift into the river often in your sleep, but last night you moved through it as if it were your home. I know you have no understanding of what you do, as does Hoonan, but there have been no weavers since the killing, and it will never be safe for it to be discovered that you are one."

"I have no idea what you are talking about," I said.

"I know. The Kirkillian have been second for many generations because of the killing. We have always been stronger than the other families, and we have always trained the seers. Our Hans were often Prime once, but they became lazy and used the seers' abilities to help sway the council to their side. At first it was only gently done and no one noticed, but then we had a greedy Han who disliked negotiation and pushed harder.

"Finally, the other families realized what he did and turned on him. They killed many of us and destroyed

341

many of our worlds and took others, until finally a settlement was negotiated, and we gave up a large part of our land, and the weavers and the seers who had worked against them were all killed. There have been no weavers allowed to be trained since."

"But that was a long time ago. And if weavers need to be trained, then how can I be one?" I asked.

"I suppose you aren't really one, but you appear to be because of the easy way you enter the river,"

It was incomprehensible.

CHAPTER 21

In which I try to see you all, before our · *time began*

We arrived at our ship and I knew I was still not entirely well, it would be several months until I was. I could still suddenly lose all my energy and feel totally exhausted after feeling very lively only minutes before. Not having slept long the night before and after the change in atmosphere of the journey, it happened then, that sudden draining, as soon as we were on board.

"I'm tired," I said to Amee, and she looked at me.

The Kirkillian had left us as soon as we arrived, and we were alone with only a couple of crewmen dressed in green uniforms nearby.

"Yes, you have gone pale," she replied, priding herself on learning how to see things about me, like happiness and sadness and illness.

The crewmen flanked us as she led me away along a wide corridor that seemed to be far too long for me just then, and I was very relieved when finally we entered a dimly lit large room, where I immediately lay down on the big, comfortable sleeping platform and fell asleep, without taking any notice of my surroundings.

I woke up to find Amee and Celina there, ready to feed me a small meal, and then I had to dress formally for a dinner. It seemed ridiculous on a spaceship. The Kirkillian was already getting ready, though, and I didn't want to claim illness when I wasn't ill really. So, I had no choice but to hurry. But I was disconcerted to find we were apparently sharing the room. I had always had my own room for the day and evening, one where I could do whatever I wanted and lie down alone if I needed to rest.

My luggage is always there and unpacked for me now, though sometimes I take an inordinate amount of time to find anything because it is always put away in different places, all the accommodations I visit being differently furnished. But Celina always knows where everything is, and she was there to help me. I was allowed to remove the net. They are used for protection from the power of seers, and I was told I would need to wear one now when I slept.

When I was dressed, Amee pinned a small thing to my waistcoat. It was one of the pieces I had worn to the council meeting, I remembered, but not very pretty. It was a worn-looking, dull brown square encased in a frame and attached to a clip.

If I was given something to wear, I wore it. If I was given something to hold, I held it. If I was told to fly, I flew. I didn't bother asking a lot of questions. If something happened often, then I eventually found out what it was all about. I still knew so little of their world and its manners that I was in no position to question almost anything. It was only much later that I discovered what the little square was—one of the keys to the Gates of Time.

We left the sleeping room through large double doors I had not noticed before and entered an elaborately decorated reception room, amazingly large considering we were on a spaceship. Several members of the crew awaited us there with Hoonan and Essen, and some members of the Laurentian embassy from Heinget. The crew was introduced as ship captains, merchant fleet commanders, a ship manager, and a battle admiral. Other odd titles I cannot recall were given to the rest.

Then we formed up into a kind of procession and moved through even larger doors out of that room into a wide corridor. Suddenly I stumbled sideways, feeling the corridor move, and I knew we were going somewhere very fast. When the corridor finally slowed and stopped, I wondered where my stomach was and had premonitions about the size of the ship we were on.

We passed out of the corridor and through a huge opening and stepped out into a world—I can't describe it any other way. I gasped, overcome by it, unable to comprehend what was before me. Enclosed ramps and walkways radiated out from where we stood and were lined with crewmen and women standing to attention. Laurentians of other houses in their own colors occasionally broke up the lines of dark green spreading out of sight in all directions.

And hanging out there among the radiating arms were ships. Certainly fifteen or twenty, all larger than the tiny human one I had traveled to Heinget on and many immensely larger than the Dellier's ship I had traveled to the Laurentian homeworld on.

"Where are we?" I asked, overwhelmed.

"At the center of the second ship of the Laurentians, the Kirkillian battleship."

Kio paused and looked about him coldly as if he were about to unleash Armageddon on some recalcitrant planet of the Metjhan. "What we mainly use it for is a mobile, trading-ship repair and docking facility. It's hardly ever been used for anything else."

I looked at Kio, disappointed at him making something so awe-inspiringly phenomenal and overpowering sound mundane. But he merely looked calmly out at the world, knowing it was his, and I, standing there beside him, looked back out at the lines of uniforms radiating away from us.

Standing there then I realized that I was not a casual visitor. I was one of that world's deities, like the Han Kirkillian, like the captains and the ship manager who stood deferentially behind me. And I understood for the first time that I truly was second there on that world ship. I had been told I was second in his house, but it had meant nothing to me. At the council meeting I had felt much like some prop rather than one of the players. There on that ship, though, I took my part in the ceremonies of welcome and the inspections that followed, behaving like some long-dead monarch or president or ancient Count of Madeleine.

Finally, Kio said a few words, and there was a faint sound as the crew spread out about us in all directions gave some sort of cheer or reply. Then we moved back into the corridor and finally entered a large dining room, where other senior members of the crew already waited.

"Your first occasion out of the house and before my family as the Dragar Han," he said quietly.

And I knew he was content to have me there, which bothered me, as it was a sign of how he felt about me. I endeavored to play my part, and having worked in the Cargo House, could have an educated discussion about the merchant fleet, which seemed to amaze everyone, including Kio. What he had previously thought I had done there all day in the Cargo House, if it wasn't to learn about cargo and cargo ships, I had no idea.

The Kirkillian himself surprised me by being quiet through most of the meal, leaving me to talk and ignoring most attempts to include him in any conversation.

I had been on many ships before, mostly human ones when I was acting governor of the southern quadrant and traveled constantly, but I knew my shipboard anecdotes would show my race as primitive, and weren't what I wanted to tell these men who lived their lives working among the stars in comfort. I was uncomfortable about where I came from and how I was seen by everyone on the ship. At that moment I was no more proud of humanities accomplishments then I was secure in my maleness, knowing I would soon be returning to a room I shared with him.

Then the Kirkillian spoke for the first time at length and told a story of his youth when he had gone hunting off the Kirkillian homeworld, secretly, against his family's orders.

"I bribed a disreputable old guide named Jero, who was famous for his hunting skills, to take me to Moradee to hunt Segedee. He had a horrible ancient wreck of a ship. There was no hygiene on it, the water was all in containers, and the air was putrid after a day. By the time we arrived on Moradee, I was beginning to wonder if the hunting would be worth the effort and discomfort of getting there.

"But I spent what was the most wonderful week for a youngster, learning to track and living off the land with the old man's assistance. And I killed two Segedee myself, with no help from him, and found the ruins of an old family lodge from before the killing. I would not have missed that week for anything, and I screamed foul abuse at the people who found me and wanted to take me home. But when I was forced to leave, I had no objection to returning in their working ship and immediately spent half a day eating and washing myself.

"Amazingly, Jero kept his ship going for years after that, though eventually it killed him by blowing up, from dishonor at its awful state I've always thought." He said.

We all laughed at his story, and several crew members reminisced about their own early days on tramp ships and illegal transports in remote places.

He dexterously arranged our departure from the hall soon after.

Back in our room he ignored me, and Celine showed me a large bathroom where I undressed and washed. When I emerged, he was gone and I crawled into the bed as I would have in his house, but having had a good rest earlier, I lay awake for some time.

I was still not asleep when he joined me, which I did not like. Then he was there with his mane against my face, and I was filled with the scent of it and I reacted instantly as one does when its what your body needs.

When we were done, I knew there was nothing wrong with my life except what I felt inside, about myself.

"How do you cope with me not being one of your females?" I asked, in the dark.

"You smell like a female. You mate much like a female but enjoy it more. In some ways you are better to have than a female. I like having a companion who isn't trying to raise their position in the family. I am greatly pleased to have one through whom I feel more of what we are than I could through any seer.

"You suit me. Don't create problems, Orlando, where there aren't any. And there are none of your women here anyway, so whether you are mated to me or not, you will be mating males or no one."

As he said there were no human women there, and if it was only sex with them that made me feel like a man, I would never feel like one among them anyway. But that was not all; it was part of it, the part that made our physical relationship difficult. I am by nature a sensual person and reasonably affectionate and loving, I liked to touch and kiss and dally lazily with a lover. But I could not do that with him, and have never learned how to, because the cause of my inability is inbuilt in me and woven into my very fabric, not something I can change.

I would like to be able to say that my Laurentian lover, my joined partner, gradually became my friend, and I understood my lover wasn't a human man. My lover was a Laurentian, and I was human, and that the rest was words.

I think he did that, but he is a great pragmatist. I have never been able to feel that. He is too much of a man like me, in all the ways I need to be one.

He moved about, and suddenly the universe opened out above me.

"It's time you stopped seeing only what a child sees of my world, of the Kirkillian world, and the Laurentian world, of your place here."

"So, you see more? And what don't you think I see? That I should behave like your dragar and accept my female place without question." I knew it was childish and wrong to say, as soon as it was said. "I'm sorry, I should not have said that."

Suddenly, the universe I had been watching move above me was obscured by the light of a lamp turned on beside me.

"Why, Orlando?"

I lay there trying to understand myself, not looking at him, "Because it isn't true. I know you love me." It was said. "You treat me like a friend and lover now. I am the one who finds the two things impossible to be together, because when I look at you with my eyes open, I see a man, a man such as I once was and want to be still. I will never feel what you do."

"You are always difficult, but you do such wonderful things. I know that is how it is. And that Marius is right when he says you think too much."

I was annoyed to find that he and Marius had talked about me. "What else did he say about me?" I asked.

"That he wants you back. I told him he could not have you."

I imagined Marius annoyed. As I have said I always felt he regarded me as his in some way. "Will I ever be allowed to see anyone again?" I asked.

"You are Laurentian now. Our river flows through you, the ocean touches you. Hoonan and I sense it there always, now that you are well again. You wanted to come and discover us, and you have. Now you can never return to what you were. It will be better for you not to think you can."

The light went out and the universe was back above me, and I might have been floating in it, it was so vast and open and close.

"Sometimes we do things because we must and don't realize what effect they'll have. And even if we can have no regrets, they have an effect," I whispered, knowing there was some of Leonardo there in him, some of Marius and many other people I had loved and admired. But I would never have been with Leonardo, or the others as I was with him.

"I killed my best friend. That is why I am here," I said, and suddenly a veil of tears covered the universe, and at last I cried for the friend I'd lost. "He had to die, and I wanted it to be somewhere he loved with someone he wanted to be with." I let the tears flow as I hung there suspended in space. "I have no regrets. But I didn't realize until afterward what effect it would have on me."

Then I felt as if he knew everything about me. Given the knowledge because he had found a way to live with me. Because he knew from the beginning that I could never leave him. I had no way to go and didn't know enough to find the way to make us work myself. Couldn't find the way, because I had to feel something inside that I had never had to think about before when I was Count of Madeleine, which was like food, and made love to women as if they were water, which I ate and drank to stay alive and whole.

He said nothing, and I looked up and as the tears dried, I saw the universe spread out above me and gazed at it, amazed at its beauty as its bright tiny points of light moved by me. I wondered vaguely how it moved so quickly and gradually realized that it was I, on my bed, who was moving, which made me feel curious. And then I wondered where Earth was—its colonies, its explorers—where all the other humans except me were.

"Where is my sun?" I asked. "The star that lights the Earth."

After a time he said it was on the other side and that the ship would have to be turned for me to see it.

And the universe was turned for me.

We lay there side by side and watched the universe revolve slowly about us, and when it stopped, he pointed and explained to me where my Sun was. A bright star, trying to hide three small ones, and near two even brighter ones, which were hardly any distance apart.

I looked hard upon our star, but however hard I tried to see you, all of you other human beings were too far away for me to see even one of you. And at such a distance I knew I loved you more than I had ever done when you were near me. I was overcome by wanting to be among you, to sense your existence, to know again the gentle warmth of human flesh.

But I could not, and he left, and I lay alone, watching, as our star moved above me. As I traveled in a great ship across the confederation of the Laurentian, to the homeworld of the Kirkillian.

Later, while I lay there, I realized I was looking for a people who did not yet exist. Realizing that those humans who lived beneath the star above me then were none I would have recognized. For I looked upon the sun of our ancestors thousands of years ago. A sun burning before the first great human civilizations arose upon the banks of the Nile and the Euphrates.

But I knew I loved those humans who lived then, no less than I do you, who are living now, and I wanted to be with them.

EPILOGUE

You are disappointed I know.

I have not told you of the wonders of the Empire, of the fall of the Han Metjhan, of great battle fleets. I write not of being co-emperor and I have not told you of that I am most famous for. I have not yet reached the Gates of Time and opened them, its wonders are not revealed. I have told you I hold one of the keys already, but it will be years before I do more.

Perhaps I will write of such things at another time. As I said at the beginning, this is my story to tell me what I have lost and what I have become, and how I became it, of what my life has brought to me.

It was not written for you.

Orlando

About the Author

Stephen Bush used to live on the east coast of Australia, not far from Sydney, but now lives on the Ribeira Sacre, the Sacred Riverbank, in the north west of Spain.

He works in publishing and writes, and his writing has been published often under other names. He regularly writes about dogs and has run many training courses. He has also previously lived in northern Australia and worked as an accountant, and he likes the wide-open spaces.

He has too many dogs living in his house. But he loves them all.

Cyberworld Publishing

Books available in ebook and print
Books by Stephen Bush
No Regrets - A memoir of Orlando, Count of Madelaine, Consort of the Emperor and Cokeeper of the Keys to the Gates of Time.
My Sister's Funeral - A Murder mystery

Books by Gina Drew

The Koniotis Mysteries Series:-each book in this six part Cyprus set series, which travels from the islands past to its future, stands alone, but they are also all connected in various ways and form the different parts of one story.
Laughter's Echo
Salted Away

Mouflon Brigade
Amathus Armageddon
Bogus Bills
Homewrecker

Also Home of Authors Olivia Stowe and Stephen Kessel

www.ingramcontent.com/pod-product-compliance
Lightning Source LLC
Chambersburg PA
CBHW030636260626
47157CB00007B/2348